"Let's try to be friends."

"I'm trying," Marcus told her in his low, gruff voice. "You have to give a guy a few days to figure things out and get over feeling like he's had his legs kicked out from under him."

"I know." She pulled her seat belt around and he reached over to click it into place for her. "Thank you."

"I'm not going to take him from you," he said as they headed down the long driveway back to the main road.

The sting of tears took her by surprise. She wiped at them and when he handed her a handkerchief, she shook her head.

"I'm fine."

"Yeah, of course you are." He shoved the handkerchief into her hand. "I know he needs you. I know he doesn't need a scarred-up, dysfunctional cowboy for a dad."

"I think you're wrong," she told him.

And the words took her by surprise.

She hadn't expected to like Marcus Palermo…

Brenda Minton lives in the Ozarks with her husband, children, cats, dogs and strays. She is a pastor's wife, Sunday school teacher, coffee addict and is sleep deprived. Not in that order. Her dream to be an author for Harlequin started somewhere in the pages of a romance novel about a young American woman stranded in a Spanish castle. Her dreams came true, and twenty-plus books later, she is an author hoping to inspire young girls to dream.

Jill Kemerer writes novels with love, humor and faith. Besides spoiling her minidachshund and keeping up with her busy kids, Jill reads stacks of books, lives for her morning coffee and gushes over fluffy animals. She resides in Ohio with her husband and two children. Jill loves connecting with readers, so please visit her website, jillkemerer.com, or contact her at PO Box 2802, Whitehouse, OH 43571.

The Rancher's Secret Child

Brenda Minton

&

Reunited with the Bull Rider

Jill Kemerer

LOVE INSPIRED
INSPIRATIONAL ROMANCE

LOVE INSPIRED®
INSPIRATIONAL ROMANCE

ISBN-13: 978-1-335-45616-8

The Rancher's Secret Child &
Reunited with the Bull Rider

Copyright © 2020 by Harlequin Books S.A.

The Rancher's Secret Child
First published in 2018. This edition published in 2020.
Copyright © 2018 by Brenda Minton

Reunited with the Bull Rider
First published in 2018. This edition published in 2020.
Copyright © 2018 by Ripple Effect Press, LLC

This edition published by arrangement with Harlequin Books S.A.

For questions and comments about the quality of this book, please contact us at CustomerService@Harlequin.com.

Love Inspired
22 Adelaide St. West, 40th Floor
Toronto, Ontario M5H 4E3, Canada
www.Harlequin.com

Printed in U.S.A.

CONTENTS

THE RANCHER'S
SECRET CHILD

Brenda Minton

This book is dedicated to my aunt Joyce, aunt Alice and aunt Betty. And in memory of my aunt Shirley Clark. They have taught us to have fun, to be classy when it matters, to live life to the fullest and to love family.

It is of the Lord's mercies that we are not consumed,
because his compassions fail not.
They are new every morning: great is thy faithfulness.
—*Lamentations* 3:22–23

Chapter One

A car door slammed and a child's laughter rang out, followed by a woman's voice. The horse beneath Marcus Palermo skittered across the arena, forcing him to hold tight. He managed a quick look in the direction of the visitors. A woman, tall with dark hair. A little boy with chocolate-brown hair who seemed all excited as he headed for the arena as Marcus made a last-ditch attempt at controlling the horse.

He had a few seconds to wonder where this woman and boy had come from and how they'd found the place, an old farm situated down a long dirt drive and hidden from view of the road by a copse of trees. He'd only recently purchased the old Brown farm and few people knew he lived here.

The boy shouted something as he ran toward the makeshift arena that Marcus had built with cattle panels. The horse jerked his head forward and took a few running bucks across the dirt-packed pen. Marcus's hat flew off. He'd just bought that hat and he liked it. He tightened his legs, but the horse had the upper hand. The black-and-white paint gelding twisted and, with a final hard buck, sent Marcus flying. As he hit the ground, he remembered that he really didn't like ranching all that much.

After a minute he sat up, rubbing the back of his neck where it hurt the most. Slowly he became aware of a couple of things. First, the horse he'd been attempting to ride had moseyed on over to the fence. The traitor had his head down like a big old puppy dog so the kid could pet him. The woman's gaze left the boy and the horse and shifted his way, nervous and a bit guilty.

Considering she was partially to blame for his bad exit off the horse's back, she could have at least asked if he was okay. But, no, she only managed to look sheepish as she ran her hand down the horse's neck. The little boy seemed more curious than anything.

"No, don't worry, I'm fine," he muttered as he came to his feet.

He limped across the arena and grabbed the horse's reins because he was a little jealous of the attention the animal was getting. He moved the gelding away from the fence and away from the hands of the visitors. The woman moved her sunglasses to the top of her head and narrowed her blue eyes at him. He must be getting better at offending the fairer sex. It had taken only two minutes for him to earn her displeasure. "Did he break your leg?" the little boy asked.

Marcus glanced at the kid. He was maybe five, with big eyes. Those eyes widened a bit, the normal reaction to Marcus's face. Because it was a kid, not an adult staring at him, Marcus had sympathy. He half turned, giving the little boy his good side.

"No," he answered roughly. "It would take more than that to break me."

"I bet it would," the boy said in awe.

Marcus hoped the woman and kid weren't fans with the misplaced idea that he welcomed uninvited guests to the ranch for sightseeing. But the woman didn't appear to be an admiring fan. She didn't look like the type of woman who had ever witnessed a professional bull ride, let alone knew who the champions might be.

"Is there something I can help you with?" He looked down at the little boy and back at the woman, because there was something familiar about her.

She was taller than average, with long, dark hair, and had high cheekbones that made him think she had Native American ancestry. But she had startling blue eyes. The blue of a winter sky. Those eyes were boring into him like he was a bug and she couldn't figure out what kind. So obviously *not* a fan.

Fine with him. He didn't need fans. In fact, he didn't need much of anything or anyone. Which was exactly why he'd picked this property, several miles off the beaten path and far enough away from his siblings that they wouldn't always be in his business.

"Are you Marcus Palermo?" she asked, her hand protective on the boy's shoulder.

"That would be me."

"Then we need to talk." She squatted to look the boy in the eye. "Sit and don't move."

"By myself?" For the first time, the little guy looked unsure. And Marcus had to admit to getting his hackles up when a kid looked unhappy.

"By himself?" he echoed. The question earned him an answering look from the female. She straightened and met his gaze head-on, those blue eyes once again penetrating him. He didn't like feeling as if he was five and about to get in trouble.

He also didn't like the fact that his gaze landed on cherry-glossed lips that were far from smiling, yet were still cherry. As if that bright gloss was the only frivolous thing she allowed herself.

"He'll be fine," she answered. "We're going to head to the barn and talk for a few minutes. I'll be able to see him from there. Correct?"

"Sure thing," Marcus whispered.

"Do you ever talk loud?" the boy asked, looking up at him from the spot where she'd told him to sit. He had a small car, and as he stared at Marcus, he pushed the car through the dirt.

"No, I don't." Marcus walked off, leading the horse behind him. He heard the gate creak on its hinges and the footsteps hurrying to catch up.

He entered the side door to the barn and she followed him.

"Say what it is you came here to say." He ground the words out. He didn't mean to sound gruff, but it couldn't be helped. Added to that, something about this woman put him off-kilter. And not in a totally bad way.

He gave her another long look and saw the wary shift of her gaze from his face to the door. She had bad news. He could feel it in the pit of his stomach.

She stood by the door, watching first the boy and then him.

"My name is Lissa Hart. Sammy Lawson was my sister. Well, foster sister."

Sammy. He unsaddled the horse and led the animal to a stall to be dealt with later. He wouldn't put a horse out to pasture without giving it a good brushing and grain. Even a horse that had tossed him in the dirt.

It had been about six years since he'd seen Sammy. The mention of her had taken him back to a time and place, a version of himself, he'd rather forget. He needed a minute to collect his thoughts, so he made sure the horse had plenty of hay and fresh water. Finally, he turned to face Lissa Hart.

"Sammy? I haven't heard from her in a long time."

Pain sparked in her eyes and she blinked a few times. "Marcus, Sammy passed away. A little over a year ago. I thought you would have heard."

He walked away from her. Now he needed more than a minute. His heart constricted, reminding him he did indeed have one. Sammy gone. It didn't make sense. The two of them had dated for a few months until she broke it off with him. He hadn't loved her, but he had cared for her. They'd been a bad fit, in different places, rubbing each other wrong. She, like so many women in his life, had wanted more than a broken-down, dysfunctional bull rider with an alcohol problem.

It seemed like a lifetime ago.

Emotions in check, he faced her again. "What happened?"

"She had an accident. Her injuries were serious. I made it to the hospital, but…"

She closed her eyes and he understood.

"I'm sorry," he said more softly than normal, and his eyes misted with unwelcome dampness. "I tried to call her after she ended it with me. She let me know she didn't want me around."

"She had ideas about what she wanted in life."

"And it wasn't a rough bull rider from Bluebonnet

Springs, Texas." He couldn't keep the resentment from his voice.

"She told me she was afraid together you'd be combustible and you'd self-destruct. She needed peace."

"Yeah, I get that. That brings us to why you're here, and then you can leave." He got the sneaking suspicion it wasn't going to go that way.

She swallowed hard, and he felt a pang of something resembling guilt or regret. She'd lost someone she considered a sister. Sammy had been young and so full of life. She'd had dreams. And now she was gone. He muttered under his breath and wiped his eyes. Contrary to how he was acting, he wasn't heartless.

"I'm here because she wanted me to find you."

"Find me why?" He took a step toward her and then changed direction so that he could look out the door, needing to check for himself that the boy was okay.

"He's your son." The words sprang from her lips, and for a minute he couldn't make sense of them.

The boy sat where they'd left him. He was making motor noises for his car and intent on building a ramp. Marcus watched him for a moment and then turned to face the woman who had just upended his entire world.

"No." He said it again. "No. She would have told me."

"She knew you weren't ready to settle down or ready for a family. She wanted to protect him the way she hadn't been protected as a child."

"Then why are you here now?"

"Because I promised." Her words were soft, sad. She shrugged. "She had heard you were changing, getting your act together."

"That doesn't explain anything."

Her gaze dropped, but not before he saw the sheen

of moisture. "I was with her at the hospital, and she told me to find you, and if you had your life together, then I should bring Oliver to meet you."

"You waited a year."

"I had to find you. I also had to keep my promise that I would make sure you had changed."

"You waited a year," he repeated, more angry than he'd been in a long time.

"I won't let anyone or anything hurt Oliver," she informed him. "And you haven't exactly been a model citizen."

That wasn't untrue. He gave her a steady look and wondered if she would back down. She didn't. He gave her points for that—most people didn't hold up under the glare he'd perfected since childhood.

"The kid is out there alone. You should go get him. And you should leave."

"The *kid* has a name. His name is Oliver and he's your son."

His son. He gave his head a quick shake. He had a son. The kid out there who had looked up at him with a mixture of fear, awe and concern was his. And he was the last person that boy needed in his life.

Lissa cleared her throat, gaining his attention.

"We have to finish this. And just because you go all angry cowboy on me doesn't mean I'm leaving. Sammy had a will. She gave me custody of Oliver. She wanted you in your son's life. But she had stipulations."

"I'm not good at ultimatums."

One shoulder lifted in a casual shrug. "I told her you wouldn't be happy about this."

She walked back to the door of the barn and peeked out.

"I think saying I'm not happy is an understatement.

She kept my son from me. I'll admit I'm not looking to have a family, but I think a man should know when he has a child. At the very least I should have been helping out, supporting him." A light came on as those words left his mouth. "Oh. Is that why you're here?"

"For money?" In her defense, she looked pretty insulted. "I don't need your money. I brought Oliver to meet you because Sammy had some misguided notion that you would maybe grow up. I guess you told her often enough while you were dating that you didn't plan on being a husband or a father, but she thought you might change your mind."

He grabbed the brush out of a bucket and opened the stall door. The horse moved to his side, and he snapped a lead rope on the halter and led the animal to the cross ties in the center of the barn. He needed something to focus on, something other than the obvious. He was a father. The role he least wanted in life was now his.

He pretended it was anger he felt, but a good dose of fear got mixed up in the emotion. Fear of failing a child. Fear of being like his own father.

"I'm not responsible. I doubt I ever will be. So I guess you ought to take the kid and go." If he acted as if he didn't care, maybe she would believe him and leave. Maybe she would take the boy and give him a chance at a happier, healthier life than either Sammy or Marcus had known growing up.

"Go where?" the boy asked from the open door of the barn.

Marcus stroked the brush down the gelding's neck. Once. Twice. Three times. With each stroke of the brush, he took a deep breath. And then he eased around to face the little boy. Oliver. *His son.*

Because of his own father, he recognized himself in that little boy. He saw a kid who was unsure. He saw fear. He saw uncertainty. He had been that kid. And now he was the dad. He hadn't planned on being a parent because he'd never wanted to see that look in a kid's eyes.

His attention shifted from the boy to the aunt. She didn't believe in him. The fact that he cared what she thought was his third surprise of the day and none of those surprises had really been pleasant.

Lissa Hart held out her hand and Oliver hurried to her side. His small hand tucked into hers and she gave it a gentle squeeze. She didn't know what else to say to Marcus Palermo. While she certainly hadn't expected this to be easy, she found it even harder than she'd imagined.

Something about this man made her uneasy. Not afraid. She didn't think he would hurt Oliver. He seemed rough and unfeeling, but she'd seen something in his expression, in the depths of his dark eyes, that told her he felt plenty.

Sammy had fancied herself in love with Marcus, but she'd ended the relationship because he was too broken, too angry to be the kind of person she could count on. Still, her sister had wanted him to heal, and she'd wanted him to have a chance with his son.

He'd stopped brushing the horse and he focused on Oliver, his dark gaze studying the little boy, a miniature version of himself. His mouth twitched, as if he might have found humor in something. The movement drew her attention to the jagged scar across his left cheek. That scar did nothing to detract from his looks. His too-long hair curling at his collar gave him a youthful appearance. But the firm jawline, the not-quite smile on his lips—those belonged to a man. A man who had lived a hard life and seen a lot of pain.

He shifted his focus from Oliver to her, and one brow arched in what could only be a challenge. She didn't flinch or look away. Neither did he, but then he dismissed her and returned his attention to Oliver. He squatted, holding out the brush.

"Do you want to brush him before you leave?" he asked quietly.

Oliver nodded because he was a little boy and of course he wanted to stand by this cowboy and brush the horse. He looked up at Lissa, seeking permission. He didn't know yet that this man was his father. She hadn't known how to tell him, and she hadn't wanted him to be disappointed. The odds had been good that Marcus would reject his child or not be able to be a parent to him, and her main goal was to protect Oliver. Sammy had entrusted her with his care.

With Marcus watching, Lissa let go of Oliver's hand and the boy slipped away from her. Her heart clenched in agony as she realized this might be the beginning of losing the child she loved so very much.

Oliver took the brush and Marcus lifted him, telling him to run the brush down the horse's neck.

"Put pressure on it," he said, in that gruff whisper of a voice, "or it tickles and horses don't like to be tickled." Oliver grinned at that and pushed the brush down the horse's neck.

Marcus continued to hold Oliver. He spoke quietly to his son, words that Lissa couldn't hear.

Tempted as she was to move closer, she stood there, waiting. He seemed content to ignore her and focus on

Oliver. The two looked like father and son, dark heads together as Oliver leaned close to hug the horse.

"I think we can turn him out to pasture," Marcus said as he returned Oliver to the ground.

"And we should finish our discussion," she inserted.

"There's an old tire swing," Marcus told Oliver. "Want to try it out?"

"Is it safe?" Lissa asked.

"It's safe." Leading the horse to the door at the rear of the barn, he opened it and turned the horse loose. He stood there a moment, a dark silhouette against the sun, as the horse trotted a short distance away and then dropped to roll on the ground. A cloud of dust billowed around the big horse as he stood and shook like a dog. Next to her, Oliver laughed at the sight.

Marcus once again faced them, his expression still and composed. He held out a hand to Oliver. "Let's go check out that swing."

Lissa followed them outside into bright May sunshine. The house that lay a short distance from the barn was an older farmhouse, two stories with a long front porch. Beyond the house was a creek, the waters sparkling and clear.

The homestead looked a bit run-down, with faded siding, patched sections on the roof and a board over one window. It could have been any house she'd known growing up in poor neighborhoods, but instead it seemed peaceful. Maybe it was the location, with the stream, the rosebushes that had taken over and the green fields in the distance.

Thinking about the house pulled her back to her own troubled past, to the abuse with her drug-addicted mother. Life before foster care and the Simms family.

She and Sammy had lived their teen years with Tom and Jane Simms.

"It took me a while to find you," she told him as they walked in the direction of a big tree with limbs that stretched out like an umbrella, shading the yard of the old house.

"That's the whole idea, being hard to find."

He helped Oliver onto the swing and gave it a push. "We're going to sit on the porch. You'll be okay here."

Oliver grinned big. "It's fun here."

"Yeah, it is." He gave the boy one last look and headed for the house.

He didn't turn back to see if she followed. Lissa tried not to let that hurt. She wasn't here for herself. But it mattered, whether or not he was good and if he was caring. Oliver needed a real father, someone to look up to. Someone who would be there for him.

She stepped onto the front porch and glanced around. It needed paint and a few boards had to be repaired. There were chairs and an old dog sleeping in a worn-out dog bed. The animal lifted his head to give them a once-over.

"Lucky isn't much of a guard dog," Marcus told her as he pointed to a chair. "He's been following me around the country for the past ten years. He's half-deaf and nearly blind."

Lissa thought the dog was a piece of the puzzle that was Marcus Palermo. The black-and-brown hound dog fixed soulful eyes on his master and then her. They must not have appeared too interesting, because he yawned and fell back to sleep.

"Why is his name Lucky?"

"He got hit by a car when he was a puppy. I found

him on the side of the road and nursed him back to health and he's been Lucky ever since," Marcus explained as he sat on the edge of the porch. "About the boy. Are you dumping him here, like he's a stray? Or do you want money?"

"He is not a stray. He's a little boy and I love him. I'm here to see if you're ready to be a part of his life."

"You make it sound like I was given a choice and rejected him."

"Sammy gave me the job of making sure you are ready to be a dad."

"Make sure I'm ready?" A cold thread of anger sharpened the words. He was no longer the easygoing cowboy he'd been moments ago. When she looked up, his gaze was on her, as glacial as his words.

"Sammy didn't know if you would want to be a father. She also didn't know if you would be able."

"I see. I guess I do have more negatives than positives. Bad-tempered, dysfunctional and a recovering drunk. Not much hope in all of that."

"She loved her son and wanted him safe." Lissa didn't add that she wanted Oliver safe. She wanted to protect him and make sure his future was secure.

"So you think I should have to jump through your hoops in order to be his dad? Because the way I see it, I could just take you to court."

She knew that, but on hearing him say it, emotion rolled through her, settling in the pit of her stomach and making her heart ache. Her gaze settled on Oliver as he worked to keep the swing moving.

"It would be unfair to Oliver to do this without taking time to allow him to get to know you. To bond with you. I need to know that you're responsible and that you'll be a good dad."

"You need to make sure I'm not my father," he said without animosity, as if he was removed from the situation with his father, a known cult leader.

"Okay. Yes. And I do have legal custody."

"I'm going to be honest here. I don't think you should leave him with me." He glanced her way and then his attention turned to Oliver. "He seems like a good kid. Anyone in their right mind would want him. I know *you* want him. And, well, I don't want to mess that little boy up. He's already had it rough. Why make things worse for him?"

"Because he's yours," she pointed out. "Because he deserves to know he has a father."

"Not everyone knows how to be a father. Some people don't deserve the title."

Marcus watched as the little boy got off the swing, gave it a push and then struggled to climb back on the moving tire. The dog suddenly took interest in his surroundings and the visitors. He stood, shook from head to toe and trotted off the porch and across the yard to Oliver.

The rangy old dog, some type of coon dog, she guessed, obviously held more appeal than the swing. Oliver jumped, rolled across the ground and then giggled as the animal licked his face.

"Lucky. Enough." Marcus whistled. The dog stopped licking, but he didn't return to the porch. Instead, he plopped on his belly and stretched out next to his new friend.

"You should give yourself a chance." She found herself uttering the last words she'd wanted to say to him.

He scoffed. "No, I don't think so. Give myself a chance to what? Mess that kid up? He's happy. Let's keep it that way."

"Don't you want him to know that you're his dad?"

He pushed himself to his feet and leaned against the post. "No. I don't want him to know. I'm sure you know plenty about my family. I told myself a long time ago that I wouldn't be a part of continuing the family line."

"And yet you did. That little boy is your family."

"And he's got you. You look like a perfectly normal, responsible adult, and you love him. If it's money you're worried about, he isn't going to go without. I'll make sure of that."

She glared at him. "Money doesn't replace a parent or parents, Mr. Palermo."

He met her gaze with a fiery look of his own. "I'm Marcus. Mr. Palermo was my father. And that's a good enough reason for you to take the boy and go."

She stood and walked past him, her shoulder brushing his. He didn't make a move to chase her down and stop her. She kind of wished he had, because she thought if he'd give himself a chance, he had a shot at being a good dad.

Oliver resisted when she told him they had to leave, but Marcus Palermo had already gone inside. What kind of man could turn his back and walk away without even offering a goodbye to his child? She knew the answer. A man who had been damaged, just as Sammy had warned. A man who didn't want to look too closely at what he was turning his back on.

She considered pounding on his door, demanding he care. But a person couldn't be forced to care. She'd learned that lesson at an early age.

Chapter Two

The next morning, Marcus woke with regrets. He stumbled to the kitchen and poured water into the coffee-maker before heading out the back door to the one thing he'd actually done to the old farmhouse. He'd added a porch with a swing, and he spent many a morning there watching the sun come up.

Nothing said *home* like a porch swing.

He loved the start of a new day when the sky turned from inky black to gray, and then that big orange ball peeked up from the horizon, the colors bursting forth like God sweeping a whole handful of crayons across the sky. Not that he would have shared that thought with anyone. No one knew how he felt about faith or life or art.

Art, another of his ventures and something he kept hidden in the upstairs bedroom, away from prying eyes.

He had a son. He had rejected the boy and it had cost him. Last night he'd lain awake thinking of that little boy's eyes, his face. He'd been a funny kid, rolling on the ground with Lucky. Marcus thought of his nieces, Issy and Jewel. With a sigh, he took a seat on the porch swing and buried his face in his hands. *Father, if it is Your will, take this cup from me.*

Jesus had uttered those words in the Garden of Gethsemane just before he was taken into custody. He guessed having a son didn't quite match up to what Jesus had been about to endure. But what Jesus had done had been the ultimate act of obedience, of giving himself up for others.

Marcus could admit to being torn. He had given his son up because he felt he wasn't the dad Oliver needed. He wasn't what any kid needed. It hadn't been easy to watch his son take hold of someone else's hand and walk away. Like a coward, he'd headed inside so he wouldn't have to meet the boy's dark and questioning eyes.

Oliver would be better off without him. He'd be better off with the woman, Lissa Hart. She seemed decent. She seemed to care. She would meet a good, honorable guy, get married, and they'd be a family. He'd meant to make himself feel better with the thought; instead, he felt worse. His son would be someone else's family.

He leaned back in the swing as the sun peeped up over the eastern horizon, and he called himself a fool. He knew better than anyone that appearances were an illusion. His dad had been the master of the game, creating a facade that fooled people until they were too far into his web to escape. His own family had been victims of the deception.

Jesse Palermo's wife, mother to his children, had preferred walking away from her own flesh and blood to staying with a madman. Marcus bore the scars of his dad's abuse—his broken voice, the jagged line down his cheek and the emotional baggage.

His sister Lucy and his twin, Alex, had worked

through their pain and married. Their youngest sister, Maria, seemed to have survived. Only because she'd been a little girl when Jesse died.

Marcus had been drifting for the past ten years or so, since their illustrious sire had died on the back of a bull he'd challenged Alex to ride. Marcus had made some money, sowed his wild oats and done his best to outrun the past. And he had a son. A boy named Oliver. A boy who would be better off without Marcus, because the only thing Marcus knew about being a father was what his dad had taught him. Jesse Palermo had beaten his children. He'd controlled his family and his congregation. He'd ruined every life he'd come in contact with.

A car barreled down his drive, tossing up dust and invading the early-morning peacefulness. He groaned when he recognized the old International wagon. His aunt Essie's pride and joy. It wasn't quite seven in the morning, so he doubted this was a pleasure visit. He headed inside for whatever lecture happened to be forthcoming. His skin was thick and she'd told him on more than one occasion that so was his head.

She met him on the front porch. Knocking on the door to seventy, she was a spitfire with long, graying hair pulled back in a braid. Today she wore jeans, a T-shirt and her apron. She'd obviously been at the café she owned before heading to his house on whatever mission had brought her.

Marcus sighed. He wasn't fooling himself. He knew what had brought her out here. The same thing that had kept him up all night and had him doubting himself this morning.

"Aunt Essie, I just made coffee."

She had a spatula in her hand. She must have carried it out of the café with her, but she went ahead and waved it in his face.

"You!" After decades in America, her Brazilian accent was normally undetectable, but today was a different story. "You've pulled stunts in your life, but *this*? Oh, I should paddle you, Marcus Palermo."

He drew in a breath and exhaled. She could only be talking about one thing. Or one person. "How'd you find out?"

"Yesterday afternoon Mindy rented a room above her store. The young woman showed up with a boy that looked a lot like you and Alex when you were little. This morning that young lady came in my café, and wasn't I surprised?" She waved the spatula a little too closely to his face. He grabbed it from her hand and tossed it onto the counter.

"Imagine my surprise when she showed up here," he countered.

"So you sent her on her way as if the boy, your flesh and blood, doesn't matter."

He recoiled at the way she described his decision and her eyes narrowed, as if she'd spotted a chink in his armor.

"What, Marcus, you don't want to take responsibility for your actions?" she demanded. She'd been more a parent to the Palermo offspring than their own mother and father, and he wasn't surprised by her questions. He wasn't even offended. Truth was, he did feel guilty.

"I sent her away because the boy does matter," he told her as he spun on his heel and walked back to the kitchen. "Coffee?"

"There you go, shutting yourself off, acting as if none of this concerns you. As if you don't have emotions."

"It concerns me," he said as he poured her a cup of coffee. She took it and gave him a long look. "What about this concerns you?"

Wrong thing to say. He knew it when she moved closer, her lips thinning with displeasure.

"What concerns me is that there is a boy in need of a father and you're acting as if it isn't your responsibility."

"I'll support him. I'll give him whatever he needs."

"But not your time. Or your love. The two most important things you can give a child." She started to ramble in Portuguese, which he spoke little of.

He poured coffee in his favorite mug and tried to ignore the memories that the cup evoked. He hadn't even thought about it when he'd pulled it from the cabinet. Sammy had given him the mug with the verse from Lamentations, about God's mercy being new every morning. She'd wanted him to remember that each day was a fresh canvas. He guessed that might be one reason he loved mornings. They did feel new. A fresh start. Every day.

New, even though the old baggage kind of held on and wasn't easy to be rid of.

It bugged him that he'd pulled that mug out of the cabinet. He looked up, wondering if God was telling him something and wishing He hadn't bothered.

"He's your son, Marcus. That's as clear as that ugly nose on your face." Aunt Essie had resumed English, like someone had pushed a switch.

"My nose isn't ugly," he replied. "And that boy deserves better than a dad who might or might not be his own father's son. I won't do that to any woman or any child. That's why Sammy kept him from me. I don't know why she made the decision to have his guardian introduce him to me after she was gone."

A wash of grief flooded him, bringing the sting of tears to his eyes that he'd regret later. Aunt Essie's expression softened and she put a hand on his arm, giving a light squeeze.

"I'm sorry. I'm sure you cared about her." Essie patted his arm. "You are Jesse Palermo's son, but that doesn't mean you are going to be the same kind of father he was. You are your own person. And if there was good in him, I prefer to think that's what you have in you. My nephew wasn't a bad man. Power and alcohol changed him."

He closed his eyes, willing away the dampness. He didn't cry. His dad had beat the tears out of him years ago with the old phrase that he'd give him something to cry about. After a few good, sound beatings, he'd no longer cared to find something to cry about.

"I did care about her, but together we were combustible. It wasn't a good thing, the two of us. Two kids with similar pasts and a lot of anger. We were both getting our acts together. She was further along that path and she didn't want to be pulled backward."

"Okay, so the two of you didn't work. That isn't the boy's fault. The woman is at the café with the boy, Oliver. And I refuse to let you throw this away. He's your son. He needs you." She gave him a quick hug. "And I think you need him. You have ten minutes to get your act together and get to town."

She left with one last warning to do the right thing. He'd tried to tell her that yesterday he'd done the right thing. He'd sent Oliver off to live a life with a woman who obviously loved him. A woman who seemed to know how to be a parent.

A woman who had sparked something foreign inside Marcus. She'd looked at him with those sky blue eyes of hers, and she, too, had challenged him to do the right thing. And he'd wanted to.

Which resulted in the decision he'd made. He'd sent her on her way. But she hadn't left town. Why hadn't she left? Because she was stubborn, that was why. Because for some reason she thought he should be involved in Oliver's life. For what purpose?

Thunder rumbled in the distance and gray clouds rolled from the south. He'd seen the forecast and knew they were in for some serious rain. The kind of rain that could only cause trouble. It seemed that the weather was the least of his concerns. He had to get to town and convince Lissa Hart to leave.

He didn't want himself tied to the woman. That was another good reason to send her back to where she came from. Having Oliver in his life clearly meant having Lissa there, as well. If one was trouble, the two together was catastrophe. As if on cue, lightning flashed across the sky.

The rain started as Lissa stood with her cell phone on the covered porch of Essie's café. Her mom, or foster mom, Jane Simms, continued to talk.

"You have to give him a chance." Jane was repeating what she'd already said more than once. "Oliver is his son. And it will be easier if you honor Sammy's wishes. If he comes back later and takes you to court, well, you don't want that for Oliver."

"No, I don't."

"You have vacation time. It wouldn't hurt you to take time off."

The wind blew the rain across the porch, the drops pelting Lissa's face. She wiped away the moisture and glanced inside the café, where Oliver was digging into his biscuits and gravy. He waved happily.

"I know and I need the time off, for more reasons than this."

"Is he still calling you?" Jane asked, speaking of a fellow nurse Lissa had dated for a short time.

"Not as often." She wanted to cry over the entire situation, but that wasn't her style. She would work through this, because on the scale of disasters she'd faced in her lifetime, this definitely didn't rate highest.

"His problems aren't yours," Jane reminded.

"I know. It's Troy's past that is the problem. And my past." She had fallen for a smile and sweeping romantic gestures, not realizing the baggage that came with both.

"It's okay to have goals, Lis. It's okay to want more. And it is okay to stay here and give this man a chance with his son. You're a good judge of character. That's why Sammy trusted you to know if he was ready to be a dad."

"I don't really want this responsibility. I love Oliver. I don't want to hurt him, and regardless of how I go with this, that could happen."

"But no matter what happens, you'll protect him," Jane countered. "I know you will. You've been more than an aunt to that little boy since the day he was born."

She sighed, holding the phone tight to her ear as thunder rumbled across a sky heavy with clouds. It was May. Of course there would be storms.

Neither she nor her foster mom spoke for several

long moments. As much as they had loved Sammy, they'd also known her faults. She had struggled, even after Oliver's birth. Neither of them wanted to speak of the past, not when it meant dwelling on the Sammy who had slipped into old behaviors and left her son too often with Jane or Lissa.

She'd been trying to straighten up and do right. That was what they focused on. She'd been working so hard on being better, for Oliver's sake.

"Don't dwell on it," Jane spoke softly. "You've taken a lot on yourself. And Sammy left a large hole in your life, along with this burden. You know I'm praying for you."

"I know you are." She looked anxiously up at the sky again. "I'd better let you go. It's raining harder and making it difficult to hear. I'm going to go back inside with Oliver."

"Give him kisses from his Gee Gee."

Lissa smiled as she said goodbye and she felt better. Jane always made her feel better. She was a true mother, even if she had come late to Lissa's life. Her own mother had failed Lissa for the first fourteen years, but Jane and Tom Simms had picked up the pieces and given her a future. They were the parents she turned to. Her own mother was someone she occasionally reached out to, hoping to find her better.

As she entered the restaurant, the wind picked up and so did the rain. Big drops splattered the windows and bounced off the cars parked along the front of Essie's. A flash of lightning lit up the early-morning sky and Oliver gulped as he swallowed a bite of biscuits and gravy. Wide-eyed, he looked up at Lissa as she sat down across from him.

"Is it a tornado?" he asked in hushed tones.

"No," she assured him. "Just rain. We always need rain in the spring."

A woman ran out of the kitchen. "Land sakes, it's gonna flood. I heard it on the news."

The waitress hurried from a table where she'd just delivered an order and took the older woman by the hand. "Bea, it isn't a flood. It's a storm. We get them in the spring and they pass. Look, there's a little boy and you don't want to scare him. Head on back to the kitchen. I left an order for you to cook while Essie is gone."

The woman, midfifties and wearing a floral-print dress, orthopedic shoes and athletic socks, focused her wild-eyed attention on Oliver. Her lips pursed and her eyes narrowed.

"Why, doesn't he look the spittin' image of the Palermo twins? I reckon someone is in big trouble and that's why Essie went roaring out of here in her old Scout. She said Marcus was about to get his ears boxed."

The waitress tugged on the woman's arm. "Bea, back to the kitchen."

Bea remained standing, wringing her hands in her apron. She glanced at Oliver and then at the windows. Lightning flashed across the sky. She trembled visibly.

"Is the little boy scared?" Bea asked the waitress, Libby. "I remember Marcus and Alex hiding under tables when it stormed. They were little like that."

"He isn't afraid." Libby tried to move the cook, but Bea wouldn't budge.

The bells chimed, signaling that the café door had opened. A breeze too cool for mid-May swept through the café and the rain became a deafening roar. Lissa didn't have to look to know who would be coming through the door. She knew because the woman, Bea, glanced from the door to Oliver and back to the door. She knew because Oliver stopped looking worried and grinned big.

"I'm going back to the kitchen," Bea announced. "Marcus is in big trouble."

Marcus nodded a greeting to a few people, pulled off his hat and headed in their direction. He half grinned at Oliver as he pulled out the empty chair at their table.

"Mind if I sit?" he asked as he folded his lean, athletic frame into the seat. He'd taken off his hat and he dropped it on Oliver's head.

Lissa started to ask if it mattered that she did mind. Instead, she forced a smile and shook her head. "No. Of course not."

At her terse response he grinned and nodded at the coffee cup on the table. He turned the cup over for the waitress to fill and leaned back as if he didn't feel the tension. But even Oliver felt it. The boy glanced from Marcus to Lissa and back to Marcus.

"Are you enjoying your biscuits and gravy?" he asked Oliver.

"Yeah. They're the best." Oliver took another big bite. "Can I see your dog again?"

"Maybe," he answered.

Lissa wanted to hurt him for being so noncommittal. She wanted to yell at him for invading their lives and turning everything upside down. But then, hadn't she been the one doing the invading? Because she'd made this trip, none of their lives would ever be the same.

"Hey, Oliver, want to come back to the kitchen and help me make today's dessert? You can even taste the pudding to make sure it's good." Essie, owner of the café and Marcus's aunt, approached their table. She wiped her hands on her apron and appeared to be completely innocent of interfering.

"Can I?" Oliver looked from Essie to Lissa. And then his gaze drifted to Marcus, and for the first time the boy seemed confused and unsure of the situation. "Aunt Lissa, are you okay?"

"Of course I'm okay. And yes, you can go with Miss Essie. I think that would be fun. When you get back, we'll leave."

He gave her a quick hug, and the feel of his small arms wrapping around her neck was the sweetest thing ever. He wasn't hers, but she loved him as if he were. Marcus Palermo could take him from her. She'd known that when she came here. She'd known for the past year that her time with Oliver might be limited. It had been a constant source of stress.

Essie gave them both a long look that held a lot of meaning, then she walked off with Oliver's hand tucked in hers. The two were discussing chocolate pie and brownies. Oliver glanced back as he walked through the door to the kitchen.

"Surprise," Marcus whispered as the doors to the kitchen closed. They weren't alone. There were still people in the café sending them curious looks that they didn't try to disguise.

"Yes. I didn't expect to see you this morning."

"Imagine how I felt when my aunt showed up at my place to inform me there was a woman in town and she had a little boy that looks a lot like me. Why are you still in town?"

He had a point. A good one. "I couldn't leave. I

wanted you to have a night to think about Oliver and being a father."

"So you planned on giving me another chance?" He arched a brow at her, clearly questioning her honesty. Or her sanity.

Lissa didn't quite know what to say.

She had wanted to go on, to forget Marcus and Bluebonnet Springs. But Oliver had been in the back seat of the car, his dark eyes intent on her face in the mirror, and he'd asked about Marcus and wondered if he'd been a friend of his mommy. Pushing aside her feelings of protectiveness, for Oliver's sake she'd searched for a place to stay. For one night, she'd told herself. To give Marcus a chance.

She didn't want to get ten years down the road and have Oliver ask her why she'd kept him from his father. She also didn't want to settle into her life as Oliver's mom and have Marcus show up out of the blue one day and take him.

"You could give a guy a chance to catch his breath. This did come out of nowhere," Marcus said. The admission seemed pulled from deep inside. "It's hard for me to imagine Sammy keeping this from me. I know we weren't a good match. But he's mine. That's pretty obvious."

"So, does a new day make things different for you?"

"His mercies are new every morning." He spoke so softly she almost didn't hear the words she hadn't expected from this hardened cowboy. "Nothing is different. But everything has changed."

"Meaning?"

"I don't know how to be a father. I didn't plan on getting married or bringing kids into the world."

"You can't undo what already is." Her heart ached for the little boy who at that moment was eating pudding and didn't know that his father was sitting there trying to figure out if he could be a part of his life.

He toyed with the spoon next to his coffee cup. "It isn't that I don't want him. But I don't want to hurt him. He's better off with you."

"He's your son."

He sat there for a long minute looking at her. "Right. My son that Sammy didn't tell me about. That speaks volumes."

"She was afraid."

"Of me." One brow arched. She understood what he meant. Sammy had given birth to his son and then decided he wasn't suitable to be in his child's life. And later she'd regretted that decision.

Meeting him changed everything for Lissa. She hadn't expected to like him. She hadn't expected a lot of things about him. Like his thoughtfulness. Or the depth of emotion in his dark eyes.

"Time goes by and what seemed like a good decision starts to look like a bad one. Sammy regretted not telling you. And then she ran out of time." She closed her eyes to regroup. It had been a year. She still missed her friend. Her sister. "And now you're about to make the same mistake. What looks like a good idea today, five years down the road, might be the worst mistake of your life."

"Valid point," he said. "But if I allow you to tell him I'm his father, and I hurt him… Five years down the road, we can't undo the damage. Speaking from experience, that kind of hurt can't be undone."

She wasn't here to share stories, but she understood

the damage an abusive parent could do to a child. She understood the scars, invisible and visible.

She understood how it affected relationships.

"You should at least get to know him."

"How would that work, me getting to know him? How would you explain to him who I am and why he is spending time with me?"

"I'm not sure. We don't have to tell him you're his dad. Not until you're ready. Or until we think he is ready."

She glanced toward the window. The sky had darkened and, if possible, the rain came down harder.

"This rain is only getting worse."

He was right. The rain was coming down in sheets. After the previous week of rain, she knew that the creeks would rise. The roads back to San Antonio would be a nightmare.

Before she left, she had to put all of her cards on the table. He deserved the whole truth, even if it meant losing Oliver. She reached into her purse and pulled out the letter.

"You should read this. Sammy left it with her will."

He took the paper, but he didn't open it. Instead, he slipped it into his pocket. "I'll look at it some other time."

"Sooner rather than later, Marcus."

"Right."

"Fine, here's my number." She wrote it on a napkin and handed it to him.

Thunder crashed and the windows rattled with the force of the wind. He glanced at her number and back to the storm raging outside. "You might ought to stay in town."

"I'll be fine. It's just a little rain. And it might let up before I leave. I have to pack up and check out of our room at the B and B."

She stood to retrieve Oliver from the kitchen, but Marcus pushed himself out of his chair first. "I'll get him."

It was a start, so she waited where she stood and watched as he headed for the kitchen.

He had stories. She didn't want them. She didn't want to be affected by a man her foster sister had deemed "too broken." She'd always had a soft spot for broken things. It was her reason for becoming a nurse. Because as a nurse she had a reason to care, a reason to fix broken people. Fix them and send them home. Once she sent them home, they were out of her life. And then she had new people to care about, to help.

Lissa knew her own hang-ups. She had lived in a broken and abusive home with a mother who never put her child first. A mother she had tried to fix. And she'd failed. Time and again. Six months ago she had promised herself that she wouldn't be used. Ever again. She wouldn't enable. She wouldn't give money. She would always care—she would pray for the woman who had given her life—but she wouldn't give her the power to hurt her.

She and Sammy had been from similar backgrounds. As teens in the Simms home, they had made a pact to never be abused again, or tie themselves to broken men who would wound them the way their own mothers had been wounded. And they wouldn't have children with men who would leave scars.

When Sammy had met Marcus, she'd been drawn to him in a way she'd deemed unhealthy. She'd never introduced him to Lissa, but she'd told her about him and about how easy it had been to fall for his charm. She'd lost herself a little, and when she realized that, she'd broken things off.

A few minutes later Marcus returned with Oliver. His aunt stood in the doorway of the kitchen, her mouth a firm line of disapproval. Marcus squatted, putting himself at eye level with his son. Lissa watched, wondering if Oliver suspected that this man was his father.

"You be good, okay?" Marcus said. She heard the rasp of emotion and knew he cared. That he cared spoke well of him. If only he realized that.

"I'll be good. Can I come back and see your dog?" Oliver took a slight step forward. "And could I get a hat like yours?"

Marcus nodded and he looked up, meeting her gaze. He stood and backed up a step, putting a hand on his son's head.

"We'll be in touch?" Lissa asked.

Again he nodded. She took Oliver by the hand and left. Even though he'd said they would be in touch, she wondered if he meant to keep his word or if this was an easy way to say goodbye.

Chapter Three

A couple of hours after saying goodbye to Lissa and Oliver, Marcus was in the field, feeling thankful for a break in the clouds and for the help of his twin.

"How much rain are we supposed to get?" Marcus asked Alex as the two of them moved cattle from twenty acres along the creek to higher ground. They had opted for ATVs over horses. The rain had slacked off for a short time and they wanted to get the job done as quickly as possible.

"They're saying up to a foot of rain toward the weekend. This is just the appetizer," Alex responded as he moved his four-wheeler the opposite direction in order to keep a few steers from bolting back toward the creek.

Marcus glanced in the direction of his house. If they got that much rain, his house would be under water. The creek was coming up fast. He had sandbags, but he knew he couldn't control the rise of water if there was a flash flood.

"We'll do what we can to keep the water out," Alex called out as they moved the cattle through the open gate.

A cow spooked. Marcus went after her, turning the

four-wheeler hard to the right to stop her. She moved back to the herd and Alex closed the gate behind her. As they headed for the barn, the rain started again. They hit the throttles and raced side by side, stopping after they'd reached the safety of the equipment barn.

Alex was laughing as he climbed from the four-wheeler. He took off his hat and shook it. "Wow, this makes a guy want to build an ark."

Marcus shrugged out of his raincoat. "I hate rain."

"But you hate it more when we're going through a drought and everything dries up." Alex sat sideways on the seat of the ATV. "So, when are you going to tell me about your kid?"

"I guess I kind of thought it wasn't any of your business."

"Really? I'm your brother. Your twin. It seems to me I'd be the person most likely to listen if you need to talk. You had to know that everyone in town would be talking about how much that little boy looks like you."

"I guess I hadn't thought about it. And no need to analyze my mental condition, brother, I'm fine."

"Of course you're fine. But you have a son. That's huge."

"Yeah, it is." He sat there thinking about Oliver. "He seems like a pretty great kid. And I don't want to mess that up for him."

"I get that. But we don't always get to choose how things work out," Alex responded. "Well, we should make a run for the house before the rain picks up again."

"You can head home. I'll do the rest of this myself. I'm sure you want to see Marissa." Alex's wife of five months. He'd found her standing on the side of the road in a wedding dress. She was a little bitty thing, but fierce, and she'd convinced Alex to give up his single ways. They'd married in December, a year after they'd first met.

Alex wasn't Marcus. As kids they'd been different as night and day. The same went for the two of them as adults. Alex thought things out and let things go. Marcus had always battled it out and held on to his anger. When it came to their father, Alex had tried to reason. He'd searched to find ways to solve their problems. Conversely, Marcus had gone at Jesse and he'd paid physically for his efforts.

Marcus's phone buzzed. He glanced at the unfamiliar number and answered. "Marcus Palermo."

"Marcus, Guy Phipps here. We've got a car in the ditch just south of the old crossroads bridge."

"Who is it?" He glanced at his brother. Alex had moved closer, pulling out his phone as he did. Probably worrying about his wife. Or their sister Lucy. Even Maria, if she was on her way home from college. She'd begun her summer break just a few days ago and planned on heading home.

"Not from around here. Name is…" Guy paused. "Name's Lissa Hart. She's got a little boy with her. She said to call you."

He took a deep breath and made eye contact with Alex, who now appeared worried. "Are they hurt?"

"Nothing serious. Doc is here. He's checking her shoulder. The little guy might have bumped his head." Guy paused again. In the background, Marcus heard sirens.

It shook him. Marcus could willingly get on the biggest and meanest bulls in the country, a ton of pure rage and power. It might get his adrenaline going, but it didn't shake him. It didn't make him feel weak as a kitten and helpless to do anything.

"Guy, are they taking them to the hospital? Do I need to meet them somewhere?" Marcus glanced at Alex, who had followed as he walked away, wanting privacy, wanting to put on a mask, as if this didn't matter. Alex wore a worried expression and Marcus knew his own would match. The two of them might be different, but they were the same. The twin thing wasn't just a myth.

He knew Alex would feel his concern. And from that troubled look in his dark eyes, Marcus understood Alex felt his brother's guilt. He'd sent the kid away. He didn't know how to be a dad, so he had sent his son on down the road in the middle of a torrential rainstorm with floods predicted. Proof that he didn't deserve to be a parent. He wasn't any better than his own father, putting his own feelings ahead of the safety of a child.

And Lissa. He hadn't given her a second thought once he'd said his goodbyes. At least, he'd told himself he wasn't going to give her a second thought. It counted, that he'd intended to forget her. But even now, those blue eyes of hers triggered a memory. She'd challenged him to care. For his son.

Few people got away with challenging him. Few people had the backbone for it.

On the other end of the line the first responder was giving him information. He had to focus. "Doc said he's going to drive them back to his office if you want to meet him there. The boy is asking for you. He's a tough kid." There was a smile in the first responder's voice.

"Put him on the phone." Marcus waited and pretty soon a hiccup over the phone told him Oliver was there and fighting tears. "Hey, little man. You okay?"

"I hit my head."

"I bet that hurt."

"It did. They said I wasn't uncon…uncon…" He sounded like a boy trying to be brave.

"Unconscious?" Marcus supplied.

"Yeah. So I'm okay."

"Nothing else hurts?"

"Nope," Oliver said on a sniffle.

"Is Lissa okay?"

More sniffling and then, "Yeah, I think. She says her shoulder hurts. She's not crying, though. Doc said she's tougher than a bull rider. I think you're a bull rider."

"I am a bull rider," Marcus told his son. *His son.* "Listen, I'm going to see you in a few minutes. You're tough. You've got this."

"Yeah, I'm tough." The boy sounded like he meant to convince himself.

"I'll be there in a few minutes, so you keep being tough and you take care of Lissa. She's not as tough as she's pretending to be."

He ended the call.

"Let's go," Alex said. "I'll drive."

"I can drive. I want to grab a couple of blankets from the house." Marcus headed for his truck.

"They're fine," Alex called out to him. "If they were in bad shape, Doc would send them to Killeen."

"I know that." Marcus opened his truck door and found his keys in the ignition. Alex climbed in on the other side.

"You should take your keys out."

"Yeah, I know. But spare me the lectures."

"So you don't want me to tell you that you care about

this kid and you shouldn't let him walk away?" Alex reached to turn up the heat.

"I want you to stay out of my business."

Alex gave him a thumbs-up. "Right."

"Don't talk."

His twin zipped his lips.

Marcus might have grinned at the ridiculous gesture, but he didn't have an ounce of humor in him. He had sent his kid away in this weather. His reckless decision had put Oliver and Lissa in danger.

It took fifteen minutes to get to the scene of the accident.

Flashing lights and scattered emergency vehicles lined the road. Marcus pulled behind a first responder and got out. The rain had picked back up. He saw Lissa sitting in Doc Parker's car. Oliver sat huddled against her, his face pale and a bandage over the right side of his forehead. Doc leaned in talking to them.

The car she'd been driving now sat on the back of a tow truck. The driver's side was dented and the tires on the passenger's side were flat. Alex said something to him about seeing where they would tow the car.

When Marcus appeared behind Doc, Oliver noticed first and big tears rolled down his cheeks. Marcus pushed away memories of his sister looking much the same way. He hadn't been able to help Lucy, but he could help Oliver. At least for today he could handle things and make sure the child wasn't frightened and didn't feel alone.

And then he made eye contact with Lissa and he could see in her blue eyes that she was being strong for Oliver. He recognized the flicker of pain that flashed across her features, tightening the lines around her mouth. But she managed a smile as she raised her left hand in a half-hearted wave.

"The roads are a mess," she informed him with a hint of humor in her voice.

"Yeah, I've heard." He leaned against the side of the car. "How are they, Doc?"

"Oh, not too bad all things considered. I think Miss Hart has a dislocated shoulder. Actually, she's a nurse and that's her diagnosis. I would concur. Mr. Oliver has a good bump on his head, but I think he's okay. I'll take them back to my office. We'll get that shoulder back in place and I'll turn them over to you."

Turn them over to him? He started to object. He was the last person they should be relying on. But Oliver looked happy with the news. And Lissa Hart looked… relieved?

Lissa kept her left arm around Oliver. Her right arm she kept at her side. Every bump jostled it and sent a shooting pain to her shoulder. She cringed and Oliver snuggled closer.

"It's okay," she encouraged, trying to smile.

"Marcus is going to be with us." Oliver said it with satisfaction, as if Marcus Palermo solved all of their problems.

The way she looked at it, Marcus was just another problem. He was too handsome. He was too much of a loner. He didn't need or want anyone in his life. And the little boy sitting next to her wanted and needed a father. He would have to be told the truth, and when that happened, she knew he would want to stay with Marcus.

"I know he is going to be there." She bit down on her lip as they hit a few potholes. The first responder had warned her that a ride with Doc Parker could be worse than the accident. She now understood the warning.

The car stopped at what appeared to be an abandoned convenience store. "What is this?"

Doc had already gotten out and was opening the door to help her. "My office."

"Oh."

"Don't worry, it's better than it looks. I know, an RN like yourself, you're used to city clinics and hospitals. This serves us just fine."

"I'm sure it does." She eased herself out of the car and waited for Oliver. He had been so brave, but he now had big tears in his eyes. One broke loose and slid down his cheek. He swiped it away and managed a fierce look.

"Are you okay, sweetheart?" She leaned close to the little boy.

He nodded and sniffed away the tears. "I'm good. I'm going to be a bull rider someday. Like Marcus. So I have to be tough."

She wanted to sigh at that revelation. Oliver needed male role models. That was all. He was attaching himself to Marcus not because of the connection but because he represented everything a kid like Oliver wanted. Marcus was tough. He had lived an exciting life. He was a world champion. Of course Oliver wanted to be like him.

Doc cleared his throat as he looked from her to the little boy. "We'd best get you inside and put that shoulder back in the socket. Marcus will be here any minute. He just had a hard time keeping up with me." The last was said with a grin and, she thought, a bit of misplaced pride.

He led them through a dismally decorated waiting

room to a small exam room. Lissa gave Oliver what she hoped to be a reassuring look.

"Oliver, do you want to sit out in the waiting room? I bet Dr. Parker has a book you can look at."

Doc rubbed a hand through thinning gray hair. "Books. Yes, I should have books. I keep meaning to get more. I have young ones that come in and books are something they love to take home with them. I can't deny a child a book. And it's Doc, not Dr. Parker."

He walked away mumbling about books and toys and a shopping list. Oliver followed him out of the exam room, leaving Lissa alone. She closed her eyes and said a quick prayer. For her shoulder. For the doctor. And for the situation with Marcus and Oliver.

Her peace was short-lived. She heard male voices from the waiting room. Doc's more gentle voice resonated through the door. She couldn't make out his words. There were footsteps in the hall, a door closed, more talking. She heard Oliver telling them about how hard he hit his head and that he was sure he must have a headache. She smiled at his matter-of-fact assessment of his condition. He was fine, she assured herself. He wouldn't be talking and laughing if he wasn't okay.

And then the door opened and Marcus Palermo charged through, looking ragged and worn. Without greeting her, he took off his hat and hung it on a hook. He brushed a hand through curly, dark hair and then he seemed to remember her presence.

"What happened?"

"I'm fine, thank you. So is Oliver." She didn't have the patience for overbearing, take-charge men.

"I'm sorry—" he shook his head "—I shouldn't have let you leave in this weather."

"You didn't have a choice. I'm an adult and I made the decision." She grimaced as a hot flash of pain hit her shoulder, payment for what should have been a carefree shrug.

"It wasn't safe," he said as he took a seat on the rolling stool next to the exam table.

"I'm twenty-eight. I know how to drive in the rain. Could you please go sit with Oliver? He's alone. I don't want him to be alone." She also didn't want to be told what she could or couldn't do. Her short relationship with Troy Larson had taught her that there was a fine line between a caring man who wanted to spend time with a woman and a controlling jerk who didn't trust her out of his sight.

"Oliver isn't alone. He's with Doc and my brother, Alex." He pinned her with his dark gaze. "Doc said your shoulder is dislocated."

"Yes. It's happened before and it isn't too bad this time. I'm more worried about Oliver. If you could sit with him. Make sure he isn't nauseated. Watch that his speech doesn't slur."

The door opened and Doc stepped inside the cramped room with the green carpet and mustard-yellow walls. He glanced at his watch and then at her.

"Well, young lady, let's get this shoulder taken care of so we don't miss lunch. Essie has the best enchiladas on Tuesdays."

She nodded toward the door. "Cowboy, you should go. This isn't going to be pleasant."

Doc cackled at her warning. "You think I haven't reset a bone or two for these boys? Marcus could probably set this shoulder with his eyes closed. He only lets me do it because he's polite. Shy, quiet type, you know."

She closed her eyes and nodded. "Yes, he is quiet."

"Well, I can't fix everything," Doc said softly. She wondered what he meant by that. "Now, let me see."

He felt her shoulder and then gently rotated her arm. She took a deep breath, knowing what would come next. Still, she wasn't prepared. Not for the bolt of lightning-deep pain or the arm that encircled her, holding her steady. Marcus smelled of rain, soap and aftershave, the kind of spicy scent that made a girl think of mountains and lakes. For a brief moment it took her mind off the pain in her shoulder. He was strong. Definitely the kind of guy a girl could lean on. But just for a moment.

Doc handed her a couple of pills and a glass of water. "I'm sorry about that. No way to do it without causing a lot of hurt. I'm going to put some ice on your shoulder and we'll put that arm in a sling. I guess you'll know when it's time to start exercising it a bit. And I guess I don't have to tell you not to drive. From the looks of your car, it won't be going anywhere for a while."

She briefly closed her eyes. "I need to call my insurance. I can get a rental."

"That won't be possible." Marcus gave her a sympathetic look. Maybe a grimace. She wasn't sure. "Not only is your car totaled but the bridge is going to be under water."

"I'm not sure what to do," she admitted as the full impact of the situation hit home.

"For now you stay put." Marcus's voice, soft and raspy, had an edge to it. And she got it. He wasn't any happier about this than she was. He probably thought he'd seen the last of her.

Doc cleared his throat. "If I might be so bold, Essie is in the waiting room. She heard about the accident on the scanner and she came right over. She's a bit nosy. But she's ready to take you to her place."

"Doc, could we have a minute alone?" Marcus asked.

"You and me?" Doc didn't show a hint of amusement, but a knowing twinkle lit his eyes.

"Doc," Marcus's tone held a warning.

Lissa cringed. Controlling men. They were all the same. When he'd dated Sammy, had he asked her where she was going? Who she was going with? When she would call him?

Doc looked from one to the other of them and sighed. "Right, I'll go check on that young man of yours."

Lissa watched Doc slip through the door, closing it tightly behind him. Marcus pinched the bridge of his nose.

"Stay with Aunt Essie," he said finally. "The flooding is going to be worse. The next few days could get pretty bad. You obviously can't drive with your right arm in a sling."

Stay. She knew that this was the fork in the road. There were many in life, and this time the choice was hers and it would affect not only her life but Oliver's. And Marcus's.

"Fine, I'll stay. But I have conditions."

"Name your price."

She shook her head at the reference to money. "There is no price. I'm not after money. I'm after your time, Marcus. While we are here, you have to spend time with Oliver. And at some point we have to tell him that you're his father."

"I don't know how to be a father."

Of course he didn't. But what man did? It happened to everyone. People decided to have children. They became parents. It wasn't as if they knew how to do it beforehand. It was on-the-job training.

"Maybe you don't know how, but you'll learn. I'll be here and I can help."

A muscle ticked in his jaw. "That's a lot to put on a man who, until you showed up, hadn't planned on having a family. Ever."

"I understand. But you do have a son. He's sitting in that waiting room and he thinks you're the best thing ever."

"He's a good kid," Marcus said softly in his gruff way. She realized now it wasn't that he was gruff. It was his voice.

"Yes, he is."

She sighed, knowing the decision she had to make, and knowing that it meant eventually losing Oliver to this man, his father. "I have vacation time," she told him. "I'll give you three weeks to get this figured out. And I'll help you as much as I can. But I don't want to lose Oliver, either." And she hoped that in the end she wouldn't lose him, not completely.

"I understand."

Her heart pounded hard against her ribs as she realized she'd just given this man a piece of her life. She'd given him a part of her heart. The part that belonged to a little boy.

As she tried to process her emotions, he took her hand gently in his and held it briefly, before shaking it to seal the deal.

That gentleness undid some of her fears and multiplied others. She'd come to Bluebonnet Springs thinking it would be easy to discount him as a parent. He would be the angry, difficult man that Sammy had described, and Lissa would have walked away with Oliver, thinking she had done her best.

But he wasn't that man. If the eyes were the mirror of the soul, then he wasn't cruel and unfeeling. He wasn't a monster. He had been wounded. Deeply. And he cared for his family. Very much.

Chapter Four

The rain continued to come down, and by Thursday, as Marcus made his way up the long gravel drive to Essie's house, it looked as if the ponds had turned to lakes and the ditches were streams carrying debris all the way to the main road. They were in trouble. They all knew it. Farmers were moving cattle away from the spring that ran through town and the countryside. Roads were being closed left and right.

The rain they'd had since Monday was mild compared to what was coming over the weekend.

The house came into view, a two-story ranch house with large windows, a lot of stucco and wood trim, and warmth. Essie's house always felt like home. The Palermo kids had all done their share of running to Essie's. And then Jesse had dragged them home. Essie, like most people around town, hadn't liked to cross her nephew. For the most part she had avoided him.

He parked beneath the portico at the side of the house and got out. The sky was heavy with clouds and the air was thick with humidity. He hurried up the steps to the side door that led through the breakfast sunroom to the kitchen. Essie smiled a greeting and went back to making coffee.

"I closed the café. People don't need to be driving to town in this, not for my biscuits and gravy." She explained her presence without looking up from the coffeemaker.

"They'd drive through a blizzard for your biscuits and gravy," he assured her as he gave her a quick hug. "How are your guests?"

"Sleeping. Lissa had a restless night and finally slept in the recliner. I have a casserole in the oven and cinnamon rolls are ready to eat. Which do you want?"

"Both," he told her as he grabbed a plate and snatched one of the rolls. "But I'll start with this."

"I'm sure you've already had a full day."

"Been up since five this morning. Fed, moved cattle, loaded up my horses and took them to Alex's place." By Alex's place he meant the Palermo ranch. But he was content to let it be Alex and Marissa's home.

"It's only going to get worse," Essie told him as she poured two cups of coffee. "Have you seen the radar?"

"Yeah, and thanks for the optimism. I thought you would be praying for it to stop."

"I'm praying, but sometimes it rains and the only thing you can do is have the buckets ready. I told Lissa they're welcome to stay here as long as they need."

"Thank you."

She gave him a look over the rim of her coffee cup, her dark eyes saying more than words. She was wanting to know how he could have walked away from a child.

"I didn't know," he defended. "Do you think I would have left a kid on his own if I'd known?"

"I would hope not. But what you did isn't as important as what you do going forward."

"I know that. I'm a different person." A completely different person. He was a new man with new faith. That didn't make him whole, but he could at least look at the situation with those new eyes.

The only person he couldn't make it right with was Sammy. Because she was gone. The thought settled like a heavy weight in his chest. They'd both been too damaged to make a relationship work, but he should have done better by her. He should have called.

He guessed this was a real lesson in thinking things through and knowing there would always be consequences. And the consequence appeared, sleepy-eyed and dark hair tousled. He had a thumb jammed in his mouth and he wore red plaid pajamas that were a little too big on him.

"Good morning, Oliver." Aunt Essie swooped his son up and hugged him tight. "Are you hungry?"

It was a shame Essie had never had kids of her own. Instead, she mothered everyone she came into contact with. Including Bea, her cook and chief problem maker at the café.

Oliver nodded as an answer to Essie's question and pulled the thumb from his mouth. He let his dark gaze settle on Marcus. He was waiting.

Marcus cleared his throat. "Morning, Oliver. How about coffee?"

Essie rolled her eyes. "He's five, Marcus. He drinks milk."

Marcus winked at his son. "I knew that, but I like to get Essie all riled up. I'll pour you some milk and get you a cinnamon roll."

Marcus pulled milk out of the fridge and got a glass.

"I like chocolate milk," Oliver informed them.

"I think I have cocoa." Essie went to the cabinet. "I'll measure it into the milk and you can stir."

Oliver nodded and stuck to Essie's side as she produced the container of chocolate powder, and Marcus set the glass of milk on the counter. He leaned a hip against the counter and watched.

They were stirring the milk when Lissa appeared. He glanced her way and quickly averted his gaze. She was bleary-eyed with her dark hair going in all directions. She might not have slept a lot, but he guessed she'd slept hard. She noticed his amusement and frowned.

"You're not allowed to laugh at me. It isn't like I can untangle this mess." She lifted her left hand to try to smooth the strands that framed her face.

"You look fine," he said. As far as lines went, or compliments, that probably rated bottom of the scale.

Behind him, Essie chuckled. He shot her a look as she pulled the casserole from the oven.

Lissa glared at him as she continued to brush her fingers through her hair. He reached out, smoothing the silky strands of hair, letting them slide through his fingers. It was about the worst thing he could have done, making that connection with her, touching her. He'd meant to help. Instead, he stood there all tangled up in something he hadn't expected. Her breath caught as he slid his fingers free of the strands of hair. Blue eyes caught and held his attention.

Behind him the pan banged on the counter with meaning. He stepped back. "It looks fine. I can braid it for you, if that would make it easier."

"No." She shook her head. "I'll leave it down."

"Did you manage to get any sleep?" he asked.

"Some… Enough. But the shoulder does feel a bit better today." She cleared her throat. "That casserole smells so good."

"It's ready," Essie piped up. There was a smirk this time when she made eye contact with Marcus. He didn't like this version of his aunt. She usually minded her own business. Now it felt as if she had a plan, a plot, and he was the victim.

He needed something else to focus on. That would be Oliver. The little boy looked kind of lost. Marcus ruffled his hair.

"Want to help me set the table, little man?"

Oliver nodded and followed him the way Lucky the dog sometimes did. As if he was just waiting for something good. A pat on the head, a bone. Marcus knew that this boy, his son, wanted and needed more from him.

He pulled plates from the cabinet and silverware from the drawer. He handed the forks and knives to Oliver.

"Can you take those to the breakfast room?"

Marcus led Oliver to the sun-filled breakfast room. It might mean losing his man card, but he loved the room with the white trim and pale yellow walls. Ferns hung from hooks in the ceiling, and potted plants filled the corners. The window seat, cushioned with aqua-and-yellow pillows, looked out over the field. Essie's cat, Midas, stretched and graced Marcus with a contented feline look.

Essie had placed the casserole on a trivet in the center of the round table. Marcus sat down opposite Lissa and then realized that more was required from him. Oliver stared at the casserole with big eyes and anticipation. Essie had gone back to the kitchen for napkins, so Marcus took over serving.

Oliver's eyes widened at the portion of casserole and the cinnamon roll with icing that Marcus piled on his plate.

As the boy dug in, Marcus was amazed and a bit lost. He'd missed out. He'd missed five years' worth of breakfasts. Five birthdays. Five Christmases. Walking. Talking. Every single thing that would have meant building a relationship, precious moments stolen from them both.

Two days ago he had been in denial. Today he got swept up in the anger and unfairness of it. It didn't matter that he believed his son would be better off without him. What mattered was that he was the dad and he should have known his son. He wanted to blame the woman sitting across from him, but it hadn't been up to her. And as mad as he was about the situation, he understood why Sammy had blocked him from Oliver's life.

A hand touched his arm. He glanced down at the woman seated next to Oliver. Her eyes were warm and met his with compassion. She gave his arm a squeeze, transferring that compassion with her touch. He shook his head, clearing his thoughts.

Without asking, he served her a portion of the casserole. And then he grabbed his coffee and left. Because he couldn't look at Oliver without feeling guilt. Without feeling angry.

He walked through the house to the covered front porch, where he stood sipping his coffee, trying to get his better self back. The door behind him opened. He expected Essie. Instead, Lissa stepped out to join him. She was the last person he'd expected to come chasing after him. She was probably the last person he *wanted* chasing after him. For any reason. She made him question himself a little too much. She made him want things he had told himself he didn't want.

He'd spent a lifetime building himself up as a happy bachelor. Okay, maybe not happy. A bachelor. Single. Living for himself. No worries about hurting people or letting them down. He didn't want or need a woman in his life.

At least that was what he'd been telling himself for a long time.

"You should go eat," he said, once again staring out over the rain-soaked farm.

"So should you. And yet you're out here fighting with the past and someone who isn't here to argue back." She stood next to him now. Man, she smelled good. Like sunshine.

"Yeah, well, I do like to argue. And I have every right to be angry."

"You do." She agreed, and that surprised him. "When Sammy found out she was pregnant, I told her to call you, to give you a chance. She said she couldn't do it… that she'd had a lifetime of men with commitment-phobia and she wasn't going to have you in her life just to have you walk out on them."

"I wouldn't have walked out."

She shrugged. "Maybe not."

"What made you decide to find me now, after all this time?" He glanced down at her. She was only a few inches shorter than he was, which made it easy to look her in the eye, easy to see her distrust.

"I don't know. I love Oliver and I don't want to lose him. But it was never right to keep him from you."

"I missed out on five years. He doesn't even know me. I'm a bull rider you decided to visit one day. He has to wonder why."

"I'm sure he does. And we'll tell him."

"When?"

"Soon." She moved away from him. "Have you read the letter?"

"No, I haven't."

"You should."

Yeah, he guessed he should. He had it in his pocket, a crumpled piece of paper with a lawyer's signature on the bottom.

He skimmed the letter, wishing he had read it sooner, read it somewhere private. Instead, the words jumped out at him as Lissa stood by the door to Essie's, her expression concerned and distrustful, all at the same time.

Sammy hadn't trusted him to be a father. She had given Lissa custody and the power to decide if he was capable of parenting his son. He raised his head, making eye contact with the woman who held his future in her hands. A woman who clearly didn't like him any more than Sammy had.

"I guess I can fight you. It would take a DNA test and not much else." He wasn't even sure why he uttered those words. He hadn't planned to keep Oliver. He knew the boy was better off with Lissa.

But he'd been considered unfit. And that made him mad. It made him want to fight.

"Yeah, I guess you could." She stood a little taller, and he guessed she was trying not to show her fear.

He shoved the letter back into his pocket. "This should never have happened. It shouldn't be you here giving me ultimatums. It shouldn't be me trying to figure out which end is up."

"I know that. But we can't go back and undo what Sammy did. We can only figure out what is best going forward."

"I guess so. But I wish I knew what it was you wanted from me. What kind of hoops do I have to jump through to earn your approval?"

"Come back inside, have breakfast with your son. Be a dad."

Be a dad. He'd met men who were fathers, real fathers. He'd watched them with their sons, encouraging them, disciplining without anger. They were men he looked up to. And the type of man he'd never considered becoming. Until now, when Sammy had ultimately put the ball in his court. And a son in his life. He followed Lissa inside and found himself wishing he wasn't a scarred-up, angry Palermo. If he wasn't, he might have tried to come up with a response that made her smile, something better than "Fine."

After the breakfast dishes were cleared, Lissa made a phone call to her foster parents. She'd called them on Tuesday, but she'd promised to keep in touch.

"How are you doing?" Jane asked, her voice bringing a sheen of moisture to Lissa's eyes. She quickly blinked it away.

"I'm good. I'm taking your advice and staying. I know you all could come get me. And I'll have a rental car as soon as I can get somewhere and find one. But you were right. For Oliver's sake, I need to see this through."

"Do you feel more optimistic about his father?"

The question brought the conversation to a standstill. *More optimistic* probably wasn't the way she'd put it. She was dangerously attracted to him and yet she knew better. Her last relationship had been a disaster. Troy had been a dysfunctional disaster, the product of a son raised by a controlling father. It felt like a repeat, even if Marcus wasn't anything like Troy. If anything, he was surprisingly gentle. It didn't make sense that this was the man Sammy had walked away from and refused to tell he had a son.

She wished she'd questioned her foster sister a little more, asking questions about why the relationship had ended. She wished she'd pushed for answers. Something more than two dysfunctionals don't make a positive.

No, she had to keep her thoughts focused on what was best for Oliver. She had to make the right choices for the little boy.

She told her foster mom that same thing. "It isn't that I'm optimistic. I just see that there might have been two sides to Sammy's story. And I want to do the right thing for Oliver."

"And you don't want to lose our little man in the process."

That part hurt the most. "Exactly."

The call ended and she stood on the covered front porch, watching as rain poured down in seemingly limitless amounts. The gray sky didn't show any signs of blue. The clouds were heavy and hung low. Fog rolled over the distant hills.

It was quiet here. The kind of quiet that made a person feel as if they were alone on the planet. She might have felt peace if she hadn't been worried about what the future held for herself and for Oliver. It wasn't as if she'd lit out for Bluebonnet Springs with no thought toward the future, no prayers for guidance. But now everything felt different. Marcus wasn't who she'd thought he would be. In Bluebonnet Springs, Oliver had family. Aunts, uncles and cousins. She didn't know what she'd expected to find here, but it wasn't this family looking out for each other.

The door opened behind her. She wasn't surprised that it was Marcus. He eyed her suspiciously. It seemed this was going to be their relationship, circling each other, questioning, worrying.

"Everything okay?" he asked as he moved to her side.

"Yes. I just wanted to touch base with my family. I wanted to let them know I'm staying so we can work this out."

"You think a few weeks will fix this situation?"

"I'm an optimist." Or at least trying to be one.

He half grinned at her words, and the faint sign of amusement caught her by surprise. "Yeah, me too."

She laughed. "Right."

"I even think this rain will let up a bit and maybe we won't have to build an ark to get out of Texas."

"I hope you're right about that."

He had a cowboy hat in his hand and he placed it on his head, adjusting it a little. His slightly long hair curled out from under, making him appear younger, less hard around the edges.

"I have to run over to my place to check on my livestock, and then I'll swing by my brother's place to assess things there. Oliver is curled up on the sofa watching a cartoon."

"Is that an invitation for me to go with you?" She regretted the words the moment they left her mouth.

He pushed the hat back a bit and gave her a long look.

"I don't have to go," she said.

"You can go. But fair warning…it might not be fun and you'll definitely get wet. Might want to see if Essie has a raincoat you can use."

She nodded and slipped into the house to see what she could find. Maybe she'd find her common sense. Essie seemed to have plenty of that. She might lend some, in case Lissa's had taken a long leave of absence.

Essie did have a raincoat. When Lissa stepped back outside, Marcus had disappeared. She heard a truck start and waited on the front porch as he drove to pick her up.

She stepped off the porch expecting to race across the lawn to the vehicle. Instead, he pulled close and jumped out to open the door for her.

"You didn't have to do that," she told him as she climbed in.

In response, he closed the door and hurried back to the driver's side. "I do have some manners."

"I know you do." She met his gaze. "Let's try to be friends."

"I'm trying," he told her in his low, gruff voice. "You have to give a guy a few days to figure things out and get over feeling like he's had his legs kicked out from under him."

"I know." She pulled her seat belt around and he reached over to click it into place for her. "Thank you."

"I'm not going to take him from you," he said as they headed down the long driveway back to the main road.

The sting of tears took her by surprise. She wiped

at them, and when he handed her a handkerchief, she shook her head.

"I'm fine."

"Yeah, of course you are." He shoved the handkerchief into her hand. "I know he needs you. I know he doesn't need a scarred-up, dysfunctional cowboy for a dad."

"I think you're wrong," she said, and the words took her by surprise. It was more than a platitude; it was the truth.

"I'm not wrong." He pulled onto the road. "I know myself better than anyone. I want him to know that I'm his dad. I want to spend time with him. But he needs you in his life."

"I think he might need us both. As the adults in his life, we have to find the best way to give him stability."

There was silence except for tires humming on wet pavement. Lissa studied the strong profile of the man sitting next to her. She couldn't see the left side of his face, but she wondered about the scar on his cheek. He glanced her way, caught her staring.

"Was the scar from bull riding?" she asked.

"It's a gift from my father," he said simply and kept driving.

"What?"

"The scar on my face. My father did that. I've always heard that the fruit doesn't fall far from the vine. If that's the case, I'm his son and I can't outrun the fact that his DNA is in me. I'm not going to subject another kid to the life we led when he was alive."

Lissa's heart constricted. It made her sad that he believed that about himself, that he would be a father like his own. But what could she tell him? She didn't know him well enough to reassure him otherwise.

She thought of another old saying and she smiled. "The proof is in the pudding."

"What?" He gave her a quick glance and then returned his focus to the road, steering around water that covered their lane.

"I don't know what it means. But if you want to throw out old sayings, I thought I'd toss out one of my own."

He grimaced and made a grunting noise that might have been a chuckle. "I think the point of a saying is that it should fit the situation. My dad was evil," he told her. "He wasn't a good person. I'm his son. The fruit doesn't fall far from the vine."

"But the proof is in the pudding," she repeated. "I don't know what proof is in the pudding, but I'm saying we should look at who you are and how you really treat those around you instead of insinuating you're evil just because your father was."

"That's real nice of you to think that." He hit his blinker and a moment later turned onto the back road that led to his place. "But I'm sure Sammy filled you in on exactly the kind of person I am. If you thought differently, you would have found me a little sooner. Sammy would have called me the day she found out she was pregnant. So there's the proof that is in the pudding."

"So Oliver is destined to be a horrible person, a terrible man and a bad father because your dad was a terrible person?"

He grinned at that. "Oh, good one. I think you get the point for this set. No, he isn't destined to be bad. He had Sammy and he has you. You'll make sure he grows up to be a decent person."

At one point Lissa could have left town, taken Oliver, and that would have been the end of it. But she had stayed and now their lives seemed to be intertwined. And the nurse in her, the person who cared and wanted to fix others, wouldn't let her walk away.

She knew better than to take Marcus on as a project. She knew one or both, maybe all three of them, would be hurt in the process.

But she was committed. She had a few weeks to show him he could be a decent father, that he wasn't destined to be his father's son any more than Oliver was. If they believed in redemption, and she knew they both did, then they had to believe hearts could change and the past didn't have to control the future.

Rather than finding reasons he couldn't have Oliver, she would help him to discover the reasons he *could*.

It seemed like the perfect plan as long as she could keep her own heart intact in the process. Marcus might be rough around the edges, but he was also chivalrous and kind. And when he smiled, she forgot that a relationship with a broken man was the last thing she wanted.

Chapter Five

From his parking spot next to the house, Marcus could see the normally lazy creek already out of its banks. With the rain still coming down, it would only get higher. He got out of the truck and Lissa joined him, standing so close that for a moment he was distracted by her. And that couldn't happen.

He needed to move his tractor and ATV to higher ground. The barn sat on a slight rise, and he didn't think water would get in there.

"Wow, there's a lot of power in that water." Lissa whistled low as they walked toward the creek.

"Yeah, enough to tear down a building or move a vehicle."

"Will it rise up to your house?"

He glanced back at the hundred-year-old home. "I guess it's probably gotten up there more than once. But that old house is solid."

He got lost for a minute, thinking of the Brown family who had lived there for nearly a century. Passed down from generation to generation, they'd built onto this house as the family grew. The house had history. A good history. He guessed that was what he liked about the place. It was rambling, ancient, but folks had been happy here. He couldn't imagine losing it this way.

"You okay?" she asked, her voice soft.

"Yeah, I'm good. Just thinking about that house. I'd hate for anything to happen to it."

"It means a lot to you, this house? Has it always been in your family?"

This was why he avoided conversation. People wanted to dig into his past, figure him out. Women were especially bad about digging. The scar. His voice. Those things attracted women who liked fixer-uppers.

He didn't need fixing.

But she was giving him that intent, questioning look, so he would give her the story she wanted.

"The house and property belonged to the Browns. When I was a kid, I used to walk down here, escaping my house and my dad. Mattie Brown made the best peanut butter cookies. And tea. She used to make me some kind of herbal tea. I don't know what she put in it, but it helped…"

He caught himself and shook his head. She didn't need that much information about his life. "I enjoyed visiting. They were a decent family. They liked each other. When it came up for sale, after all the kids moved away, I decided it shouldn't go to a stranger."

She was walking toward the back of his house, and he followed. The rain started to come down in sheets again and thunder rumbled in the distance. A second later the two of them were running. He reached the back door first and opened it for her. They stepped inside, dripping wet. It was a small space and they were face-to-face, both with water dripping. She swiped at her face with her hand, and then she touched his face, her hand brushing across the scar that he'd prefer most people didn't notice.

He stilled beneath her hesitant touch and she withdrew her hand. He grabbed a towel off the shelf over the washer and handed it to her.

"Liked each other?" she asked as she handed him the towel.

He blinked, confused.

"The people who lived here?" she clarified.

"I guess families should like each other, shouldn't they?"

In all the years he'd known Mattie and George Brown, he'd never seen them raise a hand to a person or an animal. George had worked with Marcus, teaching him to train horses. He hadn't realized back then that George was teaching him patience. Old and a little hard of hearing, George had taught Marcus to trust. There had been few people in his life whom he'd given that trust to.

The one person he still didn't trust, not completely, was himself. He didn't trust himself to not be like his own father.

"I had a neighbor." Lissa's voice broke into his thoughts, bringing him back to the present. "I called her *Tía* Theresa. She wasn't my aunt, but she would have been a wonderful aunt. She lived in the apartment next to ours. When things got rough in our apartment, I would sit in the stairwell. Theresa would join me on the steps, bringing me cookies or food." Lissa took a breath, then went on. "She told me about her husband—he'd been a police officer. He'd always treated her right, she said. Never laid a hand on her. Some men are like that, she would tell me. Some men don't hurt their women or their daughters. Not that the men my mother had in our apartment were husband or father. They were just the men she brought home."

The words she'd spoken hung between them. He didn't have to ask. He knew she'd been hurt.

"She hot-lined my mother," she said after a while. "She's the reason the state took me into custody and I went to live with the Simms family. Sammy and I were foster children together. It changed our lives. Because of the Simms, we had a family. I still have them."

He stood up, uncomfortable with the stories they were sharing and needing to shake off whatever it was about her that rattled him. He shook his head at that. He wasn't a liar, not even to himself. What it was about her was possibly everything. From her smile to the soft way she spoke and then her story. It connected them in a way he hadn't expected.

Or wanted.

The only way to sever the connection was to send her and his son packing and never see them again. That had seemed like a good idea, until it hadn't. As much as he didn't trust himself to be the man anyone would count on, he also didn't want to be the dad who walked out on his son.

He'd learned a long time ago that some things took hard work, and it appeared that parenting would be added to that list. He might not have learned the art of parenting from his own mother and father, but that didn't mean he had an excuse for not trying.

"I need to start moving equipment before that creek comes up any farther." He pulled a jacket off the hook by the door.

He thought she'd stay put. Instead, she grabbed the rain jacket she'd borrowed from Essie.

"I'll help."

Of course she would.

He gave her a long look, shook his head and walked out the door. He walked fast, letting her hurry to catch up with him.

She laughed, the sound light and a little breathless. "Oh, wow, you're running because we shared our stories and that let me in a little too close for comfort, didn't it? Emotion is your Kryptonite. You're better with the surface stuff. A smile, a joke, a teasing look, maybe dinner."

"I don't do one-night stands, if that's what you're insinuating." He checked back to see if she was keeping up. "I don't do relationships. Period. I haven't dated since Sammy."

As the information slipped out, he rubbed a hand over his face and groaned.

"Really?" Now her tone was wistful, as if she'd just learned the one great truth.

"Really," he bit out. "Now, if you don't mind, I have work to do."

"Why?" she prodded, and he knew what she meant.

"Because it's raining, and if I don't move some equipment, it could get flooded."

"Dating."

"Yeah, I knew what you meant. I just hoped I could sidetrack you. And you know why I don't date. I've been working on my life and that meant not dragging someone else into the mess."

"How's that going?"

"You can see for yourself." He hurried under the roof of the equipment shed. She was right there with him.

"Yes, I can see."

She was standing too close and he almost forgot his vow to work on himself and not get tangled up in relationships that always ended with someone getting hurt. He didn't want to hurt her. And he didn't want their relationship to be awkward, not when it might hurt Oliver.

Step one in being a dad meant putting his son first. Ahead of his own crazy, mixed-up emotions. If he kissed her—and he was tempted—that would confuse the issue. It would put his priorities off balance.

Trouble was, he really wanted to kiss her. And she was looking at him like she might want to kiss him back.

The right thing to do here was to put distance between them. Self-sacrifice at its best. "I need to get busy."

"How can I help?" she asked.

She could go back to Essie's. Or even to San Antonio. She grinned at him knowingly, as if she could read his thoughts. That smile was becoming familiar. It showed that she'd survived her childhood and she still found things to laugh about. Still found ways to enjoy life. She enjoyed goading him.

"You could let me get some work done," he grumbled.

"I can't leave. I don't have a car." She patted his chest with the palm of her hand. "Let's get something straight, cowboy. I'm not chasing after you the way the girls did back in your rodeo days. I'm here to help you build a relationship with your son. End of story. The last thing I want is a damaged male with an overinflated ego."

Of course he was the last thing she would be looking for in a man. The ego she'd talked about took a bit of a hit, but he shrugged it off. Instead of arguing, he climbed into his tractor and leaned down, reaching for her left hand. She took the offer and he pulled her into the cab of the tractor with him. "Don't get any ideas. I'm not letting you drive a piece of equipment that cost me a small fortune."

"I wasn't going to ask." She said it sweetly and he knew she'd been tempted.

As they drove through the field, he used the tractor to pick up a bale of hay.

"How much land do you have?"

"Five hundred acres," he answered.

"That's no small amount." She had been watching the landscape roll past. Now she turned to look at him. "You've done well with bull riding."

"Yeah, I've done well. I made good investments."

"Did you?" She didn't push. Her gaze darted to the rain-soaked fields, the cattle grazing at the top of the hill. "And here I thought you couldn't climb out of the bottle long enough to feed yourself, let alone a couple hundred head of cattle."

"Thanks for the compliment."

"In a way it is. I was wrong about that. You obviously feed your cattle."

"Yes, I feed my cattle. And I haven't been climbing in any bottles. Not for several years."

"Did you ever want to do anything else, other than ride bulls or ranch?"

To her it probably seemed like a logical question. People must have other dreams and ambitions. She didn't know what it meant to grow up with Jesse Palermo controlling a person's every action. As a kid he hadn't dreamed of anything other than escaping.

"Nope, it's always been this for me. I'm dyslexic." The admission slipped out. Not normally what he considered a conversation starter.

"I didn't know that," she responded.

"It isn't as if I tell everyone I meet." Or anyone, really. His siblings knew. Essie knew.

"Are you saying that is why you didn't have other goals?"

"No, it's just a part of who I am. I spent my childhood acting out, getting in trouble and definitely not studying."

It was only lately that he learned he knew about more than livestock. He had a gift with the stock market. He'd invested his earnings and he'd seen a pretty decent return on his investment in the last couple of years.

He didn't know her well enough to trust her with that information. *Trust.* That was something he was working on.

His phone rang, saving him the trouble of having to answer the questions he knew she would have asked. She was that type of female, the kind that couldn't let anything rest. He would have liked to say that bothered him, but it didn't.

Sitting next to her, he didn't feel much like Marcus Palermo, the brawling bull rider. He felt like someone who ought to be thinking about growing up.

Lissa half listened to the phone call as the tractor bounced across the field. Rain that had let up returned, heavier, bouncing off the windshield of the tractor. Deftly, as if he didn't have to think through the actions,

Marcus moved big, round bales of hay. After several minutes he ended the call and turned the tractor back toward the barn. He drove through the open gate and up the drive to park on a hill a distance behind the house.

"I paid too much to have that tractor taken downstream."

"Do you think that will happen?"

"They're expecting a pretty good crest at midnight tonight, and if this rain doesn't stop, it'll get even higher. They're stacking sandbags in front of some stores in town, hoping to keep the water out."

He parked the tractor and reached up for her hand. "Careful, the ground is slick."

She eased down, careful of her now throbbing shoulder. When he gave her a questioning look, she managed a grimace that she hoped resembled a smile.

"Pretty sore?"

"A little," she admitted.

"I have a heating pad inside. While I get some things moved, you can take a break, maybe have a cup of tea that will help."

"Tea that will help?"

"Chamomile." He walked off as he said it and she hurried to catch up, ducking through the door beneath his arm that held it open.

Big tough bull rider, scar down his left cheek and a broken voice, but he drank a tea known for its calming properties. He led her through the kitchen to the living room. The house was another surprise. It was sparsely furnished but cozy. The walls were shades of pale blue and a light gray. The furniture looked as if it belonged in a seaside cottage.

As she wandered, examining the paintings on the

walls, he pulled a heating pad from the closet. She accepted it and followed him back to the kitchen to watch as he started a pot of coffee and made a cup of chamomile tea.

His movements were spare, efficient, controlled. Not once did he smile. He needed to smile. Oliver was a funny kid who liked to joke. What if Marcus didn't understand that about his son?

What if Marcus lost his temper? What if he didn't hug Oliver, tuck him in at night or comfort him when he was afraid?

She told herself to stop. She could go through dozens of "what if" questions. She could spend her life worrying. But what good did worry do?

"What happened to your voice?" She asked the question she'd been wondering about since she'd met him.

The microwave dinged. He pulled the cup of tea out, stirred in a spoonful of honey and handed it to her. "Let it steep a few minutes. And my voice is none of your concern."

"Isn't it?"

"Do you think it will affect my ability to be a dad? Is that the reason for all of the questions? Are you scoring me on my emotional state, my parenting, my ability to be an adult?"

"No, of course not."

He gave her a long, steady look devoid of anger. "It isn't something I talk about. Ever."

"I see."

He took the heating pad from her and plugged it in next to the table. "Sit down."

She did as he ordered, sitting with the cup of chamomile tea between her hands, warming her. He adjusted the temperature on the heating pad and settled it on her shoulder. His touch was firm yet gentle. She thought she felt his fingers trace a path across her back. Maybe it was her imagination, that featherlight touch.

She glanced up at him. "I'm not scoring you. And my question wasn't connected to your ability to parent. I genuinely wanted to know. Maybe the nurse in me. Or maybe—" she paused to think through the words she'd planned to say "—as a friend."

"My dad did this," he whispered close to her ear. "And I didn't want to continue the cycle of abuse. I don't want to take a chance that I would leave a child with scars. Oliver is a funny, happy kid. He should stay that way. Every time I get angry I worry that it might be the time I can't control my temper."

And then he walked out the back door, closing it firmly behind him. For the few seconds the door was open, she heard the rain coming down and in the distance the drone of an engine. With the closing door, there was silence once again.

She sat there alone, thinking back to what he'd told her. His father had maimed him, stolen his voice and left him emotionally scarred, as well.

She wanted to go after him, to tell him she was sorry. Sorry he'd been hurt. Sorry she'd pushed him for answers. But she knew when to let a man go. And this one needed to be set free.

Contemplating her next move, she sat there with the tea he'd made her and the heat soaking into her stiff shoulder. As she finished the tea, she realized Marcus didn't know himself very well. He thought a damaged voice, a scarred body and a nightmarish childhood made him a bad person. He'd probably spent a lifetime living up to that reputation, to his past, making sure everyone knew he was damaged goods.

What he failed to see, what she saw, was that he cared. He cared enough about Oliver to turn him over to Lissa. He cared enough about her, a stranger who had shown up on his doorstep with news that had to be shocking, that he would care for her well-being.

As she sat in silent contemplation, the sun came out from behind the clouds. The golden light streamed through the kitchen. And outside she heard a child's laughter. Oliver's laughter.

She unplugged the heating pad and went out the back door in search of Oliver and Marcus. She found them in the front yard. Another man, a carbon copy of Marcus, and yet not, had joined them. Alex Palermo, his twin, had short hair, no jagged scar on his cheek. And he smiled. Truly smiled. He saw her and tipped his hat in a greeting.

A break in the clouds meant the rain had slowed to intermittent sprinkles. She spotted a patch of blue and rays of sunshine streaking across the sky. Maybe the forecast would be wrong and the rain would miss them this time.

"Lissa, did you see the dog?" Oliver hurried to her side, catching hold of her left hand. "He plays dead with his tongue out. And it's funny. You have to watch."

"I'll watch," she promised. "How did you get here?"

"Alex stopped at Aunt Essie's and I wanted to see you and Marcus. She told me if I wore my seat belt I could ride along. But I'm supposed to stay out of the way."

"He isn't staying out of the way," Marcus grumbled, but she saw the tug of his mouth, a hint of a smile.

There was hope for him yet. She'd never been one to

give up on a challenge. But the challenge might be in keeping her perspective. She had to turn Marcus Palermo into a father and nothing more.

Chapter Six

Marcus looked at the three people who had invaded his life. And his kitchen. His twin, Alex, had poured himself a cup of coffee and seemed to be settling in for a cozy visit. As if they had time to sit for a cup. If anything, they needed to be on the road, seeing who of their neighbors needed help getting to higher ground.

Oliver had brought Lucky in with them and he made quick work of trying to get the dog to learn to roll over. The dog plodded around, leaving muddy footprints everywhere. Marcus could have told the boy that the dog played dead because it was the easiest trick in the world for an aging hound dog who didn't much care to get off the porch.

Instead of dissuading him, however, he got a box of dog treats out of the cabinet and handed them to his son. "Try this. Sometimes it just takes a treat."

"Hmm," Lissa murmured with meaning.

"Can't teach an old dog new tricks," he told her.

In response she laughed. "With a treat?"

"Probably not." He managed to keep a straight face,

but she caught his eye and winked, almost undoing any hold he had on his self-control.

Alex handed him a cup of coffee. "Well, what's the plan?"

He didn't have a plan, other than hitting the road and trying to figure out who needed help and how best to get things done. Those were the thoughts of a man who didn't have a child. He realized that as he stood there with a cup of coffee, watching Oliver play with Lucky. The dog had sprawled out on the floor and occasionally raised a paw in something that resembled shaking.

He looked down at his coffee and wished, for the first time in a long time, that it was something a lot stronger than coffee. As if he knew, Alex poured milk into the cup and gave him a long and meaningful look.

Marcus raised the cup in salute. "Thanks."

"Anytime."

His phone rang. He grabbed it off the counter and walked out the back door. "Pastor?"

"Marcus, any chance you could head your stock trailer to town and load up some belongings? We've got a couple of houses on West Street that are going to be under water by nightfall."

"You got it." He would gladly do something that would keep his mind off whatever other thoughts or temptations were running through his mind. "I'll be there as soon as I can get Oliver and Lissa back to Essie's."

"She's in town at the café, cooking like a madwoman and serving meals to the workers and those who are trying to pack up and get out."

"I'll bring Lissa to help her out. Hopefully, the water won't get up to the café."

"That's our hope. And our prayer." Pastor Matthews spoke as solemnly as Marcus had ever heard. "You're doing okay?"

The question forced him to be honest. "I've been better. I could use a few of those prayers, if you've got some to spare."

"You know I do. Marcus, you can handle this."

"I guess I can handle whatever comes at me."

The sun had gone behind the clouds again and he headed back inside as more rain began to fall. He caught Lissa in the act of straightening a picture that hung on the wall in the small dining area.

"It's fine, leave it." He looked for his brother and Oliver. Both were missing.

"You did this, didn't you?" She touched the painting of a barn nestled in a field of wildflowers.

"Mighty nosy, aren't you?"

"Curious, not nosy. I'd like to say the painting takes me by surprise, but maybe not. You're not as tough as you'd like everyone to think, cowboy."

"I'm tough enough." He walked off, grabbing his coat from the hook by the door. "We have to go. The water is rising and a few houses will have water in them pretty soon. I'm taking my trailer to empty them out."

"I can help."

He shook his head. "Nope. You're not going to do heavy lifting. And I don't want Oliver there getting hurt. I'll drop you off at Essie's café. She will probably put you to work."

She froze up as he spoke and he stopped, knowing he'd done something wrong. "What?"

"That's very nice of you to want to keep us safe, but

I prefer when men discuss things with me rather than giving me orders."

He scratched his thumb along his chin and nodded. "I apologize."

Her expression softened. "No, I'm sorry. I do understand why this is the best plan. We all have our pasts and it's just…" She shrugged.

"Don't apologize," he assured her. "I get it. And if you seriously want to be out in the rain loading furniture into the back of a stock trailer…"

He gave her shoulder a meaningful look.

She grinned. "No, I don't. Let me get Oliver."

"I'm going to hook the trailer to my truck." He nearly bumped into Alex on his way out the back door.

"Where's the fire?" Alex asked, following him to his truck.

"No fire, just a flood. Pastor Matthews asked me to bring my trailer to West Street."

Alex pulled keys out of his pocket. "I'll head home and get mine. What about Oliver and Lissa?"

"I'll drop them at the café."

"Essie's cooking like a madwoman, I imagine. I'd guess Lucy and Marissa are with her."

Marcus shot his brother a look and wasn't surprised to see that gooey love-struck expression on his face when he mentioned his wife. He wasn't surprised that Alex had fallen, maybe surprised it had happened so quickly. They were different people, he and Alex. Twins but nothing alike.

A few minutes later he backed his truck up to the stock trailer, watching in the mirrors to get it lined up and close to the hitch in the bed of the truck. He jumped out, slipping in the mud as rain poured down. Wouldn't it be nice if they could have a break just long enough that they didn't have to do all of this in a downpour? But then, if that happened, they might not have to worry about a flood. Period.

After hooking the trailer to the truck, he turned to find Oliver and Lissa were there. They'd located an umbrella and were huddling together.

"Get in the truck." He opened the door and motioned them inside. "This rain is crazy. The two of you don't need to be out in it."

"I wonder if this is how Noah felt?" Oliver asked as he buckled up in the back of the truck.

Marcus grinned at the serious look on his son's face. Son. That was still going to take some time to get used to. And it made earlier temptations, old temptations, seem like the worst decisions ever. A few years ago he wouldn't have been a candidate for fatherhood. Not in the condition he had been in.

The last thing this kid needed was a dad who climbed back in the bottle every time he felt a little bit stressed.

Fortunately he had put that life behind him.

If he was going to be a dad, he'd have to find a quick route to being the kind that Oliver deserved. He'd have to be a dad his son could trust. He just wasn't certain how a man went from being footloose to tied down and dependable.

"I'm not sure about this," he mumbled to himself more than to the woman sitting next to him.

She sighed. A quick look in the back seat and he knew why she wasn't responding. Rule number two, don't discuss stressful things in front of children. He had a lot to learn about parenting.

And from the tense woman sitting next to him, he

had a lot to learn about Lissa Hart. He wanted her stories. What made her bristle when she thought someone was taking control? It should have bothered him more that she'd managed to get under his skin in such a short amount of time. Surprisingly, it didn't.

Marcus let them out at Essie's café. Lissa hurried up the steps of the café and through the front door with Oliver squeezing in ahead of her. The bell chimed at their entrance. Before she could think, Oliver was hurrying through the not-so-crowded diner in search of the woman who really was his aunt.

Sooner or later, preferably sooner, they'd have to tell him. For now, Essie was a sweet lady who had taken them in and given him permission to call her aunt, and she made yummy food.

Lissa pulled off the raincoat, mindful of her shoulder. Oliver had disappeared into the kitchen. She was alone and she could take a breath and figure out her next move. She shouldn't have let it bother her, that Marcus wanted to tell her the plan. It had felt like taking over. She knew it had been more about what worked best.

It all went back to a childhood where she'd never felt in control of her situation. Life before Jane and Tom Simms had meant never knowing what would happen next. She'd wondered who she would come home to, what her mother's mood would be and how she would get through a night without someone knocking on her door.

She wanted more for herself. She wanted more for Oliver. She wished he had better memories of his mother. Because Sammy had started to spiral out of control after she had her son. She had been clean and sober for years, and then something had happened.

At the back of Lissa's mind she had always wondered if that something had been Marcus Palermo.

"Lissa, good morning. Oliver told us you were out here." Marissa Palermo, Alex's wife, smiled a greeting, but the smile dissolved. "Are you okay?"

"Of course." She managed what she hoped was a cheerful expression. "I'm here to help."

Marissa locked arms with her and they headed for the kitchen. "We can always use help. Essie is making chicken and noodles and she's going to open in an hour. She wants potatoes mashed and biscuits cooked. I hope you're up for a long day."

"With plenty of coffee, I can handle it."

For the next hour they worked hard. Even Oliver pitched in to help. He was the potato masher and Essie told him he mashed those potatoes even better than Bea Maxwell, the cook who seemed to have a penchant for saying whatever came to her mind.

"You're just saying that because he looks like the twins," Bea grumbled. "And they always were your favorites."

"I take exception to that," Lucy Palermo Scott called out to Bea as she put the finishing touches on the pies they would serve for dessert.

"Watch yourself, Bea." Essie hugged Bea. "We need to focus on cooking."

"I know, I know." Bea waddled off to the sink. "I hope I can wash my hands without getting in trouble."

Lissa sneaked a peek at Oliver. He didn't seem to be listening at all. He was busy mashing potatoes and eating pudding off the spoon Marissa had placed in front of his mouth. The moment cemented for her that this was a family. They were laughing, loving one another and teasing in a fun way. They weren't at all what she'd expected from the offspring of cult leader Jesse Palermo.

His control over his church had been legendary. He'd been a world-famous bull rider, a minister of his own brand of the gospel and a father. What had been hidden had been the abuse of his family. But they'd survived. She could see that in this group of women. They were all survivors.

"Let's get this on the buffet." Essie called out the order and the women started to move, including a few from the community who had come in to help.

Lucy moved to Lissa's side as the women worked to get food to the warming trays. Oliver was given serving spoons to carry out. Lissa was very aware that Lucy had something to say. It was obvious in the way she watched the others leave.

"Do you plan on taking him back to San Antonio?" Lucy finally asked. "If he's my nephew, I want to know him. And he deserves to be here with his father, with aunts and uncles and cousins."

Lissa blanched at her candor. Apparently, Lucy didn't sugarcoat things. But neither did her brother.

"I don't plan on taking him. I plan on honoring Sammy's wishes. She wanted him to know his father. She just never got around to…"

Loss hit her again, the way it often did.

Lucy briefly touched her shoulder. The gesture was sweet, but Lissa knew that the other woman wouldn't switch loyalties. And neither could Lissa. She'd made a promise, to do what was best for Oliver. Somehow she'd thought it would be easier. She thought she'd show up and find a man unfit to parent. What she'd found was a man who hadn't planned to parent, but a man who was loyal and caring. It made the whole process so much harder than she'd expected.

"Marcus is a good man," Lucy defended. "None of us are without baggage, without a past. But few men will defend or care for their loved ones the way my brother does."

"I understand you feel strongly about your brother. But Oliver…" She nearly choked on the emotion that welled up from her heart.

Lucy's expression softened with understanding. "What was Sammy like?"

"Not perfect. She had her baggage and her past."

"What was she like as a mother?"

"She struggled." Lissa looked down at the tile floor. "But she loved her little boy."

"I'm sure she did. But I'm also sure that you love him, too."

"I do." She swiped at her eyes and gave herself a minute to get her emotions under control. "I don't want to hurt Marcus. But I also don't want Oliver to be hurt."

"Then I guess we both want the same thing. I just hope that you'll give Marcus a chance."

Give Marcus a chance. Lissa wished it didn't sound as if Lucy was connecting her to Oliver's father. It wasn't about her feelings for him. Because she didn't have feelings for him. She was there to introduce Oliver to his father. A man she would probably see from time to time, but they wouldn't be connected in any way.

Period.

A few minutes later she had to remind herself of that belief. Marcus had arrived and he'd taken a seat with Oliver and an older gentleman Lissa didn't know. He buttered a biscuit for his son and must have known she was watching. With a smile he made eye contact with her.

She told herself again, no connection. Nothing happened when he smiled and winked like that. She didn't feel a thing. Because she wouldn't feel anything. Jane had told her to wait because someday the right man would convince her that he was worth her time. The right man would be a partner. He wouldn't control. He wouldn't take over. He wouldn't hurt her with his hands or his words.

The right man would make her feel as if the future with him at her side mattered, that it made sense.

She could trust herself because she would know that man when he stepped into her life.

It would be the right time, the right man, the right place. Not this man, this place or this time. Even if there was something about Marcus Palermo, the way he helped his son at the buffet line, the way he stopped to talk to the older people, taking time, truly listening. He didn't believe himself to be good enough to be a little boy's father. If she was going to lose Oliver to him, she knew she would have to help him to realize he could be the person his son needed.

They were not a team, but they were two people who cared about a young boy. It mattered that they could get along.

She could see good in him. She wasn't so naive that she couldn't also see that he was charming, and her ability to resist him seemed limited.

A man who was kind to his son, to the elderly and to animals. It was a lethal combination.

Chapter Seven

Water rolled over the top of the bridge Marcus had crossed more times than he could count. He hit the brakes and stopped his truck. Next to him, Lissa looked a little bit nervous. He glanced in the back seat of his truck and smiled at Oliver. The boy didn't have a clue. In five-year-old fashion he was talking to a toy he'd brought along for the ride to church.

"I guess we won't be going this way." He stated the obvious.

He guessed Essie, who had left earlier for Sunday services, must have taken the back route to town. He dialed her number as he backed away from the bridge. When she answered, he felt a serious sense of relief.

"Making sure you're okay."

His aunt sighed. "Well, I guess I have enough sense not to cross a low-water bridge. And I already told first responders. They are on their way out with barricades. I took the county line road to get to town. It's about the only way."

"We'll be late for church," he told her and Lissa at the same time.

A few minutes later they were on the best route to town. It would take an extra ten minutes, but at least they'd get there safely. When they finally pulled into the church parking lot, it was packed. Definitely more than the usual Sunday crowd. Probably several people staying in the shelter the church had set up. Others were there to pray that the rain would stop.

Lissa's phone dinged. A text this time and not a call. He watched as she peeked at the phone and slipped it back in her purse. She'd done that several times. He didn't like games. Even if it didn't concern him, he wanted to know the truth. He wanted, for her sake and Oliver's, to know that she was safe.

"Going to ignore it again?" he asked, realizing that might have sounded a tinge jealous. He hadn't planned on jealousy, but for some reason he seemed to feel responsible for the woman who had been taking care of his son.

Responsible. Yes, much easier than thinking of himself as jealous.

"I'm not ignoring anything," she answered. "And it isn't any of your business."

Lissa tossed her head toward the back seat, as if warning him the conversation was off-limits with the child in the truck. He was starting to think that was her way of avoiding any conversation she didn't feel comfortable with.

He wanted to talk about those phone calls because she had to have a reason for ignoring them. Either she didn't want him to hear her talk to her boyfriend or she was hiding something else. He might be late to fatherhood, but it mattered that his son and the woman caring for him were both safe.

"We're going to discuss this," he said as he pulled his keys from the ignition.

"Nope." She got out of the truck and opened the back door for Oliver. The boy hadn't said much since they'd left Essie's. As a matter of fact, he hadn't said too much since yesterday. Mostly he gave them both some serious questioning looks, and he seemed a little bit upset.

Marcus got the feeling they needed to talk to Oliver, tell him what the situation was and let him adjust. No more of this taking time, letting him get settled.

As they headed up the sidewalk, Oliver hurried ahead of them, still clutching the toy he'd had in the truck.

"We have to tell him."

Lissa faltered at his words and he reached for her arm, steadying her. "Right. I know we do. I just wanted to give it time."

"I think we don't have a lot of time. I know you want to take him back to San Antonio with you. And I know full well that with Sammy's letter and her will, you feel as if you have that right. But he's my son. I'm going to make some decisions that you might not like. The first one is that we need to tell him. Soon. And you have to understand that I won't let you walk away with him, not without a fight."

So much for the cowboy who wasn't sure if he was ready to be a dad. He hadn't been sure. He still wasn't all the way in, but he also wasn't going to let his son down. Walking away from Oliver would definitely be letting him down.

Her careful gaze shifted to his face, to the scar on his cheek. "I guess we know where we both stand."

"I guess we do."

He started toward the church, knowing she had a

hurt expression on her face and tears swimming in her blue eyes. He'd spent a lifetime being cold, shutting out his feelings, pretending he didn't care. He tried to call on all of the tactics he'd learned over a lifetime of finding it easier to not feel. It might have worked if their fingers hadn't brushed as they walked. The cold and standoffish routine was difficult to achieve when you noticed a woman's tears and you were tempted to reach for her hand.

"Stop looking at me like that," she warned as they climbed the steps. "You don't have to worry. I'm not going to fall apart."

He blinked back his surprise. He didn't go around with his heart on his sleeve or emotion in his eyes. He was the ice man, that was what they had called him when he rode bulls. Nothing scared him. He had faced the meanest bulls in the world and he'd conquered them. But this woman could take him to his knees, she made him want to protect her.

"If you keep looking at me like that, people will get the wrong idea." She poked at his arm.

He rubbed the spot and grimaced. "Sorry. I really don't want to hurt you, Lissa. Would it be better if I said something about how good you smell?"

Reaching for the handrail, he headed up the steps, taking them slower than he would have liked. He looked back and she was standing at the bottom of the steps, hand over her heart.

"Was that a compliment?"

He shook his head. "Nope."

"You're just trying to make me smile. Right?"

He glanced inside the sanctuary and raised a finger to his lips. "They're praying."

He eased into a pew and scooted to make room for Lissa. Oliver had found a seat a few pews in front, with Lucy, her husband, Dane Scott, and their daughter Issy.

Next to him, Lissa's hand stole to his and her fingers, soft and feminine, curled around his roughly calloused ones. She gave a light squeeze and bowed her head, her lips moving softly as she prayed.

Thread by complicated thread she was undoing his resolve, his plans and his composure. She made it difficult to sit through that sermon and keep his mind focused. Somehow, though, he managed to pray for guidance, because he knew the coming weeks wouldn't be easy. They could all be hurt in the process of figuring out what would be best for Oliver.

After church they stood and made their way forward, to Oliver and to the rest of his family.

"You must have slipped in after we started." Lucy smiled from him to Lissa. "Lissa, I think Doc is looking for you. Something about setting up a clinic here at the church and he might need your help. I think he has a little bit of a crush on you."

Marcus ignored that comment. But then he couldn't ignore his little sister Maria. She came barreling up the aisle, nineteen and still the most exuberant member of the family. She wrapped her arms around him and hugged tight.

"Hug me back, Marc." She gave him another squeeze.

He did his best not to stiffen in her embrace. She was a hugger and nothing he said could ever stop her.

"Don't call me Marc," he grumbled at her. "Welcome home, squirt."

"You even sound like you mean it."

He did mean it, but he decided not to encourage her. "When did you get home?"

"Early this morning. It took me forever to get here, avoiding flooded roads and bridges."

"She brought a friend with her," Lucy interjected. "His name is Jake."

Maria gave her a look and kept talking.

"I met Oliver." Maria gave him what passed as her serious look. "He's a cutie. Chip off the old block, but a lot more charming."

"Quiet," he ordered.

"Chip off the old block," Lissa repeated. "That's another one we could use."

"Stop." He couldn't help but give in to the smile that tugged at his lips.

"Was that a smile?" Maria stepped closer and peered at him. "I think it might have been. Have I been gone that long?"

"You've been gone long enough that you brought a friend home to meet the family," Lucy interjected, with a look at Marcus that meant she was sparing him their little sister's questions by distracting her.

"So where is this friend?" Marcus surveyed the room and didn't see anyone unfamiliar.

"Helping stack sandbags in front of Essie's." Maria slipped her arm through his. Concern darkened her eyes. "How are you doing?"

"I'm fine." He didn't pull away, but he was aware that his younger sister always knew him a little better than anyone.

"They're serving lunch in the fellowship hall. I have to find my crew." Lucy shot him a look, as if to make sure he followed her meaning. "You should find Oliver. I think he went with Dane to get Jewel from the nursery."

He hadn't thought about Oliver. Another point against him. A dad should think about his child, know where he was, consider his well-being. Things like food were important.

"Come with me." Lissa took him by the arm. "I'm here for two more weeks, Marcus. I'm not going to leave you to sink or swim."

He was obviously drowning, but he wasn't about to tell that to the woman at his side. Not when the drowning had as much to do with her as it did trying to figure out how to be a father. Both had him in over his head, out of his depth and a few other sayings he could think of. Sink or swim, she'd said. She had no idea how fitting that was for his current state of mind.

Lissa clasped her hands behind her back as they walked down the hallway in the direction of the nursery. The church, once the church where Jesse Palermo had pastored, was now a shelter for abused women as well as a community church. Several of the classrooms had been turned into dorms for those seeking a way to build a new life. With the threat of flooding, single women from the community were being offered cots in the living areas.

It was symbolic in so many ways. The church Marcus's dad pastored had left broken lives behind, and this church was rebuilding lives and the community. Lissa admired Marcus—it had to take a lot of strength to put that behind him and to be there helping. She'd learned that he gave to the mission of the church and also helped with construction projects.

People had been forthcoming with more information about Marcus and the Palermos than she really needed. She realized that some were trying to give her advice and others thought there might be something between her and the remaining single Palermo twin.

Some less helpful folks had told her about Marcus's years of alcoholism and how he used to turn to the bottle when life got tense. She thought they were more interested in stirring up trouble than in truly helping.

But she hadn't ignored their carefully veiled warnings. A man who had once stayed drunk more than he stayed sober. Could he take care of Oliver? What if he turned back to his old ways?

Several feet from the door, Marcus stopped, his expression unreadable, his eyes cool and detached. Or that was what a person might think if they didn't look too closely. In the past week she'd learned a little about how to read him. She saw that he was never really without emotion. He might not smile and laugh, but the feelings were there, beneath the surface. And what she saw right now was a man afraid of how his life had changed.

"What in the world am I doing?" he asked, his raspy voice gruff.

"Becoming a dad," she challenged.

His gaze darted to the door at the end of the hall. The nursery. She could see that he was torn.

"This is crazy." He yanked off his cowboy hat and brushed a hand through his hair.

"It isn't," she encouraged. That hadn't been the role she'd expected to take in this situation, that of encourager. She hadn't wanted to trust this man or cheer him on.

Especially when he'd made it clear he would fight

for his son. She knew if it came to it he would take her to court. And he would win.

"You came here hoping to find me unable to care for my son. You were probably right in believing that, so don't start acting supportive now."

"We should get Oliver. They're serving lunch."

They entered the nursery and she watched with a pang of envy as Marcus lowered himself to the floor to sit with his son. They talked about the toys, about Lucy's little girls, Jewel and Issy, whose father had already taken them to the fellowship hall. And then Oliver mentioned a pig that sometimes ran through town and he wondered if he would ever see that pig.

Marcus guaranteed him he would. Lissa wanted to tell him that adults didn't make promises they weren't sure they would be able to keep.

But she didn't have a chance. Marcus swooped his son up into his arms and told him it was time for lunch. Before she could object, he had the little boy on his shoulders. Oliver pulled the hat off Marcus's head and placed it on his own. "Can I stay up here?"

Lissa started to protest, but it came out as a squeak. Marcus glanced at her, amusement dancing in his dark eyes for a brief few seconds.

She shrugged, because she wasn't going to be the naysayer. Marcus turned his head a bit to look at his son.

"You'll have to duck or you'll hit your head as we go out the door."

"I can do that," Oliver assured them.

They entered the fellowship hall, Oliver laughing as Marcus told him about a summer picnic at the church complete with bounce houses.

"We don't have to go home yet, do we?" the boy

asked as Marcus lifted him from his shoulders and placed him back on the floor. The white cowboy hat covered his eyes and he pushed it back to look up at them.

"No, not yet," Lissa assured him.

People were going through a line, filling plates with food. Oliver didn't hesitate. He left them and headed for the food line.

"This is why we need to tell him."

She sighed. He was right…she needed to tell him. It just hadn't been her plan to get stuck here. She hadn't planned to witness the child she'd been raising become attached to the man who was his father. She didn't know what she'd expected. She'd loaded Oliver up and told him she had someone she wanted him to meet.

"This can't continue," he whispered close to her ear.

"I know, Marcus. I do know." Lissa was aware now that Oliver was talking to Pastor Matthews. She smiled at what she saw. "Look at him."

"What?" Marcus asked.

"The way he's standing. He's so much like you. Even down to the way he stands and the way he talks."

Marcus glanced from her to his son and a corner of his mouth quirked up. "Yeah, chip off the old block. Pretty cute kid."

The tension of moments ago evaporated.

"If you do say so yourself," she teased.

At that, a full grin spread across his face, revealing dimples she'd never noticed before. And that grin slayed her. She hadn't expected the power behind his smile, the way it changed him. She cleared her throat, uncomfortable with the thought, the way that smile tugged at something deep inside her.

One minute he had her convinced he couldn't possibly be responsible enough to be a father, and the next moment she wanted to help him achieve that goal.

"Are you okay?"

"Of course I am," she assured him. "You should help him with his plate."

He gave her a knowing look.

"I get that he's everything to you." He placed a hand on her shoulder. "This is a mess, you know. We can't undo the past, but it shouldn't have been like this. I didn't want to be my father. I should have been there five years ago. I should have been there last year. You could have called me."

When Sammy died. Lissa closed her eyes briefly, feeling guilty because she should have called him. She should have allowed him to be there for Sammy, for Oliver. Instead, she'd listened to her sister, granted her the last wish and promised to see this plan through to the end. Lissa should have known it would cause them all more pain in the end.

"I am sorry," she told him. "I should have called you when she had the accident."

"But you didn't," he said, and then seemed to become aware of their surroundings. The hurt, the anger, all of the emotions that had flitted across his face suddenly disappeared. From a distance, anyone would think he didn't care, that he wasn't affected.

However, she knew the truth. It was in the dark depths of his eyes. The pain of the past, the anger, the confusion.

"I'll get him a plate. And you. Go sit down and I'll bring you one, too." He gave her a brief quirk of the lips, his version of a smile. "Step one in becoming a father. Kids have to eat."

"No peas. Oliver doesn't like peas."

"Neither do I."

Unwittingly, she had given them a connection. Of course, half the little boys, and maybe grown men, across the country would say the same about peas. She could have added that she didn't like them, either.

But she didn't.

Maria, the youngest of the Palermo siblings, waved at her from a table in the corner. She was seated with Lucy's stepdaughter, Issy, and with the little girl Lucy and her husband, Dane, had adopted, Jewel. The child, eighteen months old, was Maria's biological child whom she'd asked her older sister to raise. The Palermo kids had been through a lot, but what Lissa saw was a family that had begun the healing process and they had a lot of love for one another.

Her foster parents had given Lissa and Sammy that family bond. They were the grandparents of Oliver. They were the home they went to for holidays. They were the people Lissa counted on, even now.

She sat down at the table with Maria, who was busy cutting meat and helping Issy, blind since birth, with her food.

"Can I help?" Lissa offered.

Maria flashed her an amused look. "That's very brave of you. But of course you can help. With these two, we always accept help. If you can make sure Jewel keeps her food on the tray of that high chair and not the floor, that would be great. Is Marcus bringing you a plate?"

"He is." She looked away, uncomfortable with the

questions she saw forming in Maria's eyes. Questions about Marcus. About her relationship to him.

She was here because Sammy wasn't. Sammy, who had gone to the store to pick up a few things while Lissa watched Oliver and had died in a car accident. She'd lived long enough to tell Lissa to give Marcus a chance to be a dad.

If Sammy had lived, would the two of them, Marcus and Sammy, have found each other again? Would they have been a family?

"That's about the sweetest picture ever," Maria spoke, catching her attention and thankfully distracting her.

She followed the younger woman's gaze and had to agree. Marcus had a tray and was heading their way. Next to him, still wearing Marcus's hat, Oliver carried his own tray. They were talking, with Marcus leaning down to catch what his son had to say.

"Yes, the sweetest." Lissa could admit the cowboy made it easy to drop her guard. She had to keep things in check and remember that this man had a history of leaving broken hearts in his wake.

She hoped and prayed that Marcus Palermo could be the father Oliver deserved. And she also prayed that her heart wouldn't be shattered beyond repair in the process.

Chapter Eight

One thing Marcus really disliked was being the center of attention. With Oliver tagging along next to him as they made their way to the table, they were getting plenty of attention. An arm bumped his and he side-stepped before realizing it was Lucy.

"Calm down, it's just me. And get that cornered look off your face." Trust his older sister to see right through him and not give him space.

"I don't like crowds." There, that ought to keep her out of his business.

Instead, she gave him a curious look that bordered on maternal. Oliver had left them. He was pulling out a chair and setting his tray on the table. Lissa leaned to listen to something he said.

Lucy cleared her throat to get his attention.

"Marcus, if you need anything...if you need to talk, I'm here." Lucy, now the family therapist, stood on tiptoe and kissed his cheek. He'd been right about that maternal look softening her expression.

"Who are you?" he mumbled, and she didn't seem

at all troubled by the question. Instead, she gave him a parting grin and headed for the table.

Of course, he wouldn't escape her. Her daughters were at the table with Maria and Lissa.

He ought to ask if there was going to be another little one at the family table next spring. That would get her off his back. And then he realized he liked the idea of another baby at their holiday table.

He'd learned something about himself in the past six months or so. He did like babies. He liked kids. And with that thought, his gaze shifted to Oliver. His son. It got him in the solar plexus, whatever that was. It felt safer than saying it affected his heart.

"I got you a plate." He set it down in front of Lissa, ignoring Lucy. "Oliver assured me you like lasagna. He also told me to get you a double helping of peas. I didn't."

She tickled Oliver and then kissed his cheek. "He would do that to me. Thank you for not listening to him."

Across the table from them, Lucy made a choking sound. Marcus glanced at her, but she pretended to be helping Issy with her food. It was new, this teasing version of his sister.

Lucy had found some happiness. And peace. It was written all over her face, shone from her eyes.

He guessed that was what all the Palermo siblings wanted, for the others to be happy. And Lucy was happy. He searched the room for Alex, because Marcus's twin had found the same for himself. Who could have known that picking up a bride on the side of the road would work out so well for a man?

"Can I have my chocolate cake now?" Oliver asked as he pushed green beans around his plate.

Marcus glanced at Lissa to see what she would say, but she arched a brow, returning the question to him. He looked at his son's plate, still filled with chicken, vegetables and mashed potatoes.

"I think you have to eat at least part of the good food before you get dessert," Marcus answered. "Now, I'm just guessing at that, but I know that I always eat my dinner before I tackle dessert. You won't get strong eating cake."

"If I eat ten bites of each thing?" Oliver looked pretty hopeful, and ten bites of each thing would pretty much clean his plate.

"I think that's a deal." Marcus poured ketchup on his own mashed potatoes and ignored the look Lissa gave him, a pretty disgusted look if he was to guess.

He wasn't going to explain to her about a real dislike for mashed potatoes. When he was a kid, they were required to eat everything on their plate. Ketchup, he'd discovered, made some foods go down a little easier.

He was finishing up when the outside door flew open and a first responder rushed in carrying a child. Throughout the fellowship hall, people froze, their gazes glued to the scene, the man in his yellow vest, the child, pale and unmoving. Next to Marcus, Lissa moved quickly to her feet and hurried toward the scene that everyone else suddenly seemed to understand. People rose. Many murmured. Marcus hoped they were praying, because the child, a little girl, didn't look good.

"Watch Oliver," he said to Maria as he pushed back from the table. She nodded, her eyes large as she watched Lissa hurrying through the room with the first responder.

Marcus followed them down the hall to Doc's make-shift clinic. He stopped at the door and watched as Lissa leaned over the child, who appeared to be a year or two older than Oliver. It got him in the gut, watching that little girl and thinking about his own son.

Lissa had a stethoscope and she helped the child to sit as she listened to her heart, her breaths. Tears were streaming down the child's face.

"My mommy?" She leaned into Lissa's shoulder.

Marcus made eye contact with the first responder, who shook his head only slightly before answering. "We're looking for her."

No promise that she would be okay or that they would find her. Marcus knew what had happened. The wet clothes of the child, the search. The mom must have driven through water and she hadn't gauged the depth or the power behind the swiftly moving force. He wanted to go help search. He should be helping.

"Marcus, could you find Doc? And if the two of you will leave, Pearl and I will find her some dry clothes to change into. We'll need blankets, too. And a heating pad if you can find one. Her temp is low."

"The water was cold." Pearl shuddered as she spoke and then her teeth started to chatter.

Marcus grabbed a pile of blankets and handed them over to Lissa. "I'll see what I can find."

"I want my mommy." The little girl was full-on cry-ing now. And Marcus wasn't good with tears. It brought back too many memories.

"I'll be back."

The first responder followed him from the room. "Doc is at the search site. In case they do find the mom."

Marcus wanted to spew just about every curse word he'd ever been paddled for saying. And then some. Instead, he stopped and said a quick prayer that they'd find Pearl's mommy.

"How'd they get the little girl out?"

"Her mom got her out the window. She told us she grabbed a branch, but the car went under. I don't think we'll find her mom alive."

"Family?"

"Not from around here. They were on their way to Oklahoma, where the mom has family."

Marcus went from wanting to say some strong words to wanting to hit something. "Okay, let's see if we can find out the name of those relatives and give them a call."

The dining room had cleared out except for the Palermo family and a few others. Pastor Matthews stood in the little group and he clearly didn't have good news. His face paled and he shook his head.

"Did they find her?" the first responder asked.

"They're still looking, Joe," Pastor Matthews assured him. "They found the car and she wasn't inside. So that gives us hope that she got out."

"I pray she did. That little girl is about the age of my Sara." Joe brushed at his eyes. "Okay, I have to get back to work."

"Let's pray before you go," Pastor Matthews offered. Joe took off his hat and Marcus joined the two men. As the pastor prayed, a few others joined their circle.

After praying, Marcus searched for Oliver, who was a short distance away, tears swimming in his dark eyes.

"What's up, buddy?" Marcus squatted to put himself at eye level with his son.

"That girl's mom died?" Oliver was sobbing now, tears streaming down his cheeks. And Lissa wasn't there. Lissa the comforter. It wasn't what Marcus did. He was an action man. He wanted to solve the problem, not look it face on.

"No, kiddo, they're still looking for her and we just prayed that they would find her." Because he couldn't lie to his son. "And the little girl is okay. Her mom saved her."

"But her mom might not come back."

"I think she will," Marcus told his son. Then it hit him that Oliver was thinking about his own lost mommy.

He stood, and as he did, he picked Oliver up and held him close. Little arms wrapped around his neck.

"I'm sorry, Oliver." Sorry he hadn't been there for his son. Sorry that Sammy was gone. And sorry that he was a rotten excuse for a human being.

As much as Marcus didn't believe he was fit to be anyone's father, he realized he needed to be the man his son could count on.

"I miss her." Oliver didn't cry anymore; he just held on tight and let Marcus carry him from the room. His family didn't stop them and didn't ask questions.

Marcus didn't know what else to do. He wanted to comfort his son. He wanted to make things right for him and for the little girl down the hall. Life wasn't fair. Sometimes it took some real skill to get over the past, the hurts, the failures.

"I want Lissa," Oliver said softly, his cheek against

Marcus's shoulder. Marcus had been thinking almost the same thing. Lissa had become his anchor, too.

He didn't want to add her to the list of people he had failed.

"We'll give her a few minutes and then we'll see her." He started to put Oliver down, but the boy held on tight to his neck.

"No."

"Okay, little man, I'll carry you."

They stopped at the door to the clinic. He could hear Lissa's soft voice. He heard a child sobbing and Pastor Matthews saying something gentle and comforting. He continued to hold Oliver as they stood outside the door.

The door opened and Lissa stepped out. She swiped at her eyes and then somehow managed a smile. "Hey, you two."

"Did they find her mommy?" Oliver asked. "If she's sad, I could let her play with my toy truck."

Lissa leaned in to kiss Oliver. "That's very sweet of you. We found her a teddy bear and she's resting now. They're still looking for her mom."

"We prayed they would find her." Oliver reached for Lissa. She took him, holding him tight.

Marcus knew that expression. She needed the hug as much as the little boy needed it. Sighing at the realization, he stepped close and wrapped them both in his arms. Surprisingly, it wasn't bad. Especially when Lissa relaxed in his embrace, snuggling close.

He'd spent a lot of time chasing after fame on the bull-riding circuit, chasing wealth and even chasing women. However, he'd never experienced what that moment brought to him. Right here, right now, he felt like the person they needed.

"Thank you." She stood on tiptoe and kissed his cheek.

Just like that, she undid his calm. She rocked his world a little. It was the simplest thing on the planet, a kiss on the cheek. But it wasn't simple. Coffee was simple. A sunrise fell into that category. Maybe even a quiet evening on the porch. But a kiss from Lissa—that complicated things.

Lissa had needed his presence and the hug he had offered. His embrace had seemed something of a sacrifice. It wasn't like him to give of himself that way. That made it all the more special.

"You all should go. It will be getting late. Oliver needs a bath and clean clothes. He'll need dinner and a bedtime story."

The demands put them back on firm footing. She could see it in Marcus's eyes.

"I think those are things you should do."

She laughed a little. "You can manage. You run the water. Make sure it isn't too hot or too cold. He can handle the washing and dressing parts. But then it's story time. This is why I'm here…"

She didn't finish because Oliver eyed her curiously. He didn't know what to think of her turning his care over to someone who had been a stranger just a few days ago.

"Right. Okay, we can do this." Marcus gave her a long look. "You'll call if you hear something?"

"I'll call." If she heard something about Pearl's mother. That was what he meant.

They left and it wasn't easy, watching them walk away together. They were bonding. She told herself that was the way it should be. But her other self argued with that because she didn't want to lose Oliver. She didn't want to honor the letter Sammy had left.

It just wasn't fair. Her foster sister had given birth to Oliver, but she had neglected him and left his care to Lissa. She should have a say in who would raise him. She leaned against the wall and took deep breaths to get past the anger and the hurt.

Several hours after Pearl had been brought to the clinic, Doc Parker returned.

"Lissa, I'm glad as anything to see you here. And how is our little patient?"

Pearl had fallen asleep. Her tearstained cheeks were pale, and she sometimes cried a little as if she dreamed of the accident that had pulled their car into the water. But she was otherwise unharmed. Lissa put a finger to her mouth and pointed to the child.

"Sleeping. They're trying to get a state caseworker here, but with the roads…"

"Ah," Doc whispered. "She's a cute little thing. No idea where she is from or where they were heading?"

"None."

He shook his head and eased closer to the bed to study the child. "We'll keep praying."

"Of course we will," Lissa responded.

Doc eyed Lissa over the top of his wire-framed glasses. "So, do you plan on letting Marcus be a part of the boy's life?"

Of course everyone had guessed. It wasn't a stretch. When a person saw Oliver and Marcus together, it was obvious they were father and son.

"Yes, he'll be a part of Oliver's life. As much as he wants to be a part of his life."

Doc raised his glasses to the top of his head and gave her a look that could only be disappointment. "Don't let his gruff demeanor fool you. Marcus Palermo cares. Deeply. He's loyal to a fault. And he isn't going to just let you walk away with his son."

She knew that. A month ago she had convinced herself that the cowboy Sammy had described was the type of man who wouldn't want to deal with a child. She'd convinced herself he would just sign over custody. It had been easy to believe. Until she met him. Now, although she wasn't sure of his parenting ability, she was positive he would fight for his son.

"His voice?" she asked. She needed to change the subject, and she did wonder about Marcus and what had happened to him during his childhood.

"That's his story to tell."

"Because Marcus loves to talk about himself," she said.

At that, Doc laughed. "Yes, he's a talker."

They both knew that he wasn't.

Doc got up to pour himself a cup of coffee. "Oliver's mom died in a car accident?"

"Yes, she did."

"That's a tough one. And you're a good woman for being there for him. I guess you could always stay in Bluebonnet. Maybe the two of you could work out a custody agreement."

"I have a job in San Antonio."

"Of course you do. But change isn't always bad. And if it's a job you're worried about, I could use a good nurse."

Stay in Bluebonnet? No, she couldn't imagine herself living in a small town. She had never considered leaving San Antonio. She loved her job. Her foster parents and friends were in San Antonio.

But if Marcus took custody of Oliver, her heart would be here. In Bluebonnet Springs.

"I don't think so, Doc. I'm just here for two more weeks."

He let out a sigh. "I'm sorry to hear that. How is it you're related to Oliver?"

"His mother and I were foster children in the same home."

"That's a tough situation." He sat on a rolling stool and faced her. "I'm sure this won't be easy for any of you."

"No, it won't be."

"Well, I know you probably have a lot of opportunities in the city, but I'm going to leave the offer on the table and hope you'll reconsider. I could use a good nurse practitioner to run the clinic when I retire."

"I appreciate that offer. And I'm not qualified as a nurse practitioner."

"It's something to work toward."

It was an offer she never would have expected. It was an open door if she needed one. She could stay in Oliver's life. She would also be stuck in Marcus's life. And Oliver's daddy was becoming problematic for more reasons than the one she had anticipated.

He was not the person Sammy had described. He controlled his temper, spoke gently to his son, and he cared deeply about the people in his life.

For the past few days he had made her feel like one of those people.

Chapter Nine

At nine o'clock, Marcus handed Oliver his toothbrush and his bear pajamas. He had to admit, he was proud of himself. He'd kept his son safe for an entire day, fed him, spent time with him, and now he was rocking the bedtime routine.

"Do you have a step stool?" Oliver stood at the bathroom sink, eyeing it with a look that said he didn't see this happening.

"Let me ask Essie," Marcus offered. He looked from the sink to the boy. "Or I can pick you up and set you on the counter."

Oliver looked at the granite top and nodded. "Okay, lift me up."

Marcus lifted Oliver, who then sat crossed-legged on the granite vanity top to brush his teeth. When he finished, he jumped back down and reached for a washcloth to wipe his face. Marcus watched, amused at the bedtime routine.

"Will you read me a story?" Oliver asked as he put the brush back in the drawer. "Lissa always reads to me."

"What does she read?" he asked, watching as Oliver brushed his hair, almost as if he meant to go out and not to bed. When he finished, he handed the brush to Marcus.

"She reads the bible storybook to me. And *The Three Little Pigs*. Do you like *The Three Little Pigs*?" Oliver reached for his hand.

Marcus took that small hand in his. Did Oliver miss Sammy? That was a stupid question. Of course he missed his mom. Marcus's own mother had skated out on her family. Even though Marcus had been a teen and he'd understood why she left, he'd missed her.

And resented her. But she'd never read to him.

"So? Will you read me a story?" Oliver asked as he led Marcus to his bedroom.

A room the little boy obviously shared with Lissa. There were twin beds covered with handmade quilts. A rocking chair held folded clothes. And the room smelled of citrus and wildflowers. Lissa's perfume, if he was to guess.

"I'll tell you a story," Marcus offered.

He pulled back the blankets on one of the beds, the one with a stuffed teddy bear and a dinosaur robot that didn't look too cuddly. He moved the dinosaur to the dresser and sat down on the edge of the bed as Oliver slid under the quilt. The little boy, eyes sleepy and big, reached for the teddy bear.

"What story will you tell me?" Oliver asked on a yawn.

"I like the story of God's people praising Him as they went against the enemy. There weren't very many of them, but God promised them the victory if the priests went before them singing praises."

"Did they win?" Oliver asked, his eyes getting heavy.

"They did win."

"Will you pray?" Oliver opened one eye. "I'm kind of sleepy. Pray they find that lady. And will you tell God to tell my mom that I'm okay."

"I will."

Marcus was glad Oliver's eyes were closed, because those prayer requests hit him hard. He brushed away the tear that trickled down his son's cheek and felt one slip free from his own eye. He might not be much of a dad, but it hadn't taken him long to realize he loved his son. If it took a fight, he would have Oliver in his life.

He prayed a silent prayer for all of them, and then he prayed for Oliver and for Lissa and the town. He tagged on the special request that God pass on a message to Sammy. Oliver was okay. He was better than okay. He had people who loved him and they were looking out for him.

There was no echoing amen at the end of the prayer. Oliver had rolled over onto his side, the bear tucked close to his chin, his thumb in his mouth.

"Good night, son." He tucked the comforter around Oliver, then left the room, flipping off the light as he went.

Essie was sitting in the living room working on a quilt. She glanced up as he walked in, and then she removed the glasses she wore for close-up work and reading.

"What are you going to do?" she asked.

"I'm not sure. I mean, I know I'm going to be his dad. I'm not sure how to take him from Lissa. She's been his mother for the past year, but she's also been in his life since the day he was born."

"I think you'll figure it out. You're already figuring it out."

"I'm glad you think that, but this was just one night. We're talking a lifetime of nights." A lifetime of opportunities to let his son down. He checked his watch. "I should go get Lissa."

"You be careful on those roads, Marcus. I've been listening to the scanner and it's treacherous. Accident after accident tonight. And the water is coming up fast."

"I'll be careful. Anything you need from town?"

She shook her head. "Not that I can think of. Let me know when you get home. Even if I'm sleeping, wake me up."

"I'll wake you up when I bring Lissa, but then I'm going on back to my place."

She had her glasses back on, but she raised them a fraction to give him a forbidding look. "You can't sleep there tonight. If the water comes up, I'm sorry, but it might take out that old farmhouse."

"It's been standing a long time, Essie." He couldn't imagine the farmhouse being gone. Most of his good memories were built around that house and the Browns.

She continued to give him a look.

He bent to kiss the top of her head. "I'll stay at Alex's."

"Good."

She went back to quilting and he headed out the back door to his truck.

The rain appeared to be coming down even harder, if that was possible. It took him twenty minutes to make the ten-minute drive to town. When he pulled into the church lot, a patrol car was leaving. He parked and jumped out of his truck, running for the nearest door of the church and avoiding puddles along the way. Pastor Matthews must have seen him coming, because he had the door open as Marcus rushed up the steps.

"Come into the ark," the pastor said as Marcus entered the building, swiping a hand over his face to wipe away the rain.

"Why's the county cop here?" Marcus asked as he shrugged out of his rain-soaked jacket.

"We had a little incident with a spouse. Your friend is a black belt. Did you know that?"

"My friend?"

Duncan Matthews grinned. Marcus liked the pastor. He considered him a friend. One of his few. But the look on his face might move him from the friend category.

"Oh, come on, Marcus, have a sense of humor."

"I have a sense of humor," he grumbled. "Is she okay?"

"You mean Lissa? The woman who isn't your friend?" Pastor Matthews nodded and they started down the hall together. "She's fine. Slow down and try not to charge back there like you think the building is on fire. She did take a blow to the jaw, but she says it isn't broken, just bruised. Doc says she's done for the night and needs to go home and get some rest."

"That's why I'm here, to take her home." He stumbled over that last word and heat crawled into his cheeks. "To take her to Essie's."

They entered the clinic and he spotted her sitting in a rocking chair, legs drawn up, an ice pack on her cheek. She sighed when she saw him, as if she knew him well enough to know what he might be thinking or what he might say.

The last thing he planned to do was say what he was

thinking. He thought she looked small, sitting in the chair curled up like that. He thought she looked like a woman who needed a hug. And he wasn't a hugger. Maybe Essie could give her a hug. Or Oliver.

Not him.

Hugging her was the last thing he wanted to do.

"You heard?" she asked when he pulled up a stool and sat next to her.

"Yeah, I heard. You're okay?"

"Yeah, I'm okay. I should have been more observant. If I'd been on my guard, I would have noticed, but I thought I could defuse the situation with words. I prefer words."

"Black belt?"

Blue eyes twinkled at him. "Yeah. Surprise. My foster mom wanted me to feel empowered."

He understood that. What he didn't understand was why he reached to move the ice pack. He didn't get why he needed to see where she'd been struck. He definitely didn't understand why he touched the bruised flesh and felt the pain deep, as if it were his own.

He closed his eyes against memories that called to mind why he cared. He knew why it mattered. He knew why it bothered him to see her flesh marred, to see the flash of pain in her eyes. He and his siblings had all suffered at the hands of their father.

"Stop. You didn't do this."

How had she known his thoughts? Did she guess that he always feared the monster deep within? What if it was sleeping, waiting to someday rear its ugly head and lash out at someone he cared about? He'd lost his temper once with Sammy. He'd called the next day and told her they were done. Not because of her, but because of him. He wouldn't allow himself to get close if it meant he might hurt someone he cared about.

"No, I didn't do this," he answered gruffly. "Let's get you back to Essie's so you can sleep. Doc, I'm taking your patient home. Need anything before we go?"

Doc looked up from the desk he'd commandeered. He glanced from Lissa to Marcus. "No, I don't need anything. I am sorry that you're taking my assistant. I guess you won't be able to talk her into staying and working with me on a permanent basis."

Lissa stay permanently in Bluebonnet? She had stepped away from him and was studying the little girl, who still slept on the bed. Her lips moved in a silent prayer. A woman of faith. Something else to like about her.

No, he didn't think he could talk her into staying. And he wasn't sure he wanted to. "Sorry, Doc, you're on your own."

He glanced at the woman standing next to him. She looked about done in and she was cradling her arm, probably to give her shoulder some relief. When her time was up in a couple of weeks, she'd probably be glad to see the last of Bluebonnet.

Until then, he guessed it was up to him to take care of her. He would put her in the category of family. That would make it easier to deal with whatever it was he felt.

They were walking down the hall when Marcus stopped abruptly. Lissa glanced up at him, wondering what was going on. He was always the strong, silent type, but since he'd arrived at the church to take her home, he'd gone beyond silent.

Brooding might be a better word.

"What?" she asked as he stared down at her.

"You can't put yourself in dangerous situations like that. Oliver needs you."

"I didn't put myself in a dangerous situation. I refuse to take the blame for being in the wrong place at the wrong time. But what I did do is protect myself and possibly keep an already abused wife from being further abused."

She poked his arm once for good measure.

He had the good sense to look contrite. "You're right, I'm sorry. It worried me."

"It wasn't fun for me, either." She winced because everything hurt now.

Marcus sighed as he stared down at her and then, before she could brace herself or object, he scooped her up and held her as if she was a five-year-old child. She tried to get loose, but his arms tightened around her and she was forced close, feeling the strength in his arms.

Suddenly, objecting became the last thing she wanted to do as she settled in his arms and felt his warmth, felt the strong beat of his heart. As they went out the door, Pastor Matthews provided an umbrella, shoving it into her hands, and then he tossed her an already damp jacket. A jacket that smelled like Marcus.

"You all be careful out there," the pastor warned, and she wondered if the warning had a double meaning.

Marcus picked up his pace as they headed for his truck.

"I could walk," she offered.

"I know you can. But you look like you might collapse. You're not heavy."

"Thank you. I think."

A moment later they were at his truck, and he managed to pull the door open and deposit her in the seat without ever letting her feet touch the ground. She pulled on her seat belt as he went around to get in on the driver's side.

Not surprisingly, he climbed in without a word. In the dark interior of the truck, barely illuminated by the distant light at the front of the church and the orange glow of a streetlight, she saw the harsh set of his mouth. He was a thing of beauty, with chiseled features, a strong mouth and dark eyes.

If she didn't know better, she might think he was mad at her. But she did know better. She knew he was worried. Upset. *For her.*

He caught her staring and quirked a brow. As they pulled from the parking lot, he turned up the radio, a country station playing softly.

"Stop staring." He finally spoke, his voice soft and raspy.

"What happened?" She felt a strong pull toward him and a need to know his stories. It couldn't lead anywhere, this attraction or the other deeper, more startling emotions. Proof yet again that she had a radar for dark and brooding men.

But she wanted his stories.

"Happened?" He peered through the rain-splattered windshield as the wipers worked to keep it clear. The road was dark and the lines nearly invisible.

"Nothing, focus on the road."

They hit standing water and the truck hydroplaned, swerving just a bit. He grimaced and kept a tight hand on the wheel.

"Relax," he told her.

"What if the bridge is out?" she asked.

"You're all about the positive, aren't you?" He kept his attention on the road.

"Sorry."

He slowed as the rain came down harder. "My dad."

The two words spoken in his raspy voice took her by surprise. She shifted in the seat and studied his face, the clenched jaw, the way his hands gripped the wheel.

"Your dad?"

"You asked what happened. My dad did this to me. I was—" he shrugged "—I guess maybe fourteen. I don't remember. Must have been the lack of oxygen to my brain as he tried to choke the life out of me."

"Why?" The word came out as a whisper. Shock made her feel cold. She shivered in his jacket, which still covered her.

"Lucy and her husband, Dane. Back then they'd been sneaking around, dating. My dad didn't allow dating. When he found out, he ran Dane off and he locked Lucy in a storage room in the barn."

"You tried to get her out."

"Yeah. First Alex tried to talk to him. Alex is always the diplomat. When that didn't work, I tried to reason with him my way. I knocked him down and thought I'd take him with my fists. Unfortunately, he was bigger and stronger. Doc guesses he damaged my larynx. He also bashed my shin with a shovel. And left the scar on my face."

Tears fell. She brushed them away, but not before he saw.

"Don't," he warned. "I would do it again."

"I know you would."

"But I'm not a hero." He slowed the truck as they neared the turn to Essie's. "I'm a recovering alcoholic.

I've never been good at being there for the people who needed me. I've let down more people than I can count."

She wanted to tell him he wasn't like his father. She wanted to assure him that she didn't believe he would ever harm his son. But what did she know about Marcus Palermo?

Nothing really.

She took that back. She knew that he was gentle with his son, cared about his family and was strong enough to carry her when she couldn't carry herself. She closed her eyes, remembering those moments in his arms. She'd felt safe.

He'd made her feel protected. More than once.

He'd also made her feel more. More unsure. More terrified of her own emotions. More drawn to him than she had ever been drawn to any man.

He parked under the portico at the side of Essie's house and told her to slide across and get out on the driver's side. She did, knowing this time he wouldn't carry her. He didn't even reach for her hand. Instead, he hurried up the steps and opened the door that led through the breakfast room.

"Are you hungry?" he asked as they entered the kitchen.

"A little."

He opened the fridge. "There's leftover potato soup."

She took the container from his hands. Strong hands. The thought unnerved her. She moved away from him, finding a bowl and then pulling out another for him. He didn't object, so she filled both bowls and heated them in the microwave.

They didn't sit down to eat. They stood side by side in the kitchen with just the light over the sink and the rain pouring down outside. Somewhere a clock ticked away the seconds. They were too close. The moment felt companionable and more. She avoided looking at him, afraid of what she would see in his eyes and afraid of what he would see in hers. She was afraid of him, but it wasn't the kind of fear that raised her hackles or made her worry for her safety.

Marcus finished his soup and poured two glasses of iced tea. He set hers on the counter behind her and carried his to the breakfast room, leaving her alone. After a few minutes she followed him, knowing he had walked away to be alone with his thoughts, with the past.

She had forced him to think back on the abuse. Unsettled by that, she stepped close, needing to comfort him. He took a deep breath, and as she slid an arm around his waist, he stiffened. She wasn't going to let him get away with that. If he was going to be Oliver's dad, he needed to learn to embrace, to hug, to touch.

Little boys might be snips, snails and puppy dog tails, but they still needed warmth and they needed affection. Marcus had obviously gotten the short end of those two things as a child.

Slowly he moved until they were facing each other. He took a breath and relaxed, and she wrapped her arms tighter, holding him close. She wouldn't lie to herself and say this was her way of comforting a man who had been hurt. The man in her arms wasn't that child anymore. He leaned forward, touching his forehead to hers.

Rain trickled down the windows and thunder rumbled in the distance. Slowly the moment continued to shift and change until it became something that stole her breath. He moved and she looked up, searching his dark eyes as he changed position, lowering his mouth to capture hers.

Softly his lips brushed hers, the touch so light it almost didn't happen. She sighed into the kiss and then his lips met hers a little more insistently. A little more desperately.

Their hands remained intertwined. He pulled a hand loose to sweep it across her cheek, holding her there for the sweet exploration of his kiss. His touch was soft, gentle and sure.

Slowly he drew back, closing his eyes and murmuring her name. His fingers loosened and he let go of her hand.

"I have to go." He took a cautious step back. "I shouldn't have done that. I'm not going to do it again."

"No?" She disliked that it came out as a question. It should have been a definite no. They wouldn't do this again.

"My days of playing the field are over," he explained, answering the question that shouldn't have been a question. "And I'm the last thing you need in your life."

"Thank you for explaining that." She could have told him it was too late. Sammy had put them in each other's lives. For better or worse.

His mouth kicked up at the corner, and an almost amused look flickered through his eyes. "You're welcome."

And then he left. As a parting shot, she should have said something like *You got that right, buddy. You're the last thing I need in my life.*

Instead, she stood at the window watching him drive away and arguing all the reasons he was right and insisting her sanity had taken a momentary leave of absence.

Tomorrow would be different. She'd be sane again. It wouldn't be dark and rainy. They wouldn't both be in this vulnerable place.

The connection would be broken, she assured herself. She sighed, her forehead pushed against the cool glass of the window as the rain continued to fall. It was dark. So dark out there in the country with no streetlights, no houses. She'd never felt so alone.

Maybe that was the place Marcus had touched tonight, her loneliness. Maybe they'd both been lonely and it had drawn them to each other.

Whatever. She could convince herself of anything, but the truth was she liked him. He wasn't at all the person she'd expected. And he was dangerous to her heart. Dangerous to her convictions.

Her first priority had to be Oliver. His future. His happiness and safety.

She'd spent her childhood being the victim of her single mother's poor choices. Oliver wasn't going to be the victim of her poor choices. Throughout her childhood, Lissa had been an afterthought. Her safety had been an afterthought. Her mother's relationships, the men, had come first.

As attractive as Marcus Palermo might be, Lissa wouldn't get sidetracked. Not when the man she found herself attracted to was the same man who could take Oliver from her.

Forever.

Chapter Ten

"Wake up. We've got to roll."

The words penetrated Marcus's sleep-fogged brain. He covered his head with a pillow. "Go away, Alex."

He brought his arm up and peeked at his watch. Five in the morning. His alarm would go off in an hour. Since he hadn't slept much last night, he wasn't even thinking about getting up an hour early with his brother, who obviously believed the saying about the early bird getting the worm.

"Out of bed."

"I don't like worms," Marcus muttered. "You go get all you want."

"Town's flooding, you slug. Get up. We have to get stuff out of the café before the creek reaches it."

That got his attention. "My house."

"Yeah, I know. If you hurry, we can make a loop and go by your place before we head to town." The door closed.

Marcus could still hear the rain. As he headed down the hall a few minutes later, he could also hear Marissa and Alex in the kitchen. They were whispering, and even without seeing, he knew they were cuddled up and talking all sweet to each other. He couldn't decide whether to be disgusted by the display or find it amusing and cute.

He was disgusted. That was what he decided when he walked into the kitchen and they were standing close, arms around each other.

"Too early in the morning to subject me to this." He poured himself a cup of coffee. "I thought we were in a hurry."

"We are in a hurry." Alex filled a thermos with coffee.

"We should check on Essie." Marcus sat down to pull on boots. When he looked up, Alex and Marissa were sharing a look. "Did I say something funny?"

"No, not at all." Smirking, Alex tossed him a granola bar. "Let's go."

Marcus headed out the door ahead of his brother, shrugging into a jacket as he went. He pushed his hat down on his head as he hurried across the yard to Alex's truck. It took his twin a few minutes longer, standing in the doorway of the house kissing his wife.

Jealousy. It came out of nowhere. Marcus had never been jealous of his brother. Well, maybe once or twice, when school had come easy to Alex. Or when he'd managed to talk his way through anger instead of fighting with their father. But when it came to women, no, he'd never been envious. The two of them wanted different things. Alex had a more settled personality. He wanted the minivan and family vacations.

Marcus had been telling himself for as long as he could remember that he didn't want those things. It was easier to shut himself off than to open up and be rejected. Or to open up and think about hurting someone.

When Alex finally climbed behind the wheel of the truck, Marcus had settled his emotions. He refilled his insulated mug with coffee from the thermos and gave a quick shake of his head at the silly grin on his brother's face.

"What?" Alex grinned because he knew. And he wasn't at all ashamed.

"I'm happy for you," Marcus admitted. He glanced out the window and sipped his coffee.

"Thanks, because I'm pretty happy for myself. We're having a baby."

Just like that, everything changed. The hot coffee scalded when Marcus spilled it on his shirt. He sat up a little straighter and gave Alex a quick look to see if the expression on his face matched the tone.

"A baby." He laughed a little, thinking about his brother as a dad.

"Well, it isn't like you don't have one of your own."

That changed the mood in the truck. Oliver had been a baby. His baby. He hadn't known that a kid with his DNA was living on the same planet, breathing the same Texas air, learning to walk and talk. "Yeah, I do have a son of my own."

"It's a lot to take in, isn't it?"

"Yeah, it's a lot. But he's a good kid."

"So you'll keep him?"

"He's my son, Alex. Not a puppy I found on the side of the road." Marcus shot his brother a look. "Is there really a question about that? I don't know how I'm going to do this, but I can't imagine him not being here with us. We're his family."

"I know that. But a few days ago, I think you weren't as crazy about the idea. Also, there's Lissa to consider. He's been with her for a while."

"I know all of that."

"I never thought this would be our lives." Alex turned onto the main road, but he kept the speed down and dodged standing water on the pavement. "We were all a pretty dysfunctional mess. But we've kind of pulled ourselves out of that pit."

Marcus shrugged it off. "Yeah, I guess we have. Thank God and Essie."

They pulled up to Essie's a few minutes later. Their aunt stood on the front porch with Lissa. The two were scanning the horizon, where there wasn't much to see but more clouds and more rain coming. Essie raised her coffee cup in greeting.

"Well?" she asked as they walked up the steps to the porch.

"We're heading to my place and then to town," Marcus said. "We thought we'd check on you all before we head that way."

"Check on me, my foot." Essie gave him a long look. "I don't guess you could load up an entire café in that truck of yours."

"I wish we could," Marcus replied. "But we can get anything out that you want."

"My pictures on the walls and the register. I guess that's about all we'll be able to take out. I'm hoping that even if the water gets up in the building, it won't take everything."

"We'll stack tables and chairs against the far wall in the kitchen." Alex gave their aunt a quick hug. "And we'll say some prayers."

"More than that, we cannot do." Essie sighed. "I've been praying for a few days now, and it doesn't look like the good Lord is bringing this rain to a stop anytime soon. I know He could. And I know for some reason He isn't. But I also know we'll make it through this the way we've made it through everything else life has thrown at us."

There was a point to that little sermon. Marcus figured it had something to do with rain and prayer, and something to do with his life. Essie pursed her lips and gave him that dead-on serious look of hers. Yeah, the message was for him. He'd make it through this. The way he'd made it through so many things. Actually, when it came right down to it, finding out he had a son wasn't such a bad thing after all.

As if on cue, the door opened and Oliver hurried out to join them. He saw Marcus and a big grin split his face. A moment later arms were wrapped around his waist.

Marcus patted the boy on the back and then made unfortunate eye contact with Lissa. Her look prodded him to give more of himself. He hugged his son to him and then scooped him up in his arms.

"What are you doing up this early?" Marcus asked Oliver.

"I heard Lissa and Aunt Essie talking." Marcus guessed his shock must have shown on his face. "She said I can call her Aunt Essie because she's an aunt and I need another aunt."

"That makes good sense," Marcus agreed.

Oliver wiggled to get down and Marcus put him back on his feet. "Aunt Essie said she can't open the café today. Because of flooding. But she's going to make pancakes. She said pancakes were always your favorite. They're mine, too. That must be because we have the same last name. Marcus Palermo and Oliver Palermo. I think that's cool."

"Yeah, that is cool." Marcus had to agree. Who wouldn't?

He met Lissa's gaze over the top of her coffee cup as she took a sip. Why hadn't he thought about Oliver's last name? He had just assumed Sammy had given him her last name. But standing there in front of him, as proud as he could be, was Marcus's flesh and blood. And he had his last name.

He'd gone through times in life when he hadn't been too proud of the name. He had thought about changing it so he wouldn't have that connection with his father. But now, Oliver having his last name changed everything.

The last thing he wanted was for his son to be ashamed of who he was. He also didn't want Oliver to ever be ashamed to have him for a father.

"We should get started." Alex gave Marcus a nudge with his elbow. "I know you want to get down to your place, but we might not be able to make it over the low-water bridge that crosses the dry creek."

"Yeah, I was thinking the same. We do need to be heading on to town. We can do more good there than at my place." Marcus put a hand on Oliver's shoulder. "Take care of the ladies, okay?"

"I thought I would go with you. I might be able to help." Lissa, he realized, had on rubber boots and a raincoat.

"I don't think so," Marcus started. She froze him with those blue eyes of hers.

"I make my own decisions, Marcus."

Okay, he got it. She didn't want him to kiss her one night and tell her what to do the next. But the anger. He didn't get that.

He put his hands up in surrender. "Fine. Do you want us to take you to the clinic? I'm assuming Oliver is staying with Essie?"

"Yes, Oliver is staying with me," Essie responded as she placed a hand on his son's shoulder. "I am leaving the search and rescue to you younger folk."

"Yes, you can drop me at the clinic at the shelter." Lissa was coming down the stairs. "I want to help Doc. And I want to be there with Pearl. They are still searching for her mother."

"Hold down the fort, Oliver." Marcus touched his son's shoulder. They had to tell him—soon, when things calmed down and they could spend time talking things out.

"I will. I'm pretty good at that. I build forts at Grammy Jane's house."

"I bet you are." He grinned at the boy's exuberance.

Oliver pointed at him, a huge smile flashing across his little face. "I made you smile. Aunt Essie said you almost never laugh. Everyone laughs. Don't they, Marcus?"

Marcus shot his aunt a look. They ought to be more careful what they say, because Oliver was obviously pretty good at eavesdropping.

"Yeah, everyone laughs." Marcus ruffled his son's hair. "Go on inside and enjoy those pancakes. Make sure you get bacon."

"Knock knock." Oliver looked up at him, waiting.

"What?"

"Knock knock. You're supposed to say 'who's there?'"

"Am I really?" Marcus blinked, confused by the way the conversation had turned.

"Say it so we can leave," Alex prodded.

"Who's there?" Marcus asked.

"Atch."

"Atch who?"

"Gesund..." Oliver bit down on his bottom lip. *"Gesundhigh."*

Marcus didn't crack a smile, but he wanted to. "Nope."

"It was a joke," Oliver told him.

"Gotta go." Marcus headed down the steps with Alex chuckling behind him.

"That kid is going to get the best of you." Alex spoke as they were driving toward Bluebonnet.

"He *is* the best of me." Marcus didn't mean to be emotional about it, but he was late to the fatherhood party. He'd ridden some bulls, made some money, bought the farm he'd always wanted. But the kid, he was everything and then some.

He'd forgotten Lissa. She hurried after them, grabbing the door when he started to get in. He moved back and motioned her inside the cab of the truck.

"You're sure you want to skip your place?" Alex asked as they headed down the road.

"I moved what was important. And the stuff upstairs should be safe."

"Paintings," Alex told Lissa. He ignored Marcus's warning look. "You saw the ones downstairs, right?"

"Yes, I did. They're very good." Lissa gave Marcus a questioning look, and he didn't feel inclined to give answers.

Alex didn't stop. "Marcus is an artist."

"Okay, end of discussion. That's private."

"He sells them at a store in San Antonio. On the River Walk." Alex grinned, enjoying himself a little too much.

Marcus turned his attention to the window. Forget it. He wasn't winning this one.

Her phone rang. Marcus watched as she glanced at the caller ID.

"Block the caller."

She looked up. "What?"

"Same caller you've been ignoring for a week now. Block it if you don't want to talk."

"I'm not answering because he wanted to give me his opinion and try to control my days, my time and my life."

She couldn't be any clearer than that. It wasn't his business. One kiss didn't give him the right to tell her what to do. He got it.

"Your life. I'm not telling you what to do."

She dropped the phone back in her purse. "If I block him, I won't know what he's up to."

That got his attention. "Are you afraid of him, Lissa?"

"Not afraid. As you know, I can take care of myself. But he does make me nervous. He has met me in the parking garage of the hospital. He says he's there to make sure I get safely to my car."

"Have Security take you to your car. I'm not making that an order, just a friendly suggestion."

And now he wanted to pound this guy. A man he didn't know. A man he would never meet. But a man who made her expression tight with fear, even if she didn't call it fear. So much for not getting involved. Without trying, she'd pulled him into her life and made him care.

They turned into the church parking lot and the conversation ceased. He willingly let it go. It wasn't his business. She wasn't his business.

An ambulance pulled in behind them. That got all of their attention. The attendants climbed out the back. As they did, Marcus noticed a woman emerging. She was wrapped in blankets, and her hair was soaked and hanging around her pale face.

"Pearl's mommy," Lissa whispered, her voice wobbly with emotion. "Please God, let that be Pearl's mom."

They got out as Pastor Matthews was running toward the ambulance. The woman sobbed, falling into his arms. They could hear him telling her she had saved her daughter.

Lissa's hand slid into Marcus's, the most natural gesture in the world. He gave her slim fingers a slight squeeze and she leaned into his shoulder, surrounding him with her warmth.

"There's your answer." He whispered the words against her hair and then, carefully, he kissed the top of her head.

"Yes, there's the answer." She smiled up at him. "You guys go rescue the world. I'll be here with Doc."

They watched the reunion between Pearl and her mother, and then they left. As they drove through town, Alex and Marcus were both shocked. The water had come up over the tracks and was rushing along the side of the café. It wasn't inside the building, but it was close. "Let's make a sweep through town before we tackle the café," Marcus suggested. "I'll check the state website and see if they have changed the projected cresting of the creek. If they haven't, the water probably won't get in the café."

"I think the rain is supposed to move out of the area later this afternoon," Alex answered. "But I'm afraid that isn't going to do us a lot of good." They drove down a side road lined with houses. The waters from the creek had become a river, rushing out of the banks and sweeping through houses that were a good hundred feet from the banks of the normally shallow creek.

"Is that Dan Godfrey on his front porch?" Marcus asked as they drove along the street above where the flooded creek had overtaken the houses and the road that ran parallel to the water.

About a half block ahead of them Marcus could see the elderly man standing on his porch, his pants rolled up to his knobby knees. He had a big box in his skinny arms and a cat sitting on the box.

"What in the world?" Alex hit the brakes and pulled his truck to the side of the road. "How did search and rescue miss him? I heard they rescued Chet Wilkins and that crazy pig of his. The two were sitting in a canoe next to Chet's house."

"If I know Dan, he probably didn't answer the door. Or he hid, thinking he's lived there his whole life and that creek has never gotten close to his house."

"Yeah, there's a big X on his door, so they did check the house. And you're right, he probably hid."

The two of them got out and headed in the direction of Dan's house. Alex yelled, telling the older man to stay put. The waters were rushing, and no way could Dan stand up against that current.

"Do you think we can get to him?" Marcus asked as they neared the house. The water was already to his knees and it would be deeper when they got to the front porch.

"I think we can stand up against the water. I like that Dan has his pants rolled up to his knees. The water is probably up to his waist."

"I'll carry Dan if you grab the box and the cat," Marcus offered.

"You hate cats so much you're willing to take the old man?"

Marcus grinned at that. "Yep."

The current pushed against them as they walked. All the time, Dan remained on the porch with his box and the cat. Water rushed around his house and was already several inches over the porch where he stood.

"Time to get you out of here, Dan." Alex took the box and the cat.

"I didn't want to leave Annie's house." The old man swiped at a tear as he mentioned his wife. "She loved this place. I had to get her doilies and the pictures of the kids. And this old cat."

"Did search and rescue let you stay?" Marcus asked.

Dan shook his head, his gray eyes faded and sad. "No, I climbed up in the attic when they came. I guess they thought I left with Billy. But Billy couldn't find me, either."

Billy was Dan's son. He lived in Killeen and got back as often as possible to see his dad.

"Is there anything else you want out of here, Dan?" Alex offered.

"No, I've got my memories. Sixty years' worth. Annie and I built this house the year we married. Back then there was money working in the oil fields." The older man looked at his house, all the emotion visible in his expression. "We had a good life here, me and Annie. Raised four kids. Had a passel of grands."

"You'll be able to come back," Alex assured him.

"No, I don't think Billy will let me. I heard him tell his wife that I'm slipping. I ain't, but that's what they think. After this they'll probably move me to the city and one of them homes."

Marcus felt for the man. He couldn't imagine leaving the place he'd built and lived in for sixty years. It was hard enough envisioning losing the home he'd had for less than a year. A home with memories built through another family, not his own.

"Maybe he'll let you stay in town, Dan." Marcus offered. "But we can't stay here right now. The water is seeping into the house and it's still coming up."

"I guess we'd better go." Dan sighed as he looked at the swollen creek. "I didn't think it would get like this. I thought a few inches, and if it came up, I'd just walk out. I didn't even move my old Ford out of the carport. I guess I won't have a truck after this."

Sure enough, water was pouring through Dan's old truck.

"It looks like you'll have to say goodbye to that truck." Alex held on to the cat and Marcus bit back a smile. That cat was going to have to ride in his brother's truck.

"Come on, Dan, time to go." Marcus scooped Dan up, and the older man kicked a little.

"I ain't no silly woman needing you to carry me out of here, Marcus Palermo."

"I know you're not, Dan. But that water is strong and you don't weigh much."

"I can walk out of here," Dan insisted in a stronger voice than he'd used in a while. Marcus set him on his own two feet. "I don't mind if you hold me steady, but

I'll not have you carrying me. What would Annie think if she was here?"

Marcus didn't argue. A man had his pride. "Come on, then."

Slowly they trudged back through the water. Dan had a hard time staying on his feet, but Marcus kept hold of him. He understood that the older man wanted to preserve his dignity. Marcus would help him do that. Besides, at least Marcus didn't have to hold on to that screaming, yowling cat.

The house Marcus grew up in was a sprawling, single-story ranch house. The stable and arena were several hundred feet from the house. Lissa walked through the stable with Oliver. Lucy had picked up Essie and Oliver and driven to the church to get Lissa. The guys were still busy in town helping people save what could be saved and rescuing those who hadn't gotten out in time.

Ahead of them, Marissa Palermo talked about the horses her husband, Alex, raised and the cattle. He also had bucking bulls.

Marissa taught at the local school, but school had let out for summer break. As she talked, Marissa touched her belly. Often. If Lissa had to guess, she would say that other woman was pregnant.

"Can I ride a horse?" Oliver hurried ahead of them and stopped at a stall door where a big, gray head stretched over the door, eager for attention. The horse lipped at Oliver's hair and then blew out a breath. Oliver laughed and backed away, but then he inched forward again, raising a hand to pet the same velvety nose that had snorted on him.

"I think maybe when the rain stops we can arrange

that." Marissa stood next to Oliver, her hand going again to her belly. "This is Granite. He's Alex's favorite."

"I like him, too." Oliver smiled up at her.

She was his aunt. Lissa realized that as she watched the two, Alex and Marissa. Oliver had no idea that he was surrounded by aunts, uncles and cousins. Marcus was right—they needed to tell him as soon as possible. Oliver deserved to know these people and to know they were his family.

The more time she spent with them, the less she worried about Oliver's future. He would have these people in his life. The more she got to know them, though, the more she felt her heart ache with loss that was eminent.

Oliver spotted a cat and took off, eager to catch it.

"Be careful, some of these cats are a little wild," Marissa cautioned. "But if you look around, you might find kittens. Just don't go in stalls with horses."

When he heard the word *kittens*, Oliver slowed his pace and started a search. Marissa sat down on the bench placed midway along the aisle. Lissa sat with her.

"How far along are you?" Lissa asked.

At the question, Marissa smiled a sweet smile. "Just a few months. We haven't told anyone."

"I think you'll have to tell them soon," Lissa advised. "You're glowing."

At that, Marissa turned a shade of pink and her hand went to her belly again. "We're just so excited. It's twins. They did an ultrasound last week and there are two little Palermos on the way."

"Wow! That's exciting."

"And frightening," Marissa added. She watched as Oliver crawled under the door of a stall.

Lissa checked to make sure it was empty and then

sat back, relaxing. The rain had slowed and was now a gentle patter on the metal roof of the stable.

"I watch him and I think, I'm going to have one like him. He's so stinking cute that I just can't wait." Marissa glanced at Lissa. "They'll be cousins."

Lissa nodded, keeping an eye on Oliver as he continued the search for kittens. At one time Marcus would have been a child living here, playing in this barn. No, she rethought that. Did he ever play? Did the Palermo children have happy memories? It would be a shame if they didn't have those good memories, having grown up in a place like this, with so much to offer.

Oliver continued his search through the barn. He stopped at a closed door and peeked at Lissa before turning the handle and slowly pulling the door open.

"I should check on him." She stood. "He's not been himself since we picked him up earlier. He might be getting homesick."

Marissa touched her arm. "Don't let him play in that room. Marcus wouldn't want him in there."

"No?"

"It's a difficult story and not mine to tell."

"Of course. I'll go get him."

Maria entered the barn as Lissa hurried to collect Oliver. The younger Palermo smiled a greeting before nodding toward the room Oliver had entered.

"Better get him out of there," Maria warned. "Marcus and Alex just pulled up."

Oliver, being five, didn't understand the meaning of *hurry*. He had found a litter of kittens. The mama cat curled around them, licking them in turns and nuzzling them as they curled against her belly.

"Can I take one home with me?" Oliver asked as Lissa squatted next to him.

"No, we can't have cats in our apartment. Remember?"

Oliver looked crestfallen at the reminder. "Yeah, I know. I like it here. There are cats and dogs and horses."

"Yes, there are. But we don't live in the country."

"No, we live in a big, big city." Oliver ran a finger over a little striped tabby kitten. "I like this one."

"He is pretty," Lissa agreed. "We need to go now."

"What have you all found?"

The soft but gruff voice startled Lissa. She jumped a little and faced the door, feeling guilty for having been caught in the room that Marcus wouldn't want her in.

He didn't look upset. His expression softened as he looked from her to Oliver. His son had worked up the courage to pick up the tabby kitten.

"Kittens, huh?" Marcus remained at the door.

"Come in and see them. There are six." Oliver kissed the kitten on the top of the head. "How does the mom get to them when the door is closed?"

"She goes up in the loft and comes down. See the little opening?" Marcus pointed at the ceiling, and sure enough the wall didn't go to the top. There was a ledge and an opening that led to the loft. It was only about six inches wide, but big enough for a cat.

"I want a kitten, but we can't have cats in the city," Oliver informed Marcus with a glum expression on his face.

"Oliver, you should put the kitten back with his mommy. She's looking for him." Lissa stroked the kitten's soft head, and then she helped Oliver return him to the mother cat.

"Have you seen the kittens?" Oliver asked, unaware of how Marcus seemed frozen at the door of the room. "You should see them. They're all colors."

"I bet they're pretty. And if you didn't live in the city, you could take one home with you." Marcus looked from Oliver to Lissa and she wanted to tell him that was unfair.

"Yeah, but we can't live in the country. Lissa has a job in San Antonio. And she doesn't really think she could work for Doc Parker. We just came here so I could meet you." Did his voice seem off? Upset? Lissa heard it, but she wanted to believe she didn't.

"You have been eavesdropping again," Marcus said quietly, as was his way.

"I hear a lot of stuff," Oliver said, not bothering to look up. His attention remained on the cats. "I know that Marcus is my dad. That's why I have his last name. And I'm the spitting image of him. Whatever that is."

"Spitting image," Lissa whispered, her throat clogged with emotions that felt like sadness, regret and loss. She was going to lose Oliver to this place and these people. They were his family, she reminded herself, and she had no claim to him. The letter gave Marcus the rights. The right to choose Oliver. The right to keep him from her.

Marcus was at her side. She hadn't noticed him moving into the room. She felt his hand on her shoulder, and then he squatted next to her, his hand sliding down her arm and then away.

"You are my spitting image," he told Oliver in his quiet voice. "But you're a far sight better than me."

"My mom said I had a dad and that I couldn't meet him because he would take me and he wasn't no good."

Oliver looked him over and his mouth drew into a frown. "I guess she meant you."

Lissa's heart shattered. Sammy never should have told Oliver those things. Why would she do that to him? She sighed because she knew. Sammy hadn't always thought about Oliver's feelings.

Marcus sat on the floor, moving so that his back was against the wall. He pulled Oliver onto his lap. "I'm really sorry your mom told you that. And I wish I had known you a lot sooner so we could work up to this whole father-and-son thing."

"Because you're sorry that you didn't want to be around me?"

Lissa looked at Marcus, unsure of what answer he would or should give a five-year-old child. His eyes reflected her surprise. Leave it to Oliver to ask the hard questions.

"I've made a lot of mistakes and I'm trying to make up for those mistakes. Oliver, I am very sorry that I didn't get to be around you."

He didn't say anything against Sammy, who hadn't told him he had a son. Lissa mouthed a silent *Thank you.* He nodded and continued to talk to his son in a quiet and comforting tone.

"Will I live here now? Instead of with Lissa? My bed is at her house. And I have a bed at Grammy and Pops's. We always lived with Lissa, though." His little face fell as he looked from one adult to the other.

Lissa felt the ache of loss as never before. She'd been holding this little boy since he took his first breath. She'd changed his diapers. She'd helped Sammy potty train him. She'd taught him the alphabet and his colors.

Marcus's gaze bored into her, questioning her without words. Oliver had revealed so much. More than she'd been willing to tell.

Oliver crawled off his lap. "You just don't want to be a dad. That's what I heard them say in town."

Marcus paled beneath the accusation. He opened his mouth. Lissa waited, wanting him to say the right thing. But what could he say to that. He had never planned on being a dad. He didn't trust himself to be a dad.

"It's something I have to get used to, Oliver." He stood, his hand going to the boy's. "I haven't been a dad before."

He looked to Lissa, clearly lost and unsure of how to handle the hurt his son was experiencing.

"Oliver, we'll talk about this. Maybe it's nap time?" Lissa reached for his hand.

Oliver ran out of the storage room and into the waiting arms of Maria. His aunt Maria, Lissa realized.

"I don't want a nap," Oliver responded, burying his face against Maria as her arms went around him. "I want my mommy."

Tears trickled down Maria's cheeks as she soothed the little boy. "How about we go to the house and have cookies and milk? I'll put in a movie and we'll cuddle."

Lissa ached to hold him, to comfort him. She had been prepared to lose him, or so she'd thought. Bringing him here, she'd known she was giving him up to Marcus. But she hadn't expected to feel this distance as Oliver picked someone else's arms over hers.

A strong arm went around her waist, offering comfort. She nodded and told Maria that sounded like a great idea. The younger woman lifted Oliver and carried him from the stable. Marissa had also left, which meant she and Marcus were alone.

And then she was in his arms and he was holding her as she cried against his shoulder. His lips touched her hair and he murmured that it would work out. They would figure this out and do what was best for Oliver.

His next words were ones she wasn't prepared for. "You have to tell me more about Sammy. Oliver was living with you. There has to be a reason for that."

She nodded, admitting that there had been a reason. She had hoped she wouldn't have to discuss the mess her best friend and foster sister had made of parenting.

Worse, the feeling that she was closer than ever to losing Oliver. And the man holding her, offering her comfort, was the man who would take him from her.

Chapter Eleven

"Let's take a ride to my place," Marcus told the woman he'd carefully set aside after hugging her through the worst of her tears. She brushed a hand across her face and drew in a deep breath.

"I guess we should talk."

Not that long ago Pastor Matthews had told him that the closer he got to God, the more his faith would be tested. He'd never been too good at tests. This time he couldn't fail. There was too much riding on his choices and the outcome.

How in the world did he part Lissa from Oliver? Worse, he couldn't let his son go. A week changed everything, it seemed. God created the heavens and the earth in six days. And in about the same amount of time He'd turned Marcus into a father. A man who couldn't begin to think of signing away his rights.

"We can drive over to my place. I need to check on things there."

She nodded and followed him out of the barn. The rain had stopped. Alex emerged from the tractor-repair shop he'd built on the property and saw them heading toward the old farm truck. He stepped back inside the garage and came out with keys.

"You might need these."

"Thanks. Don't send out a posse. We might be a while."

"Marcus," Alex warned.

Marcus raised a hand to wave him away. "I'm fine."

He wasn't going to lose his temper. He wasn't even thinking of taking a drink. At least he had that going for him. He just wanted to know everything. And the only one who could tell him the entire story was the woman walking next to him, acting as if she was on her way to walk the plank.

"I'm fine," he repeated, this time for her benefit.

He opened the door and she climbed in the truck. Blue eyes locked with his. He reached to touch her pale cheek. Her eyes closed beneath his touch, but she moved closer, curving into his palm in the sweetest way.

He felt as if she'd turned him inside out and upside down. He didn't know front from back, right from left. Somehow he had to find his old, steady self, the man who kept emotion on the back burner. Cold-as-Ice Palermo, they'd called him. That had been a million years ago, it seemed.

He closed the door and walked to the driver's side of the truck. When he got in, he turned the radio to a cowboy country station that he liked. Soulful lyrics about open roads, rodeo, sweethearts and gentle rains. All the things a man could dream about but never thought could be reality.

"She slipped," Lissa said as they drove.

Tires hummed on the drying pavement. In the west

there was a flash of red through gray clouds as the sun set on the horizon.

"Slipped?"

"After she had Oliver. She stopped working. She went out with a guy. She started drinking. You have to understand, she told me that she'd broken up with you because you were angry and wild, drank too much and she was afraid of you. That's the excuse she gave for not telling you about Oliver."

"I'm a mean drunk?" He said the words, not quite understanding. "That's why I didn't get to see my son until he was five years old? And you kept him from me an extra year."

He fought down the anger. But he had to be fair. It wasn't really Lissa he was angry with. He noticed the fear in her blue eyes. He didn't want her afraid of him. He wanted her trust. That made this about the most complicated relationship of his life.

But it wasn't a relationship. They shared one thing, Oliver. Maybe they shared a friendship. And now he realized they shared distrust.

"I knew you would take him from me. The letter gives you the right."

"You're right, it does. And I will." He couldn't begin to explain how it felt to know what was taken from him, with no thought to his feelings or Oliver's. He was going to make it right.

"I know."

"You're the one who raised him." He watched as tears gathered in her eyes and she nodded. "Not Sammy?"

It was the story of the two women in Solomon's court. The one said to split the baby in half. The true mother was willing to spare her child and give him up.

No matter what, Oliver would be split. His anger with her lessened to a slow simmer. "We'll figure something out."

"Figure something out?"

"Some way to share custody. You could take that job Doc offered. It would be easier for him to split his time between us." He had other reasons for that suggestion. It would make it easier for Marcus to see her. If he kept her near, he would see her, hear her laugh, share Oliver's big adventures as he grew up.

"I can't. I have a job. I have an apartment."

"Okay. Well, we'll have to give this time and work on something that is good for Oliver."

"For what it's worth, I'm sorry."

He sighed. "Yeah, me too. And for what it's worth… I don't blame you. I just don't want to give up my son."

"I know."

Yeah, she knew. Because she considered Oliver her son, too. He might not lose his temper, but it would have felt good to hit something.

They pulled down the road to his place. With the windows down, he could hear the water roaring.

Slowing to a stop, he sat in his truck and stared at the old farmhouse that he'd planned to spend his life in. He had known it would need work. He'd planned on reinforcing the porch and putting in new windows. It was hard to take it all in, the collapsed porch roof, the broken windows. The tree that had fallen, crashing into the roof.

He got out and headed toward the back door. It took a hard shove to get it open. And then it took a full minute to get his bearings.

As he'd expected, the floodwaters had receded and

left behind mud and silt, leaves and small branches that had come through the broken windows. A yowling sound, faint but miserable, echoed from the rafters. He stepped back into the living room and listened, waiting to see where the sound came from. When he heard it again, he followed it to the spare bedroom. He peeked in the closet and saw golden eyes glowing from the shelf. The cat hissed.

"I'm thinking about helping you out of this situation if you calm down. But I'm not interested in getting clawed up."

He pulled off his jacket and reached for the loose skin on the back of the cat's neck. As soon as he had hold of the hissing feline, he wrapped it in his jacket. The cat fought a good fight but then settled in his arms.

"I'm not fond of cats."

"Yet here you are rescuing him." He spun to face Lissa. She stood in the doorway, humor shining from blue eyes that he thought he'd see in his dreams for the rest of his solitary life. If he ever allowed himself to dream of forever with someone, she'd look a lot like this woman.

Someday she'd be married to a doctor, maybe a business owner. They'd have some cute little kids. She'd have a good, stable life. The kind of life she probably dreamed about when she was a kid. The kind of life that would make her feel secure. And where would Oliver be? He noticed the cat had started to purr. Its wet fur had soaked his jacket and the T-shirt he wore. It didn't matter, because the only thing he could think of was what the future might hold for Oliver, and for him.

"You okay?" Lissa asked.

"Yeah, I'm fine. Not sure the same can be said for

this trespasser that I found in my spare bedroom. I'd say he got caught in the creek and somehow he managed to get inside the closet and on the shelf."

"Brave cat. What about you, though? This is a lot to take in." She glanced around, making her point. His house, his dream, appeared to be trashed.

He shrugged it off as if it didn't matter. They both knew it did. It had been about more than a house, a building; it had been a legacy and feelings he'd had for a family that had shown him love.

This home had made him feel safe. In a tumultuous childhood, it had been his haven. But now, as he looked around, it looked as if the dream ended here, with the flood and devastation.

"You have insurance? You can rebuild."

Right. She made it sound easy, but a person couldn't rebuild memories. As wrong as it might sound to others, he couldn't imagine another house on this land. A new home would be an empty shell without memories of the family that had meant so much to him.

"Yes, I can rebuild." He gave her the answer she wanted to hear.

"What are you going to do with that cat?" she asked as they stood there in the kitchen.

He opened the fridge and found lunch meat. He opened the package and put it on the counter. The cat scrambled out of his jacket and attacked the meat, alternately growling and purring.

"I guess I'm going to feed it. And then name it. Lately, it seems as if animals and people find me."

"Yes, you've had your share of surprises. I guess a cat doesn't seem like a big deal after having a boy dropped on your doorstep."

She reached to pet the cat. It hissed but kept eating, allowing her to stroke its still damp fur.

Marcus leaned against the counter. "I've had to do more self-examination in the last two weeks than I've done in my life. When you first showed up, being a dad was the furthest thing from my mind. I couldn't imagine letting a kid into my life. And now I can't imagine life without him." He glanced around the muddy kitchen and sighed. "But I also have a whole new set of concerns. What kind of life can I give him? I'm a single man without a real home."

Her hands touched his shoulders. He flinched when she traced a finger down the scar on his face. No one ever touched that scar.

"I didn't come here expecting you to be a person I would trust Oliver to. But I do. You're not the only one who has had to realize some cold, hard truths." She kissed his cheek. "You're good. And kind. Oliver needs you."

"But that would mean taking him from you."

"I know." And she backed away, hurt by his words.

"Like I said before, we'll figure something out," Marcus reassured her.

He headed up the stairs. Lissa followed. As they made the turn at the landing, the cat ran past them. He guessed the animal had decided to stay. He should probably name it. And buy some cat food.

Whatever thoughts he had on the cat, it didn't matter once they hit the upstairs bedroom.

"What in the world?" Lissa stepped inside the room, spinning to take it in.

"You did this?" she asked. But it was more of a statement.

"Yeah."

She touched a canvas with a painting of an abandoned church he'd seen while driving through the country. He'd had to tramp through a field of bluebonnets to take a picture. The old building had been surrounded by evergreens and barely visible from the road.

"Amazing."

"I enjoy it." It had been his therapy for years. "Some people journal their feelings. I used to sketch. And when I got a little money, I bought paints. The last few years of bull riding, as I was getting sober, the other guys would go to the bar."

"You'd stay in your room and paint."

"Bingo."

She reached for his hand. The gesture didn't make him feel trapped, but it did something to his heart he hadn't quite expected.

Lissa realized the moment she took hold of Marcus's hand that in the short time they'd known each other, she'd become comfortable with him. The small gestures such as holding his hand, kissing his cheek, seemed natural. It felt as if they had always been.

But she knew better than to let those feelings control her logical self. She'd learned that while working in the emergency room. The first time she'd had to treat an injured child and her emotions had almost clouded her judgment, she had realized that to be effective she had to put aside some of that emotion and keep her thinking clear.

The situation with Marcus was proving to be very

similar. It would be easy to be drawn to him, to feel
something for him. But clear thinking had to prevail.

As if reading her thoughts, he pulled his hand from
hers and started moving paintings. He had a half-fin-
ished sketch of a horse standing in a field. She watched
as he moved the canvas and others, stacking them neatly
against the wall.

"What are you going to do with them?" she asked.

"Box them up and move them to Alex's. I'm afraid of
the structure of this house. We probably shouldn't even
be in here. It makes sense to get things out while I can."

With that he grabbed several of his paintings and
headed down the stairs with them. She picked up a
couple more and followed. Voices carried, a child's
higher tones, someone older, responding. As they entered the kitchen, the back door flew open and Oliver
ran through, Alex behind him.

"Hey, we thought we'd come help." Alex pulled on
leather gloves as he looked around. "This place is a disaster."

"Thanks." Marcus headed for the door, but then he
paused, as if remembering something. He shifted the
paintings and glanced back at Oliver. "Want to help me
out, little man?"

With a quick nod, Oliver slid through the door and
held it open for Marcus. And then the two of them were
crossing the mud-soaked yard. Lissa watched from the
window. She had placed the paintings she carried on
the dining room table, leaving them for Marcus to retrieve. It was better this way, better if she gave Marcus
and Oliver time alone, time to bond.

She needed time and distance, too. To let her heart
get used to losing Oliver. Her gaze slid to the tall, hand-

some man walking next to the little boy. Her heart would miss him, too. That was an unexpected outcome of this trip and the two weeks she'd spent in Bluebonnet. The small town had grown on her. The man Sammy had labeled dysfunctional had grown on her, as well.

As a friend. Just a friend. She wouldn't let him be more. Not that he wanted more. Not with her. They were too similar and, at the same time, too different.

"This is a real mess," Alex grumbled as he walked around the house.

"He doesn't think he can repair it."

Alex stepped back into the kitchen, where she still stood watching Marcus and Oliver as they loaded up the truck. Oliver said something and Marcus gave him a serious look.

"I wasn't talking about the house. He can build a new one."

"He doesn't want a new one. This house means something to him."

"I know. He used to sneak off and come over here. But anyway, I was referring to the situation with Marcus and Oliver. And you."

"It isn't a mess. It's life. Life is always messy."

"Yeah, and complicated."

Right, *complicated*.

Marcus and Oliver seemed to have forgotten the artwork. They were heading toward the barn. She stood for a few minutes watching as the two of them talked and then disappeared through the open double doors.

"You can go on out there," Alex said as he picked up the paintings she'd left on the table. "I'm going to load some of this up for him and then I'm heading back to my place to feed livestock. Tell Marcus that later I'll be in town to help some of the church members start the cleanup process."

"I'll let him know."

Alex patted her on the back and then he left. The gesture had been awkward but comforting. She smiled at the thought. Alex was a good brother. Marcus had a big support system to get him through this.

She wasn't so sure about herself. She didn't know who she would be without Oliver. She also knew she couldn't fight Marcus. She didn't have the money. And it wouldn't be right. Marcus was his biological parent.

Sighing, she started across the wide expanse of yard. From the barn she heard laughter. Oliver said something she couldn't quite hear and then he laughed again. She entered the dimly lit interior of the barn and saw the two of them working with a lasso. Marcus guided Oliver's hand as the little boy held the rope. Together they brought it up, circled it a few times and then let loose. The rope flew through the air, landing on horns stuck in a bale of hay.

"You almost got it that time," Marcus assured his son.

Oliver looked up at him, his face hidden beneath Marcus's hat. "I'm going to be a cowboy."

"Are you now?" Marcus asked. "There's a lot of other things you can be. A doctor or lawyer, maybe a policeman, or even a teacher."

"Yeah, but you're a cowboy and I'm your son."

Marcus put a hand on Oliver's shoulder. "Yeah, you are."

They were working it out. Oliver's anger that they'd hid his parentage from him. Marcus's lack of trust in himself. She didn't know where that left her. Alone, she guessed. No, not alone. She would still see Oliver. She had her parents, friends, coworkers.

She had a job offer to come here. But if she did, would that make things difficult for Oliver and Marcus? Would it complicate their ability to bond? She didn't want to do that to them.

Marcus noticed her first. He nodded his head in greeting, and when he did, Oliver looked up and noticed her. A grin spread across his face and he held up the rope as if it were a prize he'd won.

"Look, Lissa. I can rope! It isn't easy, but I did a good job."

"I saw that. I'm really proud of you." She reached to pet Marcus's dog. The animal plopped to its belly, sighing as he rested his head on his front paws. "Alex went home to feed his animals and then he's going to town to help with cleanup."

Marcus nodded. "I'm going to get what I can out of this place, and tomorrow see what I can do in town."

"How will people rebuild or replace what they've lost if they don't have flood insurance?"

"They will get help from government agencies. Some probably do have insurance to cover the damage, or at least the contents of their homes. And a lot of folks will just dig in, recoup what they can and make do."

"Maybe we can find a way to help?"

Marcus had a wheelbarrow and he tossed a couple of bags of feed in it. "We? As in you and me, or do you have a pet in your pocket I don't know about?"

"I wouldn't mind helping out."

"It takes time to put together a fund-raiser."

Meaning she'd be gone. Maybe he was right. Why would she even consider volunteering herself for something that would take weeks to pull off? By the time they could get it arranged, she'd be in San Antonio and back at work. She didn't even know what it was she wanted to arrange. She just wanted to help the small town that had become a big part of her life in a short amount of time.

"It'll work out," Marcus said quietly. "And if you want to tell Essie your idea, I'm sure she'd dig in and get it done."

They walked out the back door of the barn, Marcus pushing the wheelbarrow. He had explained that he had to feed his cattle but didn't want to get his truck stuck. He'd considered using his ATV, but then he'd have to get it from the equipment shed.

Oliver had run ahead of them. He returned, grinning big.

"Knock knock."

Marcus groaned. "Another one?"

Oliver nodded, walking backward to face them. "Yep."

"Who's there?" Marcus asked.

"Partridge." Oliver giggled as he said it.

"Partridge who?"

"Partridge who ate a pear tree."

"Nope." Marcus shook his head.

"Really?" Lissa asked. "You're not going to laugh?"

"He's going to have to do better than that." Marcus answered, but she saw the twinkle of amusement in his dark eyes.

He was enjoying this game of Oliver making up jokes to crack his seriousness. She guessed Oliver probably enjoyed it, too. It was a way for the two of them to bond.

"You're getting the hang of this parenting thing."

She gave the compliment, meaning it. She knew what it meant for her, that he would soon take her place in Oliver's life. But he was the parent, not her, she reminded herself.

They continued on through the soggy grass, the wheelbarrow tire occasionally becoming bogged down in the mud. If anyone had seem them, they probably would have thought they were a family.

But they were the furthest thing from family. And when this was all over, she feared she would feel more alone than ever.

Chapter Twelve

A contractor finally got to Marcus's house at the end of the week. He walked around the outside of the building and then he tentatively stepped inside. Marcus followed. The cat ran past them. He needed to keep it out of the house if he could. Or she. The cat was definitely a she. A pregnant she.

"It's going to have to be torn down, Marcus. I'm sorry. I know that isn't what you wanted to hear. The house had issues before the flood. Now it's just hazardous. You need to keep out, and keep everyone else out."

Including that cat.

"You're sure? Even if money is no issue?"

Tad, the contractor, shook his head. "I'll build you anything you want on this land, but this house is done. Not just because of the flood. Main supports are rotted. Some are now broken. The flood took a big chunk out of your foundation. You can't repair this house."

Marcus walked away, glad he'd left Lissa and Oliver with Marissa. He needed time to think, to come to terms with the loss of this dream. He hadn't allowed himself many dreams in life, but this one had been a constant. All the years riding bulls, the money he'd invested in the stock market—it had all been with this one goal in mind. He'd wanted the Brown ranch. Hope Acres, they'd called it.

Truth was, he'd wanted more than the land. He could have bought land anywhere, but he'd wanted this place for one reason and one reason only—the *memories*.

Because of Oliver, that dream had grown into something more. He wanted his son to know a home where people were happy, where they trusted each other and where tempers didn't mean scars. He wanted to be the man who would provide that home, that stability. He'd never thought of this house in terms of children, but with a son, he needed all that this house represented.

He stood by the creek and listened as Tad got in his truck and left. After a few minutes he headed for his own truck. He didn't have a clear plan. When nothing made sense, he drove. This time he didn't head for Bluebonnet or for Alex's place. He wanted to be far away from people who would talk sense into him.

He didn't want to look at Lissa or Oliver and feel conviction.

He wanted a drink. As the thought crashed into his brain, unbidden, he stopped the truck. In the middle of the road he hit the brakes and sat there. No cars were coming. There wasn't anyone for miles around. He sat back, brushing a hand over his face as he contemplated what he'd almost done.

Two days ago he'd met with a lawyer, asking what it would take to get custody of a son when his name wasn't on the birth certificate. Today he was thinking about falling off the wagon. He was the last thing Oliver needed. A house, no matter what it meant to him, wouldn't fix this. A house wouldn't make him the person he wanted to be. For Oliver. He shifted into gear and accelerated on down the road.

At the first intersection he did a U-turn and headed back to town. In the opposite direction of temptation.

When he pulled into the parking lot of the church, he saw Pastor Matthews with a few other men surveying the roof of the church. It needed to be replaced. It could have waited another six months or so, but the rain had brought about some weak spots and exposed leaks.

Marcus got out and joined the group that had gathered. They stood on the front lawn, looking up at the steeple.

"Marcus, glad you showed up. We're trying to decide if the steeple can handle another ten years or if we should repair it, as well as the roof." Pastor Matthews winked, giving Marcus a clear clue as to how he felt about the steeple. He had wanted it repaired for a year or more, but the men of the church had stubbornly dug in their heels and said to wait.

Marcus ignored the meaningful look the pastor gave him. "It's leaning a bit. I know you all will do the right thing. And I'll do what I can to help."

"Now that you're a family man, it appears we'll have you paying more attention to these things." Dan Wilson, Marissa's grandfather, laughed as he made the comment.

Marcus didn't respond. He didn't have words.

Pastor Matthews shook a few hands and excused himself from the meeting. "Marcus and I need to talk about some other problems around town. Maybe we can think of a way to help the folks that were hardest hit."

The other men wandered off and Marcus followed his pastor around the side of the building. There hadn't been much wind during the storm, but enough to take off some shingles.

"What's going on?" Duncan Matthews asked as he stopped to survey one of the older windows that hadn't been replaced in the remodeling they'd done over the past few years.

"I can't do this."

"Can't help the community?" the pastor asked.

"I can't do this to Oliver. I don't want to hurt him."

Serious brown eyes studied him, waiting for him to spill it.

"I'm one step away from falling off the wagon. I don't have a home." That was Marcus's truth. It was his reality.

"Oh, I see. Did you fall off the wagon?"

"Not yet."

"But you're determined to try?" He said it without a smile.

"No, I'm not determined. But it could happen. And what would that do to him?" Marcus slid a hand through his hair. "I don't want to take Oliver from Lissa. She's raised him. He has a bond with her."

"I can understand that you're worried. Would it make you feel better if I said I wasn't? You aren't the same man you were a few years ago."

Marcus clenched his jaw. "I know I'm not. But how do I take that boy from the woman who has been a mother to him?"

"How about the two of you talk and work something out? Maybe share custody…"

"She lives in San Antonio and I live in Bluebonnet." And he couldn't imagine her being gone. That was a complication he hadn't planned on. He'd never planned on a woman changing all of his plans, all of his goals.

Pastor Matthews grinned. "I guess you could marry her."

Floored would not have been a strong enough word for what Marcus felt when Duncan made that suggestion. Marriage had to be the furthest thing from his mind. And the worst possible option.

"*Marry* her?"

Duncan shrugged. "Seems perfect to me. Two people who both love a child and who seem to have some type of feelings for each other."

"I don't love her." Marcus stuttered the words.

Again the pastor lifted a casual shoulder. "Of course not."

Of course he didn't love her. "She's a thorn in my side who happened to turn my world upside down."

"Tell me how you really feel, cowboy."

The words, softly spoken in that all too familiar voice. He cringed and turned.

Lissa stood at the corner of the building. Fortunately alone. He shoved his hat back and pulled it forward, trying to find the best way out of this mess. She didn't wait; she headed his way and the coward of a pastor hightailed it out of there.

Lissa, with those bright blue eyes and a smile that said *Gotcha*, stopped in front of him. "Oh, don't get all red in the face. Of course you don't want to marry me. Thorn in the side, though? That seems a little unfair."

He sighed. "Yeah, that was unfair. Maybe I was being too lenient."

"I'm the disaster of a woman who crashed into your life and made you face mistakes, and the future. And being the cowboy you are, you'd rather have gone on your merry way as a bachelor with no worries."

"I guess that about nails it. Where's Oliver?"

"At least you're honest about your feelings for me," she said, letting him off the hook. "Oliver is around front with Lucy. Why? Do you have more you need to say to me?"

"No, or maybe I do need to say more. You're not a thorn. Or a disaster. If I was a man who could marry..."

"If you weren't punishing yourself for being Jesse Palermo's offspring."

"Yes." He had to give her points for being blunt. "If I wasn't Jesse Palermo's son. If I wasn't an alcoholic. If I wasn't a sorry excuse for a human being, and if I could ever be good enough for someone like you... I would marry you."

"That was sweet. Not exactly a proposal, but sweet. And because I don't want a roller-coaster ride of a relationship, I'm very glad you're not asking."

They stood there facing each other, and he couldn't help feeling empty as they said those words to one another. Lissa bit down on her bottom lip and looked away, and he wondered if she felt it, too. As if the two of them, because of their pasts, would always be missing out on what other people took for granted.

Or maybe he was just extra negative today because of the house, Oliver and feeling the worst case of temptation he'd felt since he quit drinking. And it wasn't alcohol tempting him. It was her. His heart did a strange stutter at the realization.

"Lissa, I..."

"I know you hired a lawyer to take Oliver. I get it.

He's your son and you have the right. I'm begging you to not take him completely." Her eyes welled up with tears.

He reached out and brushed them away, and then his finger slid down her cheek to her chin. He tipped her face, wishing he could kiss her. Wishing he could do more than be the man who hurt her.

"I'm not taking Oliver. I met with the lawyer to see about custody. He needs to be with you. I've set up a trust fund and child support. We can work on visits."

"Marcus, he needs you."

"Yeah, I guess he probably does. A dad is important. Or so I've been told. We'll make sure he spends time here. But he needs more than I can give him. I'm a recovering alcoholic who doesn't have a home."

"Right. Of course." She stood on tiptoe and kissed his cheek.

Marcus tilted his head, capturing her mouth in a last, sweet kiss.

"I have a new joke." Oliver rounded the corner of the church and skidded to a halt.

Lissa pulled back from Marcus and what had felt like a goodbye kiss. She hated goodbyes. Most especially this one. She blinked, because she wasn't going to cry. She wasn't going to let him get to her.

But it might have been too late for that. Because he had become the unexpected. Not only was he not the person she'd thought he would be, but the way he touched her so profoundly had taken her by surprise.

In two weeks he'd become a person she trusted. And against all odds, she'd let him into her heart. No. He'd taken her heart captive.

"Were you two kissing?" Oliver said it as if it had to be the most disgusting thing ever. "Gross."

Marcus laughed. "Don't worry, Oliver, I'll wash my cheek real good and I probably won't get cooties."

"The girl is the one who gets cooties," Lissa countered, because it felt safer to have this conversation than to think about the future.

The joking and the friendship proved they could co-parent Oliver. They would work out visits. They would probably see each other often. On the inside she cringed, because seeing him often might be the hardest part of this entire plan.

"What's your joke?" Marcus asked, picking up his son and tweaking his nose.

Oliver's smile split his face, exposing the dimple that made him look so much like his father. "Knock knock."

"Who's there?" Marcus almost grinned as he asked.

Lissa watched the two of them. Marcus trying hard to be serious and Oliver making a funny face, probably hoping that would tip the scale in his favor.

"Banana."

"Banana who?"

"Banana…" Oliver grimaced. He bit down on his lip. "I think I forgot."

Marcus laughed, and Oliver did, too. "Kid, I think that's the best one yet. I think we should get Alex and go ride a pony."

"I made you laugh?" Oliver grabbed his hand.

"Yeah, you made me laugh." Marcus set Oliver back on his feet and took him by the hand. "Knock knock."

"Who's there?" Oliver moved in close to his side.

"Pony."

Oliver grinned big. "Pony who?"

"Pony who wants you to ride him."

Oliver fell over laughing. A belly laugh that was contagious. "That's not even a joke."

Marcus took off his hat and put it on his son's head. "Nope, but it made you laugh. And it was definitely better than 'banana, I can't think of the rest.'"

Lissa followed the two of them, picturing them as Oliver got older. And Marcus… He would get older, too. They would probably rodeo together. Marcus would teach his son to ride and to be a rancher. And someday Oliver would choose this life over the life she offered in the city.

It unsettled her, all of these changes. For as long as she could remember, she'd maintained an orderly life. She set goals. She worked hard to keep everything and everyone in a neat box. Friends. Family. Career.

Oliver. She'd kept him in a box, too. He was Sammy's son. But deep down, he'd become her child. She loved him the way any mom would love a child. She needed to tell him that.

Marcus was offering a way for her to continue that relationship, but it meant taking Oliver from Bluebonnet and from the family here. Everything had become infinitely more complicated.

"I'm heading back to Alex's," Marcus told her as they neared the front of the church. "How did the two of you get here?"

"Marissa. She's inside giving a hand with the evening meal. I wanted to see Doc. He asked if I could help him for a few days. And since I only have a few more days in Bluebonnet, I thought I'd make myself useful."

"Do you mind if Oliver and I head back to the ranch, then? I thought we'd have a riding lesson."

"You don't have to ask permission to take your son with you, Marcus."

"No, of course not." He placed a hand on Marcus's shoulder. "But I'm also not going to take off and not discuss plans with you."

They were co-parenting. Okay, she could handle that. Step one in the two of them raising Oliver together. And *not* together. With a pang, she watched Marcus and Oliver leave, and then she headed inside to find Doc.

She met up with Marissa in the hall.

"Lissa, you okay?" Marissa asked as she approached. "Did Marcus do something?"

She smiled at that. Yes, he'd done several some-things. And it had ended with a kiss so sweet it had felt as if her heart would never recover.

"Of course—" she hesitated "—not."

Marissa slipped an arm around Lissa's waist and the two walked together. "What did he do?"

"He talked to a lawyer about custody of Oliver. I know that makes sense. I just hadn't thought about it."

"He isn't all bad, you know."

"I know he isn't. But no matter what, this is going to hurt."

"I hope that it doesn't have to hurt. And I know Marcus well enough to know he'll try to do the best thing for all three of you. He's been building himself up as the bad twin for a long time. He's the rebel. He's the one who struggled in school. He fought anyone who dared to challenge him. He rode some of the meanest bulls in the country. All to prove that he is cold, angry, bad to the bone. But he isn't."

"No, he isn't. And that's made this whole process so much harder than I thought it would be. I thought I'd come here, Marcus would be the person I'd pictured."

"Angry, dysfunctional and a drunk?" Marissa asked.

"Yes, I guess. And instead…"

"He's angry, charming, sweet."

"Stop." Lissa held up a hand. "I just want him to be a dad to Oliver."

"Of course. So you'll be leaving at the end of the week?" Marissa stopped outside Doc's office. "I think Doc was hoping you'd change your mind and stay here."

"I can't stay." She said it with less conviction than in weeks past, because leaving now meant leaving something more than a job. She was abandoning a community and people she'd come to care about in the past two weeks. She would be leaving behind the friendships. And Marcus.

"We all wish you would," Marissa said. "Some of us more than others, I think. And that's something I never thought I'd believe about Marcus. I really thought he'd be an old man living on that farm, no wife, no kids, just his grouchy old self."

"I think that's still his plan. Except he'll have Oliver."

"Right, of course. He'll have Oliver."

Lissa reached to open the door to the clinic. "I'm going to help Doc."

"For what it's worth, I'm sorry. And I think you're the best thing to ever happen to my brother-in-law."

It didn't matter what either of them said. Marcus had made it pretty clear how he felt about her. She was the thorn in his side. And she understood how he might feel that way. She'd upended his world. She and Oliver had stayed and he'd been forced to take on the role of father.

And…he'd kissed her. She couldn't stop thinking about that kiss. He might have said no to her in his life, but that kiss said yes.

Chapter Thirteen

It was toward the end of the week and Marcus didn't like to think about time slipping away. Oliver and Lissa would be leaving in a matter of days. And he would miss them. He didn't want to admit that to himself, to his twin, to anyone.

"I'm going to donate my paintings." He said it as he drove toward town, Alex in the passenger seat. Oliver rode in the back, but he wasn't paying attention.

"The guy who never let anyone know he painted is going to donate them now? For...?" Alex fiddled with the window.

Marcus locked the windows because Alex had to be about ten years old when it came to pushing buttons. Literally and figuratively.

"I'm going to put them in the church auction for the flood fund."

"I would say that's a big step toward adulthood."

"Thanks, bro," he said. "That means a lot coming from you."

Alex glanced in the back seat before he spoke. "You're also an idiot."

Marcus shot him a surprised look.

Alex didn't laugh. He didn't crack a smile. "I mean it. You're messing up."

"I'm not having this conversation with you," Marcus ground out.

"Well, too bad. Because you're going to have it with me."

"Are you two fighting?" Oliver asked from the back.

"Yes."

"No." Both brothers answered. And then they glared at each other again.

"Is Maria getting married?" Oliver asked. "I told her I'd be her ring bearer."

"Married?" This time they answered in unison.

Marcus glanced back and then returned his attention to the road. "Why do you think that?"

"Because Jake came back yesterday. He was at Aunt Essie's talking to Maria." Oliver stopped talking.

"What?" the two brothers asked.

"I'm not supposed to tell."

Marcus stared into the rearview mirror. "So you're *not* going to tell us how you know they're getting married?"

Oliver shook his head.

Alex laughed a little. "Maria said that guy only planned to stay a few days, but then all of a sudden she wanted to introduce him to the family. It sure looks like he's settled in. Lucy said he's staying with them through the summer."

"He's too old for her," Marcus insisted.

"He's six years older than she is. That isn't too old. She's almost twenty."

They let the conversation go. Oliver wasn't talking.

Marcus drove them through Bluebonnet Springs and to the work area where men from the church planned to meet up for the day. Spring Street in Bluebonnet Springs, aptly named because it ran parallel to the spring, had suffered the most damage in the flood. Several homes had significant flood damage.

"Now, you're going to be good and stay with me. Right, Oliver?" Marcus asked as he got his son out of the booster seat. "Lissa gave us all the rules for being safe. Gloves. No stepping on boards that might have nails."

Oliver nodded and the two of them hurried to catch up to Alex. They had to step around debris as they made their way. Amazing that one little creek could do so much damage.

There were several men congregated at the front of a house that had been built a hundred years ago and had probably been through its share of floods. The siding of the house had never been updated, so it was still wood. The paint, in part due to age and in part due to the flooding, had been chipped away, leaving big sections of bare wood slats. Marcus walked up to the group of men who were surveying the property. Pastor Matthews, Alex, Lucy's husband, Dane Scott, and others. Jake, the boyfriend of Maria, was there, too. Marcus made sure to give him a glare that would remind him she had two brothers who ought to be asked before he went proposing marriage.

Oliver slid in next to him, his hand in Marcus's.

"What are we looking at?" he asked.

"A mess," Pastor Matthews responded. "But not one we can't handle. The floodwaters soaked the old plaster walls in the Moore house. The linoleum on the kitchen floor peeled up and the carpet in the bedrooms will have to be taken up. The biggest problem is the mold and the plaster walls. That about sums up every house on this block."

"My dad is going to auction off his paintings to help." Oliver yanked on Marcus's hand as he made the announcement. Obviously he had been listening to their conversation in the truck. "Aren't you, Dad? You paint all kinds of pictures."

Marcus choked a little. Oliver stared up at him, eyes all innocent and sweet. Marcus didn't know what emotion to process first. His son had just called him *dad* for the first time. *Dad.* The word meant a lot. It meant responsibility, never giving up on a kid, being there for him.

And he'd just had his paintings outed to a group of men he wouldn't have considered telling.

Dane gave him a curious look. Alex just laughed. Pastor Matthews appeared to be trying to hide a smile.

But all that mattered right now was that Oliver had called him dad. He wanted to shout it to the world. He wanted to call Lissa. That thought stopped him in his tracks. She'd become a habit. Maybe more of a temptation than his old habits. She was the first thing he thought of when something happened, good or bad.

"Maybe we should get some work done." Marcus glanced around the lawn of the house. Trash from the flood littered the yards and even the sidewalks. "I have big trash bags and extra pairs of gloves if anyone wants to help me start getting some of this cleaned up. I've got the trailer hooked to my truck so I can go from here to the Dumpsters set up at the school."

Oliver yanked on his hand again. "But, Dad, tell

them about your art. Especially that bull painting. It looks like crayons, but it isn't. Tell them about that one."

"We probably need to get some work done, son," he said. But he managed to smile because Oliver had about the happiest look on his face. "You have to be careful. There could be nails and sharp metal. Don't pick up anything unless you ask."

"I could pick up sticks," Oliver offered.

"Okay, you can pick up sticks. We'll make one pile for those." Marcus handed Oliver a pair of gloves. "I found these at the feed store. They're your size."

The gloves looked just like the ones Marcus wore. They looked like father and son, and now that Oliver had called him dad, it truly *felt* like it, as well.

They walked down the block, picking up trash as they went. There were boards, tree limbs, even parts of buildings scattered where the flood had deposited debris it brought downstream.

Alex joined them, bringing extra of the large, heavy-duty trash bags. "I thought you might like company."

"I'm pretty happy with the company I have." Marcus nodded in Oliver's direction. He stopped to look around. "Some of this we could pile up and burn."

"That's probably a good idea."

All of a sudden, Marcus paused. "Hey, Alex, do you hear that?"

"What am I listening for?"

Marcus put a finger up. "Listen."

Oliver ran to his side, dropping small branches as he went.

"I hear it, too. I hear it whining." The little boy, his arms holding the few sticks that hadn't been dropped, stopped and tilted his head to listen.

"I think it might be in the ditch," Alex offered.

The boy dropped the remaining sticks and raced for the ditch as fast as his little legs could pump.

Marcus hurried to catch up with him. "Oliver, be careful. We don't know what all is down there."

Water still stood, even after nearly a week. Marcus stepped carefully and pulled away some of the branches and trash that had built up near a culvert.

"A puppy?" Oliver asked. "Can I see?"

Marcus squatted to look in the culvert. Dark and filled with debris, it didn't look like anything that an animal could live in. His son got close to his side.

Alex leaned in behind them with the flashlight from his phone. "Let me help."

Bright eyes glowed from the narrow confines of the culvert. Marcus reached in, letting the puppy sniff his hand before he managed to get hold of the animal, hauling him out by the scruff of his neck. The puppy yelped and cried, but they got him out in the light, where they had a better look at him.

"Puppy, you are in poor shape," Marcus whispered to the tiny animal. "And no bigger than a minute."

"Looks like a Labrador, although it's hard to tell with all of that mud. And he's all skin and bones." Alex ran a hand down the puppy's back. "I think you should take him to Doc Parker."

"I'm sure Doc would appreciate a four-legged patient."

"Better manners than some of his two-legged patients." Alex stood back up, grinning down at him.

Marcus stared for a moment, as if he was looking at himself in the mirror. Except for one big difference. Alex had found something that had changed his life.

He'd found Marissa. He was happy, with himself, his life, his faith.

"You okay?" Alex asked.

Marcus stood, cradling the puppy against him. "Yeah, I'm fine."

He looked around, missing Oliver, who had been glued to his side. "Oliver?"

The little boy was on his hands and knees, crawling into the round drainpipe. Marcus shoved the puppy at Alex.

"Hey, get out of there!" He reached for him, but it was too late. Oliver screamed and jumped back.

His son raised a hand, gashed across his palm. Blood and debris mixed and ran down his arm. Marcus prayed it looked worse than it was. He picked up the boy and took the handkerchief Alex had ready for him.

"Hang on, buddy, let me take a look." Marcus dabbed at the cut with the handkerchief and sucked in a breath at what he saw. The cut was deep and bleeding profusely.

"I want Lissa," Oliver cried against his shoulder. "I want Lissa."

"We'll get Lissa." Marcus trudged up the hill and headed for his truck. "Alex, can you call Lissa and Doc Parker? Tell them I'm heading to Doc's clinic."

"Want me to ride with you?"

Marcus shook his head. "We're good. Can you unhook the trailer off my truck? I'll get Marcus into the seat. There's a towel in the back seat that will work better than this handkerchief."

Marcus gently settled Oliver in the seat and buckled the seat belt. The little boy was sobbing, tears dripping down a face that was dirty from working in the yard.

"I unhooked the trailer. Do you need anything else?" Alex appeared at Marcus's side. The other men were behind him. "I don't mind going with you."

"I'll head over, but I'll call you after Doc has a look."

It took less than five minutes to get to Doc's clinic.

"Here we are," he told Oliver. The little boy didn't look good. His face was pale and the tears had dried up. "Hey, you're okay, little man. I promise, you're fine."

"I don't like blood." Oliver shuddered.

"I don't blame you, but in a few minutes Doc will have you all cleaned up. I'm sorry, Oliver. I shouldn't have had you down there."

"I thought there might be another puppy. Like a brother."

He unbuckled his son and pulled him into his arms. As they headed for the door of the clinic, Lissa hurried out to meet them.

"Lissa is here," Marcus said as he reached for the door, trying to be careful not to jostle Oliver. He didn't know what to do when the little boy started to cry again. "Did I hurt you?"

Oliver shook his head. "I just want Lissa."

Of course. Marcus understood that. He wasn't much of a comforter. Lissa was. He could vouch for that. She took Oliver from him and held him close.

"What in the world did you do, wrestle with glass?" She whispered close to his ear she cuddled him against her.

"I had to save the puppy and see if it had a brother," he explained. He glanced over her shoulder and looked at Marcus. "Where's the puppy?"

"The puppy is in the truck. I'll get him in a minute. We want Lissa and Doc to check you out first."

Oliver sniffled and wiped his face with his good hand. "Maybe Doc could help him, too?"

As if on cue, Doc Parker appeared in the doorway. "What's all this ruckus? Oliver, are you having a bad day?"

Oliver nodded. "And we found a hurt puppy. Marcus needs to get him so you can fix him."

Doc laughed at that. "I'm not much of a veterinarian, but I can take a look after we've taken care of you. Let's get you to an exam room."

Marcus stepped back. Lissa handed Oliver over to Doc and remained in the waiting room, her blue eyes bright, focused on him.

"I'll get the puppy." He couldn't help that his voice was gruff with emotion. He'd never felt this helpless in his life. He'd never needed to be away from a place as much as he wanted out of that clinic.

"Marcus."

"He called me dad. I didn't know it would feel like this, to go from Marcus to dad." It had all become real in the last hour or so. The word *dad* had changed things in a way that Oliver showing up in his life hadn't.

"Don't you leave," Lissa said with meaning, as if she knew what he was thinking.

"I'm not leaving. I won't leave."

She disappeared through the door and he sat down, needing a minute to get his head on straight. On his watch, Oliver had gotten hurt. Marcus knew that kids got hurt. But he couldn't shake the image of Oliver, pale and hurting and wanting Lissa. Not him. *Lissa.*

Lissa found Marcus sitting on the tailgate of his truck holding something in a horse blanket. She sat down next to him and reached for the puppy. The animal squirmed in her lap but then turned to lick her hand.

"Is he okay?" Marcus asked as they sat there.

"Yes, he is. He needed ten stitches. It was deep and it needed to be cleaned out. Doc gave us antibiotics, just because of the floodwater and not knowing what all could have been in that muck he reached through.

"What about you? Are you okay?" she asked.

He gave her a sideways look. "I'm fine."

Right. Of course he was. Lissa didn't push. She knew he'd been shaken, but she suspected there was more to it than the gash on Oliver's hand.

"I'm glad you're okay, because he's asking for you. I don't want you going in there looking like you just poured a bowl of cereal and discovered there's no milk."

"I'm sure that isn't the look on my face." He rubbed his hands down his face, as if that would relieve the tension from his expression.

"Oh, it is the look. I promise it is. Doc said you can bring the puppy in and he'll take care of him."

"I think he's hungry more than anything. He's skin and bones."

She lifted the puppy and gave it a good look, and then she smiled. "It is a cute thing. Good thing you have plenty of room for animals. Oliver has already decided he wants to keep it. I told him you'd have to at least try to find the owners and, also, he'll have to make sure it's okay with you."

"With me? If Oliver is keeping the puppy, it's going home with him."

"We can't have pets. The puppy stays with you and the cat."

He hopped off the tailgate and walked away from

her. She let him go. When he turned, she saw all of the confusion, worry and pain written into his expression.

"When are you leaving?" he asked.

"Two days. But we'll be back. Remember, you want weekends and to share holidays, summer breaks. It's like an amicable divorce."

"Is there any such thing?"

Lissa shrugged. She had never thought about it before. Now that she did, she realized everyone got hurt. There was no party who walked away completely unscathed.

Marcus narrowed the distance he'd put between them. "When he got hurt, it wasn't me he wanted. It was you. You're the one who makes him feel safe. You make him feel secure. I'm just fun for the time being because I have an old dog and ponies. Dogs and ponies aren't going to sustain him forever. When he gets sick or hurt or even lonely, he's going to want you."

"I think you're trying to find a problem when there isn't one." She gave him a long, level look. "He's a typical little boy. He asked for the person who has been a mom to him. If you're worried about how you handled this, you did what any dad would do. You didn't panic and you got him to the doctor."

"Oh, I panicked," he admitted drily.

"He didn't know it."

"No, I guess he didn't." He stepped a little closer and she could see the anguish in his eyes.

"You are his dad. And he does need you."

"But he needs you more. He needs a mom." He nodded in the direction of the clinic. "We should go in. I don't want him to be alone, wondering where we are. He worries, you know."

"I know." She had stayed awake with him the nights he'd cried himself to sleep and the nights he'd awoken with bad dreams.

They walked back through the clinic, Marcus carrying the puppy, who whined pitifully from inside the blanket. From room two she could hear Oliver telling Doc Parker all about the way they'd heard that puppy crying and then rescued him from the pipe under the road. When they entered the room with the puppy, Oliver's eyes lit up. He was sitting on the bed, his injured hand bandaged and cradled in his other arm. She knew it hurt. But the puppy seemed to take his mind off the pain.

"Can you fix him, Doc?" Oliver asked as Doc Parker peeked inside the horse blanket.

"That's a fine-looking pup, Oliver. Looks like he might be a Labrador. Chocolate-colored, I'd say. But first we need to wash the mud off him and see how he looks."

"He was holding up one leg," Oliver offered. "But we got him out of that hole in the ground."

Doc took the puppy. "I'm taking him to my utility room to clean him up, and then we'll give him a real examination. But I think he's going to be just fine, Oliver. I think, more than anything, this guy needs something to eat."

"Me, too," Oliver said.

Doc left and Oliver lost his mojo. He curled up, holding his arm.

"Knock knock," Marcus said as he pulled up a stool and sat down next to the bed.

Oliver grinned. "Who's there?"

"Interrupting cow."

"Interrupting cow—"

"Moo," Marcus said before the boy could get out the word *who*.

"Hey!" Oliver said. "You didn't let me ask. Interrupting cow—"

"Moo," Marcus said again.

"What are you doing that for?" Oliver was still laughing.

"I'm an interrupting cow," Marcus told him.

They both laughed, and then Oliver leaned forward and threw his good arm around Marcus. "You're a funny dad."

Lissa's heart melted and she brushed away the tears that trickled down her cheeks. This was why she had come. She'd come here to give Oliver this gift. The gift of a father. If only Marcus could see that he was a dad. He was exactly the man Oliver needed. He might be a little broken, a little banged up emotionally, but deep down, he was good.

It felt as if her heart was colliding with her common sense as she watched him with his son. She'd come here knowing what she wanted for her life, and now what she wanted looked a lot like the man sitting with Oliver telling knock-knock jokes.

Doc returned with the puppy. He had a towel wrapped around the little dog, and sure enough, it did look like a chocolate-colored Labrador. He handed the animal over to Oliver, cautioning the little boy to hold tight but to watch his own injured paw.

"Is his leg hurt?"

"I think just a sore paw. Nothing appears to be broken. Now, I'm not a vet, so I would watch him over the next couple of days. Give him water and small amounts of food."

"I'm going to name him Buddy." Oliver leaned down and the puppy licked his cheek.

"I think that's a real good name. Now, don't forget to keep your hand clean and dry. Lissa will watch for infection." Doc looked from Lissa to Marcus. "Anything else?"

"I think we're set." Marcus picked up the puppy and handed it to Lissa. "You might want to make sure you can have pets."

"Marcus." Her warning came too late. He simply hadn't thought. She'd already told him she couldn't have pets.

"But Buddy can't live in an apartment." Oliver scooted to the edge of the bed. His dark eyes were bright with tears. "He's a country dog and he wants to stay here. He likes to run in fields and play fetch."

"Oliver." Marcus shook his head. "I don't know what to say."

"You're my dad." Oliver sobbed into Marcus's side. "I want to ride horses and learn to rope."

"You'll get to do those things," Marcus promised. "And I'll learn when to keep my mouth shut."

Doc Parker stood at the door watching them. "On-the-job training is how parents learn. You can buy books, attend seminars, but none of it is going to make sense without real-life experience."

Marcus picked up Oliver, holding him as Lissa stood back, the puppy wiggling in her arms.

The whole situation seemed more complicated than ever. Because they were all in over their heads and feeling things they hadn't expected to feel.

Chapter Fourteen

Marcus pulled up to the community church as the bell pealed across the countryside. He loved the sound of church bells. The good old country kind that a person could hear a mile away on a clear summer morning. As he got out of his truck, he spotted Essie. Lissa and Oliver had just arrived, as well.

Oliver saw him, said something to Lissa and then ran for Marcus. Little arms went around Marcus's waist, holding tight. Who would have thought in the matter of a few weeks that his son's hugs would change everything for him?

"Can I see Buddy today?" Oliver asked when Marcus picked his son up.

"I think that's an option, little man. Alex and Marissa invited us for lunch, and Buddy is there waiting to see you. How's your hand?"

Oliver held out his hand, palm up. Marcus had to give Doc credit, his seams could rival the ones sewn by the quilting circle.

"Lissa said you had to doze down your house. Does

that mean knock it down to the ground?" Oliver looked at him, eyes narrowed.

"I'm afraid so."

"Will you build a new one for us to live in?" Oliver asked, the question coming out of left field.

Marcus stopped walking toward the church to stare down into dark eyes that matched his. "I haven't really decided. I loved that old farmhouse. It meant a lot to me."

"If you build a new house, can Lissa live there, too?" Oliver asked. "Is it going to be a big house? With a dog door for Buddy and Lucky? And I'll have a bedroom they can sleep in. And Lissa can have her own room."

Marcus lowered Oliver so the two of them could walk side by side. He had to admit, he liked it when his son tried to match small steps to Marcus's larger steps.

"I'm sure it can have a dog door." He avoided answering the question about Lissa. He also wouldn't say yes to the dogs sleeping with Oliver, although he figured it would probably happen.

"I bet I could crawl through a dog door," Oliver continued, totally oblivious to the fact that Marcus was lost in thought. "Knock knock."

Marcus jerked his thoughts back to the present and his son. "Who's there?"

"Dog."

"Dog who?"

Oliver stopped walking. "Dog who got stuck in the doggy door."

"I think you're totally missing the point of knock-knock jokes," Marcus told him. "Hurry up, we'll be late for church."

Lissa and Essie had gone on ahead of them and were

now waiting on the church steps. Lissa looked… He paused because he had to decide how she looked. Like a painting, that was how he had to describe her as she stood on the steps of the church, the breeze lifting her hair around her face, her expression soft as she watched Oliver. The face of a mother.

The face of a woman that in any other lifetime he would have fallen in love with. He guessed a man couldn't have everything. He could dream. If it was that easy, he'd dream himself up as a man who could be the person she wanted in her life.

"Lissa, we're going to Alex's for lunch today." Oliver reached for her hand as they hurried up the stairs.

Marcus watched as she bent to talk to Oliver, straightening his collar and brushing a hand through his hair. When she looked up, her eyes were misty with unshed tears. He couldn't be the man she was looking for, but he could do one thing for her. He could make sure she felt secure with Oliver.

They sat with Marcus's family. It wasn't easy to focus on the sermon. Not with Oliver and Lissa next to him, knowing that he had to take care of things. Today. If they continued on the way they were, it would only get more difficult. He wouldn't want to let go. Funny that the sermon should be about letting go. Letting go of our dreams in exchange for God's plans. Letting go of insecurities for the peace that God gives. Letting go of fear, because we are more than conquerors through Christ who strengthens us.

But the sermon was also about allowing God to be in control. That was the part he had a hard time with. His entire childhood had been controlled by a man with a quick temper and a hard fist. He was old enough and had come far enough in his faith to understand that God gave free will. It was still difficult to let God take control of his life.

He didn't feel good about the fact that he'd never been so glad to have a sermon end. When he got up to head out, Essie followed.

"Ants in your pants?" she asked.

"Aunt in my business?" he whispered back.

She laughed. "That's a good one. And you bet I'm in your business. I didn't pay enough attention when you were young, so I have a lot of lost time to make up for."

"I'm fine. And you paid plenty of attention. When he allowed it."

"The sermon was about control. That bothers you, doesn't it?"

"Not at all." He stopped to look around for Oliver. His son was talking to Lucy and Dane's daughter Issy.

"That boy is something else. If you mess this up, Marcus, I'm not sure what I'll do with you."

"I'm not going to mess this up. I'm going to do the right thing for my son. He belongs with Lissa. He deserves the kind of life she can give him. And they deserve a secure, happy life."

"You're doing the easy thing for yourself," Essie snapped. "I have to go. I suddenly have a bad headache."

She hurried away and he would have guessed her head was just fine. He turned and Lissa was behind him. From her narrow-eyed expression, she'd overheard the conversation with his aunt.

"What is that all about?" she asked.

"No beating around the bush?" Marcus sighed. "I think you and my aunt are cut from the same cloth."

Her mouth quirked at the corner. "Thank you for the compliment."

"You're welcome."

"Should we talk now or later?" she asked.

"I think later." He searched the church and spotted Oliver at the doors with Issy. The two were talking, becoming cousins.

He hadn't thought about it, about the family Oliver had gained when he became part of the Palermos. They'd always been dysfunctional. Growing up, Marcus had been a pariah of sorts. He had gotten used to the fact that girls wanted to date him because they'd considered him a bad boy. Parents hadn't wanted their daughters to be seen with him.

He searched for his sisters and saw them talking with people from church. Alex and Marissa had taught children's church today. When had this happened? When had they all become so functional and respected? They were a family. A good family.

"Are you okay?" Lissa asked.

"I'm good, just had a moment." Nothing had changed in that moment. It had just been a realization of sorts. "I think it would be easier if you go sooner rather than later."

"You want us to leave?"

"Isn't that your plan? To leave today?"

She looked confused. "Yes, of course. We can leave right after lunch. But I'm not telling Oliver. That's on you."

"Don't worry, I'll tell him. And it's June. We can spend more time together this summer. Before school starts in August."

"Of course you can."

He had avoided relationships for most of his life, but he knew an angry woman when he saw one. He decided escape was his best bet. "I'll meet you at the ranch."

He watched as she went to gather up Oliver. She bent to tell him they were leaving. He heard her tell him they would see Issy at Alex and Marissa's. Marcus joined them, thinking he might be able to make it easier.

"We have to leave now?" Oliver complained as they crossed the lawn to the parking lot. He was glancing back, looking for all of his new friends.

"You want to see Buddy, don't you?" Marcus asked.

Oliver nodded, but he didn't look too thrilled, or convinced. "Issy said she'd show me her pony again."

Marcus helped Oliver into the rental car. "I bet she will. How's that hand?"

Oliver looked at his hand. "It's still good. I bumped it and thought it would bleed again. But it didn't. Does that mean I can ride a horse?"

"I'm not sure. It might. I'll meet you at Alex's." He closed the door and Lissa was still standing there, her expression thoughtful. "What?"

She shrugged. "I think you want us to leave because you don't want to say goodbye. You love him."

"He's my son."

Her gaze softened. "Oh, Marcus, you're such an idiot."

"Yeah, I guess I am." He kissed her cheek. "Meet you at the ranch."

He walked away, wishing he didn't have to. He wished he could be the hero who saved the day. Just once. He didn't want to be the man who always felt as if he'd failed the people in his life. He wanted to be the dad a son could count on. Lissa made him want to be the man a woman could count on.

The ride to the ranch took fifteen minutes. It felt more like an hour. As he pulled up to the ranch, he saw Lissa getting out of the car, then glancing into the back seat. The wind lifted her hair and swirled her floral skirt around her legs.

He headed her way to see if she needed help.

She was the one thing he knew he wouldn't get past. He'd dealt with his childhood, the loss of his voice, his parents. But her... He shook his head as he got out of his truck. He wouldn't get over her.

Marcus walked up behind her and peered over her shoulder.

"He needs a nap. He hasn't been sleeping well," Lissa said, indicating the sleeping child in the back seat.

Marcus nodded, understanding. He hadn't been sleeping so well himself. "I'll carry him inside."

He scooped his son up from the booster in the back seat of the car. Lissa hurried ahead of him to open the front door so that he could carry Oliver inside. Maria had gotten to the house early and she brought a blanket to cover her nephew.

"Where's Jake?" Marcus asked quietly.

"On his way back from visiting his parents. Marcus, give him a chance. He wants to talk to you all."

"I am giving him a chance. I just don't want you to be hurt."

She kissed his cheek. "I won't be hurt. I love him and he loves me. This is the right plan for my life. I know where I'm going and what God wants. And Jake is part of the plan. We aren't rushing into anything, but we know what we want."

"Good." He gave her a quick hug. "But tell him he owes us a conversation, Alex and me."

"Of course he does." She glanced down at her sleeping nephew and her lips pulled up. "He's not just an eavesdropper. He is a blabbermouth."

"He is." He felt a tug on his heart.

Maria looked up, studying Marcus's face. "Don't mess this up."

"My family has a lot of faith in me."

"I have faith in you. You don't have faith in yourself. And sometimes I wonder if you've ever given anything to God," she said with far more wisdom than he expected from his little sister.

"I try, Maria. I do try."

He left his little sister to care for his son, and he went in search of Lissa. He found her on the front porch. She smiled when he walked out the door, and she patted the seat next to her. He couldn't sit next to her. If he did, he'd never want to let her go.

Marcus realized the flaw in his plan. He wanted to make things right for her, but he also didn't want to lose either of them. They were going back to their lives in San Antonio. He would resume his life here in Bluebonnet Springs. He and Lissa would see each other on occasion, and Oliver would spend time here. But it wouldn't be the same.

Never in a million years would he have imagined this goodbye being one of the hardest in his life. It had been easy three weeks ago. Now he wasn't sure what it felt like to have a broken heart. He doubted he had ever experienced one. But what he felt at that moment, telling her goodbye…it was pretty close.

Lissa had known coming to Bluebonnet Springs that this would never end well. In the past few weeks she'd suspected it would end worse than she'd expected because she hadn't expected to feel anything other than resentment for Marcus Palermo. That had changed as she'd gotten to know him. She took a breath at the inadequacy of that word. She'd fallen in love with him.

She watched as he paced the porch and then faced her, an anguished look on his face. She wondered if she wore the same expression because she knew that was what she felt.

"You might as well tell me what it is you want to say. If you've changed your mind and you want him here with you, I understand. He is your son. Just tell me because I want time to lick my wounds before I have to leave." She couldn't look at him. She couldn't accept the hand he offered.

"Don't be ridiculous, I'm not taking him from you."

At those carefully spoken words in his gruff whisper of a voice, she looked up. "Okay, then what is it?"

"I talked to a lawyer about giving you legal custody. But I want more than that for him. I want you to be his mom."

Her heart stopped. "You what?"

Red flooded his cheeks. "No. Not like that. I want you to adopt him. I want him to know that no one can take him from you."

"You want me to adopt him?" She shook her head, not getting it. "You're his dad."

"And that won't change. But you need to have the title of mother. You are his mother."

She pinched the bridge of her nose and fought the sting in her eyes. "I don't know what to say."

"Say you will allow me to do this."

He was giving her Oliver. In a way that made him legally hers. *Theirs.* They would share Oliver. He wasn't proposing love or marriage. Silly her, his words had tripped her up. He was proposing a partnership.

"I thought you would want this," he said softly. His gaze, dark and melting, connected with hers. "This is something I can give you. You will legally be his mother. You will call the shots. If there comes a time when you think I'm not the best thing for him…"

"You're such a silly man." She leaned in and kissed his cheek, fighting the urge to tell him what she really thought, and felt. "Thank you for doing what you think is right. But I don't think a day will come when you aren't fit to be his father. You just proved that you're a dad, that you care about him, that you're willing to sacrifice to make him happy. I hate leaving, because he will miss you." She drew in a breath and allowed herself to admit the truth. "I'll miss you."

She got up and walked inside.

Maria was waiting for her inside. Oliver was sleeping and Marcus's little sister had obviously guessed what her brother had been up to.

"Is he playing the martyr?" Maria asked. "He always has, you know. He pretends he doesn't care. I think he cares too much."

"That might be it. And he doesn't trust himself," Lissa told the younger woman. "I don't know how to convince him…"

She stopped herself from saying the words. If she couldn't say them to herself, she wouldn't say them to someone else.

Maria's expression turned all ornery little sister. "Maybe you should tell him."

"I don't think so." Because she'd overheard his opinion of her. He might think she was a great mom for his son, but to him she was a thorn in his side.

She brushed hair back from Oliver's face and he blinked, waking up to smile at her. "Hey, almost time for lunch."

"Is it chicken?" he asked.

"I think it is." She smiled at the question because he asked it several times a day. He loved chicken.

He sat up, yawned and stretched. And then he looked at her, reaching to trace a finger down her cheek. His eyes narrowed and he looked at the other cheek.

"Why are you crying?"

"Because we leave today. Remember? And I think we will both be sad when we leave."

Oliver nodded and then he hugged her. "But we can always come back. Aunt Essie said so."

"Right, we can always come back." She reached for his hand. When she turned around, Marcus was there. He didn't look as if he would cry, but he also didn't look like a man ready to say goodbye.

Chapter Fifteen

The dozer moved over the cleared land. All traces of the home he'd bought were gone. Nothing but bare dirt. Marcus couldn't help thinking of those days as a kid when he'd hightailed it to this house, to the front porch with its old rocking chairs.

The memories had kept him solid through a lifetime of ups and downs. The memories weren't gone. It had taken him a while to realize that he still had pieces of the Brown family. They were *his* memories, the life lessons they'd taught him. The faith they'd encouraged him to find. He could train just about any horse he got hold of—because of the Browns.

One of those horses happened to be under him at the moment. A solid red chestnut. She had a splash of white on her nose. That was it. She would make a good little horse for Oliver. That was why he'd bought her.

He hadn't seen his son in three weeks. Not since a pretty June day when Lissa had brought him down to go fishing. She'd kept her distance, acting as if they didn't even know each other. It had unsettled him. And then she'd told him they were going on vacation with her

foster parents. She hoped he wouldn't mind. A week
in Florida and then she'd be back to work. So it might
be a while before he saw Oliver again. She had smiled
and told him she would leave him the whole month of
July, if Marcus wanted.

It had felt all wrong, that visit had. Oliver hadn't
talked much. Lissa had been distant. Marcus had felt
as if he had royally messed up. He had felt that way a
time or two in his life. When he overrode a bull and got
tossed. When he had pushed too hard against his dad.

But this time it cut him to the core unlike ever before.

Alex pulled up, getting out of his truck with that silly
grin he wore most of the time these days, now that everyone knew Marissa and Alex would have a baby in
the fall. And Lucy, a month or two later.

Maria was planning her wedding to the pretty boy
from Fort Worth.

Essie seemed to be dating Marissa's grandpa Dan.

The whole world was going crazy.

"What has you looking like you ate lemons for breakfast?" Alex asked as he approached the arena.

"Nothing. What do you think of Pepper?"

"You named the horse Pepper?" Alex teased.

"Red Pepper."

Eyebrows shot up. "Gotcha. She's pretty small for
a big boy like you. You might try riding a grown-up
horse."

"Go. Away." He turned Pepper in a tight circle and
then took her around the arena again.

"You've convinced me. You've definitely moved up
to pony class," Alex called out. "So, are you going to
build a house or just sleep in our spare bedroom for the
rest of your life?"

"I guess if you want me out, I can move in with Essie."

Alex put a booted foot on the rail of the arena. "I don't think Essie wants you, either. And before you ask, Lucy doesn't have room."

"Why don't you all just take me down a dirt road and leave me. Maybe someone will take me in."

"I doubt it. You're mangy and bad-tempered. Rebuild your house, Marcus. You need a place for your son to visit. And maybe someday, when you're thinking straight, you'll start dating. I hear Oliver's mom is a decent catch."

"Go away. I'm giving you thirty seconds to get back in your truck and go."

Alex laughed. "Right. I'm scared." He rested his arms on the top rail of the fence. "You know that twin thing people are always talking about? You know, feeling each other's pain. Knowing when the other one is in trouble."

"It's a load of horse—"

"Horse tack. Yeah. I knew you'd get all angry." Alex pushed his hat back and Marcus, for the first time in a long time, got the feeling he was looking in a mirror. "Marcus, you're unhappy. You're like a horse with a burr under the saddle. You've convinced yourself you can't have what you most want and it's eating at you. It all comes down to trust. Trust God. Trust yourself. Trust a woman to know her own mind."

"Your thirty seconds are up."

At that, Alex settled his hat back on his hat and headed for his truck. "See you at dinner. Tell Oliver and Lissa hello for me."

Oliver and Lissa? Marcus shook his head and guided

the horse on another circuit around the arena. The little mare had an easy gait. She knew her leads. She didn't fuss. He knew she'd make a good first horse.

And then she took him by surprise, rearing up a little and then bucking like a maniac. Burr under the saddle. No. Alex wouldn't do that to him. He held on, wrapping his legs around her middle and holding back on the reins so she couldn't get her head down to pitch him.

When she finally settled, she was shaking. He slid from the saddle and gave her a careful look. She gave herself a good shake and then her head went down as if asking for forgiveness.

"Hey, cowboy, that was quite a ride."

He paused and then faced the woman and little boy standing outside his arena. This time, unlike that time almost two months ago, they were both smiling at him. And he knew two things. One, that the little boy with dark hair was his son. Two, the woman with the brilliant blue eyes had upset his apple cart. He actually knew three things. He had missed them the way he would miss a breath if it was taken from him.

He led the horse to the fence.

"You didn't get thrown." Oliver made the statement sound as if it was the biggest surprise of his life.

"No, I didn't. I didn't expect the two of you."

"We surprised you." Oliver grinned as he said it.

"You sure did. Hey, do you want to brush Pepper? She's pretty good. Usually. And she's yours."

"My own horse?" Oliver didn't wait. He climbed over the fence and landed with a thump next to Marcus. "Can I lead her?"

"You can." Marcus handed the reins to his son, but he stayed close beside them. "Lissa can come, too."

"I don't climb fences," she called out to them.

As they approached the side door to the barn, Oliver looked up. "I call her mom now. Is that okay?"

"What else would you call her?" Marcus took the reins from his son, scooped the boy up and put him in the saddle. "What do you think of that?"

"I like her a lot. And I'm glad I can call her mom." Oliver was quiet for a minute. "I have a mom and I have a dad. You just don't live in the same place. But you both love me."

It sounded like something he'd seen on a children's television program. Marcus wasn't sure he liked that any more than he liked not seeing them more than once a month. But he had made the right decision. He knew that. He'd given Oliver a mother. He'd given Lissa her son.

He'd given them open doors and opportunity.

He tied Pepper and helped Oliver down. Without waiting for instructions, Oliver found the brush and went to work.

"I think my mom wants to talk to you," Oliver said over his shoulder as he stroked the brush down the mare's neck.

Ginger lipped at Oliver's sleeve, but she minded her manners the way Marcus had known she would.

"Does she really?"

Oliver nodded. "I think you're in trouble. I heard her talking to Grandma Jane about your thick head. I didn't think your head looked thick. But if it is, maybe Doc Parker can help. I think my mom is going to work for him."

Maybe there was something to having a boy who made eavesdropping a serious skill. "Is she really?"

Oliver nodded, but he kept brushing. Marcus stood there for a minute watching his son. After he'd assured himself that Oliver was fine, and with a few final instructions, he headed for the door. Lissa stood there watching them, her hand on Lucky's big head as the dog panted and pushed against her. Buddy, the Labrador they'd rescued after the flood, was still at Alex's. Lucky didn't appreciate being moved and preferred his home with his barn.

"I guess you've taken up eavesdropping, too?" Marcus asked her as he closed the distance between them.

"When necessary. But he didn't tell you anything I didn't know, since it is my plan." Lissa reached for his hand. "What he doesn't know is that I came here to talk to you."

"Did you now?"

He leaned a bit closer, inhaling, because she smelled good. She smelled like sunshine and wildflowers. No wonder Lucky had glued himself to her side and wouldn't budge.

"Don't." She pushed him back.

"Don't what?"

"Don't sniff at me like that hound dog. It's weird. And I need space. Because when I'm done talking, you will either tell me to stay or tell me to go."

"I see." He lost the walking-on-sunshine feeling of a few moments ago. With Lissa looking all serious and giving him ultimatums, maybe he'd just turn tail and head back to the barn and Oliver.

"No, you don't see."

"Okay, I don't see." He studied her face. Brilliant blue eyes, pretty mouth in a firm line. He knew when to tread lightly. "This is one of those conversations where no matter what I say, I'm in trouble. Right?"

"Not exactly. If you choose wisely, you won't be in trouble."

"Are you taking a job with Doc Parker?"

She poked his shoulder. "Getting ahead of the program, Palermo."

"Hmm, okay."

"I came here to tell you some very hard truths about yourself."

He laughed at that. "And you think you're the first one to ever do that. Lissa, women have been telling me those same things for years. It won't faze me."

"You're wrong." She shook her head. "No, they're wrong. And these are not those same truths."

He started to open his mouth to argue, but something about that spark in her eyes warned him to keep quiet. Rather than talking, he put his hands up in surrender.

"First of all, you are trustworthy. Everyone who knows you has a story to tell about you and how you were there for them or helped them out in a time of need. There are people all over Bluebonnet Springs, and I'm guessing all over Texas, who will rat you out. Second, you need to learn to trust yourself. So what if you were tempted to drink. You didn't. That matters. You are a man your son can count on. You're the man he can model his life after. You're a man of faith and a man of integrity."

"Why do you think I need to hear this?" He was truly curious. And he wanted to keep her there next to him for a little longer.

"Because you doubt yourself. You did everything you could to push us out of your life because you think you are not the man we need. You believe you're not the father your son needs."

He quirked a brow. "Can we go back to the 'we' part?"

"Marcus, you told Pastor Matthews no way would you marry me, that I'm a thorn in your side."

"I didn't realize I had asked you to marry me." Now he was confused. "Or that you'd asked me."

"You're impossible. And I'm not going anywhere, you impossible man. I'm staying here. I'm going to work for Doc Parker because your son has been sad every single day that he hasn't been here. He misses you. He misses your family. He misses his dogs and that pregnant cat."

"She has kittens now."

"Stop trying to distract me."

He held his hands up again. "No way would I do that. So you're staying in Bluebonnet Springs."

"Yes, because your son needs to be here, near you. He needs to see you every day."

He nodded and he very nearly went down on one knee. He was trying to decide his next move when she reached for his hand. She didn't look at him; instead, she focused on interlocking their fingers together. Hopeful. He was starting to feel it again. It was a lightness in his soul.

Who knew?

"I'm not leaving," she said again.

This time he did go down on one knee.

Lissa looked at the man kneeling in front of her. She didn't know what to say or what to do.

"Get up." She pulled on the hand that she still held. She tried to pull free. He wouldn't budge.

He grinned up at her, his dark eyes shining, his smile lopsided and sweet.

"What are you doing?" she whispered.

"Finding out just how serious you are about staying in Bluebonnet Springs."

"I'm very serious."

"I'm glad to hear that, because I've decided not to let you go. I'm scarred up, a recovering alcoholic, sometimes angry, always unpredictable—"

"Obviously," she interrupted.

He put a finger to his lip. "Shh, my turn. I want to be the man that you can trust. I want to be the father my son can look up to. Lissa, you are more than a thorn in my side. You're the woman I want by my side. Forever." He cleared his throat and his words came out raspier than normal. "When I saw you standing there at the fence, everything felt right for the first time in weeks. You were here. And I think you're supposed to be here. I think if there is something we can trust, it is God, and we can trust that He didn't make a mistake when He sent you on this journey to find me."

"Stand up," she whispered, this time because she couldn't stop the flow of tears. "Please stand up."

He came to his feet and he moved close. Slowly, ever so slowly, he leaned down and his lips touched hers. She clung to his shoulders, thankful for his strength, thankful for his presence. Thankful that she had taken a chance and trusted.

He continued to kiss her, backing her against the side of the barn and holding her close as if he treasured her. That was what he made her feel—treasured. He had no idea that he was the man who could be that person for a woman. But she'd unearthed the truth about Marcus

Palermo. She had found her way to his heart and he'd stolen hers.

"I love you, Lissa Hart. You are my heart. I'm never going to let you go. And I'm going to build you a house on this land. We're going to fill it with kids and we're going to make memories. We're going to teach our children to laugh, to love and to have faith."

"That's a lot of planning you're doing, Marcus."

"Too soon?"

"I'm the one calling the shots here, remember?" she whispered against his shoulder. "I came here to tell you how the cow ate the cabbage."

"Did you really?"

"Yes, and you took over. The way you always take over."

He kissed her again and then he moved away from her. "Okay, what else did you want to say?"

She pointed and his eyes widened when he saw that they had an audience. The eavesdropper in chief stood in the doorway of the barn.

"Oliver?" Marcus smiled at his son.

"Knock knock."

Marcus groaned. "I hope this is a good one."

Oliver nodded. "It is."

"Okay," Marcus said. "Who's there?"

"Mary."

Marcus laughed and Oliver grinned. Lissa watched, loving them both so much she couldn't stand it. She had missed Marcus. She'd missed his quietness. She'd missed his dry sense of humor. She'd missed him.

"Mary who?" Marcus asked, his gaze sliding her way, and she just smiled because they both knew how this one would go.

"Mary my mom and then we'll be a family." Oliver laughed and jumped, forcing Marcus to catch him or be knocked down. He caught his son and held him tight. With his free arm he pulled Lissa close and she tumbled against him.

"Oliver, I think the answer is yes," Marcus answered as he held them both close. For the first time in weeks, everything felt right. It felt as if Lissa and Oliver were exactly where they belonged.

Oliver leaned in close. "She told Grandma Jane she loves you."

Marcus whispered to his son. "I love her, too. And I'm glad the two of you decided to come back here and force me to admit it."

"Sometimes it's hard to admit the truth," Oliver said in a singsong voice.

"You're right, sometimes we just need help." Marcus spoke in his soft, gruff voice as he took Lissa by the hand.

The three of them walked back up the hill. And she thought they did look very much like a family. A father, a son and a woman who loved them both to distraction.

Epilogue

On a warm day in March, Lissa stood on the hill looking down at the house Marcus had built for them. It was a replica of the old farmhouse but larger and with the wraparound porch she'd suggested. It was also a little farther from the creek than the original. Today it would become her home. And eventually there might be more children, because Oliver said he needed a brother and a sister. He actually thought a couple of brothers and one sister, because girls can be trouble.

"Are you ready?" Marissa asked as she placed the veil on Lissa's head.

She and Marcus had decided to get married there, on the ranch, because it felt right. They were starting their lives where so many memories had been made. They'd built a steeple-shaped arch by the creek and wildflowers grew profusely in the field. It was the most perfect spot they could think of to become husband and wife.

Maria kissed her cheek. "You're a beautiful bride."

Lissa took the spray of bluebonnet flowers from her soon-to-be sister-in-law. In six months they would celebrate Maria's wedding. She wanted a fall wedding.

And by then, Marissa and Alex's little girl, Bella, would be walking and she'd be able to toss flowers down the aisle. Today the little girl was content on her great-aunt Essie's lap, with her great-grandfather Dan sitting next to them, giving her his finger to grab hold of.

Lucy led Issy, who would be their flower girl. Jewel would help. Which meant she would throw flowers at the people gathered to celebrate. She seemed to love throwing flower petals. Lissa didn't mind at all. She had told Lucy to relax and let the girls do what they wanted.

Today was her wedding. She didn't care if the flowers got tossed or if the music went flat. She didn't care if the cake fell. Of course, like every bride she wanted a beautiful wedding. She was even happy to see her birth mother, although her foster father would walk her down the aisle and her foster mom had helped pick her dress. They had been the constants in her life. They'd been the first to teach her about unconditional love.

Through their love for each other, Tom and Jane Simms had taught her the truth about marriage. They'd taught her that real love wasn't perfect—it took work, sacrifice and communication. Real love included understanding and forgiveness. Tom and Jane were celebrating their fortieth anniversary. They knew a little bit about love and making marriage work.

If the wedding ceremony itself wasn't perfect, it wouldn't matter. What truly counted was that she had the people around her who mattered most. She knew that God had blessed her beyond measure.

And as the song "Never Alone" began to play, she knew she would never be alone.

She smiled at Tom, her stepfather, and together they stood and watched the flower girls, bridesmaids and groomsmen, including Oliver, make their way down the small rise to the creek. She dabbed at her eyes and drew in a breath. Tom patted her hand on his arm.

"This is good," he told her. "You're going to be fine. Remember, God is in it. Keep Him at the center of this marriage and you'll be fine."

She nodded. "Yes, we will be."

"Time to become Mrs. Marcus Palermo." He sounded choked up and she noticed tears in his eyes. She leaned against his arm and whispered her thanks to him for being her father.

He led her down the path to Marcus, told Marcus to take care of their girl, and then he took his seat next to Jane. They both nodded and smiled, giving her their blessing.

But it was the man next to her who mattered most. He was her future. He was her other half.

"I love you," he whispered.

"I love you back."

Pastor Matthews cleared his throat. "My turn to talk."

He started the ceremony and the rest was a blur. The only thing that mattered was that God had brought them together. God had made them a family.

And the rest of their lives was ahead of them.

* * * * *

REUNITED WITH THE BULL RIDER

Jill Kemerer

To my sister, Sarah. You'll always be my hero! And to my brother-in-law, Rich, and my nieces, Eva, Cecilia and Calista. You make life fun!

Also I heard the voice of the Lord, saying,
Whom shall I send, and who will go for us?
Then said I, Here am I; send me.
—*Isaiah* 6:8

Chapter One

Tonight was no ordinary night, not for Amy Deerson, at least. She was about to meet the little girl she'd been asked to mentor. When the pastor called yesterday, she'd jumped at the opportunity to spend a few afternoons each week with a neglected child. At four years old, the girl was too young for the church-sponsored mentor program, and the pastor had suggested a private arrangement due to the circumstances. But first, Amy needed to meet the girl's father. He had the ultimate say in whether she spent time with his daughter or not.

Taking a deep breath, Amy got out of the car and approached the church's entrance. It was still chilly for late March in Sweet Dreams, Wyoming, but it wouldn't be long before wildflowers bloomed. Just thinking about flowers, crafts, tea parties and other things small girls enjoyed put a bounce in her step. *Don't get ahead of yourself.* This was the initial meeting. Until the dad agreed, it was not a done deal.

She'd prayed for so long to make a difference in a kid's life, and God had answered.

Amy headed down the staircase to the meeting

rooms. The low hum of male voices quickened her pace. What would the girl look like? Would they hit it off right away? And would the dad be cute?

Cute? Really, Amy? Who cared what the father looked like? A romance would be inappropriate given the situation. And, anyway, she'd been scorched at love twice. She would *not* put her heart on the line again.

The hallway walls were filled with pictures of kids doing crafts at previous vacation Bible schools. Excitement spurred her forward. Life was falling into place. Business was booming at her quilt shop, she'd finally gotten up the nerve to submit a portfolio of her fabric designs to several manufacturers and now this! She'd never intended to remain single, but that's how life had worked out. Helping this little girl would ease the longing in her heart for a child of her own.

She peeked into the preschool room. Hannah Moore, the pastor's wife, was standing next to their toddler son, Daniel, and a young girl.

It's her!

Dark blond hair cascaded over the girl's shoulders. She looked woefully thin under a purple sweater and striped leggings. Amy couldn't see her face, but she stood stiffly near Daniel, who was pushing a toy dump truck on the colorful ABC area rug. As much as Amy longed to join them, she continued toward the door at the end of the hall where Pastor Moore was waiting with the father.

Entering the conference room, she greeted the pastor then turned her attention to the man sitting at the end of the table. Her stomach plunged to her toes, the sensation worse than the roller coaster incident in eighth grade.

No! This can't be... He can't be...

Her knees wobbled to the brink of collapse. Unable to hear a word the pastor was saying, she shook her head, her gaze locked on familiar blue-green eyes. Every instinct screamed for her to run, to get out of there, to make sense of the fact Nash Bolton was in the room.

Nash. The man she'd loved completely. The one she'd thought she'd marry. The guy who had left town over a decade ago—no goodbye, no explanation. The jerk who had never come back.

It hit her then… The little girl she'd been asked to unofficially mentor?

His daughter.

She was having a nightmare. She'd wake up and be in her bed under her favorite quilt—

"Thank you for meeting us tonight," Pastor Moore said.

It wasn't a nightmare. And yet it was.

She blinked a few times and sat in the nearest chair, forcing herself to focus on the pastor's face. In his early thirties, he had a kind air about him.

"Sure." She hoped her lips were curving into what could pass as a smile.

Pastor Moore gestured to Nash. "Amy Deerson, this is—"

"We know each other." Nash's deep voice was firm, and its familiar timbre unlocked memories she'd thought long gone.

She dared not look at him. Couldn't handle whatever she would find in his expression. Regret? Sarcasm? Pity? Didn't matter—her feelings for him *were* dead. She'd been over him for a long time—years and years. The shock of seeing him had sent her into a tizzy. That was all. In a few minutes, she'd be fine.

"Good." The pastor took a seat opposite her. "I've had such a strong feeling about you helping little Ruby."

Ruby. The girl's name was Ruby.

"Amy has been training for several months to be a mentor. She's passed her background checks and is willing to devote the extra time you mentioned Ruby needs. And with none of our other trained mentors available to help at this time, well…it seems ideal. With your permission, I'll tell her about Ruby's situation. Or would you like to?"

Nash brought his fist to his mouth and cleared his throat. He looked older, his face harsher than she remembered. And he'd filled out. Still wiry, but with more muscles in his arms and chest. Gone was the young cowboy she'd loved. In his place was a chiseled man.

Their past flashed back. The day they'd met. Their first kiss. His big grin and slicing sense of humor. The future they'd planned. Oh, how her heart had overflowed for him. And then he'd disappeared, leaving her devastated.

And now he was back. And she—out of all the women in this town—had been asked to spend time with *his child* when all she'd wanted was to marry him and be the mother of his babies? *God, You wouldn't be this cruel. This is a joke, right?*

"Pastor," Nash said, "could you give us a moment, please?"

"Of course." He stood. "I'll see how it's going in the preschool room. Be back in a few minutes."

Amy straightened. She wanted to look away but didn't. It had been ten years. She'd moved on. And the fact he had a daughter made it quite obvious he had, as well.

"I didn't know, Amy. I never would have agreed to come if—"

"If you'd known I was involved." She hated how snippy she sounded. And that his full lips and high cheekbones still made her chest flutter. His cropped brown hair gave him a maturity his previous waves had not. The laugh lines around his eyes were a kick in the gut. He'd been carefree, rising to the top of the professional bull riding circuit while she'd nursed a broken heart. And he hadn't cared one bit.

He hadn't loved her.

He'd loved someone else and had a baby with her.

"So, she's your daughter." She was surprised she wasn't yelling at him.

"No."

No? What was he talking about?

"She's my little sister."

"I know that's not true," she snapped. "You're an orphan."

"Yeah, about being an orphan." He shifted his jaw. "Not quite."

Nash had known moving back to Sweet Dreams was dumber than climbing on the world's meanest bull while recovering from a broken rib, but he'd done both anyway. The bull hadn't been nearly as scary as the thought of running into Amy. He'd been in town a mere week and already his worst fear had come true. Except this was even worse than running into her. This was…horrible…beyond bad.

He'd loved Amy more than anything on earth. That's why he'd had to leave all those years ago—to protect her.

But now another female needed his protection. He

would give Ruby all the love and normalcy he'd missed out on as a kid, and if it meant living in the same town as Amy, so be it.

He just hadn't planned on running into her this soon. In fact, he hadn't put any thought into what he'd do when he eventually *did* run into her, which was inevitable in a small town.

How could he tell her everything that needed to be said in a few minutes? It was hard to concentrate with her big coffee-colored eyes shooting knives his way, not to mention her long dark brown hair tumbling over her shoulders, reminding him of its silkiness. Creamy skin, curvy figure—she looked even better than when he'd left, and she'd been a knockout back then.

"What do you mean, 'not quite'?" Her clipped words told him loud and clear how hard this was for her. He owed her…so much.

"I wasn't an orphan. I lied to you." It had been the only lie he'd told her. And it had torn them apart. She just didn't know it.

"I see."

He hesitated. "The pastor will be back soon, so I'll give you the condensed version. My mother had me when she was fifteen years old. She was a drug addict and, at times, a prostitute. She told me she didn't know who my father was—could have been any number of guys. I haven't seen or talked to her in over ten years. In December I got a call saying she'd died of a heroin overdose. That's when I found out I had a little sister."

The chaos of the past four months gripped his muscles in relentless tension. He shrugged his shoulders one at a time to relieve it, which didn't work. Amy stared at him with a mix of disbelief and disgust.

"How did you get custody of her then? Wouldn't someone close to her, someone she was familiar with, raise her?"

"You'd think so, right?" He flexed his fingers. "Needless to say, my mother didn't leave a will. Ruby's father is like mine—unknown. Our mother was turning tricks for drugs at the time and had no idea who he was. Believe me, the courts and I did our best to find out. We had little to go on. No one else wants the kid."

Amy's face looked ready to crack into a million pieces. "Do *you* want her?"

"Yes."

"A child isn't a duty."

"Exactly." He lightly thumped his knuckles on the table. "That's what I told the judge when I petitioned to be her guardian. I couldn't let her grow up the way I did." He hadn't meant to admit the last part. When they'd dated, he'd purposely not discussed his upbringing with Amy. He hadn't wanted her to know the depravity of his youth. Since he'd moved to Sweet Dreams from Sheridan, Wyoming, when he was thirteen, hiding his childhood hadn't been difficult to do.

What did it matter now? He'd lost all rights with her the day he'd skipped town.

"What do you mean?" she asked.

He had to get back on track. "Ruby's been growing up in a bad—I'm talking highly dysfunctional—environment. The night our mother died, the police went to the apartment she'd been living in. Ruby was there, alone. No food. Heat was turned off. Electricity, too. Who knows how long she'd been there by herself? Believe me when I say the only stable times in the girl's life have been when she was in foster care while our mother was in jail."

Amy's eyes widened, and she blinked rapidly. Then she lifted her chin. "Why here? Why bring her to Sweet Dreams?"

Because he'd had no other choice. Ten years ago he'd purchased a home nearby, but that had been when he'd still believed he could have it all, including Amy.

"I own property outside of town. As soon as the court awarded me custody, Ruby's therapist recommended I get her settled as soon as possible, and she was adamant about Ruby needing stability. I'd bought the house and land before…well…before I left, but I've never lived there. I've been renting it out. The therapist urged me to raise Ruby here permanently."

"Back up." She brought her hand in front of her, palm out, fingers splayed. "You own a house here?"

"Yeah."

"I guess I didn't know you at all." She tucked her lips under as if trying to get her emotions under control. "Not an orphan. Bought a house—I'm assuming when we were still together. What else didn't you tell me?"

Regret thundered through his veins. He wished he was on a bull, in the chute, ready to be released into the dirt arena. It was the only place he'd ever been able to escape. He imagined wrapping his hand with the rosined rope…

"Never mind. I don't want to know." She turned her head to the side, exposing the pale skin of her neck.

"The reason I left—"

"No." She held her hand out. "You don't get to do this now. I'm not interested in your confession. It's too late. I'm here for one reason—to mentor a little girl.

Whatever you want to get off your chest will have to stay there."

"You would still help her?" Nash had to give it to her—she was courageous. He'd always admired her quiet strength, her morals, the way she'd soothe anything bothering him. And he'd thrown it all away.

"I don't know." Her dark eyebrows formed a V. "It's a lot to take in."

"She's withdrawn, malnourished, fearful. She was placed with a young couple while the courts decided if I could be her permanent legal guardian. I visited as often as allowed. It took a long time before she warmed up to me. The day I gained custody was the day we moved here. The therapist thought it would be best. No more temporary living arrangements."

"So you're here to stay."

"Yes."

"For as long as Ruby needs."

"Forever. Dottie Lavert will help out when she can. Clint's nearby. Wade isn't far. Marshall, too." Clint Romine, Wade Croft and Marshall Graham were his best friends—practically his brothers—from his time at Yearling Group Home. They'd all been sent to the group foster home as young teens, and they'd stayed friends as adults.

"Good. Sounds like you don't need me."

"I wouldn't be here if Ruby didn't need someone. The therapist wants her to have a positive female influence. A consistent presence—someone who can give her a better understanding of how a caring woman acts. Basically, the opposite of our mother. It's too much to ask of you, though. Like I said, I never in a million years would have dreamed…"

"What? That I would want to help a child?"

That you wouldn't have a houseful of kids of your own. And he knew she didn't. Clint had told him she was single. He had no clue why. She was the most nurturing person he knew.

"Clint told me you keep busy with your quilts and the store. I didn't think you'd be willing to give up so much time for a stranger's kid."

"Yes, well, I like children, and I want to make a difference. I just think the situation is too bizarre for me to be Ruby's mentor. It would be uncomfortable for us both."

Exactly. This had been an extremely uncomfortable ten minutes.

"I agree. Hopefully, the pastor has someone else who can help. I'm not looking for a babysitter—I retired from bull riding and I'll be spending all my time with Ruby until she starts school next year—but given the circumstances…well…she needs more than me."

Amy wrapped her arms around her waist and didn't reply.

The problems he'd faced over the past four months galloped back. Learning his mother was dead. Retiring from the profession he'd loved. Figuring out how to live in one spot when all he'd done was travel for a decade. Raising Ruby, who was emotionally stunted, when he had no idea how to be a parent. And this meeting—he'd been so hopeful the woman would be exactly what Ruby needed. From what the pastor said, no one else was available. A clawing feeling gripped his throat.

He wasn't equipped for any of this. And he really hated failing.

"I hope you were able to catch up." The pastor

walked back in, a big smile on his face. "Amy, now that you are more aware of what Ruby has been through, do you have any questions? Concerns?"

"Yes."

The hair on the back of Nash's neck bristled.

"As Nash mentioned, we knew each other a long time ago. In fact, we dated. Given this information, don't you think someone else should be paired with Ruby?"

"Well, it depends." He cupped his chin, rubbing his jaw. "I'm assuming it wasn't an amicable parting."

Amy quickly shook her head. Nash looked away.

"If you both can put your personal feelings aside and keep Ruby the main priority, then I don't think there's a problem. But if there is any revenge in either of your hearts, I urge you to decline. You won't be able to support Ruby the way that she needs. We must all work together for her. She's been through enough. Wouldn't you agree?"

"Yes," they replied at the same time.

"Since you dated some years ago, I'm guessing you've both moved on, so I don't think it will be an issue. And it's up to you two how much interaction you want to have. Amy, why don't you meet Ruby before making any decisions?" The pastor tilted his head, watching her response. She considered for a moment before nodding. He smiled. "Good. I'll take you down there. Nash, you wait here, and we can talk more when I get back."

Nash tracked Amy's moves as she left the room. An ache spread across his chest. She would never agree to help Ruby.

Lord, I can't do this alone. Please have mercy on me.

He'd given Ruby a nice house, clothes, food and love,

but he couldn't give her a mother. The only woman he'd ever wanted was Amy, and he'd never forgive himself for leaving her in such a cowardly fashion. He hadn't given her a warning, hadn't even said goodbye.

Moving back to Sweet Dreams and glimpsing Amy occasionally would have been punishment enough, but being in regular contact with her?

He couldn't imagine a more painful scenario.

She'd been his. And he'd forfeited all claims to her.

He should be glad Amy wouldn't agree to this arrangement. Would make life easier for him. But where did that leave Ruby? He could not let his baby sister—the child he now considered his daughter—to grow up as damaged as him.

"You must be Ruby." Amy crouched in front of the play kitchen where the tiny blonde stood. The girl flinched, backing up to the wall. Amy ached to put her at ease. "I'm Amy."

Ruby's mouth slackened, her blue-green eyes opening wide with distrust. Nash's eyes. She resembled him in other ways, too. Wide forehead, high cheekbones. But Nash's nose was longer, while Ruby's was a perfect button.

Hannah and little Daniel were coloring pictures at one of the children's tables. Amy wasn't sure what to do. The girl's body language shouted fear.

"Would you like me to read you a book?" Amy gestured to the beanbags next to a small bookshelf.

Ruby didn't blink, didn't move. Her lips trembled.

"It's okay." She longed to touch her cheek, to reassure her, but she sensed any physical contact would terrify the girl. "Why don't I pick one out, and you can come over if you'd like?"

She crossed to the shelf and selected a Curious George picture book. Then she lowered her body into one of the beanbags. How she would get out of it, she had no idea. Boy, it was low to the ground. Ruby hadn't moved but still stared intently at her. Amy plastered on a big smile and waved for her to come over.

Ruby didn't so much as twitch.

Maybe if she started reading it, the girl would join her. She read the first five pages out loud and peeked over the cover. Still staring. She read five more pages. Ruby had drifted a few feet in her direction. Progress. She continued until the end. Ruby stood about three feet away, her eyes locked on Amy's face.

"You know, pretty soon you'll be able to go to school, and you'll learn how to read."

"I know some letters." She spoke with a lisp.

Amy nodded, encouraging the sign of interest. What this child must have been through. Left unsupervised with no food or heat. Disgraceful.

"Do you see any letters you recognize on the cover?" Amy held the book out.

"*E. O.*" She pointed to the letters.

"Good job! You're very smart. Do you want me to read another book?"

She didn't respond.

"Why don't I pick one out?"

Pastor Moore and Nash came into the room. Ruby raced to Nash, wrapping her arms around his legs as if she never wanted to let him go. The sight made Amy's stomach clench. Ruby trusted Nash. It was obvious.

And if Amy had to guess, the child didn't trust another living soul.

"Hey, RuRu, how do you like this fun place? We'll be coming to church here every Sunday." He hoisted her into his arms, settling her on his hip. She let her head fall onto his shoulder and wound her arms around his neck. "Us grown-ups have to talk a few more minutes, so you stay here and color with Daniel, okay?"

She buried her face in his shoulder.

"Honey, I will only be gone a few minutes." His voice was soft, tender. He glanced at Pastor Moore, then Amy. "Would you give us a sec?"

"Of course." The pastor waited for Amy to join him, and they went back to the conference room. "What did you think?"

"I think you were right to contact me. I know it's not the church's traditional program, but she seems… well…a bit traumatized."

"Yes. She's been through a lot. Tell me, Amy, do you see yourself as being her mentor? Now that you know her situation? Not to mention the man who will be raising her is someone from your past?"

Ruby's face, demeanor and adorable lisp all came to mind. Yes, she could see herself as the girl's mentor. She longed to make life better—normal—for the sweet child. To earn Ruby's trust would mean the world to her.

But interacting with Nash?

No.

Just no.

Sure, she'd moved on and didn't need to know Nash's reasons for leaving, but the hurt was still there. Even if she and Ruby only met privately, looking in the girl's eyes would be like looking into Nash's. Amy didn't know if she could do it.

But how could she admit to the pastor all the thoughts churning in her brain?

"I have a lot of mixed emotions about this. If it was anyone but Nash, I'd be setting up a schedule tonight. She's so teeny. And four years is a dear age."

"Are you over him?" the pastor asked gently.

"Yes." She nodded too quickly. "Haven't seen him in a decade."

"I see. Are you worried you won't be able to handle a long-term commitment with Ruby?"

Was she? Any arrangement with Ruby meant interacting with Nash. What if she got mad at him, or he blurted out the reason he left and it devastated her? Would she still be able to give Ruby the attention she needed?

"Kind of. This is all sudden."

"Let's pray about it." He bowed his head, and Amy clasped her hands. "Heavenly Father, You are all-knowing and almighty. Please give Amy and Nash clarity about what is best for Ruby. If Amy isn't the person You have in mind to help, make that clear, and lead another of our church members to step forward and answer the call. Above all, we pray You will heal Ruby's hurts and comfort her. Lead us to support Nash as he navigates the new waters of fatherhood. In Your name we pray."

"Amen," Amy whispered. The reference to answering the call pierced her conscience. It had been more than a year since she'd begun praying about mentoring a child. How many times had she prayed to be paired with a young boy or girl? Too many to count.

"If you're willing, let's ask Nash and Ruby to meet us

here again tomorrow night. It will allow you to spend a little more time with her before making your decision. If you want to help, you and Nash can work out a schedule then. If not, I'll talk to him about other options."

"I think that's a good idea. Are there any other mentors who could help Ruby?"

"Not at this time, but a few of our retired ladies might be willing to spend a Saturday afternoon each month with her."

Amy frowned. Would a few Saturday afternoons be enough for Ruby?

Nash came back into the room. His Western shirt and jeans couldn't hide the fact he was built out of rock-solid muscle. It wasn't as though she was attracted to him—she merely had eyes. He was a good-looking man. Who'd broken her heart and left her so he could ride bulls and be a superstar.

"Ah, Nash, good. Amy and I were talking about not rushing into this. Would you be willing to come back tomorrow night? Given this new development, I think you both could use some space before making a decision."

"Sure." He crossed his arms, then quickly uncrossed them. "And if it's a no?"

Pastor Moore smiled. "We have options. None as good as Amy, but don't worry. We won't let you and Ruby down."

"Okay. Does seven work for you?"

Amy nodded. Why was she even considering this setup? No one—*no one*—would fault her for saying no. If it was anyone else, she'd do it. She ignored the voice in her head telling her she was only thinking of herself. Maybe she was, but who could blame her?

After murmuring goodbye, she hurried out of the

room and stopped in her tracks. Ruby stood with Hannah and Daniel in the hallway. Her blank expression turned Amy's legs to lead.

If only the child would smile or cry or…something. Amy had been around a lot of children during her years teaching Sunday school. She was used to the highs and lows of their moods. However, she couldn't categorize Ruby's emotional state. She seemed completely unengaged with the world. No joy, no hope—nothing.

As much as Amy wanted to avoid Nash, she also wanted to brighten this little girl's life. Give her a reason to smile.

She had a lot to pray about.

"Guess what?" She approached Ruby, bending to speak at her level. "We can read another story tomorrow night. How does that sound?"

Ruby looked at her blankly. "I like the monkey book."

"I do, too." Amy straightened, surprised at the emotion clogging her throat. "See you tomorrow."

If she agreed to this, she'd lose her heart to Ruby. Maybe already had. Losing her heart to a child she could handle. But losing it to Nash again? She would never let that happen. Not when her life was finally falling into place.

Chapter Two

Nash clipped the walkie-talkie to his belt and strode to the barn the next afternoon. Breathing in the cool air, he let the sun's rays soothe his agitation. Ruby had fallen asleep watching cartoons. Normally, the girl didn't nap—she fought sleep something fierce—so the fact she'd conked out was a blessing. He'd only been her guardian for a week, and already the role felt impossible.

He wasn't a dad. He was a broken-down, retired bull rider. Sure, he'd risen to the top of his profession and made gobs of money, but he didn't know how to do domestic. At thirty-one years old, he had a lot of life left to figure out, like how he was going to spend his days from now on. Inspecting his property would be a start.

Snow must have thawed recently for the ground to still be soft. This part of Wyoming tended to be dry. He checked the walkie-talkie again. If Ruby woke up and he wasn't there… Her terrified face from two nights ago still bothered him. He'd put her to bed, read her a story and gotten ready to leave. She'd clung to his arm, shaking her head, her eyes wild. He'd asked her what was wrong, but she just kept repeating, "Don't go." So he'd stayed until she fell asleep. An hour later, she'd woken up, screaming. Scared him half to death. He'd cradled her in his arms, wishing he could have been there for her from birth to protect her. It had taken another hour before she'd stopped shaking.

Sometimes he wished his mother was alive just so he could chew her out. But she wasn't, and he was left to fix her mistakes. Not that Ruby was a mistake…but her upbringing had been disastrous.

Could he fix Ruby?

Yesterday he'd bought the walkie-talkies and showed Ruby how to use them. He'd said, "If I'm not in the room with you, all you have to do is press this button and holler for me. Then take your finger off, and you'll be able to hear me talk." They'd practiced until she was an old pro.

He chuckled. He'd probably be at her beck and call from now on. Not that he minded. The girl was as cute as could be. His mission was to help her find her smile. He wanted to keep it there. Make her forget a lifetime of trauma and neglect.

He slid open the barn door and counted the stalls as he walked through. Enough for ten horses. He already owned six. His friend Wade had been boarding them for him while he was on the road competing. The other outbuildings held his equipment. The property had one fenced-in pasture and plenty of land for any number of operations.

Lately, he'd been thinking about opening a training facility for young bull riders. But he wasn't sure if he should. Just because he had the property to train kids didn't mean he had the ability to teach. Maybe he'd be better off breeding horses. He certainly wasn't running a cow-calf operation like their friend Clint. Which reminded him…he hadn't talked to Marshall in a while. He'd better call him soon.

After shutting the barn door, Nash went back into the house. A pang of regret hit him every time he entered. Before moving back, the last time he'd been inside had been the day he'd bought it as a surprise for Amy. An engagement present. He'd been planning on proposing to her the next week. Then his mother, once again, had destroyed his life.

The diamond ring still sat in its box in his top drawer. He really should sell it.

Like he ever would.

He checked on Ruby, asleep and curled up in a tight ball like a dog afraid of getting kicked. He kissed her soft cheek before going to the kitchen. The company he'd hired to paint and decorate the house had done a good job. He'd given them free rein and a blank check. Just told them to make it feel like a family lived there and to make sure Ruby's room was fit for a princess. If only money could fix all of his problems, but the millions in the bank couldn't win Ruby's trust or buy Amy's forgiveness.

Amy was going to say no to helping Ruby. And while her refusal would be best for him, it definitely was not best for Ruby.

The girl hid apples and packages of crackers under her pillow and in her closet. He'd found cookies in her shoe. The therapist had warned him it might take a while for her to believe she'd always have enough to eat. Whenever he found food, he was supposed to gently remind her she was safe with him and he would always provide for her.

He sat on one of the bar stools at the island, dropping his forehead into his hands. The enormity of the situation threatened to overcome him.

I'm not qualified for this. What if she always hoards food and wakes up screaming? What if she never smiles? Is too scared to go to school? What if she's been damaged beyond repair?

He raised his head toward the ceiling.

God, I need You.

Ruby had no one but him.

He'd handle it. He had to.

Amy girded her shoulders and entered the church at 6:55 pm. She'd spent the past twenty-four hours talking to her mom, her best friend, Lexi Romine, and the Lord. Lexi and Mom thought she should decline being Ruby's mentor. The Lord, it seemed, had other plans.

Every time she prayed, she kept coming back to Isaiah 6:8: "Also I heard the voice of the Lord, saying, Whom shall I send, and who will go for us? Then said I, Here am I; send me." She'd prayed for so long to help a child. How many times had she thought *Here am I, Lord. Send me*?

And now that the opportunity was here, she couldn't justify turning it down. Every time she tried, her argument fell flat. She kept thinking of the Old Testament story about Joseph. If Joseph could forgive his brothers for selling him into slavery and then provide for them so their families didn't starve, couldn't she move past her issues with Nash to help Ruby?

Maybe this was her cross to bear.

But could she bear it?

With her back straight and head high, she strode to the preschool room. This wasn't for Nash. It was for Ruby.

Maybe Nash didn't keep his promises, but she kept hers. She'd promised the Lord she would do His will.

She believed this was His will.

After entering the room, she halted at the sight of Ruby on Nash's lap. The child held a stuffed sheep in the air and was pretending to make it dance. She wasn't smiling, but the fact she was playing was a good sign.

"Hello, Ruby." She waved. "Who is this sheep? He's quite the dancer."

She immediately clutched the animal to her tummy like a wild rabbit stilling at the first hint of danger.

Nash took the sheep out of Ruby's hand. "I think this is Sheldon. Sheldon the sheep. Is that right, RuRu?"

She turned to see his face. A hint of a smile lifted her lips, and she nodded.

"Or it could be Samantha." Amy slowly approached them, trying to be as non-threatening as possible. "Are you sure it's a boy?"

He flipped the sheep over twice then sniffed its head. "It smells like a boy. It's not all flowery like a girl." He held it up for Ruby to smell. She took a sniff. "What do you think?"

"Boy," she said.

"Well, it is very nice to meet you, Sheldon." Amy held her hand out and pretended to shake the animal's paw. "Would he like to sit on your lap while we read a book?"

Ruby didn't respond.

"Should we try another Curious George? See what trouble that silly monkey gets into today?"

Amy selected a book and folded her long legs to sit in the beanbag, grunting as she sank the final inches. Ruby brought the stuffed animal over. She didn't sit, though.

"Stay?" Ruby asked Nash, her gaze full of worry.

"I'd hate to miss the story." He folded his legs to sit cross-legged on the carpet. The process looked painful. Ruby, clutching Sheldon, settled on his lap, and he tickled her side.

"Daddy!" She giggled and squirmed. Nash stopped teasing her, kissing the top of her head instead.

Daddy? Amy ignored the pitter-patter of her heart at the sight of Nash in such a paternal role. Maybe if she and Ruby met privately, the arrangement would work. They could make cookies and color. They could go to the library and check out books or stop into The Beanery for hot chocolates.

If she was going to be part of Ruby's life, it had to be on her terms. And that meant spending time alone with Ruby. No Nash allowed.

After reading two books, she asked Ruby if she wanted to pretend to bake a cake. Ruby followed her to the play kitchen, and Nash declared he'd be back in a few minutes. He had to speak to the pastor. As soon as Nash left, Ruby became expressionless, the way she'd been in the hallway yesterday.

"First we need flour and sugar." Amy pointed to the fake boxes of food. "Can you find them?"

She stood with her arms glued to her sides. *Okay.* Amy grabbed a box and pretended to pour it into a plastic bowl. "Mmm… I love cake batter. Here's some butter. Throw it in." She handed plastic butter to Ruby, who let it fall into the bowl.

"And eggs. My cakes always have eggs. Let's crack them." Amy tapped the plastic egg against the table and pretended to drop it in. Ruby ignored the egg in front of her. "We're ready to mix." She found the plastic hand-mixer and gave it to the girl. "Give it a good stir."

She obeyed, but Amy got the impression she was merely going through the motions, that she wasn't enjoying herself.

Hannah and Daniel entered. "Hello, you two. Ruby, would you mind staying here with Daniel and me while Amy talks to your dad for a minute?"

Ruby just stared at her.

"I won't be long." Amy found Sheldon and gave him to Ruby. "Here. Make sure this sheep doesn't get into any trouble." Although she hated leaving her, she went to the meeting room.

"Well, I trust you've both had time to pray about the situation." Pastor Moore waited for her to sit. Nash was in the same spot as yesterday. "What do you think?"

She considered for a moment. The previous twenty minutes solidified her opinion. With patience and a woman's touch, Ruby had a better chance at coming out of her shell. And Amy wanted to be that woman.

"I would like to spend more time with Ruby." Amy watched Nash. He jerked to attention. "But I don't know if you'll be comfortable with my suggestion."

His eyes darkened. "What is it?"

"Would you be okay with me spending time with Ruby alone? I'd love to show her around my studio, take her to the library, that sort of thing."

He bowed his head. "I'm not sure."

"I don't know if I can agree if it's going to be the three of us all the time. It's a bit intimate given our history."

He blew out a breath. "I understand. Really, I do. I'm thinking about Ruby. I know you'd be good for her, and frankly, I'd prefer she spend time alone with you. But she's going through a lot. What do you think, Pastor?"

He'd prefer not to be around her, either? Why the words hurt, she didn't know. It's not as if the past ten years hadn't proven the fact.

"I think you should follow your instincts, Nash." The pastor addressed Amy. "Ruby is afraid of strangers. It will take time for her to get used to you. She might need Nash with her until she's comfortable."

Amy swallowed the sour taste in her mouth. It wasn't as if she didn't know the pastor had a point, but she was already going out on a limb by agreeing to this. Couldn't they cut her a break?

"I guess we could do a trial run," she said. "Say, a few afternoons next week and see how it goes? If we aren't feeling it, we'll go our separate ways."

"Works for me," Nash said gruffly.

Pastor Moore stood. "I'm here if either of you need to talk or have additional concerns. Feel free to call. Why don't I let you two work out the details of next week?" He left the room, and the air felt charged as soon as he was gone.

With no idea what to say, she fixed her gaze on the map of ancient Israel hanging on the wall. Nash remained silent, as well.

"How weird is this for you?" Amy finally asked him.

"Really weird." His throat worked.

"Gives me a new appreciation for what divorced

parents must go through. Coming up with a visitation schedule, figuring out drop-offs and all that."

"Except we were never divorced," he said. "Or married."

The words hurt, she couldn't deny it, but Nash seemed unsure of himself, and Amy had never seen this side of him. He'd always been quick with a joke and oh, so confident.

He massaged the back of his neck. "Sorry... Thank you for agreeing to help Ruby. I know you don't want details, but what I did back then was unforgivable. I at least want you to know I hated leaving you."

Then why did you?

She didn't want to know.

"It was a long time ago." She waved the apology off like a pesky fly. "Which days work best for you?"

Storm clouds brewed in his eyes, but he accepted the change in subject. "Any you have free. I have nothing going on."

"So you really retired?"

"I did."

She wanted to ask what he planned to do next, but she stopped herself. She didn't need personal information from him. She'd stick to business—to Ruby. Which reminded her...a few things had been niggling in her mind.

"Does Ruby know you aren't her father?"

"Yes. I explained I'm her much bigger brother. It took several supervised visits at her foster home before she'd even speak to me."

"But she calls you Daddy."

He shrugged, a smile briefly lighting his face. "When I told her she was going to live with me, I asked her what she wanted to call me. She said, 'How long am I going to live with you?' I told her forever. She replied, 'Daddy.' I tell you, my heart melted into a puddle right there on the linoleum floor of the courthouse."

Amy's heart was growing squishy, too, and that wouldn't do. *Remember the days after he left? How you sat by the phone hoping he'd call? And don't forget how awful it was to read about him winning the event in Houston. Going on with his life as if you'd never meant a thing to him.*

"Yes, well, that's good." She reached into her purse for her planner. Opening it, she scanned the next week's schedule. "Why don't we do Tuesday and Thursday, say, three o'clock? You can bring her to my apartment. It's above Amy's Quilt Shop. Just go around the back and up the stairs. I have a studio I think she'll enjoy."

All the brightly colored fabrics, the work tables, sewing machines and art supplies were sure to please the girl. She'd plan a few simple crafts for them to do.

"You don't have to work at three?" He frowned.

"No, I hired a high school girl to work afternoons."

"Tuesday and Thursday then. Listen, Ruby is shy around…well, everyone. She might have a hard time being in a strange place without me."

"You could go to The Beanery after you drop her off. If she gets upset, we'll join you and get a hot cocoa or something."

"That might work." His face cleared, and his shoulders relaxed. "Does this mean you'll make a final decision next week?"

"Do you really want me to spend time with Ruby? Or do you feel cornered into it?"

"I want Ruby to trust other people. I mean, she'll be

going to school soon, and I don't want her scared of her teachers. Would it be easier on me if someone else was her mentor? Yeah. But I'm grateful you're willing to try. She needs more than I alone can give her."

So having a different mentor would be easier on him, huh? She bit back a nasty retort. The insecurity in his eyes pacified her irritation. Her decision wasn't about Nash anyway. It was about trusting God even when the circumstances didn't make sense. She'd always wondered if she would step up and take care of an enemy if put into the position of being a Good Samaritan.

She'd regret it if she didn't at least *try* to help Ruby.

"Then, yes, let's see how the visits go, and I'll give you a firm answer next week."

"Wade's delivering my horses soon." Nash sat in a white rocking chair on his front porch Tuesday afternoon. Clint Romine, one of his best friends, sat next to him in an identical chair. Ruby was picking pasque-flowers from the yard. He still had a little time before he had to take her to Amy's place. He had no idea how their meeting would go, but he feared the worst. Those early visits with her at the foster home had been terrible. But maybe Ruby was in a better mental place now. He hoped so.

"How long has it been since you've ridden Crank?"

"Four months. I'm itching to saddle up. Could ride for days, I think, and I'd still feel as restless as a mountain lion."

"You've been traveling the circuit since we graduated high school. Of course you're restless." Clint lived outside of Sweet Dreams with his pretty new bride, Lexi, who happened to be Amy's best friend. Another complication Nash didn't know how to handle. Would his move back to Sweet Dreams be awkward for Clint and Lexi, given how he'd treated Amy years ago? He'd worry about it another day.

Nash sighed. "I've got to figure out what I'm going to do now that I'm here."

Clint stared ahead, slowly rocking. How could he sit there so calmly? Nash was about to bust out of his rocker. He didn't care if the decorator claimed the chairs cozied up the porch; they made him feel like a grandpa. A sprint up the drive would go a long way to helping him let off some steam. But the sad truth was he couldn't sprint if he tried. His body had been so beaten up and battered that he had trouble even jogging.

"Thinking about ranching?" Clint asked.

"No."

"Breeding horses? Wade could help with that."

"Maybe." He stood and paced the porch, his movements choppy. "I've been thinking about something different. I'm not sure it would work."

"What's that?"

He stopped at the column nearest Clint and leaned against the railing. "I might open a training facility. For young bull riders."

Clint considered it a moment. "I could see it."

"But I don't have the experience to teach kids."

"What are you talking about?" Clint laughed. "You have more experience in your pinky finger than anyone I know."

"Yeah, but that's riding bulls. Not *teaching* kids to ride them."

"You'd be great. What would you need?"

"Steers. Bulls. A practice arena. Chutes. Equipment. Insurance—a lot of insurance."

"There you go."

"But knowing what I've been through, do I want to encourage kids to follow in my footsteps? You know the injuries I've sustained. And I was fortunate."

"It's a dilemma, that's for sure. I guess you'll have to pray on it."

Last year, Clint's response about praying on it would have annoyed Nash. But after he'd had a string of bad rides and broken his ankle and ribs for the umpteenth time, he'd spent a few months at Wade's secluded ranch—a thirty-minute drive from Sweet Dreams—and gotten right with his Maker. He prayed about everything now.

"Will you pray about it, too, brother?" Nash asked.

"Of course." Clint rose, nodding toward Ruby. "How's she doing?"

"Better than I expected. When I first met her, she was so skinny her bones pushed against her skin. She was terrified. Skittish." He shivered thinking about her back then. "I'm really sorry I missed your wedding, man. I never would have—"

"Don't say a word, Nash." Clint shook his head. "I understand. I would have been furious if you'd have come to the wedding when you found out about Ruby. She needed you."

Ruby approached, eyeing Clint with distrust and avoiding him. She thrust a bouquet of purple blooms in Nash's hands.

"For me? Well, RuRu, these are the purdiest flowers I've ever seen. Thank you kindly." He winked at her. "And don't worry about Clint here. He's one of my best buds. We lived together when we were teens. You'll meet my other friends, Wade and Marshall, soon enough."

Ruby hid behind his leg. He knew her well enough to assume her gaze was fixed on Clint.

"I've got to be going." Clint tipped his Stetson to Ruby. "Good to meet you. Maybe your dad will bring you out to the ranch sometime. We have lots of horses and cows and dogs. You like dogs?"

No answer. Thankfully, Clint didn't seem to need one.

"Thanks for coming." Nash clapped him on the back. "Don't be a stranger."

"Bye." Clint waved and ambled to his truck.

"Well, what do you say we get these in some water before we head over to Miss Amy's?" Her eyes had questions—a lot of questions—but he couldn't read her mind. "What's wrong? You're worried about something. I can tell."

He opened the door for her, and they went to the kitchen, putting the flowers in a mason jar with water.

"You a little scared of her?" He boosted her to sit on the counter.

"No."

"What is it? You can tell me anything."

"How long do I have to stay?"

He smiled at her lisp whenever she said her *s*'s.

"You don't have to stay at all. But if you want to, you'll be there for one hour. And I'll be three stores down, slurping coffee. You and Amy can join me if you want, but I'd like for you to give her place a try without me first."

She gulped, her eyes wide and fearful. "One hour? How much is that?"

He almost laughed. He'd forgotten that little kids didn't have a strong sense of time. He pointed to his watch. "When this small hand goes all the way around once, an hour has passed. Maybe you need a watch of your own. We can order one for you. But right now, we've got to skedaddle if we want to be on time."

He picked her up, grabbed his keys and carried her to the garage. After strapping her into her car seat, he backed out and drove toward town. Despite the assurances he'd given Ruby, he had a bad feeling about this visit. Ruby already seemed fearful. What if she made a scene at Amy's? If she did, he wouldn't be able to leave her there, and then Amy would back out.

If Ruby was upset about staying with Amy, he wouldn't force the issue. The kid had been through enough. He just hoped his uneasiness didn't mean his fears were about to come true.

Chapter Three

Amy hummed as she fluffed the throw pillows on her couch. Ruby would be here any minute. She rushed to the other side of the open living space where she kept her private sewing and art studio. If she wasn't cutting material, quilting or making patterns for her weekly blog, she was drawing designs for her own fabric line. Well, hopefully, her own fabric line. She should be hearing back from the fabric manufacturers within a few weeks. How many years had she dreamed of stocking the designs she'd drawn? She shook her head. None of that mattered right now. Her sole goal today was to make Ruby comfortable.

A knock on the door made her pause. *Lord, please give me the wisdom to help her.* She'd show Nash his fears about leaving Ruby were off base. She'd been around young children her entire life. She knew what little girls enjoyed. It would just take a while for Ruby to get used to her. No big deal.

She opened the door. Nash held Ruby in his arms. *Oh, my.* He looked every bit the cowboy she remembered in his hat, jeans, jacket and boots.

"Come in. I'm so glad to see you again, Ruby. Let me take your sweatshirt." She waited while Nash helped Ruby out of her pink hoodie. "I'll show you around my place."

After hanging the hoodie on a hook near the door, Amy veered left to the open studio. She stopped next to the floor-to-ceiling shelves, which held fabrics in a rainbow of colors. In the center of the space, Ruby clutched Nash's hand.

"You did all this?" Nash let out a low whistle. "Everything is so organized. You actually make all those quilts you sell?"

"Most of them. I consign a few local artists' quilts, too." She shouldn't be so pleased at his reaction. He seemed to fill the room with his charismatic energy. He used to draw her like iron to a magnet. She gestured to the rack holding her latest creation. "I'm trying a new pattern."

He and Ruby inspected the rust, cream and navy design. "Patriotic. I like it. Reminds me of the Fourth of July."

"I'm hoping to finish it in June. Red, white and blue quilts always sell well in the summer."

"Speaking of this time of year…" He looked down at Ruby. "Pretty soon you and I will be watching rodeos on Friday nights. Sounds fun, huh?"

Her eyes gleamed almost aqua as she nodded up at him. The sight touched Amy.

"I can't wait for cotton candy and barbecues." He rubbed his stomach. "Mmm-mmm. Makes me hungry just thinking about it. In fact, I'd better get something in my tummy before it growls and scares the neighbors. I'll be heading over to The Beanery. Text me if you need me."

He kissed the top of Ruby's head. Then he nodded to Amy. "I'll be back in an hour. You girls have fun."

As soon as the door clicked behind him, Amy let out a sigh of relief. She couldn't help it. The room felt more spacious, less combustible without him there. She brought her palms together and turned her attention to Ruby.

"I have a ton of markers. Why don't we color?"

Ruby gazed intently at the door, her face white as a fresh snowfall.

"He'll be back before you know it." Amy tried to reassure her by gently taking her hand, but Ruby yanked it out of her grasp. Her lips trembled, grew blue around the edges. Tremors shook her shoulders. The poor thing was petrified!

Amy knelt beside her. "Ruby, what's wrong? It's okay. You're safe with me."

Her eyes were so wide, so fixed on the door. Amy clearly wasn't getting through to her. What should she do? The way Ruby had flinched at her touch, Amy didn't want to scare her further, but she had to divert her attention away from the door.

Why was she so upset? Nash told her he'd be back in an hour. The child knew he was going down the street to the coffee shop.

Amy stood up, raising her face to the ceiling. *What now?* Whatever was going through Ruby's mind was so frightening, she couldn't move.

"Honey, why don't we go get a hot chocolate with your dad?"

Ruby blinked, shivering. Then she looked away from

the door at Amy. Tears began to drip from her eyes to her cheeks. She didn't say anything. Simply nodded.

Amy tried not to let her disappointment show as she helped Ruby into her hoodie. Whatever had happened to this girl in the past had clearly traumatized her. Nash had mentioned neglect and malnourishment, and Amy had brushed over those words as if they hadn't mattered. She should have paid more attention. She'd been so caught up in her own past she hadn't asked the necessary questions.

The psychological damage must have cut deep. Was Amy qualified for this?

She led Ruby to the staircase. "Hold my hand, okay?"

Ruby tucked her tiny hand in Amy's. The gesture pinched her heart. If only she *could* help this girl. She needed more information. And that meant, as much as she didn't want to, she'd have to find a way to meet privately with Nash.

The coffee was perfect—strong with a kick to it. Same as he liked his bulls. He grinned at his own inside joke. The Beanery was quiet. He hadn't been in here before. Looked new, rustic. Smelled great, too. He took a drink. Leaving Ruby hadn't been too bad. She hadn't thrown a fit or anything. So why couldn't he dismiss the nagging worry in his brain?

He smacked his forehead. He hadn't stopped to ask Ruby if she wanted to stay. He'd just left.

He should have asked her. Why hadn't he thought to ask her? His knee was bouncing triple time. *Get yourself together, man.*

He checked his watch. He'd been gone seven minutes. Fifty-three minutes to go. It was times like these that made him wish he was a reader. A book would help pass the time.

The door clanged open, and Ruby raced to him, her face beaming. A lead weight dropped in his gut. If they were here and it had only been seven minutes, the visit couldn't have gone well.

He swung her onto his lap and gave her a big smile. She didn't need to know his emotions were churning. "To what do I owe this pleasure? I thought I was picking you up in an hour." He noted the tear stains down her cheeks and fought back a groan. "You were worried I'd be lonely, weren't you? That's awfully nice of you to be thinking of me."

She rested her cheek against his chest, and he brushed her hair from her face, holding her tightly. Amy stood behind the chair across the table. He mouthed, "What happened?"

She shook her head quickly and mouthed, "Later."

"Can I get you a hot chocolate, Ruby?" Amy asked. "With whipped cream?"

Ruby nodded. If she wasn't so fragile, he'd remind her of her manners. But right now *please* and *thank you* were the least of his worries. If he couldn't leave her with Amy for ten minutes, would he ever be able to leave her anywhere?

A vision came to mind of kindergarten in another year, and instead of Ruby waving happily as she walked into school with a backpack and a lunchbox, he saw her trembling, crying, unable to enter. Some of the bull riders' wives homeschooled their little ones. Would he be forced to do the same?

Homeschooling?

Him?

The coffee threatened to come up. He didn't think he had it in him to homeschool. Maybe he should call the therapist.

"Here you go." Amy beamed at Ruby as she set the cup down. Nash could see the worry in her exquisite brown eyes. And he recognized her tic from all those years ago—she rubbed her index finger and thumb together whenever she was out of her element. For a second he felt sorry for her. Wanted to make it better, like old times.

Old times. The best days of his life. Even better than winning his first Professional Bull Riders World Championship at the age of twenty-three. Every minute with Amy had been like a dream.

Ruby reached for the cup and licked the whipped cream.

Amy smiled, scrunching her nose at the girl. He had to avert his gaze at all the affection in her expression. He used to be the recipient of it. The past ten years suddenly felt bleaker than he remembered them.

"I was wondering," Amy said, tracing the rim of her mug, "would you two mind if I came over later? I've never seen your house." She gave Nash a charged look, and he instantly understood. They needed to talk but not with Ruby around. And the only place they could reasonably expect privacy was in Ruby's domain.

"Sure." He knew she was going to back out of their arrangement, and he didn't blame her. He suppressed a sigh. "How about seven-thirty?"

"Great." She sipped her cocoa. "How is it, Ruby? Chocolaty enough?"

"Mmm." She sat on his lap, happily slurping her cocoa. He had to hand it to the kid—she bounced back quickly. His spirits sank, realizing how much hope he'd put into Ruby spending time with a woman. Would take some of the pressure off him. Not to mention, he hadn't had more than a minute to himself while Ruby was awake since the day he took custody. If she couldn't handle being with someone as nice as Amy for short periods, what chance did he have at giving her a normal childhood?

Amy began talking about the daily coffee flavors, and they chatted about other changes in the town. Anyone who walked by would think they were having a pleasant visit. A couple of old friends catching up. And he was glad she could be civil, even if they'd never be friends.

By the time they'd all finished their drinks, he didn't know what to do. He hadn't begged for anything since he was a small boy, but thinking about Ruby's future made him desperate enough to contemplate begging Amy to reconsider.

He just wished he had another choice.

"She's out."

Amy waited for Nash to join her at his kitchen island. She'd arrived an hour ago, and she'd tried to engage Ruby by asking her about the toys in the living room, but Ruby hadn't seemed interested in them. Only when Nash had suggested watching a Disney movie had Ruby's face lit up. Thankfully, she'd fallen asleep halfway through *Frozen*. Not that Amy had anything against that particular cartoon; it was just hard to be in a family-type environment with Nash, especially given what she needed to ask him.

She needed the full story of Ruby's past.

Her mind had been so preoccupied, she hadn't had time to truly process his gorgeous house or the fact it was exactly the type of home she used to dream about, back when she still had hopes of getting married and having kids of her own. She'd thought she'd be raising a family in a place like this with property not too far from town. She'd thought wrong.

"Are you sure she won't wake up?" She didn't want Ruby to stumble in on them discussing her.

"I don't think she will. She woke up briefly when I pulled the bedspread over her, but I stayed until she fell asleep again."

One look at his face and all the questions she'd rehearsed earlier vanished. His eyes always changed to gray when he turned melancholy. Seeing the slate shade brought a ping of sadness to her heart. She'd always done her best to soothe his blue moods. But that was then and a lot of life had happened since he'd left. He would have to deal with his moods himself.

"I take it she fell apart when I left her at your apartment earlier."

"I wouldn't say she fell apart." Sitting on a stool, she folded her hands on the counter. "It was actually worse than falling apart. I don't know how to describe it except she almost seemed catatonic. It scared me. I didn't know what to do. She was terrified. Couldn't stop staring at the door after you left. Her face turned white. She trembled. When I suggested meeting you at the coffee shop, she finally snapped out of it."

He frowned. "What did she do then?"

"Tears started falling, but she listened to me and held my hand all the way to The Beanery."

He drummed his fingers on the counter. "Makes sense in a way."

"It doesn't to me, and that's why I'm here." She raised her chin. "I need to know more about her childhood."

Fear flashed in his eyes.

"I need to know it all." Amy wasn't backing down on this. Either she had all the facts to come up with a realistic way forward to spend time with Ruby, or she had to walk away.

"You're not going to like it."

"I'm well aware of that."

"This needs to stay confidential. I want her to have no baggage in this town. I don't care who knows I'm really her brother raising her as my daughter, but no one needs to know the horror this kid's been through."

"Agreed. You have my word I will not tell anyone the details you share."

"I've told you about our mother." He crossed his arms over his chest, leaning forward. "She went through cycles of heavy drug use and court-mandated rehab. When she was using, she'd do anything—and I mean anything—to get money for her fix. Prostitution. Theft. You name it. She had no sense of time, no sense of reality. Since Ruby had no father or siblings living with her, the poor kid had to rely on herself when our mother was higher than a kite. Inevitably, our mother would get picked up by the cops and thrown in jail for whatever she was guilty of, and while she served time, Ruby would be placed in foster care. But our mother would get out and she'd be clean, so she'd get custody again until the cycle repeated."

"How often did this happen?" Amy's mind was spinning from the scenario. She pictured Ruby small, hungry, scared. She also pictured an unstable drug addict not taking care of the girl.

"Too often."

What did that mean? Every two months? Once a year? She sighed. It didn't really matter. "So walk me through the things she had to endure."

"Being left alone in a filthy apartment with limited food. Could have been a couple hours. Sometimes, I'm sure it was days."

"Days? But she was practically a baby!" Amy brought her hand to her chest. *Horrible.* "She needed a babysitter. No young child should be left alone in a house for any length of time."

"Trust me. I know." He exhaled loudly. "Then there was the fact our mother used around her. Ruby grew up around drug paraphernalia. I guarantee Ruby witnessed her shooting up. I'm sure there was emotional abuse, as well."

Tears threatened at the thought of sweet Ruby going through all that.

"And this went on her entire life?" Amy sniffed.

"Yes. Up until mid-December at least."

"If her case workers knew all this, why did they ever let her return to her mother?" The injustice of it made her want to wring someone's neck.

"They want to keep families together, and they didn't know all of it."

If they hadn't known all of it, and he hadn't seen his mother in a decade… "How do *you* know this is what happened?"

He bowed his head briefly before meeting her eyes. "From experience."

It took a few seconds to register, but when it did…

She shook her head slightly, her gaze still locked with his. "I see."

And she did. These new facts sliced open her heart. She'd thought she'd known Nash when they'd dated. She'd always sensed the pain under his easy smile. Understood there were things so awful from his past he might not ever be able to share them. But she hadn't known this.

"You could have told me," she said softly. "You know, back then."

He looked away.

Apparently, he disagreed. She straightened, forcing herself to get her head back to the here and now, not stuck in the way back when.

"Now that I know more about her past, I think she's terrified of you leaving her." The more Amy thought about it, the more obvious it became. "She is much more comfortable with me when you're in the room. But the instant you left today—well, I think she has no idea if she'll be left by herself, dragged to another home or if she'll ever see you again. How long have you had custody?"

"A little over a week. But I've spent time with her almost every day since December."

Amy sagged on the stool. She hadn't realized… No wonder Ruby was so scared. Amy never should have pushed for her own agenda, having Ruby come to her apartment without Nash.

"Well, spending time alone isn't going to work until it sinks in you will always come back for her."

"You're right." He stretched his head back. "Listen, there are a few other things you should know."

She braced herself.

"Since she never knew when she'd have food, she hoards it. I find all kinds of snacks in her bedroom. Sometimes under her pillow or stuck in a shoe. And if she wakes up and I'm not around, she screams. Loud. I bought walkie-talkies so I can go outside if she naps, which she doesn't do very often."

"That breaks my heart."

"Mine, too." He tapped the table, raw honesty pouring from his expression. Then he pointed to the living room. "I bought her all those toys, but she won't play with them. Barely looks at them."

"I noticed the same earlier."

"The therapist told me this is common in severely neglected kids."

"Will she overcome any of this?" Amy held her breath. *Please let him say yes.*

"Most likely. If she feels secure. That's why I moved back. Called the pastor when Dottie told me about the mentor program."

Something in his tone, the dip of his shoulder, clued her into something she'd missed since seeing him again. He didn't want to be back here. He never would have stepped foot in Sweet Dreams again if it hadn't been for Ruby.

Because of me. Because I'm here.

Her heart hurt all over again. Ten years and the wound hadn't fully healed.

"All these questions... Does this mean you still want to help her?" The question came unexpectedly, and Amy almost jumped.

Knowing what Nash had told her, did she still want to help Ruby?

Yes!

The intensity of the thought surprised her. But she had to protect her heart where Nash was concerned. She couldn't trust him with it. She might not even be able to trust herself with it. She was willing to take that chance if it meant bringing sunshine to the little girl who'd only known darkness.

"I want to help her. But I think we're expecting too much of her too soon."

"What do you suggest?" His eyebrows drew together, and he clasped his hands tightly.

"In the pastor's office, we all agreed that Ruby's needs come first, right?"

"Yes," he practically growled.

"Then you and I are going to have to put aside our issues to let her get used to me."

"I'm not following."

"The three of us are going to have to spend time together if Ruby's ever going to trust me enough to be alone with me."

He looked nauseous. Irritation flared in her chest. *Welcome to the club, buddy. It isn't easy for me to be around you, either.*

"You'd really do that…given what I put you through?"

She gave him a firm nod. "Yes. But we need to make it crystal clear to Ruby we are only friends, and there will never, ever be anything romantic between us. I don't want her to be confused about my role in her life."

"Of course. Never, ever will there be anything romantic between us."

"Then we agree." She should be thankful. But his *never, ever* had been more forceful than hers.

"Agreed." He rounded the island and stuck out his hand. She placed hers into it, and his rough, warm skin caused the hair on her arms to rise. He smelled familiar, like aftershave and leather. She snatched her hand back.

Never, ever.

Wouldn't be difficult as far as she was concerned.

"For how long?" he asked.

"For as long as it takes."

Chapter Four

"I'm going to soak up a few rays while you create your masterpieces. I'll be sitting out here if you need me." Nash slid open the patio door while Amy and Ruby dipped paintbrushes into a cup of water. Once he closed the door and sat in a wrought iron chair, he glanced through the glass at Ruby. Her paintbrush was raised and her eyes locked on him. He waved. She didn't wave back, just resumed sloshing her paintbrush on the paper. A good sign.

The cool wind whooshed under his collar. He welcomed it. Being cooped up indoors had never been his style, and hovering in the kitchen for the previous hour, trying not to notice Amy, had ramped up his nerves. He was still attracted to her. Maybe even more than before. When they'd dated, he'd been young and brash and out to prove something, and now...well, he had nothing left to prove. He'd thought being the best bull rider in the world would wipe away his childhood, make him feel like *somebody*. But rather than giving him an identity, all those championships had merely hammered home the fact he was alone. No loved one to celebrate with.

No wife to shower with his financial blessings. As a result, he'd taken more and more risks. And grown hollow inside.

Having Amy around reminded him of the emptiness all too well.

He'd forgotten her rich laugh, the way she always smelled like she'd just baked cookies, the sweet way she had with people. Her patience with Ruby had nearly choked him up earlier. He hadn't realized how overwhelmed he'd felt since finding out Ruby existed. Only two days had passed since Amy had agreed to mentor Ruby. Once the painting session ended, they would talk to Ruby about Amy's role in her life. They'd keep it simple.

Although every cell in his body wanted to stand, to pace, to *do something*, he forced himself to sit there for Ruby's sake. He'd remain where she could see him. Didn't want her thinking he'd abandoned her or something. Amy's insight about Ruby being afraid he'd leave made sense. Growing up, how many times had he felt the same?

But sitting still was hard. He longed to check the stalls in the horse barn again. Nothing but the best for his horses. They'd be arriving tomorrow. Most of them were retired rodeo horses he'd purchased over the years from washed-up cowboys no longer able to support non-competing animals. Nash had been paying Wade to pasture them. In a way, Wade had pastured him, too. For the past decade, one of Wade's empty guest cottages had been where Nash crashed when not touring. Wade owned a lot of prime land in Wyoming and oversaw a lucrative horse breeding business as well as a cow-calf operation. Wade's employees took good care of Nash's horses, and he never worried about them, knowing they were living the good life.

Yesterday he'd organized the tack room, supervised the hay delivery and checked the pasture and fences with Ruby by his side. She liked the outdoors. Acted more like a normal kid outside than in. He'd been the same way.

The sliding door opened, and Amy poked her head out. "We're done. Come and see Ruby's picture."

He pushed himself to stand, wincing as his hips adjusted. His injuries had all healed, but most days his body felt like it belonged to an older person, not to a man in his prime.

"Let's see what you made, RuRu." He stopped behind her chair, and she looked over her shoulder at him, hope and fear in her expression. He recognized it well. As a kid, he'd never known when his mother would scream at him for no reason. Living with her had been tumultuous in every way. That's why he'd been so grateful for Hank, the man who'd introduced him to bull riding. As a kid, Nash had spent his summers traveling to rodeos with the cowboy who'd briefly dated his mother.

"It's a bunny," she whispered as her slender shoulders slumped. He frowned. Did she think he'd make fun of her or something?

"I love how you made the bunny blue and purple." He knelt beside her, kissing her forehead. "You did a bee-yoo-tiful job."

Her shining eyes met his, and she wrapped her arms around his neck so tightly he almost choked.

"This painting is a keeper." He patted her on the back. "We're going to have to figure out a place to hang it."

"Thanks, Daddy."

Amy had been cleaning the supplies. She packed everything into a large quilted tote bag.

"You know who else we need to thank?" He tweaked her nose. "Miss Amy. She's a good art teacher, don't you think?"

Ruby's face fell, but she nodded once.

"Do you want me to say thanks with you?" He kept his arm around her waist.

"Yes."

"Okay. Ready?" He held his finger up. "Thank you, Miss Amy."

"Thank you, Miss Amy," Ruby mimicked politely.

"You are very welcome, Ruby." Amy smiled. "I enjoyed painting with you. In fact, I have lots of fun projects for us to do together."

She gave him a pointed look. That was his cue. Time to talk to Ruby about her. He'd keep it simple, the way Amy asked, but his memories and regrets warred in his mind.

"Here. Have a seat, Amy." He pulled a chair out for her, and they all sat around the kitchen table. Nash turned to Ruby. "I know this has been a lot of new stuff for you, RuRu. Now that we're settled in here, I want you to have some girl-time now and then. Don't want you stuck inside with an ornery old cowboy like me every second. Miss Amy would like to spend more time with you."

"Don't you want me anymore, Daddy?" Ruby's stricken face was like a kick to the ribs.

Nash inwardly groaned. *God, why didn't I anticipate this? I'm clueless at this dad stuff.*

"Of course I want you, Ruby. Why would you think

I don't?" He plucked her out of her seat and set her on his lap. "I'm your daddy. Forever. Remember? You will always live with me. I will always want you."

"And I don't have to live at Miss Amy's?" Her forehead was creased with worry.

"No! Is that what you thought? No, Ruby. Amy is our friend, and she knows you've been through some rough patches and wants to make life a little happier for you. That's all."

Amy reached over to place her hand on Ruby's. "Your daddy is right. I'm not here to take you away. You'll always live with him. At church I signed up to hang out with a little boy or girl, and the pastor thought I'd enjoy spending a few afternoons with you each week. Your dad and I are old friends—just friends. I'm here for you, not for your dad."

As if he needed to be reminded.

He tried to appear upbeat. "What Miss Amy is trying to say is she's not my girlfriend or anything."

"When I said I'm here for you, Ruby, I meant it. And it's just a few times a week. Do you have any questions?"

Ruby looked like she had plenty but was too scared to ask them.

"Well, if you think of any, you can always ask me. We can talk about anything you'd like. I'm a good listener." Amy stood, picking up her tote bag and waving at Ruby. "And now I'd better get out of your hair. See you soon, Ruby."

"I'll walk you out." Nash followed her to the front door, pausing on the porch. "What's next?"

"That's up to you."

Her fresh-baked cookie smell hit him full force,

made him want to lean in and touch her hair. He backed up a step. "Next week, Tuesday again?"

She shook her head, her pretty brown eyes intense. "I would like to see Ruby more frequently until she's comfortable with me. I'm worried too much time between visits won't serve her well. What about Saturday? The three of us could have lunch at Dottie's Diner or something."

"Good idea. Dottie's Diner. Saturday." He tried to pretend he was pleased for Ruby's sake, but the ping of hope in his chest wasn't about Ruby. He liked being around Amy. And though they would never be a couple again, he didn't mind hovering around the edges of her warmth.

He just had to be smart enough to douse any fantasies of a future with her. They didn't have one, and he'd best not forget it.

"You'll have to bring her to the Easter egg hunt," Amy's mother said. "It's a week from Saturday. Mark it on your calendar."

Her mother, Ginger Deerson, was practical. Outspoken, but practical. And Amy needed a dose of honesty right now. Because watching Nash interact with Ruby had thawed a tiny patch of her heart. What if that spot spread through the whole thing? It would be a disaster.

"I'll mention it, Mom." Amy sipped hot tea in her parents' living room. She'd driven there after leaving Nash's. The one-story brick house looked the same as it had her entire life, and it always comforted her. A safe place in a stormy world. Being around Nash was throwing her emotions into hurricane conditions.

"I finally heard from your brother. He thinks he'll be home later this summer."

"Really?" It had been months since she'd seen Matt. Older than her by two years, Matt was currently on a sea tour as an officer of the navy. "Did he say when?"

"You know him. Can never get a straight answer. At least you fill me in on your life." Mom clicked a pen and jotted notes on her ever-present scratch pad. "I'm not a hundred percent sold on you being around that bull rider so much, but we'll make sure Ruby melds right in with the Sweet Dreams community. Does she like animals?"

"Animals? I think so." Amy let the part about "that bull rider" slide. Mom had never liked Nash. Thought he was too wild for her. She'd wanted Amy to find someone dependable, someone who held a steady job with benefits. Well, a few years ago Amy had found Mr. Dependable, and she'd fared no better with John Mc-Cloud than she had with Nash. Both men had seemed on the verge of proposing. Both men had skipped town.

She still didn't know why they'd left her behind.

Mom rapidly clicked the pen a few times, which meant she was scheming. Her short brown hair had been curled and locked into place with super-hold spray. "Dooley Hill found a batch of kittens in the barn. He's trying to find them all homes. Maybe Ruby would like one."

"Maybe. I don't know." Her mother was the activity director at Sweet Dreams Senior Center. She knew everyone's business, including Amy's. Meddling aside, Amy loved her. Without her parents' love and emotional support, she didn't know what she would do. "It's not really my place to get her a kitten."

Her mother waved, scoffing. "You're doing the man

an enormous favor after the way he treated you. It certainly *is* your place. Find out what color kitten she wants, and I'll have Dooley set one aside. They're still too young to leave their mama, but they'll be weaned in a month or so. I'm pretty sure he said they were tiger-striped or black, but he might have a calico in the bunch, too. I'll ask." She grabbed her cell phone and texted Dooley, an eighty-year-old regular at the senior center.

"Dooley texts?" Amy's mind was officially blown.

"Well, of course he does." Mom's tone was incredulous. "Who doesn't?"

"Clearly I'm out of touch. But back to Ruby…she might not be ready for a cat."

Mom pulled her are-you-crazy face. "What is there to be ready for? It's a kitten. Little girls love kittens. Remember Renaldo? You dressed that butterball up and pushed him around in your plastic shopping cart for hours. The two of you had more fun together."

Renaldo had been an extremely obliging feline. Amy had loved that cat. Maybe she should take one of Dooley's kittens for herself.

And maybe she was avoiding the real reason she was here.

"Mom, I have a question for you, and I need you to take about thirty seconds and really consider it before answering."

"Thirty seconds?" She scowled. "What is that supposed to mean?"

"Just that you tend to toss out answers first and reflect on what you said later." She didn't want to offend her mother, but…

"You got me." Mom laughed, setting the pen and her phone on the arm of the chair. Her oversize navy

T-shirt hung loosely, hiding the evidence of her love of desserts, which Amy had unfortunately inherited. "Go ahead. Shoot."

Was this wise? Asking her very biased mother for her opinion? She decided to go for it.

"Why do you think Nash left?"

Mom opened her mouth to reply, then closed it. After a few seconds ticked by, she folded her hands in her lap. "I think he was selfish. Maybe he thought you would hold him back. Or he might have met another girl on the road. You always had morals, and I think they made you attractive to him, but they also could have pushed him away. Who knows? Maybe he liked the limelight, wanted to be a big star."

Hearing her mother's opinion was hard, but it wasn't anything she hadn't told herself many times.

"Why?" Mom studied her. "Don't tell me he wants to get back together with you."

"No." She shook her head. "Seeing him again dredged up all these things I've pushed away for a long time. Like how he left. And then John…"

"John was a coward, Amy. I never would have encouraged you to date him if I'd known he was going to quit his job and move away with no warning. You wouldn't have been happy with him."

"I don't know about that. He was a nice man. I don't think I would have been miserable, but you're probably right. I wouldn't have been very happy either." It had been a few years since she'd dated John, and Amy didn't miss him one bit.

"Did he ever give you any explanation?" Mom had badgered her about John for months after he left, but Amy had been so hurt and embarrassed, she'd refused to say anything. Eventually her mother had stopped asking.

"Yes." She remembered every word John had said that night. "Sweet Dreams stifled him. He didn't want to be a bank manager."

"Well, what *did* he want to be?" She might as well have said, "Who does he think he is?"

"I have no idea. He said he was crashing with a friend in Miami until he figured it out. He mentioned running a fishing charter in the Keys."

"And that was it?"

"Yep."

"A fishing charter. John? I'm not seeing it. Had he ever been on a boat?"

Amy shrugged. "I don't know. Doesn't really matter."

"Do you miss him?" Mom reached for her pen again.

"No."

"And Nash?" The pen clicked.

"It's been ten years, Mom. We're not getting back together. In fact, we told Ruby we're friends and there isn't anything romantic between us."

"Good. Don't want that little one confused. Losing her mama must have been difficult enough. I don't want you confused either."

"That makes two of us." She hadn't told her mother all the details about Ruby, only what Nash had approved.

Mom's phone dinged. "Oh, good. Dooley says he has three tigers, one black-and-white kitten and no calicos. Too bad. Little girls tend to love those calicos. Are you staying for dinner?"

"Sure. Want me to help?" They rose and went to the kitchen.

"Why don't you chop the lettuce for a salad? Oh, and Amy?"

"Yeah?" She opened the fridge, glancing back at her mother.

"Be careful. You have a big heart, and I don't want to see it broken."

Amy found the lettuce. At least she and her mom agreed on something. She had no intention of letting her heart be broken. She'd be careful, just like her mother advised.

"Whew! That went smoothly." Nash wiped his forehead and set his hat back on his head. "Thanks for coming to help."

Clint, Wade and Marshall stood along the fence, watching the horses get used to their new pasture. Nash had visited them at Wade's whenever he could. And now they would be here full time. He was looking forward to caring for them.

Horses, his buddies and rodeos had always made sense to him. Women? Not so much.

"I see Crank is as rowdy as ever." Clint, tall with dark brown hair and piercing blue eyes, watched Crank prancing along the fence line. "He's showing off for Dixie."

"He's always showing off for Dixie." Nash chuckled. Crank was his go-to horse, his favorite, the one he rode as much as possible. Dixie and Crank, still in their prime, were the youngest of his horses, and they were the only ones he rode. The other four were enjoying their twilight years being pampered.

"I've never seen a horse so similar to its owner." Wade's blond hair was streaked from the sun, and his blue eyes were set in a permanent squint. Made him look like he was always smiling. Wade shook his head. "What a showboat."

"Showboat? Me? No way. I'm a serious, respectable gentleman."

"Gentleman?" Marshall let out a guffaw. "If you're a gentleman, then I'm a royal prince."

"You wound me, Marshall." Nash pretended to clasp his heart. "I hold doors open for ladies and say please and thank you and all that."

"Speaking of ladies…" Wade had his innocent look on, but it wasn't fooling Nash one bit. He was going to ask about Amy, but Nash wasn't talking about her. Period. Wade grinned. "You and Amy were quite the pair back in the day. How are things between you now?"

Nash gave Wade the stink eye then turned to Marshall, the easiest going of the bunch. "So you're really working for your sister's husband? I thought you weren't keen on cowboying anymore."

Marshall's face fell. He and Marshall were about the same height, but Marshall had always been stockier. Pure muscle. His dark hair and scruff gave him a rugged air. "Belle needs me. Now that she's pregnant, she's scared. I don't mind."

"But I thought you liked working for the Beatty Brothers." Clint, usually quiet, shifted to face Marshall. "You've got serious skills fixing big machinery. You sure you can't just visit Belle now and then?"

"No. I told her I'd be there for her, and I'll be there for her." Marshall's tone left no room for arguments. Nash had never fully understood Marshall's devotion to his twin sister, Belle, but lately it made sense. He'd be there for Ruby, too, no matter what.

They let the subject drop. Wade addressed Clint. "It's nice to see you again. You finally broke away from the bride. How is life at Rock Step Ranch?"

Clint colored. "Perfect. Twister's going to be a fine herding dog."

"The honeymoon must be over if you're talking about a border collie and not Lexi," Wade teased.

"Lexi's great. I still can't believe we're married. She's planning about a bajillion weddings here in town. She's happy, which makes me happy." Clint looked around. "Hey, where's Ruby?"

Nash had been keeping an eye on her and pointed a few feet away where she sat cross-legged in the grass, watching the horses as if she couldn't get enough of them. He'd introduced her to his friends earlier, and she'd sat on the picnic table, watching them unload horses and get everything settled in the barn. She hadn't made a peep.

"I've got a good little helper here." Nash was surprised at the emotion welling up within him. Her tiny fingers were picking apart a blade of grass, and her long hair played in the breeze. He loved that girl. "Feeding and mucking stalls will be much easier with Ruby helping."

She glanced up at him with shining eyes. He winked at her. Shocking how much earning her trust meant to him.

Wade laughed. "Looks like she approves."

"I almost forgot." Clint smacked his thigh. "I'll be right back." He jogged off in the direction of his truck.

Marshall ambled over to Ruby and crouched next to her. "I don't know if you like candy, but I brought you some just in case." He handed her a small white sack. She stared up at him through wide eyes and held the bag. He pointed to it. "Go ahead. You can open it."

She gulped but made no move to open the bag.

"Maybe later." He smiled at her and rose.

Clint loped back, slightly out of breath, and handed Ruby a stuffed brown horse. "From Lexi and me. Welcome home, Ruby."

She hugged the horse to her chest but didn't say anything.

Nash went over and lifted her into his arms. "What do you say, RuRu?"

"Thanks." The word was barely audible.

"Now I feel like a jerk. I didn't bring her anything." Wade sighed, kicking at the dirt. "Ruby, would you like a real pony? I can get you one. Just say the word."

"Wade! You can't promise her a pony!" Nash rolled his eyes skyward.

"I like ponies." Ruby's lashes curled up, revealing innocent and hopeful blue-green eyes.

Wade got close and kept his voice low. "I'll talk to your dad about it. Don't you worry. Next time I come, I'll bring you something real nice, sweetheart."

"You don't have to bring gifts," Nash said, although it warmed his heart they all cared.

"I want to. This pretty little thing should have a nice gift from her uncle Wade. I never thought I'd be an uncle."

"You could get married and have a few kids of your own." Clint grinned.

"No way. Not me. Married, kids—you fooling?" Wade let out a loud laugh. "All this talk is making me hungry. Who's up for pizza? I'm starving."

"I'm in," Marshall said.

"Same here." Clint pulled his keys out of his pocket, and they began making their way to their trucks.

"We'll be out in a minute. Let me grab Ruby's coat." Nash and Ruby walked hand in hand toward the house. Wade's comment about never getting married or having kids had been Nash's motto for a decade. Now that he had Ruby, he couldn't say *never*. God had given him a precious gift with this little girl. But marriage? He'd wanted one woman, and he couldn't have her.

One precious gift was enough in a lifetime. He'd make the most of what he had and not think about what he didn't. It was the only way he'd gotten this far in life. It was the only way he'd make it through the rest.

Chapter Five

"Howdy, puddin'!" With a pen tucked behind her ear, Dottie Lavert stopped in front of their booth at Dottie's Diner. Amy wasn't sure how she'd gotten the nickname puddin', but Dottie had been calling her that her entire life. "Hope you're keeping hotshot in line here, and, land's sake, if it isn't little buttercup."

Amy pressed her lips together to keep from laughing. She'd forgotten Dottie called Nash hotshot. Apparently, Ruby was buttercup. This would be the second time the three of them were out in public together. Would the people in town assume Amy had gotten back together with him?

Let them think what they wanted. She knew the truth. Besides, she doubted anyone even remembered she'd dated Nash all those years ago.

She was here for Ruby. Unfortunately, Amy hadn't made much progress with the child to this point. It wasn't as if she'd spent a ton of time with her, though. Ruby would get used to her. Eventually.

Nash, sitting across from her and Ruby, shimmied

out of the booth and gave Dottie a big hug, lifting her off her feet. "Missed you, lil' mama."

"I just saw you a few days ago. It sure is good to have you back, hon." Her smile grew from ear to ear. Nash lowered her to the ground then took a seat. She dabbed under her misty eyes before getting down to business. "Okay, kids, what'll it be?"

Amy trailed her finger down the laminated menu until she found the kids' section. Turning to Ruby, she asked, "Do you like hamburgers? Or hot dogs? The chicken fingers are good."

"If you're in the mood for breakfast, I can make a stack of flapjacks with whipped cream on top, butter-cup." Dottie's pen was poised above her small pad of paper. "And some crispy bacon. How does that sound?"

Ruby nodded.

"Are you sure?" Amy asked her. "If you'd rather have something else…"

"Whip cream," Ruby said decisively.

Amy caught Nash's eye. He shrugged, grinning.

Oh, my. His smile had always done her in. Her heart was beating way too fast. She pretended to study the menu.

Nash ordered a double cheeseburger with fries, and Amy took a chance on the daily special. The diner's home cooking was always delicious, but she wasn't all that hungry.

"Mom told me Dooley Hill has kittens needing homes." Amy looked at Nash. "Might be something to consider, you know, if your barn has mice."

"Uh-huh. Mice. Sure." He glanced around the diner.

Ruby tapped Amy's arm. "Do kitties live in barns? Do they eat mice?"

"Some do." She shifted to see Ruby better. "And some live in people's houses. They're called house cats. They curl up on your lap and purr and go potty in a litter box. But cats are independent. They aren't like puppies. You have to let them warm up to you."

"Oh."

"Why? Do you think you'd like a kitten of your own?"

"Yes." She wasn't jumping up and down in her seat or anything, but her eyes held hope—so much hope. Amy wanted to squish the child to her chest and never let her go. Ruby turned to Nash. "Daddy, could I have a kitten?"

He didn't answer. In fact, he seemed awfully distracted. Amy frowned. Either that or he didn't want to be seen with her. She waved to get Nash's attention. "Nash."

"Hmm?"

"There are tiger-striped kittens and a black-and-white one. They won't be weaned for another month, but if you're interested, I'll let Dooley know."

"A cat?" He grimaced. "What would we want one of those for, RuRu?"

"I like kitties." The simple words were innocent, straightforward.

"Litter boxes get stinky. Might need rubber gloves to deal with it. I don't know…"

"I'll clean it, Daddy."

"We'll have to think about it." Nash excused himself to say hi to someone who'd walked in.

Disappointment at his lack of interest coiled inside her. Was she boring him?

"I like any color kitty, Miss Amy," she said earnestly.

"I do, too." She pushed her irritation away and concentrated on Ruby. "If you had to choose, though, which would be your favorite?"

"The fluffiest." Her *l*'s sounded like *w*'s.

"I'll tell you what, I'll ask Dooley which is the fluffiest. Then if your daddy says you can have a kitten, Dooley will save it for you. Now, why don't we draw while they cook our food?" Amy picked up the crayons Dottie had dropped off. She selected the red one and handed the small box to Ruby. Flipping over her paper placemat, she drew a tree and a sun.

Ruby watched. "Can you draw a horsey?"

"I can try." She sketched a rough outline of a horse, pleased the topic had loosened Ruby's tongue. Maybe Ruby was getting used to her. "What color would you like it?"

"Brown." Ruby handed her a crayon.

"I have an idea." Amy gave her the brown crayon back. "Why don't you color it in?"

"I'm no good." She put the crayon on the table, ducking her chin.

"Why do you say that?" Amy stretched her neck to try to see Ruby's face. "You don't have to be good at coloring. It's fun. You can scribble or stay in the lines. It's up to you."

"I'll get in trouble." Ruby glanced up. "Bad girls scribble."

"No. You won't get in trouble for coloring or scribbling. Not with me. Why don't you try?" Amy held her breath as Ruby's fingers inched toward the crayon. She picked it up, checking Amy's reaction. She nodded to her. "Go ahead. Color anywhere on the paper you'd like."

Ruby clutched the crayon in her fist. Amy made a mental note to show her the proper way to hold a pencil later. As Ruby brought the crayon to the placemat, Amy inwardly urged her on, but the tiny brown dot Ruby made must have spooked her. She dropped the crayon and backed into the corner of the booth.

"Where's Daddy?" Her voice held a tremor.

"He'll be right back." Had Ruby been punished for coloring? Amy scrambled to come up with her next move. She pointed to the brown line. "What a great start. I think I'll color a cloud on my paper."

Amy took the red crayon and drew a cloud. Then, with the green crayon, she filled it in, purposely scribbling outside the lines. "There. Perfect."

Ruby scooted closer. "Clouds aren't green."

"Today my cloud is green. Sometimes I draw yellow clouds or pink ones. That's the fun of coloring. You can make things whatever shade you'd like." Their drinks arrived, and she thanked Dottie before turning back to Ruby. "Did you get in trouble for coloring?"

She hung her head.

"When you're learning to do something, you don't have to be perfect. It doesn't always come out the way you want. But you keep trying and you get better. It's okay to make mistakes. Like scissors—have you ever cut anything?"

"I cut the tater bag open."

Amy had to refrain from putting her arm around her. A potato bag. She could only imagine why a small child would need to open a bag of potatoes. She had the urge to tell Dottie to double the whipped cream on those flapjacks and bring an extra serving on the side, as well.

"Tuesday I'll bring some safety scissors, and I'll teach you how to cut paper. We can make a paper chain."

Amy continued to color as she watched Ruby from the corner of her eye. The child was discreetly tucking sugar packets into her pockets. Should she say something? All that raw sugar wasn't good for anyone. Nash's warning about hoarding food hadn't included any advice. Should she tell Ruby to put the packets back?

Nash returned, sliding into the booth. "Sorry about that. I've been trying to reach a local farrier, and Clint told me I could probably catch him here today. What did I miss?"

"Nothing much. Just coloring." Amy's annoyance returned. Surely Nash could have called and left a message with the farrier. He knew how difficult it had been for Ruby to be alone with Amy before.

Now she was just being petty. She wanted to confide in him about the sugar packets and coloring situation, but it wasn't the time.

"Did I tell you I've got the horses out to pasture? Wade, Clint and Marshall came out yesterday to help."

"I got a pony!" Ruby's eyes lit up like fireworks.

"A pony?" Amy plastered a grin on her face although she wasn't sure itty-bitty Ruby was ready for a pony. "What color is it?"

"Brown and it has a white dot on its head."

"It's not a real pony. Not yet, at least." Nash winked at Ruby. "Did you decide on a name?"

"Brownie."

"Brownie?" Nash pulled a face. Amy almost warned him not to say anything, that Ruby could name her horse anything she wanted. "Now you've got me hungry for brownies with chocolate frosting and sprinkles all over them."

Amy relaxed. Her fear had been for nothing. Nash always seemed to know exactly what to say to Ruby. Maybe she was being too hard on him for his apparent lack of interest today.

"Good name," Amy said. "I can't wait to meet this Brownie."

Dottie set huge plates of food in front of them. "Y'all just holler if you need anything. Is that enough whipped cream, buttercup?"

With shining eyes, Ruby nodded to her.

"You tell your daddy to bring you around more often." Dottie turned to Nash. "Seeing as you've got time on your hands, you should stop by Monday morning. Big Bob, Jerry Cornell from Rock Step Ranch and Stan Reynolds have a standing coffee date every Monday at seven thirty. They'd love to catch up with you. Buttercup can have breakfast at the counter with me while you gab."

Amy spread a paper napkin across her lap, certain Nash would never in a million years agree to have coffee with three old-timers. He'd always resented authority.

"Thanks, lil' mama. I'll be here."

Amy almost choked. Nash hanging out with Big Bob, Jerry and Stan? Did she know him at all anymore? Obviously not.

"Want me to cut your pancakes for you, Ruby?" Amy reached over to slice them into small squares. The melting whipped cream slid to the side. "By the way, the church is having an Easter egg hunt next Saturday. Maybe we could all go together."

Nash squirted ketchup on his plate. "Ooh, that's a great idea. RuRu, I'll help you find the eggs if you'll give me all your Snickers bars."

"What's Snickers?" Ruby nibbled on her bacon.

"Just the most delicious candy bar on the planet." He grabbed the burger with both hands and met Amy's eyes. "You still coming this Tuesday?"

"Yes. Ruby and I have plans to make paper chains. I'll come over Thursday, too."

His face brightened in relief. Maybe he was just having a hard time adjusting to fatherhood. His move back could be difficult for him, too. Which made her wonder…how much of Nash's humor was an act for Ruby's sake? And what was it costing him? She'd known him once, but this man had a lot of layers she didn't recognize.

He could keep his layers. She didn't need to know him. He certainly didn't seem all that interested in getting to know her.

His brain might get addled if he didn't get out and socialize more often. Nash watched the countryside pass by on his way to town Monday morning. In her car seat behind him, Ruby clutched Brownie. Church yesterday had been a relief. He'd reconnected with a few people he recognized from high school, and he'd enjoyed introducing Ruby. Sure, a small crowd formed around him afterward, and he'd signed a few autographs, but he was used to it. Had been signing autographs for years.

The only downside to church had been his distraction during the service itself. Amy had sat with her parents on the other side, three pews up. He'd tried not to stare at all the dark hair cascading down her back, but time and again he'd failed. Maybe if he had something to do with his days besides taking care of Ruby, he'd have less time to linger on his memories of Amy.

For years he'd been busy traveling, competing and keeping up with the business side of his career. Stripped of the hustle-bustle, his life now loomed wide open, and the solitude was getting to him. He missed having a purpose. Missed the camaraderie with his bull riding buddies.

That's why he'd latched on to Dottie's invitation to join her husband and the other guys. He'd always admired Big Bob Lavert. Shortly after Hank had died, Nash had been sent to Yearling Group Home for teen boys. Big Bob and Dottie had run Yearling, and they'd been more parents to him than his own warped mother, who'd been incarcerated at the time. Big Bob had taught him how a man of integrity acted.

Sometimes Nash still missed Hank. He'd never forget the summers he'd spent with his mother's ex-boyfriend. He'd learned everything he'd needed to know about competing in rodeos from the cowboy, and the training had launched his career. Although Hank had been a compulsive gambler and an alcoholic, he'd gotten Nash out of the terror of living with his mother for three months every year. For that, Nash would be eternally grateful.

He turned onto Main Street and parked near Dottie's Diner. He got out and opened the back door to help Ruby. The wind was blowing strong this morning. As he lifted her up, she let out a cry, pointing to Brownie. He grabbed the horse and hurried them both inside.

"Whew. The weather is ornery today." He set Ruby down near the counter. She hopped onto a round, red vinyl–topped stool bolted to the floor. Dottie came out from the kitchen and grinned. Her light gray hair had poufy bangs and was twisted up in the back with a clip. He tipped his hat to her. "Hey, lil' mama."

"The fellas are back there. I'll take a break with buttercup here." She leaned over the counter in front of Ruby. "I made some waffles. You like them?"

Ruby, beaming, nodded.

"Good. I think a glass of chocolate milk will help them go down. What do you think?"

Nash squeezed Ruby's shoulder. "I'll be right over there if you need me. Remember what we talked about—don't take the sugar packets. Oh, and make sure that horse stays in line."

"What have I always said about horses in my diner? None allowed." Dottie crossed her arms over her ample chest. "Oh, wait. Are you talking about the one you're holding? He looks harmless enough. He can stay."

Ruby hugged Brownie tightly.

"I'm just teasing ya, buttercup. I'll be right back with the food."

Nash headed to the booth in the back where the men were drinking coffee and laughing about something. Big Bob started to get up, but Nash waved him down.

"Dottie said you might join us, but we didn't know if you'd show up." Big Bob looked bigger and older than Nash remembered, but his eyes were shrewd and kind. "Fellas, this is Nash Bolton, two-time PBR world champion, Touring Pro Division champion and runner up at the World Finals. He also rode the meanest bull alive and lived to tell about it. Nash, I don't know if you remember Jerry Cornell and Stan Reynolds."

"Good to see you again." Nash shook their hands and slid into the booth next to Stan.

"What was riding Murgatroyd really like?" Jerry leaned forward. His wiry frame reminded Nash of Hank and the cowboys he'd spent all those years with. He'd toured with the best of them.

"It was like trying to hop on a comet," Nash said. "That rotten bull lit me up good."

"Oh-ho! You hear that, Stan? A comet." Looking pleased with himself, Jerry sat back and slurped his coffee.

"I heard you, Jerry. Don't get all smug. I never said Murgatroyd was easy."

"You implied it. Didn't he compare the beast to a dairy cow, Big Bob?"

"You did, Stan, and it's time you eat those words."

"I'm not eating nothing." Stan threw his wadded up napkin on the table. "I don't care what you say. Night Fright is meaner and bigger than Murgatroyd."

Nash sat back in his seat, thoroughly enjoying this exchange. This had been what he'd missed for months—smack talk mixed with an obsession of all things rodeo.

"Well, Nash rode Night Fright, too, so let's get his opinion," Big Bob said. All three men looked at Nash expectantly.

"Night Fright is a tremendous bull. Strong. Cunning. He knows all the riders' tricks. But I figured him out. Rode him the full eight seconds and then some. Murgatroyd, on the other hand…"

An awed silence descended for a moment.

"You see?" Jerry smacked his hand on the table. "Night Fright isn't all he's cracked up to be, so you can stop yammerin' on about him."

Stan glared. "He just said he's strong and cunning."

"You know what bull to really watch out for?" Nash made sure he'd caught their attention. When they'd leaned in, he continued. "Trombone."

"Trombone," they echoed.

"He'll be the one to beat in another year or two."

"You don't say?" Stan pulled a small box out of his chest pocket and tapped out a toothpick.

Big Bob gestured for the waitress to bring Nash a cup of coffee. "You hungry, son?"

The waitress poured a cup, and Nash ordered eggs, home fries and sausage patties.

"How you liking that property?" Jerry asked. "You're out near Four Forks Road, right?"

"Love it." Nash took a sip of the piping hot brew. "I think Ruby's going to be a little country girl. She's happy out there."

"I hear you got your horses in," Big Bob said. "You gonna put up more fence?"

"I'm going to have to. I need more pasture. Who do I talk to about installing some?"

"Roscoe Lovey," Jerry said. "He's the best around. Fastest, too. You putting up cattle?"

"No. I'm not sure what I'm doing yet. Been thinking about maybe… Nah, never mind." He felt the heat rising up his neck. Why was it so hard to admit he'd been thinking about teaching kids how to ride bulls?

"What were you going to say?" Stan sucked on the end of the toothpick.

"I'd have to wait until Ruby's in school, anyway, but… I've been thinking about opening a training center. Teaching kids how to ride bulls."

The three men stared at each other for a second then

turned as one to him. Their grinning faces told him what he hadn't dared expect. The idea was good.

"That's the best plan I've heard in a long time," Jerry said. "Some of these kids are like pronghorns running across the plains. Smart but skittish. If they had someone teaching 'em proper, they'd have a shot at the big time."

"I agree with Jerry," Big Bob said. "Having someone like you show them the ropes would make a big difference."

"I'm not sure," Nash said, toying with his coffee mug.

"You should at least talk to Billy Jacobs. He took over the high school rodeo program last year. I'm sure he could use some help if you wouldn't mind sparing a bit of your free time. Might give you an idea if working with kids is for you."

"I'll consider it. I've definitely got plenty of free time." Talking to the high school coach might be smart. Something still held him back, though. "I don't know if I should encourage anyone to ride bulls. Doctors wanted me to retire about seventy-two times. It's dangerous. I'm beat-up, and I'm only thirty-one."

"They're going to ride anyway, Nash." Big Bob leaned back, his hands on his impressive stomach. "You could help them avoid the injuries."

Nash frowned. "There's no avoiding the injuries. It's the most dangerous sport in the world for a reason."

"That's why it's so excitin'." Jerry got a faraway look in his eyes. "Makes me feel alive watching you young bucks get in the chute. Wish I was younger, so I could take a ride myself."

"Well, I'm thinking about it, but I'm not committing to it. Not yet, anyway."

"If you need help, we'll be over." Stan flicked the toothpick onto his plate.

"That's right," Big Bob said. "You need anything, just holler."

"Thanks," Nash said. "I might take you up on it. I'll keep you posted."

The other men started discussing the bull riding season, and he looked over his shoulder at Ruby. Dottie was pretending Brownie was trotting on the counter. His chest swelled. He hadn't had a home in ten years. Hadn't really had one before that either, with all the traveling he'd done even as a teen. But with this community, he could give one to Ruby. The Lord had blessed them.

Amy's pretty face came to mind.

What if he messed this—living in Sweet Dreams near her—up?

He couldn't. Not this time.

Saturday morning Amy searched the crowded church lawn for Nash and Ruby. Everywhere she looked stood happy families. Young mothers holding babies. Dads playing with toddlers. Grandparents smiling as school-age kids chased each other. Everyone seemed to be tending to small children. Everyone except her. The ache in her chest grew, and it had already been gnawing at her since opening her mailbox earlier.

She'd ripped open the envelope from a fabric manufacturer and read the dreaded words, "We regret to inform you…doesn't meet our needs at this time."

Rejected.

All these awful feelings of incompetency had

flooded her, and they hadn't left. It was as if a bully was chanting, *What did you expect? You didn't actually think you were good enough to have your own fabric line, did you?*

She could actually feel her face falling. She pasted her smile back on. No one needed to know she'd failed. God knew best. Maybe she wasn't meant to have a fabric line.

A man bumped into her, his towheaded toddler giggling from his perch on the man's shoulders. The guy apologized. She murmured she was fine.

But she wasn't fine.

No fabric line. No family of her own.

Oh, God, help me not want these things so much.

She spotted Nash in his cowboy hat, and her spirits sank lower. His eyes crinkled with laughter, and he was signing a paper someone held out for him. Autographing things for his fans.

Ugh. He had it all. The adoring crowd, the career he'd always wanted and a beautiful girl to raise as his own.

It wasn't fair.

Nash caught her eye and hitched his chin for her to come over. She almost rolled her eyes. A dozen people crowded around him. What did he need her for? She certainly wasn't going to ask him for an autograph. She debated going back to her car and driving to Lexi's for a whine session.

But then she spotted Ruby, and the child had that blank look on her face Amy had come to know all too well. This crowd probably scared the sweetheart. Amy hurried over to where they stood.

"Hey, Ruby, why don't you come over here? We need to get your plastic bag." Amy held her hand out, not knowing if Ruby would take it. Although Amy had spent Tuesday and Thursday with her making paper chains and reading picture books, Ruby still shied away from physical contact. To her surprise, Ruby gripped her hand and huddled next to her legs. Amy crouched down to look her in the eyes. "What's wrong, honey? Are you okay?"

Ruby's bottom lip pushed forward, and she gave her head a small shake.

"Come on. We'll get your bag and sit over there until the egg hunt starts. No one will bother us." Amy led her by the hand to the table set up near the sidewalk.

"Well, hello, Amy. My subway tile quilt is going much better than the dresden plate design. I don't know what I was thinking, taking on such a complicated pattern. Thanks for helping me. I see you've brought a friend to the egg hunt." Mrs. Jenkins, a retired librarian with short white hair and a welcoming face, handed Ruby a plastic grocery bag. "What's your name, sweetie?"

Ruby's hand tightened in Amy's.

"This is Ruby Bolton, Mrs. Jenkins." Amy gave the dear woman a big smile. "And this is her first Easter egg hunt, so I'm going to give her some pointers."

"Oh, right, Nash's little girl." Mrs. Jenkins gestured toward the church landscaping. "Look over there. Hope you get lots of eggs, Ruby. Don't let those boys push you around. Check under the bushes, too."

"Thanks, we'll keep that in mind." Amy led Ruby to a patch of grass on the outskirts of the lawn. Then she sat down cross-legged and, to her shock, Ruby sat in her lap. Amy closed her eyes, savoring the moment. *Thank You, God.*

"I never hunted eggs." Ruby stretched her neck back to see Amy. "Are they real?"

"No, honey. They're plastic. Each one has a surprise inside. That's why it's so fun."

"What if someone steals 'em all? Will the boys take mine?" She seemed on the verge of tears.

"There are lots of eggs here. I'll hold your hand the entire time, okay? I won't let anything happen to you or your eggs."

Ruby leaned back to rest against Amy's chest. Amy had to remind herself to breathe. This precious little girl finally trusted her enough to sit in her lap. Amy wrapped both arms around her, giving her a small hug. It didn't matter Ruby wasn't her child. This was almost as good. Before long a whistle blew.

"It's going to begin soon. We'd better go to the starting line." They walked hand in hand to the orange line someone had spray-painted on the lawn. Using a bullhorn, the pastor told everyone the rules. Nash loped over to them.

"Sorry about that." His eyes were all apologies to Amy.

She drew her shoulders back. She wasn't sure how she felt about him being a celebrity in Sweet Dreams. Did he care more about his fans than keeping an eye on Ruby? He should have noticed how upset she was. Maybe Mom was right and the lure of the limelight was why he'd left.

He rubbed his hands together and said to Ruby, "Are you ready to find some eggs?"

"Miss Amy's helping me. Don't let boys steal my eggs, Daddy."

He gave Amy a questioning look, but she didn't elaborate.

"I'll string up anyone who dares think about taking your eggs." He cracked his knuckles. Children and their parents crammed next to them behind the line, everyone waiting for the hunt to begin.

"On your mark. Get set. Go!"

All the kids ran, scattering in different directions. "This way, Ruby." Amy guided her to the shrubs around the church. Ruby saw a pink egg and quickly scooped it up. She held it in her hand as if it were pure gold.

"Oh, I see another one." Nash pointed to the birdbath. Ruby ran over and grabbed the purple egg.

Amy held the bag open, and Ruby dropped it in. She saw another one, but a little boy found it before she got there, and her eyes filled with tears.

"Not all of the eggs are for you, RuRu. They're for all the kids."

"Let's check over here, Ruby. Not many kids went this way." Amy held her hand as a few tears dropped, but when Ruby saw three eggs in the grass, she tore away and practically dove on them. Then she cradled them to her chest, her face triumphant.

"I got them!" She dumped them into the bag, too. They searched for several more minutes, finding eggs here and there before calling it quits. The three of them returned to the lawn near the parking lot and sat on the grass with the other families.

As Nash showed Ruby how to open the eggs, Amy memorized the look of wonder on her face when candy or stickers or erasers fell out. Ruby shoved as many pieces of candy in her pockets as they would hold and left everything else in the plastic bag, which she gripped tightly. Soon everyone headed to the small pavilion for hot dogs and chips.

With full plates, Amy and Nash sat across from each other at the picnic table. Ruby, next to Nash, couldn't stop peeking inside her bag full of prizes. Moments later Amy noticed the girl slip her hot dog into the bag.

"Ruby, why don't you eat your hot dog now?" She kept her tone light. "It won't be good if you try to save it for later."

Ruby's eyes filled with tears.

"Oh, don't cry, honey." Amy's spirits slid to the ground. "I didn't mean to hurt your feelings. I don't want you getting sick. That's all."

"Miss Amy's right. Food spoils, RuRu. You don't want a tummyache."

With a few sad sniffs, Ruby pulled the hot dog out of the bag. Nash teased Ruby, telling her she needed a pile of onions on her dog.

You made Ruby cry. You didn't sell your fabrics. You might never be a mother. You don't have a husband and kids like the other women here. Something is wrong with you.

Why were these thoughts attacking her now? She'd made peace with being single. She could live a happy life without children. She was thankful for the time with Ruby.

"Is something wrong, Amy?" Nash asked quietly.

Her neck grew warm. She couldn't admit she was feeling sorry for herself. Without thinking it through, she blurted out, "I heard from a fabric manufacturer earlier. They passed on my designs."

He stopped chewing midchip. "I'm sorry to hear that."

Not trusting herself to speak, she nodded. He really did seem sorry.

"Send the designs to a different company. You've got a lot of talent. Someone will want them."

"Four other companies have my portfolio. It was just…"

"A blow. I know." From his tone, she believed him.

Her emotions were entering dangerous territory. She gathered her empty plate and napkin.

"Hang in there. You'll sell the fabrics. God has a plan for you."

Stunned, she blinked. Had Nash Bolton just given her spiritual advice? He'd never been one for prayer or talking about the Lord when they'd dated.

He'd grown up.

And she didn't really know the man across from her. Aside from when she'd arrived, he'd given her and Ruby his full attention, even when people approached him in the food line.

"Amy?" Nash asked. She shook her thoughts away. "Find out if your friend still has one of those kittens. We've decided to brave the kitty litter."

Why emotion welled up, she had no idea, but she forced herself to smile. "I'll tell him to save the fluffiest one for you."

Their eyes met and understanding wove between them. She stood, looking for a trash can.

She'd never been one to share her feelings with the world, not even her closest friends. She figured they didn't need to be burdened with her petty problems. But Nash had always been able to read her.

He still cared enough to ask.

And if he cared enough to ask…

He might not be the monster she preferred him to be. Or maybe that's how he did it—got foolish girls like her to care about him. All thoughtful and charming until it didn't suit him and something better came along.

Tossing her empty plate in the trash with more force than necessary, she scolded herself.

She wasn't a girl, and she wasn't a fool, and she wasn't falling for him this time. She'd grown up, too.

Chapter Six

"**D**on't let her go too far." The mid-May breeze rippled through Amy's hair as she watched Ruby play with the kitten in Nash's backyard. A lazy Saturday afternoon—perfect for introducing the cat to her new home.

Funny how time changed things. It had been over a month since the Easter egg hunt. The weather had warmed, and Amy had grown less guarded around Nash. They'd settled into a sort of truce, where neither brought up the past and they both kept an emotional distance. As much as she wanted it to stay that way, this surface friendship kept poking holes in the emotional baggage she'd thought she'd unpacked. Questions about why he'd left kept bubbling up. She didn't know how much longer she could press them down.

Nash was in the house getting iced tea for them. The kitten had already inspected every nook and cranny of her new home and gotten into a bit of trouble when she'd squeezed her tiger-striped body behind the dryer in the mudroom. That's why they'd brought the bundle of energy outside for a while.

"Have you decided on a name yet?" Amy leaned

back against her hands as she sat on the grass with her legs out in front of her.

"Not yet, Miss Amy." Ruby's delight switched to worry.

"Why don't you pick a few names to choose from?" Amy had learned how Ruby's mind worked. The child was terrified of making mistakes, and she struggled to make decisions. The imaginative play most children engaged in was something to be feared in Ruby's world, but Amy was doing her best to make her feel safe. And, thankfully, she was slowly becoming more playful and less insecure. She'd even gotten better about not tucking away food for later.

"Okay." Ruby appeared to be deep in thought. The kitten pounced on a weed in the grass. "We could name her Tiger."

"You could." Amy bit her tongue, wishing Ruby would take a chance on a less safe name. "What other ones do you have?"

The kitten darted off after a butterfly. Ruby shrieked, chasing her. She picked her up under her front arms then scooped up her bottom the way Amy had shown her, clutching the cat to her chest. "Bad kitty. Don't run off."

"Maybe we should bring the kitten back inside for a while." Amy stood, brushing off her jeans, and waited for Ruby to join her. From the patio, they went through the dining area to the living room. Yawning, Ruby sat on the couch and kept the wiggly cat on her lap.

"I was just coming out to join you." Nash handed Amy a glass of iced tea. "Did you name the creature yet, RuRu?"

"Fluffy." With Ruby's lisp, it sounded like Fwuffy.

Amy had to choke down a laugh. The girl was too adorable. And Fluffy was slightly more original than Tiger.

"Fluffy?" He scratched his chin. "How about Fleabag?"

"No, Daddy, it's Fluffy." She hopped off the couch,
cat in her arms, and headed toward the staircase. "I'm
playing with her in my room."

Amy tucked her lips under in amusement at Nash's
raised eyebrows. *Good for you, Ruby.* She'd stood her
ground.

"Well, that's a first," he said. "She's never played in
her room by herself before."

"She's not by herself. She's with Fluffy."

"If I'd known getting her a cat would solve that problem, I would have gotten one earlier. Thanks for bringing it over." He gestured to the patio. "Want to drink
these outside? It's too nice out to be stuck in here."

"Sure." She carried her drink to the wrought iron
table and sank into the cushions of one of the matching chairs.

One nice thing about spending time with Nash and
Ruby? Amy no longer had the prickly sensation, the
one shouting for her to be on high alert, when she was
near him. Growing comfortable around him was probably inevitable with all the crafts and activities she and
Ruby did every week in his kitchen. The three of them
had ventured to other places, too, including story time
at the library and a visit to Lexi and Clint's ranch.

"I see the fence is coming along." She pointed to the
trucks in the distance. A work crew had been there all
week, installing posts.

"Yep. I want the horses to have lots of room to roam."
He got a faraway look in his eye. "Hank used to tell me

in a perfect world retired horses would have plenty of pasture and the freedom to run. Then he'd toss his cigarette butt on the ground, twist it under his cowboy boot and say too bad it wasn't a perfect world."

"Who's Hank?" Amy sipped her tea. Probably a guy he'd worked with when riding bulls.

His grave expression made her pause.

"Hank was the closest thing to a father I had growing up. He was the one who got me into riding bulls as a kid."

She didn't mean to stare at him, but Nash's childhood details had been off limits to her in the past. Habit almost made her suppress her questions. But she wasn't his girlfriend. Had nothing to lose by asking them now. And she wanted some answers.

"How old were you?" she asked.

"Must have been a couple years older than Ruby." He didn't look at her, but his easy tone didn't fool her. He was nervous.

"How did you know him?"

He let out a loud sigh. "Do you really want to hear all this? It was a long time ago."

"Yeah, why not?" She tried to sound nonchalant, but tension lined her words. She wanted to know more. When they'd dated she'd trusted he would tell her things in his own time, and she'd been content not to press. But he'd never told her...and now that he was back and they were getting along okay...she wanted to fill in some of the gaps. To understand him better so she wouldn't put him on a pedestal the way she had originally.

"Hank and my mother dated for a while. That summer we lived in a beat-up camper. Traveled to every rinky-dink rodeo in Wyoming for Hank to ride bulls and earn a little dough. I was his helper. I'd muck stalls and take care of the horses while he and my mother paid the entry fees and found their party for the night. I got to hang out with the other rodeo kids, and before I knew it I was riding calves, too."

"Wait a minute." Amy was doing the math in her head. "You were only about six, right? You were taking care of the horses while they found a party? What exactly does that mean?"

He shrugged, kicking his feet up onto the empty chair next to him, one cowboy boot crossed over the other. "Hank and my mother liked to drink, and Hank was a gambler."

"Where were you when all this was going on?" She tapped the table with her fingertips. Maybe she was reading too much into it, but it sounded a bit much for a child barely in elementary school.

"Oh, I was having the time of my life. I had three meals a day. Got to brush and feed the horses. And once Hank saw me winning belts, he told me everything he knew about riding bulls."

She pursed her lips. The time of his life? Running wild, more like it.

"He and my mother broke up—no surprise there— when summer ended. The Friday night rodeos closed, so Hank drove us back to our old apartment and left. It was a bad time for me."

"You never saw him again?" Although the man sounded like a bad influence, she sympathized with Nash just the same. He clearly cared for the guy.

"I thought he was out of our lives for good. That's the way it was with most of my mother's men, but the following May, Hank showed up at the dump we were living in and made a deal with my mother. He wanted me to join him for the summer. She'd get half of any earnings I made from competing, and Hank would keep the other half. She agreed. I think she was glad to have me off her hands."

"So you were their money maker? You were a small child."

He laughed, his cowboy hat tipping over his eyes. He pushed it back. "Not yet. No, it would be another year before I was winning enough to make it worth his while."

"Then why did he do it? Take you with him?"

Nash shrugged, a faraway look in his eyes. "He wasn't good alone. I took care of the horses, woke him up in time to get sober and ride and made sure we both ate. He was a chain smoker, an alcoholic, a gambler. He was tough on me. He'd lick me good if I came in second. Then he'd explain exactly what I'd done wrong. That's why I cared about him. Idolized him. No one ever gave a nickel about me except Hank. I spent every summer with him until I was thirteen years old, and I was making a lot of money for him by then. When I wasn't competing on the bulls, I rode his horses in other events."

"You were making money for him? Didn't you get to keep any?" This Hank guy sounded awful, but she could kind of understand why a kid like Nash would like him.

"He sent some back to my mother—never the half he'd promised her—and he'd tell me he was on a winning streak and that he'd double the money and give me a cut. He gambled everything away. Every night. It was an addiction."

She thought of her own father and how he'd raised her and her brother. He was the one who'd provided for them, not the other way around. Fondness colored Nash's words, and she could see in his tender expression he didn't hold anything against Hank.

"You loved him, didn't you?"

He turned to her. "Yeah, I did. I wanted him to be my father. I even asked him if he was, but he'd been in jail for two years when I was born, so it wasn't physically possible."

Nash's words weeks ago about not knowing his father came to mind. She hadn't considered how that must have affected him. To not know who his father was... her heart twisted. He'd had a difficult childhood, and she hadn't really known it. Maybe she hadn't pushed for more information years ago because deep down she hadn't wanted to know.

"What happened when you turned thirteen?" She sipped her iced tea.

"Hank died."

She choked, coughing. "How?"

"He was blowing through so much money. I could feel his anxieties intensifying. He wasn't much of a barrel racer, but he'd signed up for extra events to bring in cash. The night he died no one knew he'd been drinking to get his courage up for the performance. He hid it well, but his reflexes were slow. He turned the first barrel and the horse bucked him off before landing on him. Broke Hank's neck. Killed him instantly."

"Oh, no." Amy reached across the table, covering his hand with hers. "I'm so sorry."

Nash's jaw shifted. He seemed to be getting his emotions under control. "Yeah, well, what do you do? I went back to my mother, but she wasn't there."

Amy could barely keep up. First Hank died, and then his mother was gone? "Where was she?"

"In prison. She'd gotten caught selling drugs to minors near the high school in Sheridan, the town where we were living. Of course, she was also charged with possession. Since she already had a long police record, the judge didn't go easy on her to give the usual minimum sentence. She got seven years."

Amy shivered. Nash's childhood sounded like a horrible nightmare. When she was thirteen, she was going to sleepovers and doodling her crush's name in her journal. And Nash had to take care of some drunken gambler while his mom went to jail? Didn't seem fair.

"What happened to you then?"

"Hank was gone. My mother was gone. If I'd had my way, I would have been gone, too. I figured I'd do what I'd been doing—competing in rodeos in the summer to make enough money to take care of myself the rest of the year. I wanted to hire in as a ranch hand somewhere, but the government had other plans. I was sent here, to Yearling Group Home, instead."

A lump formed in her throat. He hadn't even been in high school yet, and he'd been prepared to work full-time to take care of himself? She studied his profile. Strong features, confident tilt to his head. She'd never guessed he'd gotten all his strength and confidence from such a messed up childhood. Compassion for him rose unbidden. How she wanted to shove it away, but she couldn't deny the pressure building inside her, the heavy sadness for the boy he'd been.

He turned to face her then, and his bleak eyes twisted her heart. She didn't want to care about him. If she did, she'd…

Don't feel sorry for him. Don't do it, Amy. If you want to feel sorry for someone, feel sorry for yourself from ten years ago. Remember the girl who could barely get out of bed after he left? Feel sorry for her.

"Yearling turned out great. I met Clint, Wade and Marshall there. And Big Bob cared about my rodeo aspirations. He hooked me up with his friend who competed on the summer rodeo circuit. My summers were tamer than they'd been with Hank, but I learned about discipline and doing the right thing. In many ways Big Bob made it possible for me to have my career." He took off his hat, raked his fingers through his hair and shoved it back on his head. "Enough about me. Tell me something good. How did you end up owning your own quilt store?"

Her life seemed so conventional and easy compared to his. It'd be simple to answer his question. Give him the safe tour of her life after he'd left. How she'd worked at a daycare during the day and started quilting at night. She could hide the fact she'd tried to lose her memories of him by stitching fabrics together. How every quilt she'd made had been a way to escape the devastation of him leaving her.

Or she could tell him the truth. Let him see that her life might have been tame, but her pain had cut deep.

She faced him. *Tell him the truth. Don't sugarcoat it to protect him.* He'd been honest with her. It was time she was honest with him.

"After you left, I—" her throat was so tight, she almost couldn't continue "—had a hard time with life. At first I thought you'd been in an accident or were in trouble or something. I couldn't imagine you would just…leave. No note. No call. No 'It's over.' No goodbye. I was scared for you. A week later when I saw in the paper you'd won an event, I had to accept reality. You'd left on purpose."

"Amy, I—"

She thrust her hand out. "No, nope. It isn't your turn. This is about me."

He grudgingly nodded.

"You were my best friend." Her eyes welled with tears. "I loved you. Cherished you. Thought nothing but the best of you. And then you were gone. I'd get home from the daycare and pick up the phone to tell you about something funny one of the kids said, and the receiver would drop out of my hand. You cut me out of your life, and mine became very empty."

He shifted in his seat, his face grave.

She shook away the threatening tears, swallowed the lump in her throat. "I didn't know what to do with myself. I couldn't sleep. Couldn't eat. Could barely breathe for weeks. Had no one to talk to—Lexi was off at college and we hadn't kept up with each other. Then one night, when I was about as low as a person can go, I started sewing scraps together. The rhythmic motion of the needle took my mind somewhere else."

He stood, pacing, his movements agitated and robotic. "I hate myself for that."

"I hated you, too." She rose also, rubbing her arms, and gazed at the barn in the distance. Maybe she shouldn't have told him. "I'm not trying to punish you. I just…well, I needed you to know."

He came up next to her. She dared not move or she'd fall apart. His shoulder was less than an inch from hers. All she'd have to do is lean ever so slightly and he'd put his arm around her like old times. And she remembered every detail of his arms around her—how safe she'd felt, how protected, how loved.

She squeezed her eyes shut. *Don't remember. Forget it. Forget it all.*

His arm crept over her shoulders. She hissed as she inhaled, craving his embrace and hating herself for still wanting it. She spun away from him.

"It's your fault, you know. The life I wanted? Gone. You shattered my dreams, Nash Bolton. You shattered them!"

He'd broken his cardinal rule.

He'd touched her. Soft, feminine familiar Amy. And now she was yelling at him.

Good.

He deserved her wrath. He'd been waiting for his punishment since the day he returned. And hearing her say he'd been her best friend broke something inside him. She'd been his, too. Not talking to her had been the hardest thing he'd ever done. Sometimes he'd picked up the phone, dialed half her number and hung up, his throat gripped with emotion. He'd wanted so badly to tell her about each event after it was over, the way he'd done when they were together.

He'd lost his best friend, the only person who'd ever thought the absolute best of him.

And he'd walk away again, given the same circumstances.

"I know it's my fault." He stepped back, widened his stance and hooked his thumbs in his belt loops. "I loved you."

"How can you say that? What you did was not love."

"Yes, it was. I—"

"I already told you—I don't want to hear it. There is no excuse why you couldn't have had the decency to break up with me first." She blinked back tears. "When you left, you took away my dream of a family."

He clenched his jaw. She wouldn't let him explain. Didn't want to hear his reasons. How could he get through to her if he couldn't explain?

"If you'd give me a chance, you might not think it was so lame." He stepped closer to her. The look in her eyes could have killed a rattler on the spot. His temper flared, too. "Fine. I won't tell you why I left. It's your right to refuse me. But don't blame me for not having a family. It's been over ten years. This might be a small town, but last time I checked there were plenty of single guys here. You could have married one of them and had a house full of babies. You can't blame everything on me, Amy."

"Well, I almost did marry one."

His heart ripped open. She'd fallen in love with someone else? He wanted to punch something, but he kept calm and quietly asked, "Who?"

"John McCloud."

"Don't know him." He had to refrain from cracking his knuckles. He wanted to find out everything about this guy, but what would be the point? It wasn't as if Nash had any say in the matter.

"You wouldn't know him." She stood her ground. "He was a bank manager. He moved here from Greybull several years ago. We dated for over a year. We talked about getting married and buying a little house in town."

He had no right to be jealous, but the thought of some guy making plans to marry Amy and live in a house right here in Sweet Dreams twisted his gut. It had been Nash's fondest wish for himself. He blinked away the emotions. Amy must have come to her senses and dropped the guy.

She averted her gaze. "He changed his mind. Moved down to Florida instead."

He frowned, trying to figure out what she meant.

"At least he had the decency to tell me before he left." She studied her fingernails. Her posture said, "I'm strong," but her face said otherwise.

Without thinking it through, Nash closed the short distance between them and wrapped his arms around her. The instant he registered her warm body next to his, he sighed. *This is what I've been missing. If I never have her in my arms again, I'll remember this and it will have to be enough.*

Her silky hair teased his cheek, and her fresh cookie smell weakened his resolve.

He wanted to kiss her.

He wouldn't. Couldn't.

But he wanted to.

She stepped away from him. "You're right. I can't blame you for how my life turned out." She slowly pivoted, looking out at the yard. "And I'm happy with my life, Nash. I have a successful business. Good friends. I'm very happy."

He wasn't dense. He knew what she was saying. She was happy—very happy—without him in her life.

He wished he could say the same.

How his body craved riding a bucking bull for eight seconds and hitting the dirt floor of the arena. Going through the mental checklist of possible injuries as he scrambled out of harm's way had been like scratching an itch.

Right now he had a powerful itch.

He frowned. Why would those minutes when he'd scampered to safety, assessing any pain in his body, give him relief in any way?

"Were you happy, Nash?" Amy asked quietly.

He didn't know how to answer that. All the reasons he'd thought he'd gone into bull riding might not be true. Sure, he'd wanted to be the best. Yeah, he wanted to be someone other than the son of a prostitute and drug addict. He'd had dreams of big money and fame. And he'd gotten it all.

But what if he'd competed all those years for something else? What if happiness had never been on the list?

"Sure," he said gruffly. "I loved the excitement, the danger, the thrill of the ride."

All true. Except deep down, he feared he finally understood why he'd been compelled to ride the meanest bulls, to stay on the longest.

Had he been punishing himself? For being a nothing kid, for having a mess of a mom, for losing Hank?

Whether she knew it or not, Amy had always been better off without him.

Why, oh why, had Nash gone and held her? She'd been doing so well. Keeping her focus on Ruby. Ignoring the past. Making pleasantries with Nash. Not getting too close. And then she'd blown it. Worse, she couldn't get her mind off it. Even church yesterday hadn't been enough to clear her head.

"I messed up." With a to-go cup from The Beanery in hand, Amy strolled next to Lexi on Main Street's sidewalk.

"What are you talking about?" Lexi gave her a sideways stare full of skepticism. "I'm sure you did not mess up."

They waited for traffic to clear then crossed the street to Lexi's reception hall, otherwise known as the Department Store. Lexi unlocked the door and let them inside. They went up the grand staircase to her office, and Amy promptly fell into one of the plush seats opposite Lexi's desk.

She loved this space. Lexi was a wedding planner, and her office reflected it. Feminine. Glamorous. With its dove grays and pale pinks, it instantly relaxed Amy. Sometimes it was nice to experience a contrast with her own colorful environment.

"Okay, spill." Lexi sat behind her desk, leaning in with her elbows wide and her hands clasped between them. "What happened that has you so worked up?"

"I may have freaked out on Nash this weekend."

Lexi's mouth formed an *o*.

"We've been getting along and, I don't know, I guess pretending the past didn't happen got to me or something, because all of a sudden he's sharing all these details of his childhood I knew nothing about, and I sympathized with him, Lexi. I truly felt bad for him."

"What's so terrible about that?"

Amy mindlessly turned her coffee cup in a circle on the desk. "I wanted him to feel bad for me. I don't know, maybe I resented that he didn't know how hard it was for me when he left. I wanted him to suffer. I lashed out at him."

"You're not vindictive." Lexi smoothed her long brown hair behind her shoulder. "And even if you were, he deserved it."

Amy chewed the tip of her fingernail. "It's not my style. Whether he deserved it or not, doesn't matter."

"You have every right to tell him exactly how he made you feel."

"It felt self-indulgent."

Lexi sipped her coffee and regarded the wall for a moment. "Amy, I couldn't be more blessed to have you as a friend. You listen. You care. You always want the best for me. And I want the best for you, too."

"I know you do," she said softly, getting choked up.

"Confrontation and conflict are hard for you." She leaned back, steepling her fingers. "If you feel conflicted, then give it to God. But realize you were born with a peacemaking personality. In your quest to keep things peaceful, I hope you don't lose sight of your own needs."

She'd never thought about it, but Lexi was right. "I guess I am a peacemaker."

Lexi nodded.

"It's hard for me to tell someone they've hurt me."

"I know. But if someone really cares about you, they need to know so they can apologize and not do it again."

"I know you're right." And Amy did know. She'd spent years praying for God to get her heart right, to keep Him number one in her life. "But my motives were bad. And it backfired anyway."

"What do you mean?"

"My stupid mouth opened up and I blamed him for me not having a family."

"Oh." Lexi blinked rapidly, frowning. "I'm sorry. I didn't realize a family was so important to you right now."

Her best friend didn't realize she desperately wanted children? Amy slumped in the chair. "I guess I owe you an apology, too. I assumed you knew I wanted kids. Sometimes it physically hurts me to see pregnant moms or dads with toddlers on their shoulders."

"Oh, Amy, I understand. And you don't have to apologize. I want children, too."

"I know you do." Amy stood and moved to Lexi's large board with fabrics, quotes and pictures of flowers pinned to it. She gestured to the board. "I want this, too, Lexi." She spun to face her. "I want a beautiful wedding and a handsome husband and life as a couple."

Lexi brightened, snapping her fingers. "Well, you just need a groom. What about Clint's friends Wade and Marshall? They're both very cute, and I believe they're single."

Amy pretended to gag. "You're forgetting that while you were off at college, I was dating Nash. I know Wade and Marshall. Sure, they're good-looking, but they're not my type."

"Well, Nash is out, so that leaves…" Lexi snatched a piece of paper from her drawer and started writing on it. "What about Nick Warton?"

Dare Amy confide in Lexi what was on her mind?

"I'm not going out with Nick. Nash pulled me close to him on Saturday, and it brought back all these feelings and memories."

The pen fell out of Lexi's hand. "Did he kiss you?"

"No!"

"Did you want him to?"

Yes, oh, yes! Forgive me, Lord, but yes.

Lexi shook her head. "Don't answer. I can see in your eyes you wouldn't have minded if he'd leaned in and—"

"Okay, enough." Amy went back to the chair and snatched her coffee. "It was an illusion. I was in love with him once, but I'm over him. I won't let him break my heart again."

"You know the verse about the spirit being willing but the flesh being weak," Lexi said in a singsong way.

"Yeah, well, I've had years to toughen up both my spirit and flesh. Nash isn't a bad person. He has a lot of qualities I admire. But I'm not a twenty-one-year-old girl with stars in her eyes anymore."

"He still hasn't told you why he left?" Lexi asked.

"No. He wants to, but I don't want to hear it. Whatever it was doesn't matter. It's over. And it's inexcusable."

Lexi nodded. "I get what you're saying, but it might not hurt to hear him out. It could give you some closure."

"I don't think so." Amy couldn't take the chance that what he would tell her would either break her heart all over again or tear down her defenses. Either way, she'd be the loser. She hitched her chin toward the paper on the desk. "Who else is on your list?"

"You sure about this?"

"No. I'm not sure about anything." Nash flipped through the quote again and handed the stack of papers to Marshall. A local contractor had come out to assess the cost of constructing an indoor training arena and other necessary facilities. The price wasn't what was bothering Nash. The reason behind the project was. "I keep getting this nagging feeling about it. And when I pray, I don't feel any better."

"Praying never makes me feel better." Marshall rolled up the quote and slapped it against his other palm.

"But if something's bothering you, you should listen to your intuition."

"That's what I've been thinking. Come on, let's take a walk. I've got to stretch my legs."

"Won't Amy mind?" Marshall jerked his thumb toward the house, where Amy and Ruby were making something for the kitten. This was their usual Tuesday time.

"No. The farther away I am, the happier she is." Nash hustled toward the path leading to the creek.

"I thought you two had set aside your differences for Ruby's sake."

"We did. And then we had a fight a few nights ago, and we're back to square one." Man, his hips and back hurt today. His knee, too. *Push through, Bolton.*

Marshall jogged to catch up to him. "What did you fight about?"

"She blames me for her life not turning out the way she wanted."

"She said that?"

"Not exactly, but that's what she meant."

"She's still here, though." Marshall handed him the rolled-up quote as they strode next to each other. Nash shoved it in his back pocket, wincing. Marshall stopped. "It's the third time you've made that face since I've been here. You're still in pain. When are you going to call the trainer I told you about?"

"I don't need a trainer." Nash was tempted to stomp his foot. "I walked past the gym. Picked up a flyer. It's not for me."

"Since when is working out not for you?"

"Since I saw yoga on the pamphlet. I'm not contorting these cranky bones into some weird pose. You might as well put me in a tutu and throw me on stage with ballerinas." The prairie grass rippled, reminding him to keep moving. "Come on."

"Every time you move, *I* wince. Your body is stiffer than a robot."

"I know, I know. What do you want me to do about it?"

"Make the appointment."

"Fine. I'll call him. You happy?" He glared sideways at Marshall, who was grinning like a doofus.

They continued in silence until they reached the creek. Sunlight danced off the surface, and the faint trickling of water running over the rocks filled the air.

"Marshall?" Nash bent to pick up a stone.

"What?"

"I think this is what's holding me back from making a decision."

"Wyoming?"

"No." He glared. "Training kids to ride bulls would be fun for me. I'd enjoy it. I know I would. But I don't know if I could live with myself if they ended up beat-up like me or, worse, disabled."

Marshall propped his cowboy boot on a boulder. "What's wrong with ending up like you?"

Nash could list sixty-five things about what was wrong with ending up like him, but he stuck to the relevant one. "I'm facing a lifetime of frozen muscles and creaky joints. I'm young, Marsh, and even you can see I get around like an old man. I got out of the sport before I was paralyzed or killed. How can I train anyone to ride bulls when I know what they'll be facing the rest of their lives?"

"I see your point." Marshall picked a long blade

of grass and wound it around his finger. "Maybe you need to ask yourself why you competed. You did it your whole life knowing the danger, dealing with the pain. Why?"

Punishment. Nash tossed the rock back into the water. "It was all I had. All I was good at."

"Did you ever worry about getting killed?"

Nash shrugged. "Not really." Was that true? Had he never worried about death? "I liked being number one. Seeing my name up there. I liked winning."

Marshall chuckled. "I think we all like winning."

Nash thought back to the other night when he'd held Amy and she'd lashed out at him. All he could think of was how much he wanted to get on a bull. Win or lose, every ride had been a challenge, a physical release. The only way he'd known how to escape.

He sighed. "What if I only did it to punish myself?"

"What do you mean? Quitting?"

"No, competing."

Marshall laughed. "Nope, not seeing it. You loved riding. You know you did. You had this gleam in your eye every time that chute opened."

"I did love it. But what's that saying about a fine line between love and hate?"

"Doesn't apply." Marshall shook his head. "Let me ask you something. Did you carry around a lot of guilt after you rode? Or did you feel all right inside?"

Nash had never felt guilty for riding whether he won or lost. "I felt all right."

"Well, there you go."

"But I also craved the danger, didn't mind the pain. What's that say about me?"

"I don't know, man, but I know your childhood stunk

as bad as mine. If you were punishing yourself, it was only a small part of why you rode or you wouldn't have kept winning. Ultimately, you had a gift and you used it. Be proud of that."

"What do you mean, I wouldn't have kept winning?"

Marshall stared at him hard. "If you had really wanted to punish yourself, you wouldn't have been careful, wouldn't have gotten to safety after each ride."

The impact of his words hit Nash hard. It was a sobering thought.

"So you're saying, my sense of self-preservation didn't allow me to truly punish myself?"

"Yeah. And what was there to punish, anyway? You're one of the best men I know." Marshall wiped his brow. "Has it been hard? Giving it up for Ruby?"

"No." He inspected a hole near the creek. "I was ready. And I'd give up just about anything for her."

"I know what you mean."

Nash studied him. Marshall's body bore witness to his daily workouts. He always moved with ease.

"Are the other bull riders in the same shape as you are? You know, in pain and having a hard time moving?"

Nash nodded. "Most of 'em."

"That's a shame. Too bad something can't be done to help them."

He could wish all he wanted, but his body would never be the same. And neither would the bodies of the other bull riders he'd hung out with over the years. At least he had money, this property and his little girl. Many of the retirees had no savings and nothing to fall back on.

Nash stretched his arms over his head. "Come on.

There are limits to Amy's patience. We'd better get back."

If he could just find a way to get into Amy's good graces. He preferred their truce to the curt nod she'd given him earlier. Maybe he should apologize. For not thinking how his leaving would affect her. For not taking the blame for ruining her life. For not giving her the family she wanted. For leaving her and their dreams.

Forget apologizing. It would only make it worse. Someday she'd realize he'd done her a favor. Until then, he'd be smart to leave well enough alone.

Chapter Seven

Where was the peach fabric with the butterflies? Amy was supposed to be at Nash's in five minutes. Yesterday, after the Memorial Day barbecue at her parents' house, she'd planned today's project for Ruby, but she hadn't had time to pack a bag with the supplies. At this rate, she'd never get to their Tuesday craft session. She gave up on the shelves and started searching through the bins in the closet.

The time had come to talk with Nash about spending time alone with Ruby. The girl was comfortable with her. She no longer flinched when Nash stepped outside, and she even hugged Amy every time they were together. Yes, Amy would mention it to him later.

Her cell phone rang. She didn't recognize the number but answered it anyway.

"Amy Deerson?"

"Yes?" A shade of peach caught her eye. She dug the fabric out of the bin.

"This is Louis Whitaker with Orchard Creek Mills. We've reviewed your fabric portfolio, and I have to say, we're quite impressed. Are your designs still available?"

The material slipped out of her fingers to the floor. Her pulse started racing so quickly her vessels might burst. "Yes, they are."

"We'd like to offer you a licensing contract."

A contract! Her head spun. *It's happening!* All the beautiful fabrics she'd designed would be folded and stocked in her store. How many times had she searched for the right pattern and been disappointed? How many times had she wanted to make quilts out of her personal designs? All the years of learning Photoshop, taking online design classes, blogging and creating quilt patterns were about to pay off.

"...my assistant will email you the contract. It's a rather tight turnaround. We'd like to have the final design files in July to have the production ready for next May's International Quilt Market trade show."

July. It would give her a month to make requested design changes. She wanted to jump up and down and scream, but instead she composed herself and asked Mr. Whitaker the questions that came to mind. After talking for several minutes, she agreed to review the contract and promised to call him with any questions before hanging up.

Tossing the phone on the table, she leaped in the air and shouted. Her arms were shaking. Her legs were shaking. Even her toes were shaking. She shoved the fabric into the bag, grabbed her phone and ran out the door.

She called her mom as she hurried down the steps, told her the good news and promised to fill her in with all the details later. Then she drove to Nash's as a million wonderful thoughts tumbled through her mind.

As soon as she parked, she raced to his front door.

He opened it almost immediately, putting his finger to his lips. He came out onto the porch and closed the door behind him.

"What happened to you?" he asked. "You're smiling so big your teeth could blind someone."

"I sold my fabric line." She threw her arms in the air, and to her surprise, Nash caught her by the waist. She hugged him. Who cared if this was her ex? She wanted to celebrate.

"Yeehaw!" He lifted her off her feet easily, as if she were as light as Ruby. It was her turn to laugh when he spun her in a circle. "I knew you'd sell them. One of these days you'll have to show them to me."

"I will." Her eyes locked on his full lips so close to her face. He smelled good. His cologne should be outlawed. And then there was all that muscular power holding her so tenderly. Attraction made her lightheaded. His eyes deepened to almost turquoise and the pulse in his neck visibly quickened. A tiny thrill zinged her. She affected him, too.

"Will you stay in Sweet Dreams?" Nash asked.

"Why wouldn't I?" She eased out of his embrace.

"I don't know. I guess maybe you'd have to live in a big city now that you'll be a designer."

"No, I can do everything from home."

"You're sure? You won't be missing out on opportunities by staying here?"

Her happiness dipped a notch, and she stepped back. "I'm sure I've missed out on opportunities, but in my mind, you make the best of life wherever you are."

"You've never thought about living somewhere else?"

Did he want her to leave or what? "Sure, I've thought

about it a time or two. Denver is a fun place, and Salt Lake City is so beautiful."

"Why didn't you go?" His eyes gleamed with something she couldn't put her finger on.

"I think the better question would be why. I had no reason to leave." All this moving talk was killing her mood. "Where's Ruby?"

"She fell asleep. Has a low fever. I called the doctor's office and they told me to give her some children's medicine."

"Oh, no. Poor baby. I hope it's nothing major."

"I hope not, as well. Probably too much excitement at the fair this weekend." His voice was thicker than normal, and he kept tapping his thigh as if he couldn't stand still. "I'm really happy for you, Amy."

She detected a vulnerability she'd rarely seen in him. Normally, she'd leave if Ruby wasn't around, but she gestured to the rocking chairs. "Mind if I stay a minute?"

"I'd like it if you did."

Once they'd both taken a seat, she angled the chair to see him better. She fought for the right words. Lexi's advice about getting closure kept coming back. *Lord, I didn't plan this, but I feel like it's time. Should I ask him?* A sense of peace quieted her mind.

"I'm ready," she said. "I want to know why you left."

"Oh." He gripped the arms of the rocking chair and stared ahead before turning back to her. "Are you sure?"

"I'm sure." But worries returned. How bad would it be? Had he left her for another woman? Or had he fallen out of love and been unable to say it? He could have gotten bored with their ideas for the future. Or, like her mom had said, maybe being a star was more exciting to him.

"My mother got out of prison when I was almost twenty. You and I were already dating."

Amy's mind raced with questions. What did his mom have to do with him leaving?

"She had a nasty habit of threatening me if I didn't do what she wanted. She'd used me my entire life. When I was eight, I'd found a starving dog and told her I'd take care of it and pay to feed it, that she'd never have to do a thing. She let me keep it. Now, I won't tell you how I got the money to pay for its food—I'm not proud of my life back then—but I loved Digger. Several months later, she was on a cocaine binge. She was scary when she used cocaine. Thought she saw clowns in the walls. And that wasn't the worst of it."

Amy stopped rocking and concentrated on Nash's face. What he was describing brought a sick feeling to her stomach.

"She told me if I didn't shut Digger up I'd never see him again. Digger wasn't even barking. I hid the dog as best I could, but the next day he was gone. She made good on her threat. I never saw him again." Bleakness washed over his face.

"I'm so sorry, Nash." And she was. To lose a beloved pet must have been horrible.

"Yeah, well, that was life with dear old Mom. So, like I said, she got out of prison. Hadn't seen her or talked to her in seven years. I was already on the PBR tour. You and I were making plans for the future. I was happy. Life was finally going my way."

Amy had a sinking sensation, and she couldn't look away from Nash if she tried.

"But she found me. She always found me. I was out of town, getting ready to compete. She wanted money. A lot of money. I told her no way. She threatened me. I laughed. I was used to her demands, and there was no way I was caving. But then she threatened you. She told me exactly who owed her favors. They were dangerous people. It took me a split second to make a decision. I told her we'd broken up. That I didn't have room for a girl and a career. I wrote her a check for ten thousand dollars. Told her it was the last money she'd ever get from me and if she ever contacted me again, I'd make sure she went back to jail for good. I never saw or heard from her after that."

She hadn't expected his explanation. Questions popped up one after the other.

"If she left you alone after that, why didn't you just give her the money and come back here? We could have stayed together."

He steepled his hands together and brought the tips of his fingers to his chin. "She would have always threatened you. She would have hurt you."

"But—"

"Without you, she had no leverage. She could harass me all she wanted, and it wouldn't have mattered. She'd only ever been able to get her way with me by terrorizing something I loved. I had to make her believe I didn't love you."

Amy stalked to the porch rail, trying to make sense of what he was saying. She pivoted to him. "You don't know for sure she would have hurt me."

"I couldn't take that chance."

None of this was giving her closure. She was just supposed to accept that he'd left...to what? Protect her?

"You should have told me."

He rose, too, and moved a few feet away. "No. I couldn't have. I had to make her believe we were over."

"By making sure we truly were over? I don't see how either of us could have won in your scenario." So he'd dumped her to protect her from his mother. And he hadn't told her the reason because…? That was the key Amy couldn't figure out. "Why didn't you at least say goodbye?"

"For all I knew, she had one of those druggie thugs hanging around Sweet Dreams, scoping it out. She knew too much about you, Amy. Things she only could have known if she was spying on you."

Amy let out a dry laugh. "You make it sound like she was some sort of CIA agent. From what you've told me, I find it hard to believe she had such a master criminal mind."

"She was smart, attractive and manipulative. How do you think she kept getting released? Or regained custody of me so many times? She told her parole officers and the courts what they wanted to hear. You'd be surprised at what people will do to get what they want."

"Then I guess you didn't want me all that much." She shivered, rubbing her arms. His excuse felt flimsy.

He crossed over to her, his body inches from hers. "How can you say that? I loved you."

"Not enough, apparently." She stood her ground.

"She would have hurt you."

"If you would have trusted me—"

"Trusted you? I trusted you."

"No," she said, shaking her head, the reality of what he'd told her finally making sense, "you didn't. You never even told me about your mother. I would have understood, Nash. And there were other ways we could have handled her threats."

"You say that now, but—"

"It's okay." She put her hand up, a sense of acceptance washing away the hurt. He might think he'd been noble, and she didn't have to convince him otherwise. In a way, she was glad to know the truth. She'd always wanted a man who loved her enough to fight for her.

Nash hadn't been that man.

He'd set his own terms with his mother, and Amy had been the payment. Pain shot through her temple. "It was long ago. We were both young, and our lives headed in the directions they were supposed to go. We clearly weren't meant for each other."

"You were everything to me." He gently took her by the biceps, intensity blazing from his eyes. "I loved you."

"Love doesn't walk away and never look back." She shimmied out of his grasp. "Listen, I've got to go. I think Ruby is ready to spend some time alone with me. Tell her I hope she feels better. You can bring her over to my apartment Thursday. We'll try an hour by ourselves."

With stiff movements, she strode to her car. As she drove away, she could see Nash in her rearview mirror. He was leaning against the porch rail watching her.

All her earlier excitement from selling her fabric line disappeared. She didn't want to go to her parents' house. She didn't want to think about Nash and his psycho mother.

She didn't know what she wanted.

Rewinding the clock ten years wasn't an option.

She'd do what she'd always done. Move forward. One step at a time.

* * *

As soon as the dust from Amy's tires had settled, Nash did the only thing he could—saddled up and headed out. With his walkie-talkie clipped to his belt, he rode Crank up and down the pasture fence, staying close enough to the house that if Ruby woke, he could be back in a flash.

Amy had rattled him. The fool woman didn't know what she was talking about. She'd made it sound so easy: "You could have told me. You didn't trust me."

Bah! He'd trusted her. How could he have told her his mom was alive and one of the worst human beings on the planet? *Oh, by the way, Amy, while I'm out traveling every other week of the year, you might want to watch out for some scary men who might mess you up. My mother's drug buddies will do anything for crack and heroin. See you next Monday.* He couldn't have. She was wrong.

He'd thought about quitting the tour. Staying in Sweet Dreams and getting a job. Keeping an eye on Amy every minute. Every day. But his experience had told him it wouldn't be enough. It would never be enough where his mother was concerned.

He'd told Amy about the summers with Hank, but he hadn't told her about the rest of the year, when he'd been at the mercy of his mother and her other boyfriends. He'd learned at an early age to hide when they were using. If he didn't...

He wasn't rehashing the terror of those days. No sense going back.

The wind whistled as Crank trotted along. What had Nash expected? That Amy would listen to his reasons and forgive him? Thank him for putting her safety first? He wasn't that dumb.

Still, it stung for her to accuse him of not trusting her.

And now she wanted to be with Ruby alone.

He nudged Crank to go faster. He'd been soaking up Amy's presence for weeks, and it had soothed him like the balm he applied to his sore muscles after a competition. And now she was taking it from him.

From him? He scoffed. It had never been for him. She'd only been around for Ruby. But he'd sopped up her kindness, conveniently forgetting he could never have her. Maybe a small part of him had hoped she'd forgive him if she knew the whole story.

Well, at least he knew for sure she'd never forgive him.

The blue skies and sunshine gave the appearance of a perfect day. The rest of his horses were grazing in the distance, their tails flicking leisurely. He wished he could be like them, not a care in the world. Reluctantly, he turned Crank to head back to the barn.

The agitation spiraling up his torso wouldn't go away. If he didn't have bull riding to channel his restless energy and there was no Amy around to soothe his rough spots, how was he going to handle the unwanted pressure inside him?

Lord, I don't know how to do this. I feel like a balloon about to pop. But I can't get on a bull and take a beating anymore. Being in Amy's presence—even when I wasn't talking to her—made my anxieties vanish. And now I won't have her around either. What do I do? How can I shake this—whatever it is—that's weighing me down?

What was weighing him down? Shaking him up like a can full of fizz was more like it.

He thought of Hank. The drinking. The gambling. Hank's way of escaping his pressures.

God, I can't go Hank's route, and I don't want to. I've got Ruby. I can't end up drunk, broke and dead.

The words the pastor spoke every Sunday came to him like the dry breeze. *And the peace that surpasses all understanding will guard your hearts and minds in Christ Jesus.*

Exactly what he needed—a peace that surpassed all understanding. *Lord Jesus, please have mercy on me and give me Your peace.*

He relaxed into Crank's easy stride. The trainer Marshall kept hounding him to call came to mind. Would it really be that bad to at least talk to the guy?

He didn't want the town gawking at him. If the trainer wanted him to do sprints or something, everyone would see his clunky movements. What if his shoulder popped out lifting weights, the way it had so many times when he was competing?

He didn't want to fail.

Because if he did, running away wasn't an option. Not this time.

Maybe he was a coward.

Wiping his forehead, his thoughts zoomed right back to Amy.

He didn't blame her for being mad, for her accusations. Not really. He should have called and broken up with her. He shouldn't have left without a goodbye. At the time his decision made sense. It still made sense. Sort of. But she'd deserved better. Still deserved better than a beaten-up scaredy-cat like him.

His last memory of her from before he left was standing under a full moon in the driveway of her parents' house. She'd given him a wide smile as she stole his cowboy hat and placed it on top of her head. He'd yanked her to him, kissing her thoroughly. He'd been thinking, *One more week and we'll be engaged.* He'd just had to get through one more classic…

No more regrets, Bolton. You made choices you have to live with.

The sad truth was if he had broken up with Amy, he might have gotten over her.

And even he wasn't stupid enough to claim he was over her.

He couldn't go back, but he could make new choices. Better ones.

Chapter Eight

The following Tuesday afternoon, Amy uploaded pictures for her weekly blog post. Nash was dropping Ruby off soon. Their first girl-time without him. Ruby's fever hadn't broken until Sunday, so they'd had to skip their usual Thursday and Saturday dates. It had given Amy time to finish the rust, cream and navy quilt. She'd also reviewed the fabric licensing contract, talked to a lawyer, signed the papers and sent them off. Her parents had celebrated with her by grilling steaks. The evening had been lovely, but she was willing to admit, at least to herself, it would have been even better if Nash and Ruby had been there, too.

She hadn't allowed herself to dwell on Nash's confession. He'd done what he'd felt he needed to do all those years ago, and she'd been honest when she'd said they clearly weren't meant for each other. If the past decade had taught her anything, it was that she deserved someone who loved her enough to stick around and share his life with her. At least Lexi had been right—Nash's honesty had given her some closure.

A knock came from the door. She hurried to it, opening her arms wide as Ruby walked inside.

"I'm so glad you're here. I have something really fun planned for us today."

Ruby ran into Amy's arms. What a welcome! Amy savored her embrace. Nash hung back, adjusting the collar of his T-shirt with Eight Seconds scrawled across the chest. He wore basketball shorts and running shoes. Gone was his cowboy hat, and in its place, a baseball cap. Since he'd returned, she'd yet to see him in anything but cowboy boots and jeans. Unfortunately, he looked amazing no matter what he wore.

"Come in." She waved him in, determined to treat him like any other friend in town. Tension wasn't good for Ruby. Or for her. "Want to see my fabric designs?"

He gave her a sheepish smile and took off his hat. The man was too handsome. She led him to the wire where she'd clipped printouts of her designs. The pattern was off on one, and she needed to fix the color layers of another. She made a mental note to fix them later and flourished her hand. "Ta-da."

"They're paper." He sounded surprised. "I didn't realize they weren't actual fabric."

Her friends had said the same thing, so it didn't bother her. "I sketch the early ideas, then I take pictures and edit them in digital imaging software. That's where I add the colors and make each drawing the best it can be."

Was her best good enough, though? What if Mr. Whitaker didn't like the final designs?

She'd heard of other designers signing licenses and not having their fabrics printed. She was *this close* to having her dream come true—it would be devastating for the deal to fall through.

He peered at the one inspired by Indian paintbrush. She loved the pattern. The background was tan like the dry earth, while the red flowers and green stems repeated. The collection revolved around the colors of the Bighorn Basin.

"Makes me feel like I'm out riding the land. These are incredible, Amy."

And just like that, her treat-him-like-any-other-friend-in-town idea vanished, replaced by something more than friendly. His opinion mattered to her, whether she wanted it to or not. "Thank you."

"Miss Amy, what's that?" Ruby tugged on her arm, pointing to the print with whimsical animals.

"That is my version of pronghorns. Do you like them? They're like fast deer. They leap in herds around the countryside."

"They're cute."

"And so are you." Amy bent, touching the tip of Ruby's nose. Then she addressed Nash. "Do you want to stay for a minute? I made blueberry scones. I can put a pot of coffee on."

He continued to study each printout but glanced over his shoulder. "No, I've got a meeting with a trainer. But thank you."

Good. This is what she wanted. Time with Ruby. A cordial relationship with Nash. Nothing more.

She shouldn't feel let down, but she did.

"Well, RuRu, I'll be two blocks over at the gym. If you need me or start feeling scared, you girls can text me, and I'll come right back, okay?"

"I won't be scared, Daddy."

He met Amy's eyes over Ruby's head. He looked skeptical. She smiled to reassure him. Then she walked him to the door, and he lingered a moment with his cap in his hands. Was he going to say something? If he was, he must have thought better of it, because he just nodded to her and left.

"Okay, Ruby, do you want a little snack first or should we start our project?"

"Snack!"

"Good plan. Come and see my place." The living area, kitchen and studio were all one large room. She took Ruby around and showed her the fabrics, her art space, the sewing machines and quilt racks. Ruby oohed and aahed over the containers of colored pencils, markers and various craft papers. They ended up in the kitchen. After uncovering a plate of scones and cookies, she poured glasses of milk for Ruby and herself. "How is Fluffy?"

Ruby took a bite of a chocolate chip cookie. "She's good. She purrs a lot. But her nails hurt."

"Her nails? You mean her claws?" Amy bit into a scone.

"Yeah. She scratched me yesterday." She flipped her arm over so Amy could see the skinny red welt on her forearm. "It hurt."

"It looks like it. I don't think she meant to hurt you, though."

"I told her she was naughty. I 'nored her after that."

"Well, she's only a kitten. She probably doesn't know any better."

"She should. I bleeded."

Amy fought back a smile. "Try to forgive her. And be patient. When she's older, she won't scratch as much."

"As much? I don't want her scratchin' at all."

"I don't want her to either, but she's your kitty now, so try to love her. She's never going to be perfect."

Ruby's eyes filled with tears, and she set her cookie down.

"What's wrong?" Amy asked. "Why are you upset?"

"If I would have been better, Mama wouldn't have left."

"Oh, honey." Amy lifted Ruby out of her chair and held her. Ruby twined her arms around her, letting her cheek fall against Amy's shoulder. Amy stroked her hair. "That's not true. Your mother had problems. None of them were your fault."

"I was a bad girl."

"You weren't a bad girl."

"I was. I made her leave."

Amy rose, still holding Ruby in her arms, and sat down on the couch. She settled Ruby sideways on her lap. "What happened to you and your mother was complicated. She took things that made her mind not think straight. And they made her die. Nothing you did could have changed it."

"Are you sure, Miss Amy?" Tears stained her cheeks, but the hope in her eyes was what stabbed Amy's heart.

The poor child blamed herself for her mother's death.

"I'm positive. And, listen, I know your daddy takes you to church and talks to you about Jesus, doesn't he?"

Ruby nodded.

"God loves you so much. There's nothing you can do that would make Him leave you."

"But I can't see Him."

"No one can." Amy chuckled, hugging her tightly.

"But it doesn't mean He's not there. Can you see the wind?"

"No."

"Does it mean it's not there?"

"No."

"Even if you're all alone, God's still there. He loves you. And you don't have to be perfect. You can make mistakes. God still loves you. He'll never leave you. Even if you do the naughtiest thing ever, He still loves you and won't leave you."

"Are you sure?"

"Yes."

"I love you, Miss Amy."

Amy's throat knotted. The trust and love of this little girl felt precious.

"I love you, too, Ruby."

Bare Bones Gym lived up to its name. Nash kept his phone in his pocket while he waited for the trainer. Wide planks of wood lined the walls, and the high ceilings showed exposed steel beams painted black. The air was cool but it smelled like a gym—sweaty and raw. Nash didn't mind the ambience at all. His kind of place. He checked his phone. No texts or calls. Ruby must be doing okay with Amy. For the moment, anyway.

A dark-haired guy wearing sweatpants, running shoes, a form-fitting black T-shirt and a stopwatch around his neck approached. He had to be six foot two, and he was lean but cut. He stuck his hand out. "Shane Smith."

"Nash Bolton. Good to meet you." Shaking Shane's hand, he suddenly felt out of place. He was used to honing his body nature's way, on a horse or outdoors. This gym stuff... Could he keep up without making a fool of himself? Why had he listened to Marshall anyway?

"Let's go to my office. We can talk in private before hitting the floor."

Nash had trouble matching Shane's long, quick strides. By the time they reached the office, his left hip was flaring up. He gritted his teeth. *Never show the pain.*

"Take a seat." Shane sat behind a nondescript desk as Nash sat in the folding chair opposite him. "First of all, I'm honored you called. Your ride on Murgatroyd was like nothing I've ever seen."

"I appreciate that." Nash straightened. Maybe this place wasn't so bad. "Listen, before we go further, my four-year-old daughter is staying with a friend, and she isn't used to being without me. If I get a text, I might have to leave."

"No problem. I understand. I have a two-year-old myself." Shane leaned forward. "Now, let me tell you about one of my programs. I work with several retired rodeo men. They've all had severe injuries in the past they still suffer from. I don't know if that's your case as well, but I've developed workouts designed to lessen the pain and strengthen the weak areas. I call it Rodeo Rehab."

Rodeo Rehab? The name was catchy. If it lessened his pain and strengthened his weaknesses, he was signing up. Nash grinned. "Tell me more about it."

"The first step is the one every cowboy resists the most."

Nash bristled. He knew where this was going. The doctor.

"I recommend getting a full health checkup with your doctor."

"I've seen enough of them to last a lifetime."

Shane laughed. "I'm sure you have. But you were probably getting treated for an injury. I want you to have a full picture of what shape your body is in right now. Some breaks don't heal well, and physical therapy can make a big difference in your quality of life. I tailor your workout plan based on your overall health."

"I'm healthy. Healthy as a horse." He pounded his chest.

"That's what they all say." He raised one eyebrow. "I usually recommend weekly massages and low-impact exercises until your core is strong and your muscles flexible."

"Look, I've ridden horses and bulls since I was a tyke. My core is about as strong as it comes."

"I'll take your word for it, but you'll have to take my word on this—you aren't as flexible as you need to be. I can see it in your gait. If I had to guess, I'd say your hip's likely been shattered and never healed properly, and you've dislocated the left shoulder so many times, you can pop it in and out of its socket at will. I couldn't begin to guess how many times you took a hoof to the head."

This Shane was a good guesser.

Nash shifted in his seat. "You missed the broken ankle, collapsed lung, broken hand, dislocated jaw and torn ACL. Who cares? I'm done riding, so what's it matter now?"

"It matters because you don't have to live in an old man's body. If you follow my plan, you can have a much higher quality of life."

Nash blew out a breath. Sounded good, but it also sounded like a fantasy. Maybe this wasn't for him. He hated going to the doctor. All the lecturing and tsk-tsking irritated him. He prepared to stand.

"Don't you want to be in the best shape you can be for your little girl?"

He sat back down. Man, this Shane guy really was good.

"So...what?" Nash clenched his hands into fists. "I have to go to the doctor and get poked and prodded and lectured. Then you're saying I gotta have some therapist bending my legs every which way. Next you'll tell me I have to do yoga. I don't see any upside to this."

"You don't have to do yoga. But the former rodeo competitors I work with have seen tremendous results by strengthening their cores with Pilates exercises and yoga poses."

"You're killing me, Shane." Nash covered his face with his hands and ran them down his cheeks. "Absolutely killing me."

"I'm going to tell you what I told them. Give me three months." He held up three fingers. "If you're miserable and haven't seen results in three months, quit."

"Do we ever get to do real workouts? Like kickboxing?"

"Have you tried Pilates or yoga?"

"No."

Shane grinned. "You're about to find out what a real workout looks like. Come on. We've got thirty minutes. I'll guide you through some beginner poses."

Half an hour later, Nash stumbled out of the building, feeling both energized and exhausted. His legs trembled from the poses he'd held. Downward facing dog? More like I'd rather climb a mountain with a one-hundred-pound calf on my shoulders. His stomach hurt from the planks. Even his arms felt like noodles after supporting his body weight in ways he'd never done before. But along with the pain came a sense of accomplishment.

He'd challenged his body in a very different way than when he used to climb on top of a bull. And the after-effect was similar—exhilaration, release.

Amy had never texted him, so Ruby must have been okay staying with her. Hope brought a spring to his step. He'd just worked out and liked it. He'd been able to leave his daughter with another adult for almost an hour. And, as much as he didn't want to, he was going to call a local doctor and get a full workup. He'd paid for Rodeo Rehab up front. He'd signed the three month commitment.

He just prayed it worked.

"It sounds as though she's really blossoming, Amy. I'm proud of you."

"I feel as if I'm the one who's blessed. She's such a dear." Amy powerwalked next to her mother around the high school track after supper that evening.

"That's another thing I love about you—your kindness. Didn't get it from me. You have your father to thank for that."

"What are you talking about? You're very kind. You do so much for the church and the folks at the senior center."

Her mom huffed, pumping her arms in the warm evening air. "That's different. I like doing those things."

"Just like I enjoy spending time with Ruby."

"I can see how you would. When I see her at church,

I just want to whisk the bitty thing into my arms and take her on a shopping spree. I miss those days when you were young. It would be fun to buy dolls and tea sets for a little girl again." Mom had a dreamy expression on. "Oh, I forgot to ask. How is the kitten? Is she loving it?"

"Oh, yeah, she adores Fluffy."

They kept their pace steady around the turn.

"So what's going on with you and Nash?"

"Nothing," Amy said truthfully. It was better that way. Even if her heart had been snagging and tripping every time he came to mind. His blazing eyes last week as he'd said, "I loved you," kept coming back, confusing her. "We had a heart-to-heart last week, and I think it gave us both closure."

"Uh-huh." Mom sounded skeptical.

"What? He told me more about his childhood, and I found out why he left town, and that was that."

"Oh, yeah? So why did he leave town?" Her mother's face was flushed. Amy was sure hers matched. They walked at a fast pace.

"It doesn't matter. I know. And he knows how I feel about it. Which is all that counts."

"How do you feel about it?"

She considered faking a leg cramp to avoid the endless questioning.

"I feel fine."

"Liar."

"Mom!"

"What? You're a terrible liar. Always have been. I'm glad. Means we raised you right. I know you're not fine with the reason he left. What I want to know is why." Her mom's tone took a diabolical turn.

Amy couldn't help it—she laughed. "Too bad. I might be a terrible liar, but I can keep a secret."

"True." Her mom waved offhandedly. "Another thing you didn't get from me."

They did another lap without speaking. Amy hadn't been able to concentrate on much of anything since Nash had picked up Ruby earlier. He'd said the workout had been tough but he hoped Shane's regimen would make him more limber.

She'd begun mentally putting together things she'd been ignoring. How he winced whenever he'd bend to kiss Ruby. The stiffness in his stride. He never complained about pain, so she'd assumed he wasn't in any. But she'd been wrong.

It was easy to believe he hadn't loved her enough to fight for her, but maybe she'd assumed incorrectly there, too. Maybe he'd spent a lifetime not complaining about the pain—any pain—physical or emotional.

And what did that assumption say about her? She'd believed he'd been happy with his fabulous life all these years. What if he *had* loved her the way he'd claimed?

Who cared? What kind of love did that? Just up and left?

Not the kind she wanted.

"Listen, Amy."

The hair on her arms rose. Mom only used those words when saying something Amy didn't want to hear.

"If you and Nash get to the point where you're getting feelings for each other, let me know. Dad and I will invite you all over for supper."

Amy almost stopped dead in her tracks. "What happened to 'that bull rider'?" She hadn't meant to say it, but she was curious.

"You're over thirty." Mom glanced her way. "I know you want a husband and kids. If Nash makes you happy, I want to support you this time. I'm still not sold on him, but, hey, I've been wrong before."

Amy had to blink away the sudden moisture behind her eyes. "Thanks, Mom."

"Keep praying, honey."

She'd never thought her mother would change her mind about him. Too bad it was for nothing. She didn't see her and Nash overcoming their past, especially since they were no longer spending time together.

It should make her happy. But all it did was make her sad. And as for praying…she hadn't been as regular about that, either. Between getting the fabric designs in shape, finishing up the quilt, spending time with Ruby and managing the store, she'd been spread thin.

But Mom was right. Prayer had always been her rock. She needed to make it a priority again. Trusting God's will had gotten her through the good times and the bad. She didn't have to do life alone. And she didn't want to.

Chapter Nine

"Ah, there he is." Big Bob waved for Nash to come to the back table at the diner Monday morning. "I heard you went to the gym."

"Where'd you hear that?" Nash slid into the booth, nodding to Jerry and Stan.

"Who do you think?" Big Bob held one hand up, hiding the fact he was pointing to Dottie with his finger.

"Dottie knows everything." He grinned. "I should have figured."

"Are you going to Bare Bones?" Jerry asked. "I don't even know if that Shane character can ride a horse. Never see him in normal clothes, neither. Does he own a Stetson or a pair of cowboy boots? Seems fishy to me."

"Well, fellas, I did go to Bare Bones, and I don't know if Shane owns normal clothes, but I do know this." Nash leaned in with his best conspirator's tone. "I'm pretty banged up."

Stan slapped the table and let out a belly laugh. "Son, we all are."

"Don't go speaking for me now, Stan." Jerry grimaced.

"You?" Stan said. "You're more bowlegged than a wishbone."

Jerry glared at him. The waitress slid Nash's usual breakfast on the table and poured a cup of coffee. With a wink, she sashayed off.

"Looks as though Trudy likes you, boy." Big Bob chuckled.

"She has good taste." Nash grinned before digging into his eggs.

"Hooie! Did you hear that? Good taste." Jerry laughed. "You are a handful, aren't you, Nash?"

If they only knew how tame his love life had been all this time. No girl had ever lived up to Amy, and he'd accepted his singleness. Well, until recently. Amy kept bringing life to feelings he'd thought dead, but he'd barely seen her since she'd claimed, "Love doesn't leave and never look back."

How would she know? He'd been looking back for ten years.

But his memories were as frail as plastic wrap and weren't enough anymore. He didn't want to look back. He wanted more of Amy today. Wanted access to those secret places in her soul she didn't let anyone into. But how could he get her to trust him?

He'd just have to learn more about her. Mentioning her name to these gossips would get him nowhere, though.

"When are you putting the training shed up?" Stan shifted in his seat.

Nash shrugged, taking another bite.

Jerry slurped his coffee. "Ain't you gonna teach those young bucks to ride?"

"I can't rightly say, Jerry." He spread strawberry jelly on his toast. "A part of me doesn't feel settled about it."

Big Bob considered him. "You're not competing anymore. What are you going to do about money?"

"I saved my earnings. Plus, I have my own line of chaps, boots and hats. I still get endorsement offers." But they would shrivel up as time passed. He wasn't naive about his status. New world champions got the endorsements.

The three men nodded.

"So you're looking more to fill your time, not so much to earn a living," Big Bob said.

He took a bite of toast, chewing it before answering. "That's right. I never turn down a paycheck, but I don't really need one at this point."

"I don't get it." Jerry shook his head. "You're plumb perfect to train the young 'uns around here. What's the matter? If it's a matter of bitin' off more'n you can chew, your mouth is probably a lot bigger'n you think."

Nash guffawed. "I haven't heard that one, Jerry. It's not that. My mouth is plenty big. I've spit more blood on the dirt than I have left in my body. Broken bones. Strained muscles. Had my head kicked in. I don't want these kids going in with stars in their eyes about the glamorous life."

"You could tell them about the dangers." Big Bob leveled a probing stare at him.

"But that's the problem. I don't want to discourage them, either." He sighed. "I don't know. I feel torn."

"You prayin' about it?" Big Bob asked.

"No."

"Well, get on your knees. You'll get an answer."

"What if I don't like the answer?"

"If it's God's will, you'll be okay with it. Eventually."

"A praying man is like a prairie dog…" Jerry started rambling on, but none of it made much sense.

When the waitress came around again and filled their cups, Big Bob caught Nash's eye. "You're in a position a lot of people dream about. Not worried about money. Time on your hands. So figure out what gets your engine revving. When you're excited about something and it won't let you go, you're on the right path."

What got his engine revving? Riding bulls and competing in rodeos had been his passion since meeting Hank. It had been the only thing he'd ever wanted to do or even considered doing.

Amy's words came back to him: "Then I guess you didn't want me all that much." In all the years since he'd left, he'd never once considered the possibility he'd wanted to ride bulls more than be with her.

He'd wanted her. Oh, how he'd wanted her.

But he *had* walked away without a word. And he had never let a kick in the head from a bull stop him from riding. So why had he abandoned Amy the second his mother entered the picture?

Fear gripped his chest remembering the evil look in her eyes. When she'd mentioned the men she'd send to "take care of" Amy, he'd become a young boy again, searching the streets for Digger. Watching helplessly as his mother snorted cocaine then disappeared for days on end. He still had the scar from one of her supposed boyfriends putting out a cigarette on his arm.

Shaking his head free from the thoughts, he picked up his mug. No more dwelling on it—he had other things to worry about, like his doctor's appointment this afternoon. Thankfully, Amy had offered to watch

Ruby for him. He knew he wasn't going to like a single thing the doc was going to say, but if he wanted to continue Rodeo Rehab, he had to play along.

In the meantime, he was going to spend some time online and learn more about this quilting Amy was so good at.

"This one needs more sprinkles." Amy passed the container of pastel stars to Ruby. Nash was at a doctor's appointment, and she'd been glad to offer to watch Ruby for him. They were decorating cupcakes. She'd baked them last night after spending much needed time with her Bible and in prayer. Her studies had led her to Matthew 6:21: "For where your treasure is, there will your heart be also."

For the first time she considered the fact God might have been protecting her when Nash left. Not from his mom the way he claimed—but from Nash himself. His treasure clearly had been competing, not with her in Sweet Dreams. And she'd been spared from being second place in his heart.

The thought comforted her a bit.

"Is that enough?" Ruby placed several sprinkles on the frosting.

"Do *you* think it's enough?" Amy asked.

"More." She grabbed a small handful.

While Ruby continued to carefully decorate each cupcake, Amy's mind wandered. She'd barely seen Nash in a week. Strange—accepting that she'd been second place for him had softened her heart where he was concerned. They'd been a couple of kids when they'd dated. But they'd both matured. And she found herself missing him, wanting to spend time with Ruby *and* him again.

It wasn't as if she wanted to date him—although the way he'd held her kept creeping into her thoughts—but she liked being in his company. Wouldn't mind being in it more.

Back when they'd met, he'd been thrilling, assertive and everything she'd thought she'd wanted. But the one thing she'd missed the most about him wasn't the thrilling or assertive parts—it was the easiness. He was easy to be with.

They'd always been comfortable in each other's presence. She'd been the accent color and he'd been the primary pattern in the quilt of their relationship. They'd complemented each other.

They still did. Maybe even more than before. He was solid and dependable where Ruby was concerned, but he also teased the girl and knew how to comfort her. And Amy was good at coaxing Ruby to enjoy the little things she'd missed in her neglected childhood, like tea parties and crafts and feeling safe.

She and Nash made a good team. For Ruby.

Not for each other.

She wanted to be the treasure in a man's life. Wanted to be where his heart was. She hadn't been Nash's priority before. Why would this time be any different?

If she could forget how his arms felt around her when he'd hugged her...

You're just lonely. It's been a bajillion years since you've dated anyone. Of course Nash would affect you. He's a very handsome man. With muscled forearms and not an ounce of give in his body. When was the last time any guy showed you some attention?

Several months. At least.

"Nice job, Ruby." Amy forced her attention back to the cupcakes. "Let's put them on a plate."

"When Daddy comes back, can we have a tea party?"

Hope zinged up her spine. A reason for the three of them to hang out. "Of course. We can even have it at the park if you'd like."

Ruby hopped off her chair and clapped her hands. "Yay! I love the park."

"Good. If your daddy is okay with it, we'll bring a few cupcakes and drinks with us. Why don't we pack up our goodies?"

Amy helped Ruby stash six cupcakes in a plastic container then handed her a stack of napkins and paper plates. They put bottled waters in a small cooler and tidied up the table and kitchen before washing their hands.

"Is it done?" Ruby wandered over to the rust, cream and navy quilt hanging on a rack. Amy loved how the patriotic piece had turned out.

"Almost." She took it off the rack and spread it out for her. "I'm going to wash it to make it super soft before I sell it. What do you think?"

Ruby pressed her cheek against the material, smiled and gave her a thumbs up.

She laughed. Seeing Ruby so enamored of the quilt gave her an idea. "Come here a minute." She led her to the shelves of folded fabrics. "If you were going to make a quilt, what colors would you use?"

A look of fear crossed her face.

"It's okay, Ruby. There isn't a wrong answer. I'm just curious."

Ruby tentatively approached the stacks. She pointed

to a pastel pink fabric and a lilac one. A child's quilt with a kitten pattern would be darling in those colors.

"Those are very pretty. Can't go wrong with pink and purple." Two raps on the door had them turning simultaneously. "Looks like your daddy's back."

Ruby raced to the door and threw it open. "We're going to the park and having cupcakes and you're coming, too!"

His eyebrows climbed up his forehead as he hauled her into his arms. "Is that so?"

"Yes."

He met Amy's eyes. "Is it all right with you?"

The consideration in his gaze warmed her. "Yes."

"Right now?" he asked.

Amy collected the cooler and tote bag. "We're ready."

"After you."

"How did you come up with lemon placemats?" Nash sat across from Amy at the picnic table. White frosting dotted Ruby's nose, and she was peeling back the paper from cupcake number two. He'd found Amy's blog earlier and, surprisingly, read several months' worth of posts. At first it had been to understand her better—what she did, how she earned her living—but her friendly writing style had sucked him in. He'd heard her voice in every word, and he'd gotten a better view of her world. It fascinated him.

Amy sputtered. "You read my blog?"

"Yeah. I enjoy it. Makes me want to sew a set of coasters."

"The coasters?" She gaped at him. "But that project was from October."

"Do they expire?" he teased.

"N-o-o," she said, skepticism all over her face. Her lightly tanned arms looked good against her royal blue T-shirt. She wiped her hands with a napkin. "What were you doing reading my blog?"

He shrugged. "Guess I was curious." He wanted to admit it was more than curiosity. He'd spent almost two months in her presence, and the past two weeks of not being near her had taught him one thing. He missed her. He'd take whatever he could get, even if it was reading her quilting posts.

"Daddy, can I play on the playground?" Ruby pointed to the children's playset a few feet away.

"You sure can." He helped her get up from the picnic table. "We'll watch you from here."

Ruby trotted off and climbed the ladder to the slide. He waved to her as she went down.

"So, anyway, about your quilting projects…"

"Oh, you don't want to talk about those." She waved his interest away, laughing. "How did the doctor visit go?"

Frowning, he studied her. He never realized how much she deflected attention away from herself. Probably because he'd been so busy talking about himself. "You don't want to talk about the lemon placemats?"

Her cheeks turned pink. "Well, I can't imagine you want to."

"I do." And he did. He wanted to see her eyes sparkle the way they did when she enjoyed something.

"I don't know where to start." She rubbed her thumb and forefinger together. The gesture almost did him in. He wanted to hold her hand. Reassure her. But he couldn't.

"Start at the beginning," he said. "How did you get the idea?"

Her eyelashes fluttered. Then she peeked up at him. "At my mom's. We were making lemon bars for a bridal shower, and one of the slices was so perfect. I thought bright yellow placemats with quilted sections to look like the inside of a lemon would be a fun project. The response has been great."

"I know. I saw all the pictures your readers shared in the comments. None looked as good as yours, though."

Her cheeks went from flushed to red. *Hmm.* Didn't she realize how talented she was?

"Thank you." Mindlessly, she drummed her fingertips on the table. "So what about you? Has it been hard, you know, retiring?"

"A little bit. I was injured pretty bad last year, and I knew it was time. Didn't want to admit it, but it got me thinking."

"What did you end up thinking?" Tendrils of hair blew around her face. Her lips curved into an encouraging smile.

That I had no idea what I was going to do and it terrified me.

"I've been trying to figure out what I'm going to do with my life."

She regarded him a moment. "And have you?"

"I'm working on it."

"I know this is none of my business, but seeing as how you went to the doctor…is your health okay?"

"Yeah. Nothing I didn't know, well, except for the arthritis." He scratched behind his ear. "Maybe the trainer in town—"

"Shane Smith?"

He inwardly growled. She seemed so pleased to know Shane. If the guy wasn't married with a kid, Nash might be jealous.

"Yeah, Shane. Well, he has this training program called Rodeo Rehab. I'm giving it a shot."

"I didn't realize he did that. What is Rodeo Rehab?"

"A lot of rodeo competitors are like me—stiff from repeated injuries that never fully healed. He developed a plan to improve our quality of life. I don't like some of his suggestions."

"But you're willing to try them?"

"I am."

"Good. I hope it helps. Maybe it will loosen your muscles."

"Maybe. I know it helped Shane's other clients. If it works, maybe more retired riders will sign up. About breaks my heart to see them hobbling to the competitions and rodeos." It was so easy to tell her things. He wasn't used to revealing his inner thoughts. But with Amy? It felt safe. "Can I run something by you?"

She nodded.

"I've been considering opening a training center for young bull riders. Giving them private lessons. But I don't know—"

"What a great idea!"

"You think so?"

"Yes, of course. Why? Don't you? You've got the skills, obviously. Is it the costs involved?"

"No, money isn't the problem. It's the danger."

Her lips twisted as she frowned. "Is this about Hank?"

He sat straighter. He'd never thought his indecision could be due to Hank. "I'm not following you."

"The gambling and drinking. His death." Her coffee-colored eyes captured him. He couldn't look away.

"The danger involved, for sure."

"You told me yourself kids are competing as young as six and seven."

"Some even younger. Not on bulls, of course. On sheep."

"So they're dealing with danger for years. No bull rider gets to your level unless he's done it his entire life."

The woman made sense. But what did it mean? He didn't know what to think.

"Maybe your heart isn't in it. You sounded more passionate about those retired riders hobbling around."

It wasn't that he was more passionate about it. Less fearful, perhaps? Maybe he needed to take Big Bob's advice and pray about it.

"Listen," Nash said. "I'm taking Ruby to the Dubois Friday Night Rodeo this week. Would you like to join us?"

She hesitated. He shouldn't have put her on the spot. She was busy, and she was already giving up so much of her time to help him. He just…well, he enjoyed being around her.

"Don't worry about it." He waved the idea away. "I know you're busy. How do you fit it all in, Amy?"

She crumpled the empty cupcake wrappers. "Fit what in?"

"The store, the quilts, the designs, the blog…us." He focused on her face, not wanting to miss her reaction.

She shrugged. "It's not hard."

"I imagine it is."

"I—" her eyes landed anywhere but his "—I guess I just do."

"Thank you."

"Daddy, Daddy." Ruby ran up, tugging on his sleeve. "Push me on the swing?"

"Sure." He stood, hitching his chin to Amy. "What about you? You need a push, too?"

He'd said it lightly, but he didn't move as he waited for her reply. Why did her answer feel so important?

"Why not?" Her bright smile did him in. Ruby raced ahead.

"I never told you I was sorry." He took her hand and turned to face her.

"For what?"

"For leaving you. For not saying goodbye. For never coming back."

"It's okay—"

"No, it's not. It's not okay. I'm sorry. I'll probably always be sorry. Anyway, thanks for letting Ruby and me into your life."

She looked stricken, frozen. *Great.* He'd made it worse. He should have let it go. They'd said everything they'd needed to say, and he knew better than to hope for a future with her.

He wanted her to know he'd regretted leaving her every day since he'd gone, but he couldn't admit it. Wouldn't be fair to her. He took a step toward the swings, but she stopped him.

"Nash?"

"Yes?"

"It was for the best." Her eyes shone with honesty. "God had plans for us. You would have been traveling on the circuit, and I would have wanted more than you being home for five days of the month. We both made the best of it."

Why her words tore into his gut, he couldn't say. Maybe because they were true.

He just wished it could have been different.

"If your offer still stands, I'd like to go to the rodeo with you and Ruby on Friday."

Amy turned the volume down on her favorite radio station later that night. She'd fixed the color layers of one of the designs and had settled onto her couch with a hot cup of tea. Why had she agreed to the rodeo with Nash? Shouldn't she be minimizing her time with him? Not latching on to any excuse to see him?

She couldn't even pretend she was going for Ruby's sake. She wasn't. And she hated the rodeo. Hadn't been to one since the last time she'd watched Nash perform. It had always set her on edge, worrying he'd get hurt or trampled. Ten years of not going to the rodeo had been great.

So why had she agreed?

The steaming water burned her tongue, and she set the delicate china cup and saucer on the coffee table. Was it too late to call Lexi? She checked the time. Almost eleven. Yep. Too late.

Face it, Amy, you like him.

She did. He'd been opening up to her about his past, showing her his vulnerable side. Then he'd read her blog and seemed genuinely interested. The fact he'd opened up to her about his uncertainties and asked for her thoughts about his plans made her like him even more. He cared about her opinion.

He couldn't be pretending, could he? *No.* When she'd sat across from him at the picnic table, he'd been looking at her as if *she* were the yummy cupcake rather than the ones on the table. Her heart fluttered just thinking about it.

No, stop doing this! He can't ride into town and get you back.

Did he even want her back?

She sobered up quickly. Well, he *had* apologized. And she'd needed to hear it. He'd sounded and acted sincere. So sincere she'd almost stepped into his arms and told him it was okay, none of it mattered.

But it did matter.

Rising, she pinched the bridge of her nose. Where had she put her Bible? She clearly needed some fire and brimstone. Anything to get her off these warm, fuzzy feelings that were messing with her head.

The leather-bound Bible lay on her nightstand. She grabbed it and returned to the living room. Where should she start? What book? What verse?

Closing her eyes, she searched her memory, but nothing came to mind. *Lord, what do I do? I've let go of my anger to the point I actually like this guy again. Worse, I could fall in love with him.*

Her eyes sprang open. What if she'd been in love with him this entire time and hadn't realized it? What if she'd never gotten over him in the first place?

Lord, I can't. I just can't. If I get close to him, he'll hurt me, and I've been hurt too much already.

Yawning, she set the Bible down and crept back to her bedroom. She didn't have the energy to figure life out tonight.

Chapter Ten

"Look at all the horsies, Daddy."

"Aren't they something, RuRu?" Nash carried Ruby on his hip. Amy strolled next to him as they headed toward the bleachers at the rodeo Friday night. The drive had been quiet. He'd tried to joke with her, but his humor had fallen flat. She must have added up all he'd told her about his health and his wishy-washy attitude concerning the future and found him wanting.

And why wouldn't she? He hated that his knee wouldn't bend all the way and he could barely run. As for career direction, he was no closer to a decision than before. Although, he had to admit, whenever he thought about the training center, he'd get the rush he'd enjoyed his entire life. But then doubts would creep in. And thinking of all the creaky old-timers would bring him back to reality. He still hadn't prayed about it.

"Mmm... I missed this smell." Lifting his nose to the wind, he inhaled. "Rodeo food. What I grew up on. What's your favorite rodeo snack, Amy?"

She darted a sideways glance to him. "I don't go to the rodeo."

"Ever?" He hadn't meant to sound so incredulous, but rodeo was a way of life in Wyoming. He found it hard to believe she never went.

"Ever."

Huh. And yet she'd come with him tonight.

"Why don't you like the rodeo, Miss Amy?" Ruby pointed to a small girl in a purple Western shirt and a black cowboy hat. "I like the white horsey over there."

"I do, too. Very pretty, Ruby." Amy's smile for the girl was so warm it could've baked a loaf of bread. "It's not that I don't like it. I don't know. I guess I've been too busy with other things."

Perfect. He'd taken the rodeo from her, too. She used to like it. Used to come to the local events and cheer him on. He'd missed seeing her in the stands. After he'd compete, he'd lift her in his arms for a victory kiss.

"Do you like it so far, Ruby?" Amy asked.

She nodded happily.

"Let's get something to eat," Nash said. "I see the Cheeseburgers in Paradise booth. Can't go wrong with anything on their menu."

They stopped at the rough-log structure and ordered burgers, fries and Cokes, then sat at a nearby picnic table and watched the crowd. The mountains behind them were glowing from the setting sun. Lights illuminated the arena next to them. An announcer made the audience laugh with his commentary on the kids' sheep riding event. Groups of elderly men in jeans, cowboy boots and straw hats leaned against the fence. Moms and dads could barely contain the energy of their little ones who'd been infected with the thrill of the summer night.

"Daddy, when's Uncle Wade bringing me a pony?"

A swipe of ketchup slashed Ruby's chin. Nash almost choked on his burger.

"Well, I don't rightly know if you're ready for a pony." He caught Amy's eyes, which were concerned to say the least. "I told him it was a big decision, and we'd have to think about it."

"I'm ready, Daddy." Her big eyes shone aquamarine in the pale light. "I've been helping with the horsies, just like you showed me."

"You've been a big helper, RuRu." Looking out at the crowd, he saw young children on full-size horses. He guessed a few of them would be barrel racing tonight. One girl couldn't have been much older than Ruby. "It might be time to get you riding, sweetheart. Are you sure you won't be scared?"

"I might be scared, but Miss Amy told me it's okay. When you're learning something you don't have to be good at first."

"That's right." Impressive. His little perfectionist might finally be willing to make a mistake or two. He nodded to Amy. "Thank you for teaching her that."

"I did say that, but isn't she a little young, Nash?"

He rubbed his chin. "Kids around here learn to ride about the time they learn to walk. If she's willing, I'm willing."

"But isn't it dangerous?" Amy studied Ruby with so much love and concern it almost took his breath away.

He covered her hand with his. "I won't let anything happen to her. I'll be there every second."

Her face cleared and she sighed. "I know you'll protect her."

"Can I pick the pony out?" Ruby asked, bouncing in her seat.

"We'll have to see. A small horse might be better for you. Ponies can be finicky. I want you to be safe. And we'll be going over a whole lot of rules and lessons before you get in a saddle."

"Okay!" Ruby threw her arms around Nash's neck and gave him a big kiss on the cheek.

He briefly considered buying her two horses after that sweet reaction. "You ready to watch some rodeo?"

"Yeah!"

He addressed Amy. "What about you? Are you ready to watch some rodeo?"

"As ready as I'll ever be."

He enjoyed her smile. For a brief moment he allowed himself to pretend they were a family. Just him and his smart, beautiful wife and their precious little girl. He could picture a baby in the mix. A little boy for Ruby to boss around.

These fantasies would be the death of him, but here, now, he couldn't stop them if he tried.

They threw away their trash and meandered toward the bleachers. This place reminded him of growing up. Of Hank and competing and racing around with the other kids. Of sweet-talking one of the food girls into giving him a couple of hot dogs and fries. Of sweltering nights in the camper and taking care of Hank's horses. Of getting in a chute, taking a deep breath and riding like his life depended on it because it did.

He slung his arm around Amy's shoulder and pulled her to his side. Whispered in her hair, "Come on. Let's see what these cowboys and cowgirls are made of."

Her scalp tingled where he'd whispered. Nash's arm was over her shoulder, and instead of pulling away, she'd continued her pace, pretending her heart wasn't beating as fast as the horse sprinting toward the next barrel. She'd had second, third and fourth thoughts about coming, and she'd barely said a word the entire ride here. But when Ruby asked for a pony and credited Amy with her willingness to take a risk? Amy stopped fighting it. She spiraled into their enthusiasm and threw her defenses to the wind.

Being at the rodeo with Nash and Ruby was the only place she wanted to be.

"Look at her, Daddy!" Ruby pointed to the teen girl flying by on the black horse. The girl's hair streamed behind her. "Can I have a hat like hers?"

"Well, yeah." Nash made it sound like it was a no-brainer. "We'll get you into full cowgirl gear next week. Make a trip to the Western store."

"I love the rodeo." Her matter-of-fact tone held a touch of awe.

"Me too, RuRu." He motioned for Amy to find a seat in the bleachers. She went up two rows and found a few empty spots.

"Is this okay?"

"Great." He smooshed in next to her. She was too aware of his masculine frame. The man radiated heat. She moved slightly to create space, but he filled it, too. Ruby sat on his lap, pointing to the horses every other second.

Amy tried to concentrate on the events. The announcer was quite funny. Everyone around them cheered and laughed and enjoyed themselves. As the minutes passed, she relaxed and stopped attempting to watch the riders.

What if she could have this all the time? Not the rodeo so much, but Nash and Ruby? Having his strong arms around her? Being Ruby's mommy? Having kids of her own?

The idea was so lovely she allowed herself to dwell on it for a while. The chemistry was clearly still there between her and Nash. Ruby was the most darling child in the world. Nash wasn't moving away. He planned on being in Sweet Dreams forever. No career would rip him away, and neither would his mother. So why not fantasize?

Isn't this what she'd wanted her entire life?

She let the rightness of it wash over her and had no idea how much time passed. Events came and went, and she simply enjoyed being there.

"See that rider?" Nash nudged her, his warm breath on her cheek. A cowboy was running away from a bucking bull. "He needed to get centered before they opened the chute. And he wasn't jammed up."

"How can you tell?" Her voice was hoarse. What did "jammed up" mean?

"I just know."

The next bull rider was getting ready. Nash kept up a steady stream of commentary until the chute opened. "Come on, man, be a tiger!"

The guy's hand was in the air, back and forth, and then he hit the ground hard, scrambling away from the bull.

"He did better, but his back wasn't as into it as it should have been, and I'm guessing his shoulder was bothering him before the ride."

"How can you tell?" She didn't mean to sound like a parrot, but really, how did he know this stuff?

"I just know."

The sky had dimmed to the color of ink, and Ruby's eyes were sleepy as she settled into Nash's lap.

The next rider made it a few seconds before falling off, and the bull's hind foot clipped his arm. The man clutched it, his face in agony, as he ran off to the side.

"I could see that coming a mile away."

"What could he have done to stop it?" Amy asked. "Do you think his arm's broken?"

"Yes, it's broken, and there wasn't a thing he could have done to prevent it. That's riding bulls for you."

"I don't get why anyone would want to."

"Hank used to tell me, 'The only good reason to ride a bull is to meet a nurse.'"

She laughed. For someone torn about teaching kids bull riding, he certainly seemed to know his stuff. And he was so animated. So locked into the action down there. Didn't the man realize he'd be a fantastic teacher for any young competitor?

By the final event, Ruby was sound asleep on Nash's lap. He carried her as they followed the crowd to the parking lot. When they got to his truck, Amy stood by the passenger door, staring up at the constellations while he settled Ruby into her car seat.

"What are you staring at?" He stood next to her and craned his neck back.

"I was admiring the night sky. It's beautiful."

"I agree."

"Nash?" She shifted to face him. His arm brushed hers. Her skin tingled.

"What?"

"You'd be an excellent trainer for young bull riders."

"You think so?" He sounded surprised.

"Yeah, I do. You're passionate and you know what you're talking about. Your experience would help them."

"I don't know why it's been such a tough decision."

"Probably because you know the risks. And being there when Hank died... I'm sure it left a scar."

He didn't speak for a few seconds. "It did."

He shifted in front of her, then put his hands around her waist. Her breath caught. What was he doing? Please, let him be about to kiss her...

"I know I don't have the right, but I'm going to anyway. Blame it on the rodeo." He bent his head and kissed her.

His kiss was as good as she remembered. Better. It was like getting reacquainted. She wound her arms around his neck and kissed him back. This was more than she expected—it was powerful, right.

He ended the kiss, resting his forehead against hers. "You're mine, Amy. You've always been mine."

How could she argue with that?

But then reality splashed over her like a cold bucket of water. The rodeo was what tore them apart. She hadn't been his for a decade. So how could she stand here and let him wiggle back into her heart?

Years ago he'd followed the siren call of professional bull riding and blamed it on his mother.

What excuse would he use next time?

None. She'd fooled herself twice with guys who hadn't loved her. He could blame it on the rodeo, but she'd only have herself to blame if she gave into these feelings. Not this time.

"Nash?" She stepped out of his embrace, rubbing her bare forearms.

"Yes, darlin'?"

"Don't mess with my heart."

Like he'd ever mess with her heart. Nash kicked his feet up on the couch and took a swig of bottled water.

It was one-thirty in the morning. He'd dropped Amy off a while ago, and he wasn't tired in the slightest. Annoyed? Yes. Restless? Uh-huh. Confused? Absolutely.

He couldn't be any more confused. The rodeo had kicked up all these emotions. He hadn't been away from the sport for this long in…ever. And he was tired of trying to convince himself riding bulls wasn't a part of him, like his lungs.

Rodeos and lungs—necessary for his survival.

When Amy told him he should teach the kids, that he'd be good for them, a weight had lifted from his shoulders. She had always gotten him in a way others didn't. Even *he* didn't get himself the way she did. So her advice was especially appreciated. And her insight into Hank had hit home, too. His death had left a hole.

Fact was, he missed the rodeo. Wanted to give young riders the tips and tools they needed to be successful. Big Bob had given him the high school rodeo coach's number. He could offer to assist the coach instead of starting his own business.

He'd spent his adult life responsible for one person—himself. Now he had Ruby. He didn't think it would be wise to add more people to the list. Maybe Amy was right about Hank. He'd never really thought about his death being part of his reluctance to open a training center. Seeing Hank die… He shook his head. Couldn't go there. Not tonight.

Frankly, he didn't know how he'd survived all those years riding bulls. All the chances he'd taken. The cautions he'd ignored. He'd been reckless. Only the grace of God had kept him alive and well.

And now Amy was in his life and it felt like a gift. A fleeting gift he couldn't hang onto.

Maybe he *had* messed with Amy's heart.

Who was he to fantasize about second chances and a family with her? Ten years ago he'd made the hardest decision of his life, and he hadn't looked back. No pining over "What if I hadn't left?" He'd done it. For her.

But what if he'd done it for himself?

She was right. He'd never told her about his mother. He'd kept his past from her. His childhood embarrassed him, made him feel like nothing. He'd been his mother's pawn.

Amy didn't seem to hold his past against him, but she was more elusive now. She had her own plans, her own dreams. She'd denied it, but all her fabric designing might take her to one of those places she'd mentioned—Salt Lake City or Denver. She'd said she never had a reason to leave Sweet Dreams before, but with her successful blog and stunning fabrics an opportunity could pop up.

One of these days she would put together all the pieces he told her about his past. She would come up with what he knew to be true—his scrappy childhood hadn't given him the foundation to be the kind of guy she deserved.

He'd already ruined her life once.

She deserved the best. And he was a far cry from that. No more messing with her heart.

Chapter Eleven

"Don't be mad at me." Lexi had just stopped by and was standing in front of Amy's freshly printed designs clipped to the wire. Last night's rodeo and Nash's kiss had kept her up until the wee morning hours. She'd tried to distract herself by fixing one last file.

"Why would I be mad at you?" Amy yawned, shutting down her laptop.

"I recently talked to my friend in Denver who is a buyer for a home furnishings company. I told her about your amazing designs and sent her a picture of the sample collage you gave me. Then I started thinking about it and realized that might have been a no-no since you signed a contract. Should I have kept the designs to myself?"

"Oh, no. Don't worry about it. If anything, you helped me. Orchard Creek Mills wants me to get my fabrics in front of as many people as possible. I'm sending them the final designs Monday. I'll be getting samples soon. Can you believe it?"

"I'm so happy for you!" Lexi hugged her.

"Want a glass of lemonade?"

"Sure."

Amy poured two tall glasses of lemonade and sat at the table.

"I'm putting out the feelers for potential guys for you." The way Lexi jutted her chin brought to mind espionage. Amy almost laughed.

"About that..." Amy drummed her fingernails on the table. "Let's put the mission on hold."

Lexi sprung to attention, her pretty eyes lighting up. "Why?"

"Well, last night..." She frowned, not sure how much to say. Would Lexi judge her for having feelings for Nash? Oh, for crying out loud, this was her best friend. If she couldn't trust Lexi, she had bigger problems than falling for her ex. "I went to the rodeo with Nash and Ruby."

"Oh, you did?" The words hung with too much hope.

"Uh-huh."

"And did you enjoy...the horses and such?" Lexi was clearly unsure how to proceed.

"I enjoyed the 'and such.' For sure."

She scooted forward. "Okay, I need details."

"The food was good. And I didn't want to, but I liked being with Nash..." Amy filled her in on Ruby's enthusiasm and Nash's pure joy and her own misgivings about getting too close to him.

Lexi nodded. "It sounds like you can't help it—you like him."

"I do."

"But you're worried about getting hurt again."

"I am."

"Does he act the same?" Lexi asked.

She squinted at the ceiling. "In some ways, he's the same. In others he's different."

"How so?"

"He's less brash. Humbler. Still confident as all get out, but he's more careful with people's feelings."

"Including yours?"

"Yes." Amy took a drink of lemonade. "He's actually interested in my quilts. He reads my blog."

"Really? Clint freezes every time I try to run a table setting by him. The man is terrified of fine china."

Amy laughed. "I know what you mean. When I dated Nash, he was caring and cocky, but he wasn't very interested in my day-to-day life. And I didn't expect him to be. But now that he's interested and actually asking me questions, well, I have to admit I like it."

"You should like it." Lexi nodded. "So have you two talked about the future? What does he want? I know you want marriage and kids. Does he feel the same?"

Amy shrugged. "I haven't asked him. I couldn't let myself go there."

"But if you have feelings for him…"

The pressure of his hands on her waist and his lips against hers rushed back.

"Well, you'll have to ask him what he wants, Amy. That's all there is to it."

She grimaced. "I don't know if I can."

"You're not a young chickie anymore. You're a successful businesswoman. It's okay to be clear about what you want. You can do this."

"What if I don't know what I want?"

Lexi opened her arms wide, a huge smile on her face. "Pray about it. You've given me that advice many times, and I can truly say it's the best thing you'll ever do."

"You're right. Thank you for listening and helping me. I'm kind of scared."

"Love is scary."

"Who said anything about love?" Amy tried to laugh it off, but the truth of it hit her. She could easily fall in love with Nash again.

"Not me. Nope. No mention of love here."

"I haven't shown you the surprise I'm making for Ruby." Amy padded to the table where she'd cut out all the pink and purple pieces of fabric for the kitten quilt. She'd already sewn one block. She brought it over to Lexi.

"Oh, Amy, it is adorable! And it's a surprise? Wow. I can't wait to see the look on her face when you give it to her."

"I know." She held the block out, imagining Ruby's delight when she presented the finished quilt to her. "It will take a while to make. I hope she loves it."

"She'll love it. She'll more than love it." Lexi checked her watch. "I've got to run. I'm meeting Clint at the deli. Let me know when you decide to have *the talk*. And I'll be praying for you."

Amy saw her to the door, said goodbye then collapsed on the couch. Excitement fizzed in her chest.

Her future. Nash. That kiss.

Ruby.

She covered her face with her hands. What had she gotten herself into?

Dear Lord, I need Your guidance. I agreed to help Ruby with the firm stance that I had to keep an emotional distance from Nash. And I'm failing. I have no idea what he wants. Last time I fell for him, I thought we were on the same page—that we both wanted mar-

riage and children. Lexi's right. I can't assume his fu-
ture plans include both. But how do I ask him? I'm not
ready to be in love, and I won't be with someone who
doesn't share my goals.

Maybe she should stop this whole mess in its tracks.
If she forgot about the kiss, pretended being with him
was boring, told herself he wasn't really interested in
her work...

Lord, scratch all that. Give me the courage to ask
him what he wants.

If he didn't want a wife or more kids, she'd move
on. Get over him. But if they were on the same page...

She had a lot to think about.

"Fluffy got so big, Miss Amy. Will you please come
over and see her? Please?" Ruby clasped her hands and
stared at Amy with big pleading eyes. They had finished
their sundaes and were preparing to leave the church's
Sunday afternoon ice cream social.

"How could I say no to that face?" Amy tweaked
Ruby's cheek. "Of course I'll come see Fluffy." She
glanced at Nash. "Unless you two had other plans?"

"No plans. Come on over. The cat is eating me out
of house and home. It's positively plump."

"Fluffy's not plump. She's just..." Ruby searched
for the right word.

"Fluffy?" Amy suggested. They all laughed.

"Hold my hand." Ruby took Amy's hand in hers,
and their arms swung back and forth on the way to the
parking lot. Amy savored the moment. The child had
come so far from when she first met her, and Amy didn't
take it for granted.

"Want to ride with us?" Nash opened the passenger door to his truck and helped Ruby up.

"I'll drive myself. See you there in a few." She got into her car and drove out of the lot.

She'd decided to pull up her big-girl pants and do what Lexi suggested. She was asking him the vital questions. About marriage. And more kids. And if he wanted them.

Her palms were sweaty.

What if he didn't want marriage or more kids?

What if he did?

Either way, she was terrified.

She turned down the country road leading to his house. The main thing she had to do was not let his answers affect her relationship with Ruby. The girl was too important to her. Amy wouldn't go back on her word that she was there for Ruby, not for Nash.

His long driveway came into view, and soon she rumbled down it and parked. He was just setting Ruby on the ground when Amy got out of her car.

"Come on, Miss Amy!" Ruby ran to her with her arms lifted, and Amy picked her up, giving her a kiss on the cheek. Oh, the preciousness of the girl.

"Where does Fluffy go when you're at church?"

"She curls up on my bed." Ruby fanned Amy's hair out as they walked to the porch. "She loves me."

"You're easy to love."

Ruby smiled.

As soon as they were inside, Ruby wiggled to be let down, and they went upstairs to see the cat. When Ruby burst into her room, Fluffy yawned, stretching out arms and legs before licking her paw.

"See?"

"She is bigger. My, my." Amy sat on the bed and petted the kitty. "She's still very soft."

They chatted about the cat for a few minutes before going downstairs to the kitchen.

"Miss Amy?" Ruby asked.

"Yes?"

"When I get my horsey, Daddy told me it will have a special stall. Can I show you it?" Ruby already had one hand on the patio door handle. Amy almost laughed at the excitement thrumming from her.

"Miss Amy might not want to go out there." Nash stood at the kitchen island.

"It's fine. The weather is so gorgeous I'll take any excuse to be outside."

"I'll join you, then."

Ruby opened the door and flew toward the barn. Nash matched Amy's pace.

"About the rodeo the other night..."

Her veins turned cold. Was he going to say it was a mistake? Or apologize for kissing her?

No, no, no!

"I appreciate you telling me to train the kids. You have a way of understanding me that no one else does. Not even myself."

She relaxed.

"It's obvious you're more than qualified, Nash. You should go for it." She wouldn't get a better lead-in. Question time. "Now that you're getting settled, how do you see the rest of your life going?"

His quick frown threw a shadow over his face. "What do you mean?"

"Well, I guess I'm talking about your personal life."

Her voice sounded normal, but inside she was quaking. "Hypothetically speaking, do you see yourself married?"

He slowed, staring at her. "I used to. I very much saw myself married."

She hadn't expected his answer. Couldn't look away from his eyes, more blue than green at this moment. "And now?"

"Not really something I've been able to consider."

What exactly did he mean by that? Normally, she'd wait until later to analyze his words and come up with a reasonable explanation, but not today. She'd stay on track. Get the answers she craved.

"Okay, assuming it *was* something you could consider, would you get married? Do you want more kids? Or is Ruby..." She fought for the right words. She didn't want to imply Ruby wasn't enough.

"If I had a wife, I would want more kids."

"That's good to know."

"What about you, Amy? Marriage? Kids?"

"Yes. Both." She peeked at him. He looked paler than he had a moment ago. "You don't look so good. Does the thought of marriage and more children scare you?"

He grinned, but it had no life behind it. "Me? Scared? I rode Murgatroyd, remember?"

Didn't answer her question. He might be on board with a wife and further kids, but neither seemed to have the same spot on the priority list as they did on hers.

"Miss Amy! Hurry up!" Ruby yelled, waving from the open barn door.

"Yes, ma'am!" She started jogging. At least she was perfectly clear how one of the Boltons felt about her. She wouldn't keep the sweetheart waiting.

* * *

What he wouldn't give for a chute, rosin and the meanest bull in the state. Nash paced outside of Shane's office Tuesday afternoon. They were going to review the doctor's results, and Shane would be laying out the first month's plan. Nash was ready for it. But he wasn't ready for all the other new stuff in his life.

All the changes were getting to him. No sooner had he adjusted to life with Ruby than Amy was back in it. And he'd tried to keep his heart occupied, but Amy filled every corner.

Why had she asked him about marriage and kids? He knew better than to think she meant with him. Yes, they got along well for Ruby's sake, but he didn't fool himself into thinking she'd ever take him back. The kiss the other night had been wishful thinking. Unfortunately, he couldn't forget the kiss.

"Don't mess with my heart," she had said. A clear warning she wasn't about to let him in it.

But then why had she asked him all those questions about a wife and family?

It had been all he could do not to picture her in a wedding dress.

Could he be wrong? Was she interested in him after all he'd put her through?

He'd always lived by the motto What Doesn't Kill You Makes You Stronger. And after every injury, every fall, he'd climbed right back onto the bull. He'd ridden whenever it was possible and even when it wasn't.

But love…second chances…

Had he lost his nerve?

Riding bulls day in and day out had been way easier than this.

"Come into my office, Nash." Shane rounded the corner. When Nash had taken a seat, Shane folded his hands on the desk. "How did the doctor's appointment go?"

"As expected. Bad knees. Early arthritis. Blood work is fine. Cholesterol's a bit high, but nothing to worry about."

"That's good." They discussed the particulars of his knees and arthritis for several minutes. "Are you willing to go to physical therapy?"

"I doubt there's much they can do."

"You'd be surprised."

"Well, I'll give it a go." He raised his eyebrows. "Anything a physical therapist can do for my hip? I've had three surgeries on it, and it's tight."

"Absolutely." Shane nodded. "We're going to keep your core strong while you start PT. Did your doctor refer you to a physical therapist?"

"He did."

"Make the appointment and get a regular schedule going. In the meantime, you can stand on the medicine ball."

"Medicine ball? Is this some hokeypokey remedy?"

"No, it's to improve your balance."

"My balance is fine."

Shane cocked his head. "Do I have to get out the contract you signed? Three months of doing it my way, remember?" He then went on about how core strength, balance and protective gear were helping up-and-coming rodeo competitors, as they made their way to the gym area.

Nash climbed onto the medicine ball. He fell off in fewer than three seconds. Frowning, he climbed right back on. And fell off. A fire started brewing inside him. If he could stay on a bull for eight measly seconds, surely he could stand on a dumb plastic ball for the same amount. Three more tries. Finally, he stayed on for almost ten seconds. He let out a whoop.

"We're going to keep building up your time each session." Shane gestured for him to get on the mat. "Okay, planks."

Thirty minutes later, Nash's limbs were jelly, and sweat stained his tee. For not running, kickboxing, doing jumping jacks or any other cardio, he sure felt beat. And Shane's comments about helping up-and-coming bull riders convinced him this was one of the pieces to training kids he'd been missing.

"Okay, Shane, I believe you. This, whatever it is you're having me do, is hard. I like hard. It looks as though I'll be opening a training center to teach young bull riders. I know you've got your hands full here, but I could use you, or someone like you, to get these kids in the shape they need to be. Don't get me wrong—I haven't met a teen rider who isn't compact and strong. I'm talking about the balance and reflexes. Getting their bodies prepared for the pain."

Shane was already nodding. "Count me in. I'd love to be part of any program that gives rodeo athletes the best chance to succeed while staying as healthy as possible."

"I'm guessing it will be a year before I can get everything running."

"It'll be here in Sweet Dreams?"

"Yes, sir. Right on my property. I've gotten quotes on the building. I just hadn't decided if I was going to go ahead with it."

"What changed your mind?"

Amy. Hearing her tell him he could do it, that he'd be good at it. Having someone believe in him, and not because he was a world champion, but because she knew him—the real him.

He shrugged. "Just feels right."

"I'm on board when you're ready to open. We can come up with a plan."

He shook Shane's hand, grabbed his water and headed to the door.

A plan. He hadn't had a plan in a decade. That one had blown up in his face. But his mother wasn't around to ruin this one. He'd give it a try.

Chapter Twelve

"You're becoming an old pro at using those scissors, Ruby." Amy crossed the room to let Nash in while Ruby cut out paper hearts at the craft table. Hopefully his session with Shane went well. She'd spent the morning putting the finishing touches on her files and sending them back to Orchard Creek Mills. She couldn't be more pleased with the end results. Opening the door, she waved him in. She returned to the table and nodded to the chair at the end. "Pull up a seat and join us."

"Look what I made, Daddy!" Ruby held up two misshapen pink hearts.

"Is one of them for me?" He rested his corded forearms on the table, and Amy had to look away at the sight. They reminded her of his arms around her Friday night.

Ruby's eyes sparkled as she nodded and gave him the biggest heart.

"Thank you, darlin'."

She picked up the scissors again and selected a baby blue sheet of construction paper. "I'm making one for Fluffy, too."

"Good idea. Here, make yourself a heart." Amy handed Nash a pair of scissors and a piece of paper as she addressed Ruby. "We can tie a long piece of yarn to it and you can drag it around for her to play with."

"Will she chase it?"

"Yes, and since it's paper, she'll probably scratch it up. So if you don't mind it getting ruined..."

Ruby's forehead furrowed. "I'll make two. One for scratchin' and one for good."

"Smart girl."

Nash was turning his paper like he had no idea what to do with it.

"Just draw something and start cutting." Amy shook her head. *Men.*

He set the scissors and paper aside. "I've decided to open the training center."

"You have? That's great, Nash!" Without thinking it through, she stood and put her arms around him in an awkward hug. He didn't get up, but he patted her on the back.

"Thanks. And Shane Smith's on board to plan their workouts. Want to keep the kids as healthy as possible."

"What a good idea. How long until you'll be able to open it?"

"Most likely a year."

"It will give you time to figure out all the particulars. This will be a nice way to pay it forward."

"'Pay it forward'? I'm not following."

"Hank trained you, taught you everything he knew about riding bulls, right?" She thought about the other things Hank did around him—the drinking and gambling. She chuckled. "Well, maybe don't pass on *every-thing* you saw and learned."

"That's it." He smacked his hand on the table, a big grin on his face.

Ruby flinched. "What's wrong, Daddy?"

"Nothing's wrong, RuRu. Miss Amy made me realize something. And I feel silly I didn't see it sooner."

She drew her eyebrows together. What was he talking about?

"It's not just the physical danger of getting on a bull the kids need to worry about." He leaned toward Amy. "It's the lifestyle."

Understanding dawned, and she straightened, nodding. "You can tell them about Hank."

"But not just the bad. The good, too. He cared about me."

"I know." She placed her hand over his and squeezed. His gaze met hers, and the thankfulness radiating from him made her heartbeat stutter.

"Who's Hank?" Ruby had resumed cutting the paper.

Nash's smile was soft and only for Amy. Heat rushed up her neck.

"Hank was like a father to me."

"But he wasn't your daddy?"

"Nope, but I loved him. He taught me about the rodeo."

Ruby got off her chair and climbed onto his lap. She rested her cheek on his chest. "I love you. I'm glad you're my daddy."

The picture they presented was so precious—Amy swiped her phone and took a photo. She doubted Nash had many pictures of the two of them. She'd text it to him later.

"Well, kiddo, it's time to rustle up some supper, don't you think?" Nash tweaked her nose.

Her bottom lip puffed out. "Already? I'm not done."

"You can take some paper with you." Amy selected several colors. "And I have plenty of safety scissors, so take a pair of those, too."

"What about the yarn for Fluffy?" Ruby began stacking her hearts.

"I'll find some." She measured out a length of yarn, snipped it and punched a hole in one of the blue hearts. She tied one end of the yarn to it. "There you go. Let me know how Fluffy likes it."

"I will." Ruby smiled, her eyes shining.

Amy saw them to the door, and Nash turned back to her. "I owe you, Amy."

"No, you don't."

"Yes, I do. For everything. Why don't you come over Friday night, and I'll grill some steaks? Unless you have a date or something."

A date? What was that supposed to mean? Was he messing with her? "Nash, I'm not dating anyone. I would have told you and Ruby if I was."

His face cleared. "Friday, then?"

"Sure."

He and Ruby left.

Strange. Did he really think she might be dating someone after asking him about his views on marriage and kids? She thought she'd been brave and made it obvious she was open to pursuing a relationship with him. Did she have to beat him over the head with it?

She frowned. Maybe they weren't on the same page after all.

Just like last time.

Wednesday morning Nash pulled on his boots while Ruby ate sugary cereal in the kitchen. Fluffy mewed up at her. Probably wanted some milk. Wade had just driven up, and Nash felt like a kid who'd won his first trophy. Ruby's horse had arrived, and it was a surprise for her. Funny how giving a surprise was even better than getting one. He couldn't wait to see her face when she saw the horse.

Too often lately, the face he couldn't get out of his mind was Amy's. He'd buried his feelings for her for ten years. He'd thought he was over her. Thought he could move back here and raise Ruby with only the occasional run-in and mild discomfort.

Yeah, right.

She'd hijacked his agenda—and his emotions. He valued her opinion, admired her compassion, craved her presence.

He wanted to kiss her again. All the time. Every morning. Every afternoon. Every night around sunset.

Lord, I'm about as dumb as a man can be. Help me get her off my mind.

"I've got to go out front for a minute, RuRu. I've got my walkie-talkie if you need me."

"'Kay, Daddy." She shoveled in another spoonful of cereal.

He hustled out the front door to Wade's truck and the horse trailer.

"Well, let's have a look-see." Nash rubbed his hands together as Wade rounded the back of the trailer.

"Ruby is going to love her. Gentle. Small. Older. The family I bought her from had three girls who learned to ride on her. Her name's Chantilly."

"Perfect." Nash clapped Wade on the shoulder. "Thanks, man. I always said you know horses better than anyone."

"Years of experience." He grinned. "If Ruby doesn't like her, give me a call. I have two other options."

"I don't think it will be an issue. The girl's horse crazy."

"My kind of girl."

"Mine, too." Nash chuckled. "Well, let's see the old gal."

Wade backed the horse out onto the gravel, then he stroked her back, speaking softly to her. She seemed right at home.

"She is a beauty." Nash whistled, slowly running his hand down her neck. "How did you know Ruby would want a white horse?"

"Just a coincidence." He led Chantilly toward the barn as they discussed her. When they reached the pasture fence, Wade asked, "Want to bring Ruby out?"

"You know I do. Be right back." He hurried to the patio and into the kitchen. "Get your shoes on. There's a surprise out front for you."

"What is it?" Worry lines creased her forehead.

"You're going to like it." He winked.

She scrambled to the mat where her shoes were kept and ran back to Nash. The picture she presented made him laugh—she wore a purple nightgown, her hair hadn't been brushed and her bare feet were shoved into tennis shoes with the laces trailing.

"Let's get those shoes tied before you trip and break a tooth." He crouched, ignoring his stiff joints, and tied her shoes before patting her on the head and following her outside.

When Ruby saw Wade and the white horse, she stopped in her tracks.

"Daddy, Uncle Wade has a horsey."

"I know."

Her face turned up to him with such longing Nash almost grabbed his chest.

"It's for you, RuRu. It's your horse." Once more, she was off and running. "Steer clear of its hind legs."

Circling wide around the animal, she came up to Wade and stood next to him. "Is it really mine, Uncle Wade?"

"Sure is, cutie." He grinned. "Meet Chantilly."

Nash joined them, patting the horse's neck.

Ruby lifted her arms to Wade, her face glowing with adoration, and Wade handed Nash the lead rope before picking her up. "What a mighty fine welcome, Ruby."

"A white horsey," she said, awestruck. "All mine!"

"We'll saddle her up for you, but not today. She needs a little time to get used to her new home first."

"I'll help Shalilly. I'll make sure she ain't lonely or scared."

"It's Chantilly," Nash said. "This horse is a big responsibility. You and I will be going over a lot of rules. And it might take time for her to trust you. Can you accept that?"

Wade set Ruby down, and she thought for a moment before nodding. "I understand, Daddy. Chantilly might think her mommy hated her and that's why she's here, but I'll tell her every day how much I love her."

Nash wasn't sure what to make of that comment. "This horse doesn't think her mommy hates her. In fact, she's old. She lived with three girls who all grew up riding her."

"They just threw her out?" Ruby's eyes filled with tears.

"No, they sold her to Uncle Wade. The girls all got

big and didn't have time to ride her anymore. She'll be very happy to have you taking care of her."

"I will. I'll love her and brush her and sing songs to her and read her stories…"

Wade met Nash's eyes and they both fought back laughter.

"You moved the horses to the new pasture, right?" Wade asked.

"Yes."

"Lead her around the fence line of the empty pasture and show her where the food is. The other horses will probably come up to the fence to check her out." Wade started walking backward toward his truck. "I'll get her feed and paperwork."

"You heard Uncle Wade." Nash looked at Ruby. "Let's take her around the pasture."

He held the lead rope while Ruby clutched his other hand, skipping next to him.

"I can't wait to tell Miss Amy I have my own horsey. She's going to love her. I'm going to tell Chantilly it's okay to feel sad sometimes, but Jesus is with her when she's missing her family. That's what Miss Amy told me, Daddy. And I'm going to tell Chantilly she'll always have lots of food here, and we'll never, ever leave her…"

Nash tried to keep up with Ruby's train of thought. The poor child's fears…based on her own rotten experience with their mother. He realized how much Ruby had blossomed with Amy around. A few months ago she'd barely talked, never smiled, shrank away from all physical contact, and here she was, sharing all the best things Amy taught her.

"Don't tell Miss Amy I have Chantilly, though, Daddy. I want to show her myself."

"You got it, RuRu."

"I love Miss Amy, Daddy."

I do, too.

His lungs locked up.

He loved Amy.

Still loved her. Had never stopped. And this time it was deeper, less selfish—and impossible. Absolutely impossible.

He frowned. Why? Didn't Ruby deserve to have a good mother, too? A mother like Amy?

Stop the wishful thinking!

Amy didn't want him messing with her heart. But she did want marriage and kids. What was he missing?

Had she been warning him?

Or warming up to him?

His throat felt like it was lined with sandpaper.

"I think Chantilly likes it here," Ruby said.

The horse seemed docile and sweet. When they'd taken her around the perimeter and showed her the feed station and water, they took the lead off her halter and let her settle in.

"We'll let her explore for a while." He tapped his finger against his chin. He had to run away from thinking about l-o-v-e all day. "You know what you need?"

She shook her head.

"If you're going to be a cowgirl, it's time to get you outfitted in cowboy boots, a hat and gear. I'll see if Uncle Wade wants to join us. Run up to your room and get dressed, okay?"

"Yay! Cowgirl clothes!"

"Tell Ruby I'm sorry I have to miss our craft time this afternoon, but I'll still be over tomorrow night."

Amy held her phone to her ear as she clicked open the digital files Orchard Creek Mills had emailed back to her. The repeating pattern was off slightly in one file, and another had a design element they found too fussy. They needed the files fixed and returned tomorrow.

"I'll tell her," he said. "Is everything all right?"

"Yes, it's fine." She filled him in about the files she needed to fix. "I've got to get this right for them. I have so many more ideas for fabrics, and I'm spending a ton of money to have a booth at the quilt trade show next year. I can't fail. I just can't fail at this. I want buyers to love my collection. It will open up so many doors."

"They'll love it. How could they not?"

His emotional support was like a much-needed hug. "Thank you, Nash. Listen, I've got to go. I'll be over tomorrow night."

"Hey, Amy?"

"Yeah?"

"Don't put too much pressure on yourself. Your best is good enough."

"Thanks." After hanging up, she tried to concentrate on the files, but Nash's words kept plucking at her heart.

While in theory she agreed with him, she struggled to apply it to herself. She strove to do her best—to be the best she could be—but it didn't always add up to her believing it.

She never really felt like she was good enough.

And these files brought out her insecurities.

What if she fixed everything, sent them back and Mr. Whitaker didn't like them? What if Orchard Creek Mills walked away from the contract? Until she had the fabrics in her hands, she couldn't be sure they would keep their word.

They like your work, Amy.

This excitement—this feeling of finally getting what she'd wanted after craving it for so long—was familiar. She'd had it right before Nash left town. She'd had the impression he wanted to propose. Then he had vanished. And later, when she got serious with John, she'd practically tasted the engagement ring, the wedding ceremony, the house in town, the kids.

And both times her hopes had been dashed so suddenly, she'd thought she would have a nervous breakdown.

Well, she'd come close to a breakdown after Nash.

She zoomed in on the file. Nash was wrong. Her best had never been good enough. That's why these drawings needed to be perfect. She'd give the company no reason to doubt working with her. None at all.

Chapter Thirteen

Tonight could change his life.

Nash smoothed his hands down the front of his new shirt and studied his appearance in the mirror. Not bad. And that was saying something. Ever since he'd realized he still loved Amy, he'd been a mess. He couldn't get her off his mind. He had to do something about it.

He just wasn't sure what.

He'd bought her flowers—a mixture of colorful blooms—picked out the thickest, juiciest steaks from the market, cleaned the house, bought *and lit* a scented candle and had even tossed a salad for them. Green leafy things didn't usually grace his plate, but this was for Amy. He'd endure fresh vegetables.

Should he admit he loved her and beg her to give him a second chance? Tell her he'd never let her down again? Shout that he'd changed, that he wasn't the same man who'd left her high and dry?

It all made him queasy.

He couldn't honestly say he'd never let her down again. And had he changed? He was the same old Nash. He couldn't bear to hurt her, but it wasn't as if he had the best track record of stepping up and doing the right thing. Maybe she was better off without him.

Lord, I need Your help. I don't know what to say or do, but I want to put Amy first this time.

"Daddy?" Ruby called from her room.

"What do you need?" he yelled back.

"I can't get my shirt buttoned."

"Be right there." He gave his appearance one more quick look. Good enough.

After helping Ruby button her new Western shirt—pink and white, naturally—he went out to the patio to fire up the grill. He turned the gas to medium-high and glanced through the patio door at Ruby. She was attempting to wrap a ribbon around Fluffy's neck. He went back inside before she strangled the poor thing.

"I can't get it on her, and Fluffy's being bad." Ruby threw the ribbon down and stomped her foot, clad in a pink cowboy boot.

"Cats don't like people tying 'em up, RuRu." He crouched down. "She's not being bad. Here, let me try it."

Ruby picked up the purple ribbon and gave it to him.

"You hold the fleabag while I tie it."

She held Fluffy while he got it around the wiggly kitten's neck, then loosely tied it in a bow.

"You did it, Daddy!" She set Fluffy down and hugged Nash. He held her tightly, enjoying how everything he did in her eyes was heroic. She pulled back, clapping her hands. "I can't wait to show Chantilly to Miss Amy!"

"I know you can't wait."

"Will you do the pigtails again?" Ruby held out two hair elastics. He'd watched a video on how to pull Ruby's hair into pigtails. He'd also watched a video on braiding, but it was beyond him at this point.

"You got it." He parted her hair and smoothed the sections to the side then fastened each into an elastic band. "You are the very picture of a cowgirl."

She grinned. A knock at the door propelled her into motion. "I'll get it!"

He wiped his sweaty palms down his jeans and willed himself to act normal.

"Hi!" Amy beamed, holding Ruby's hand, as she entered the kitchen. She wore a simple sundress and strappy sandals. Her hair tumbled around her tanned shoulders. She looked prettier than he'd ever seen her. His collar tightened around his neck. She gestured to Ruby's outfit. "I see you went shopping. Great choice."

"You like my boots, Miss Amy?" Ruby lifted her foot.

"I love them. I might have to get a matching pair. Then we could be twinsies."

"Twinsies!" Ruby's eyes widened. "What's that?"

"It's when two good friends dress the same. Like twins."

"Daddy, tell Miss Amy where we got the boots so she can get some just like mine."

"You are a vision tonight, Miss Amy." He met her eyes, all sparkling and brown, and his legs positively wobbled. "And as for the boots, the Western store in town will be sure to hook you up." His voice cracked on the last word. He mentally shook himself—*get it together!*

"Come on, I got a surprise!" Ruby tugged Amy's hand and dragged her to the patio.

"I'll throw the steaks on." Nash uncovered the plate of meat and found the tongs, but all he could think about was Amy in that dress.

"Okay," Amy said, "but then we need to come back in because I have something to tell your daddy."

Nash rubbed his chin, watching them stroll hand in hand to the barn. What did Amy want to tell him? Her hair waved in the breeze, and her shapely legs peeked out from under the dress. Ruby kept jumping up and turning to talk to Amy. Her patience amazed him.

He put the steaks on the grill, his mouth watering as the meat sizzled. The blue sky and hot temperature combined to make the ideal summer day. With these conditions, Ruby so happy and Amy shining like the brightest star, he'd be a fool not to tell her how he felt about her. The timing was right.

Sitting on the patio chair, he propped his ankle on his knee and breathed in the fresh air. Chantilly was still in a separate pasture, but the way she and the other horses kept checking each other out at the fence line, he figured she could join them in another day or two.

He'd called the contractor, and they'd agreed on a price and timeline to construct another barn, a new building with an indoor arena, locker rooms and additional parking space. A crew would be out next week to begin.

He flipped the steaks as Amy and Ruby approached.

"I'm going to find Fluffy. She has a bow on!" Ruby raced indoors, leaving him and Amy alone.

"Guess what?" Her red lips and big smile were blinding him. Whatever she had to say must be pretty great for her to be so happy. And if she was in a good mood now, didn't that bode well for him to declare his feelings?

"What?" He closed the grill to let the steaks cook a few more minutes.

"I got a call when I was heading out the door to come here. It was the buyer for a home furnishings company. She wants to hire me!"

Hire her? Nash scratched his neck as dread washed over him. What was she talking about?

"Lexi planned this woman's wedding a few years ago, and, since they both lived in Denver at the time, they became friends. Lexi told her about my fabrics and texted her a few pictures. Apparently, she did an internet search and loved what she saw…"

Denver. The word repeated over and over in his mind. Amy liked Denver. Thought it was a fun town. She'd said herself she'd never had a reason to move.

And now she did.

He fought a drowning sensation. If she took the job, he couldn't follow her. Ruby was doing so well in Sweet Dreams. The therapist had drilled into him that she needed stability—a real home—long term. And he'd agreed. Promised himself he'd stick it out for Ruby. No matter what.

All the words he'd been ready to say stuck in his throat. He couldn't deny Amy this opportunity. She'd worked hard to get to this point. Just the other night she'd been so stressed about failing at this.

With the heaviest of hearts, he tuned back in to what she was saying.

"…pillows and furniture, but I never thought about doing that type of work."

He clenched his jaw, took a deep breath and looked her in the eye. "You should take the job."

"What?" Her nose scrunched, and she shook her head. "No, I don't want it."

"Denver is a great city, and you worked hard for this."

"I didn't work hard for *this*. I worked hard to have my own fabric line. Two different things."

"You'll regret it if you don't go." The words came out harsher than he intended. But the thought of her moving tore him up inside. He wanted to trap her here, make her stay, but he wouldn't be that selfish.

She crossed her arms over her chest and thrust her hip out. "Are you trying to get rid of me?"

Her excitement morphed into frustration. Why was he telling her to go? Didn't he have feelings for her? Or had the friendship they'd rebuilt been a sham?

"I want what's best for you." Nash stood next to the grill. Gone was the mischievous twinkle in his eyes. He looked like a tough cowboy who wouldn't budge.

"Well, I don't want the job." She hiked up her chin. "It was an ego boost to be asked, and, yeah, I'm flattered, but I don't want to move."

"It would be a step up."

"A step up from what? In case you haven't noticed, I run a successful quilt store right here in Sweet Dreams. I sell my patterns online, have a popular blog and now can add fabric designer to my credentials. I'm sorry you think what I've accomplished is a step down."

"That's not what I meant and you know it."

"No, I don't know it, Nash. I have no idea what you think. All I know is I've worked hard for a decade to get where I'm at, and I don't need anyone telling me what to do."

"I'm not telling you what to do."

"Yes, that's exactly what you're doing." She'd been growing close to him, and once again, he'd blindsided her. He acted as if he wanted her gone, out of Sweet Dreams, out of his life.

Didn't he understand Denver offered her nothing? Everything she wanted was right here.

Nash stood with his legs wide. "There are more opportunities for you there."

"'Opportunities'?" She huffed. "What about my loyal customers—many who have become good friends? I would lose more than I would gain—my store, my friends, my family."

"You don't lose your friends and family when you move. You'd still talk to them. You'd visit."

"It's not the same." Heaviness descended on her heart. With every word, he was pushing her to go. But why? If this was the end, she didn't want to spend the next ten years wondering what went wrong. She'd done that once. She wouldn't do it again. "What's going on, Nash? I thought we're growing close."

"We are." He averted his eyes.

"You kissed me."

"Yeah."

"Am I imagining the connection between us? We get along well. Always have."

"You're not imagining it." He licked his lips. "But I'm not going to stand in the way of the career you've worked hard for."

She wanted to scream. "But that's what I'm trying to tell you—I didn't work hard to move away and work for someone else."

"If you stay here, you'll regret it." His voice was cold.

"I know I'm regretting telling you about it." Her heart was shrinking. She didn't need to be hit over the head with what he was trying to tell her, but it hurt. Once again, she'd trusted him, and once again, he'd been the wrong guy to trust.

"Forget it." He turned away. "Do what you want."

Do what she wanted? She straightened, growing more disillusioned with each passing second. What was his deal? He'd been kind and open and easy to be with ever since he'd come back to town. She knew he was attracted to her and she guessed it was more than that, after she'd caught him staring at her and the kiss from the rodeo. It was love, wasn't it?

If this was love, why was he pushing her away?

Last time he ran away.

He couldn't run away this time. Not with Ruby in his care.

Was he trying to make her leave because he couldn't go anywhere himself?

Well, then whatever he felt for her wasn't enough.

It had never been enough.

Maybe his relationships with his mother and Hank had burned him to the point he wasn't capable of loving Amy the way she wanted to be loved.

"I know what you're doing," she said. "You're pushing me out of your life. You escaped to the rodeo before, but this time you can't. Well, guess what? I'm not Hank, who used you and got himself killed. And I'm certainly not your mother, who was completely unqualified to take care of herself, let alone raise two children. I'm trustworthy, Nash. But you still don't trust me." She pulled her shoulders back, tossed her hair. "If you want me out of your life, say so. You don't need to drive me away. I'll go and never come back."

"I do trust you." He hung his head. "But I'll only let you down."

He wasn't even willing to fight for her? Red-hot fury boiled in her veins. "Well, I guess we agree on something. All you've ever done is let me down!"

She couldn't stay another second. She ran across the patio through the yard to the driveway where her car was parked. With shaky breaths she tried to remember if she'd left her purse in the house, but no, it was sitting on the passenger seat. She got in, tried to calm her trembling fingers and jammed the key into the ignition. Checked her mirrors.

Nash had followed her. He stood to the side of her car. His face had paled. His eyes were filled with panic. He didn't move, didn't say anything, but his lips looked blue and his stillness was eerily familiar.

Don't think about it. Just go!

She backed up as Ruby, arms flailing, ran out to the driveway. Tears were streaming down the girl's face. Amy forced herself to look away from the mirrors, but her heart was dying, and she could hear Ruby's wails as she drove away.

Lord, have mercy on us all.

"Make her stay! Daddy, make her stay!" Ruby raced toward Amy's car, and Nash had to grab her to stop her. She thrashed about, desperately trying to free herself, constantly shouting, "Make her stay!"

He wrapped his arms around her, holding her tightly until she stopped trying to break free. Tears streamed down her face, and her huge, gulping sobs killed something inside him. Finally, she stilled, whispering, "Don't let Miss Amy leave. Tell her I'll be good."

Nash couldn't stop the pressure building in his chest. He'd pushed Amy out of his life as easily as he'd walked away a decade ago. And this time he hadn't only ruined his life. He'd ruined Ruby's, as well.

And he had no idea why.

He carried Ruby into the house.

"Why'd you tell her to leave? She didn't want to. She said so. And you told her to go. Why, Daddy? Why?"

Why, indeed?

"I don't know. I've got to think about it. Let's give Amy time to cool off." He set Ruby on the couch. She covered her face with her tiny hands and ran upstairs, bawling. The sound of her door slamming rattled his entire body.

Smoke billowed from the patio, and he jogged outside. The steaks were black and smelled awful. He flicked the gas off and refrained from kicking the grill.

Charred meat. A brokenhearted little girl. And the best woman he'd ever met had just driven away.

It was all his fault. Every drop of it.

He tossed the black steaks onto a plate to cool off.

Amy's words about Hank and his mother kept running through his brain. He wouldn't argue that his mother had been supremely unqualified to have kids. But Hank hadn't used Nash. And Nash would never put Amy in the same category as either of them, anyway.

What did she know?

If she knew how bad his childhood had been, she'd have driven off long ago.

But she did know. Maybe he hadn't told her every

rotten story, all the twisted details, but she knew. And she hadn't left him.

She hadn't treated him differently. She hadn't judged him or looked down on him, and she certainly hadn't walked away from him.

She'd been his rock. The person he least deserved to have on his side.

Ten years ago, he'd blamed his mother for the way he had left Amy. But maybe it had been a convenient lie—the same lie he was trying to sell himself now— that he was doing it for her own good.

Could she be right? Maybe he didn't trust her.

Did he trust anybody? Or was he so messed up that he chased every good thing away? Everyone acted like he was some sort of superstar for riding ornery bulls, but he hadn't been brave.

Every thud of being launched onto the ground, each time his arm was yanked out of its socket, every bruise, kick, broken bone—all had given him a sense of relief from the yawning hole inside him.

And each time he'd cheated death, he'd known he didn't deserve another chance.

Yet, somehow he was still here.

He sat at the table, dropping his head in his hands.

God, I thought I was doing all right. I made the most of my life the only way I knew how, the only way it made sense. But I'm more empty and confused than ever. What's the point? Why am I here? Why did You make me?

He thought of his time at the group foster home. All the church services with Big Bob and Dottie. The many times Dottie had told him, "Jesus loves you. Nothing—

not one thing—can separate you from His love. Got that, hotshot?"

Dottie and her "hotshot." Maybe a talk with lil' mama would get his thoughts straight. He swiped his phone and called.

Chapter Fourteen

Amy unlocked the door to her store and flipped on the lights to the back room. Her fury had cooled, replaced by desolation. She hadn't allowed herself to cry yet, and on the drive home, she'd concentrated on all the ways Nash had failed her in the past. She should never have let him back into her life. The blame was all hers.

And she was tired of taking the blame.

She'd been convinced something was wrong with her to make Nash leave. Then she'd grown certain of it when John left, too. But the only thing wrong with her was her choice in men. They were the problem. Always had been.

But it meant she was part of the problem, too, because she kept falling for the wrong guys.

God, why didn't You equip me with the radar other women have? I need some sort of internal alert system that would say, "Hey, he's a keeper. He won't let you down," or, "Nope, don't even think about that guy. He's as unreliable as they come." Why? Why, God?

Ruby's cries kept echoing in her head. She'd broken her promise to Ruby. She'd told the little girl she was only there for her. But Amy hadn't turned around when Ruby had run out crying. The child must have witnessed their argument.

Amy's lungs kept squeezing and tightening, and it was so hard to breathe. How had everything gone wrong in such a short amount of time? Just a couple of hours ago she'd gotten the call from Lexi's friend, never realizing it would cause her life to implode.

She trudged to the showroom. The store had always brought her peace and joy. Gleaming hardwood floors, rugs, the fabrics folded and displayed just so, the quilts hanging on the walls. Her quilts. Her gaze climbed the wall to the first quilt she'd ever made. It wasn't for sale.

Memories crashed back of stitching it by hand the year after Nash left. At the time, she'd been piecing together scraps of material in all different colors and shapes. She hadn't known there was a name for it—a crazy quilt. And she never would have guessed the final product would be a thing of beauty. It had been a way out of the pain at the time.

The jewel-tone fabrics had been scraps in one of her mother's bins of craft materials for projects at the senior center. The purple, midnight blue and wine red fabrics below the center of the quilt still held her tears. She'd stitched the section after Christmas that year. Each added piece had allowed her to truly let go of her hopes that Nash would realize he'd made a terrible mistake and come back.

The colors blended together in rich imperfection, a melding of each dream she'd been forced to let go.

She took out a step stool and set it under the hanging quilt. Three steps up, and she pressed the bottom of the quilt to her cheek. The instant the material touched her skin Nash's face in her rearview mirror came back to her.

No, I don't want to remember! I want to forget!

He wasn't the man for her. He couldn't love her the way she needed, and she was done giving her love to people who couldn't reciprocate it.

She stepped down from the ladder. The crazy quilt had been scrapped together with her discarded love. Because Nash hadn't wanted what she'd desperately wanted to give him.

And he still refused to accept what she wanted to give...

She clasped her hands. She'd been trying to deny she loved him. But she'd loved him all along.

She'd always loved him.

And she couldn't keep giving her heart to someone who didn't want it.

She was worth more than that.

After locking up the store, she slowly made her way to the apartment. The quilt she'd been making for Ruby sat in blocks on the worktable. Her cell phone dinged. She swiped, hoping it was Nash, but it was a reminder from Mom to stop by tomorrow. Her fumbling fingers accidentally pressed her photos.

The first picture greeting her was Ruby on Nash's lap here in the apartment.

The phone dropped from her hands, and she covered her face, crying desperate tears.

It was really over. Her fantasy of life with Nash and Ruby—of being their family—had come to an end.

She did the only thing she could when faced with a gaping hole in her heart. She picked up the quilt she was making for Ruby and began to hand-stitch the blocks together. Tears dropped onto the fabric, one after the other.

She'd gotten over Nash once. She'd do it again.

"It's not like you to call me, hotshot. What's wrong?"

Normally he'd respond with "Nothing's wrong," but he was way past denial. "I need some straight-up, godly advice, lil' mama."

Silence greeted him. "This *is* Nash, correct?"

"Yes, Dottie, it's me." He fought exasperation. "Are you going to help or not?"

"Well, don't get your britches in a bunch. I'm not used to any of you boys asking for advice."

"Sorry." And he was. It wasn't her fault he'd screwed up his life. He never should have left Amy all those years ago. Amy was right—he'd taken the easy way out and used his mother as an excuse to avoid trusting in a future with her.

"Is this about buttercup?"

"No, it's about puddin'." He couldn't believe he'd actually referred to Amy as puddin'.

"Ah, I'm glad. Looks like you kids have patched up your problems. I always thought you were perfect for each other."

"Well, I ripped a big old hole back into those problems. But I don't know why."

"You'd better explain it to me, hon. I'm not a mind reader."

Explain it? He didn't even know where to begin. He sighed. "It all started the day I met with Pastor Moore. I can't even tell you my shock when Amy walked in to be Ruby's mentor."

"I'm guessing her shock was equal to yours."

"More, probably…" He told Dottie everything. How selfless Amy had been in helping Ruby, how he admired Amy's talent and career, how they'd become friends again and how he had deeper feelings, way deeper than he had thought possible. Finally, he admitted how he'd pushed her away.

"Well, you know lettin' a cat out of the bag is a lot easier than puttin' it back in," Dottie said.

"I guess." He scrunched his nose, trying to decipher what she meant. "Actually, I don't know why that applies to this situation."

"I don't know why you just up and left her all those years ago, hon. If you can figure that out, you'll have a good chance at figuring out why you're pushing her away now. I'm pretty sure the reason is one and the same."

"Why do you think I did it?" He held his breath, hoping for the answer, the one that would make sense.

"Oh, Nash, I could give you a hundred reasons, but if none of them are the right one, they won't matter. You need to get your Bible out and pray."

Disappointment hit him hard. Dottie was making him figure things out for himself? He wanted her to give him the answers.

"Get your Bible out. Right now. And start praying. And if you get an answer to those prayers, don't be afraid to call me anytime to watch buttercup if you need to go over and talk to puddin'. Even if it's the middle of the night. I'll understand."

"Okay, Dottie. Thank you."

"I love you, hon."

"Love you, too."

After hanging up, he did as he was told. He went

upstairs to his bedroom, grabbed his Bible and headed back down to the kitchen table. He sat and paused. *Father, I don't know what my problem is, but I'm asking for Your help figuring it out. I've got Ruby to think about now. I can't go messing everyone's lives up. I need You.*

He took a moment to let his thoughts clear. Then he opened the Bible and flipped through to his favorite psalm—thirty-seven. Trailing his finger, he found the beginning of the seventh verse: "Rest in the LORD, and wait patiently for him."

He'd found the verse last year. He'd struggled with being still—with resting—his entire life. Patience didn't come naturally to him. But taking matters into his own hands? He got that. Oh, how he got it.

When he was young, he'd wanted a mother who loved him, but he got one who abused him. Then he'd wanted a father, and Hank had showed up, but in many ways, Amy was right. Hank had abused him, too.

The night Hank died stood in his mind as fresh as if it had happened last week. The summer heat had been scorching all weekend. Dusk had fallen. The lights beamed onto the arena floor. Nash had placed second in the junior bull ride—his bull calf had been rambunctious—and he was hanging out by the chutes, joking with the other guys who'd competed. The announcer called Hank's name, and Nash had been taken aback. Weren't the barrel races going on? Hank rarely competed in those. He'd tried to peer over the chutes, but he'd had to run around them to see what was happening. The gasp from the crowd slowed his steps, and when he'd finally been able to see, Hank was on the ground, the horse scrambling to roll off him. Hank wasn't moving. He'd died instantly.

In that moment, seeing Hank's lifeless body, Nash's world collapsed. Without Hank and summers and the rodeo, all Nash had left was a drug-addicted mother. A life full of chaos.

His chest now burned with pent-up sobs. *I needed you, Hank. I loved you. You were the only man I looked up to when I was young. I wanted to be just like you. Why'd you have to die?*

He'd put the night out of his mind for almost twenty years. Refused to remember in case it broke him.

Would it break him tonight?

Did you know I did it, Hank? I became a world champion bull rider. Remember how we used to drive those lonely highways, talking about what we'd do when we hit it big? Well, I actually made it. And I never would have if it wasn't for you. I wish you'd have been there. You would have loved it. You would have chewed me out every time I came in second and told me exactly what I had done wrong. I'd have listened, too, because I trusted you. I think you were the last person I trusted with the most important parts of me. When you died, part of me died with you.

He gave in to the emotions. Cried until there was nothing left. He'd never grieved Hank, and it felt good and right to feel the pain of losing him. Finally, he lifted his head and stared at the refrigerator.

Drawings, coloring pages, cut-outs and more filled the fridge door. Ruby's handiwork. All because of Amy.

Amy.

The only person who had never—not once—given

him a reason to doubt her intentions. She'd loved him unconditionally a decade ago. And now?

The woman he'd treated so shabbily was more honorable than anyone he'd ever met. She could have been spiteful and full of revenge. Could have spit in his face when she learned about Ruby and the lies he'd told her about not having a mother. But she hadn't. Instead, she'd gone so far above anything he'd ever known to set aside her own feelings in order to help Ruby.

He loved her. He didn't deserve her, but his heart was filled to the brim with love for that woman.

A picture of three stick figures holding hands under a sun caught his eye. The scene told him everything he needed to know.

Amy was Ruby's Hank.

And for him, Amy was more. She was the difference between a glass of pure water and one of thick mud. A dreary overcast day and a spectacular sunny day. He couldn't do life without her, and he refused to pretend he could.

He didn't know how to win her back. But he had to try.

"Tell me exactly what he said, and don't leave out a word." Lexi crossed one leg over the other at six thirty Saturday morning.

Amy felt bad for waking Lexi so early but was relieved that she'd insisted on coming over. They both held matching pink floral teacups and saucers.

"I told him about the job offer, and I honestly think he tuned out most of what I said." Amy perched on the edge of the chair next to the couch. Her tea lay untouched in her hands.

"Why do you think that?"

"Because he told me to take the job." Amy hadn't slept much last night, and the bags under her eyes felt heavier than bolts of upholstery fabric. "He thinks I'll regret not taking it."

"But you don't want the job." Concern hooded Lexi's eyes. "I'm sorry, Amy. I never thought she'd offer you a position and expect you to move. I thought she'd love your fabrics and want to collaborate on pillows or something."

"Don't be sorry. No matter how many times I told him I didn't want the job and wasn't taking it, he kept pushing me to leave. I think he was looking for an excuse to put the brakes on our relationship."

Lexi raised her eyebrows and took a sip of tea. "I know all about that. Clint and I got into a huge fight before he proposed. I didn't see him for a few days. Thought he'd left for good."

"Yes, but he came back. I don't think this will have a happy ending."

"You don't know that, Amy. Remember, darkness comes before morning. Anyway, tell me the rest."

"And sometimes darkness just gets darker." Amy set her teacup on the coffee table. "I got tired of arguing with him about this dumb job offer. Then it hit me. Maybe his messed up childhood is to blame. Maybe he's not capable of loving me the way I expect."

Lexi nodded. "Clint's childhood was pretty bad, too. But he got the courage to give love a chance."

"Well, I don't see it happening in our case. I yelled at him and ran to my car. And Ruby must have heard because she came flying out the front door as I was driving away. I can still hear her wailing." Amy slumped in the chair. "I can't get her cries or Nash's face out of my mind."

Lexi cringed. "Did he look pretty mad?"

"No...he looked..." She didn't want to think about it, but his face was there. Pale, shocked, blue around the lips. She gasped, bringing her fingers to her mouth. "Oh, no."

"What?"

Amy crossed the room to the window. Why hadn't she realized this earlier? Nash had looked exactly the same as Ruby had on the first day he'd dropped her off at Amy's apartment.

Terrified. Shattered.

She tried to undo the knot of truths twisting around each other in her mind. Ruby had been severely neglected. And when Amy had asked how Nash knew what Ruby had been through, he'd told her he knew from experience.

His experience.

Ruby and Nash were one and the same.

Same mother. Same horrible childhood. Same desperate need for an anchor they could trust.

Except Ruby had gotten out of that nightmare of a life when she was still young, and the only anchor Nash had found was Hank until he died. But maybe Amy had been his anchor, too. Then his mom had intervened.

No wonder he had such a hard time with trust.

And his face last night...he *did* trust her. If she had to guess, she'd say he trusted her more than anyone else in the world. But look at how Ruby had feared Nash would leave her. It had taken time and patience for Ruby to finally believe he'd always stay.

Maybe Nash needed time and patience to trust Amy wouldn't disappear the way other people in his life had.

"What is it, Amy?" Lexi twisted in her seat.

She returned and sank into the chair. "I just realized something. I don't think I've ever truly understood why Nash is the way he is."

"Is that a good thing or a bad thing?"

"I'm not sure." She bit her lower lip. "You know how I told you Ruby was terrified of staying alone with me when I first met her?"

"Yes, the poor little thing. It broke my heart when you told me she'd worried Nash didn't want her anymore and she thought he'd just left her with you. What must have happened to her to make her think something like that."

"I know. It was so heartbreaking. And this is going to sound weird, but I think, deep down, Nash has the same fear when it comes to me."

Lexi took a sip of tea before answering. "How do you mean? He's worried you'll dump him?"

"No, not that. I think he wants to believe I won't hurt him, but given his past, he can't quite bring himself to trust it. Does that make sense?"

"Yes. Absolutely. I think you nailed it."

Amy selected a shortbread cookie from the plate on the coffee table. Lexi munched on one, too.

"What are you going to do now?" Lexi asked, brushing crumbs from her hands.

"I don't know."

"You love him, don't you?"

Amy nodded, tears threatening once more.

"But do you think he can ever emotionally give you what you need?"

Amy sighed. Ruby had blossomed with Nash's patience and constant assurances he'd never leave her. But Ruby was four. Nash was over thirty and had experienced more hardships.

"I know you want to get married and have a family, Amy. What if he never gets to the point where he can commit to you, heart and soul?"

Why did Lexi ask the toughest questions? Amy's chest felt so raw. If Nash couldn't commit heart and soul…

"If that's the case, there will never be anything between us, and I'll have to convince him to allow me to continue my relationship with Ruby."

"It will be hard."

"My life usually is hard."

"I can't argue with that." Lexi clasped her hands together. "Does he know how you feel about him?"

"I haven't said the *l* word if that's what you're asking."

"Don't you think you should before you make any decisions?"

This conversation was giving her indigestion. She'd already been brave and asked him about marriage and kids. Now she had to tell him she loved him? After he'd let her leave?

Hadn't he been the one to walk away last time? Not to mention she'd set aside her feelings to help him with Ruby. He should be the one begging her to stay, telling her he loved her, being vulnerable for once in his life.

Amy, you know the fruit of the Spirit is love, joy, kindness, gentleness and all that.

She'd been kind. She'd been gentle. He could do the love and joy part.

Didn't you ask the good Lord to send you out to the harvest? Did you only do it for a reward?

Shame sunk like a pit in her gut. Nash didn't owe her anything. She'd entered their arrangement with one intention—to spend time with a little girl. It wasn't his fault she'd fallen right back in love with him.

God, remind me You're enough. You've always been enough for me.

"If you don't tell him, you might always wonder, 'What if…'" Lexi said. "I'd hate to see you with regrets. I know how much you care about him and Ruby."

"I do care about them. More than I ever thought possible. Nash listens to me, is interested in my life, and he cares. I know he cares. I just don't know if he cares enough. As for Ruby—she's like a piece of my heart. I think I'd give just about anything to raise her as my own child."

"You have to tell him."

Amy nodded.

"Now. Go." Lexi stood, pointing to the door. "Before you have second thoughts."

"I look terrible, Lexi." She couldn't go over there with her hair an unruly squirrel's nest and her face a splotchy mess.

"Well, get in the shower and slap some makeup on. But you have to go to his house this morning and tell him the truth—tell him you love him and you'll never let him down."

Amy gasped. How had Lexi known the exact words they'd thrown at each other? Was that what Nash had really meant when he'd told her he'd only let her down? Had he been conveying his fears *she* would let *him* down?

"Promise me you're going over there. Tell him." Lexi wagged her finger at Amy.

"I promise."

"You mean it?"

"Yes. You're right. I don't want to live with regrets. It's better to be open and honest with him and lay it all out. Then I'll know where I stand, and I'll be able to move forward."

Lexi hugged her. "Call me when it's over."

"I will." Amy walked her to the door. "Thanks."

After Lexi left, Amy headed straight for the shower. She might as well follow Lexi's advice and get this over with. She just hoped she'd be the winner in love for once.

Chapter Fifteen

A tap on Nash's shoulder woke him. He lifted his head from where it rested on his arm, groaning at the crick in his neck. He'd fallen asleep at the kitchen table. Wiping his mouth, he squinted at the clock. Seven in the morning.

"Daddy?"

"What?" He shot to a sitting position. "What is it, RuRu?"

She stood before him with dark circles under her eyes and the expression of a basset hound. Her long blond hair rippled down her back. She wore a pink princess nightgown, and bare toes snuck out beneath the hem. She held a shoebox in her hands.

"Will you take me over to Miss Amy's? I have all my best things. I'll give her all of it if she'll stay."

Rip my heart open first thing why don't you, Ruby?

"Honey, that's not how it works." He lifted her, settling her on his lap. "Miss Amy spends time with you because she wants to. She adores you. It makes her happy to frost cupcakes and color and all the things she does with you."

"But she likes spending time with you, too, Daddy. Her eyes crinkle up—they look like they're smiling— when you talk to her, and she's always as nice as can be to you."

He shifted his jaw. Ruby was right. But what could he say? *Hey, kid, I know Miss Amy is all that and a bag of chips, but I blew it. More than once. And she deserves better than me.*

"I prayed last night to Jesus just like you told me to." Tears began forming in her eyes. He swiped them away with his thumb.

"I did, too, RuRu."

"Did He forgive you?"

"Yes. He always forgives us when we repent." Man, this kid was hitting home the truths this morning.

"If you say you're sorry to Miss Amy, she'll forgive you, too." Ruby caressed his cheek with her itty-bitty hand.

"It's more complicated than that."

"Why?"

Why? I don't know. Nothing makes sense anymore.

"I hurt Miss Amy a long time ago. I was her boyfriend, and I left her."

"Mama left me cuz I was a bad girl. Miss Amy said I wasn't, but…" Ruby couldn't sound more distraught. "Miss Amy's never been bad. Why'd you leave her?"

"You had nothing to do with your mother leaving. Nothing. You weren't a bad girl." His heart felt like a shredded, pulverized piece of meat. "Your mother used drugs and never should have left you. You deserved more. Still deserve more. But you need to understand something else, Ruby. Nobody is perfect. Not even Miss Amy. And it's okay to not be perfect. God loves us and

He sent His Son to die for us to take away our sins. So even if you did something really naughty, God forgives you and still loves you. Does that make sense?"

"Miss Amy told me that, too." She gave him a pitiful nod. "I want her to stay. She'll forgive you."

How could he explain to Ruby he was afraid he'd hurt Amy again? He didn't know how, but what if…

"Daddy, I don't want her to go to Denver. Can't we go to her 'partment and tell her not to go? I'll give her Brownie and Fluffy and Chantilly."

His gaze fell to the box Ruby had set on the table. He could see all of the contents. An apple. A baggie full of fish-shaped crackers. All of the paper hearts they'd cut out together. A placemat with a brown horse and red cloud scribbled on it. A box of crayons. Every eraser and sticker she'd gotten from the Easter egg hunt. The ribbon he'd tied around Fluffy.

Those simple treasures were everything to Ruby, and she was willing to give them all to Amy if she'd just stay.

Shame hit him. It was more than he'd offered Amy.

Lord, I'm sorry. This little girl has opened my eyes to the meaning of sacrifice. If You'll show me the way, I want to do the same. Amy gave me everything good. I want to give her that, too. And as much as I tell myself I'm not worthy of her and I've done too much to hurt her—I can't believe it anymore. I've got to accept Your forgiveness. I want to embrace Your love.

"Please, Daddy? Please?"

"You don't have to give Amy anything, Ruby." He took a deep breath, terrified and exhilarated at what he was about to say. "I love Miss Amy. I think she might love me, too. And here's what I'm going to do. I'm

going to take a shower and drop you off to have breakfast with Dottie. Then I'm driving over to Miss Amy's
and I'm going to tell her how much I love her and beg
her to forgive me. How does that sound?"

Ruby's eyes grew wide with hope and excitement.
"You mean Miss Amy might be your girlfriend?"

He hoped more than a girlfriend. The engagement
ring he'd purchased a decade ago still sat in his drawer.
He'd love nothing more than to see it on Amy's finger.
Hadn't they wasted enough time?

He gave her a big smile. "I sure hope so, RuRu. Now
you get dressed while I shower, okay?"

"Okay! Hurry!"

She was an old dishrag; the mirror proved it. Amy
applied another layer of concealer under her eyes. Still
puffy and dark. Telling Nash she loved him would be
much easier if she looked her best. An impossible task
at the moment. Swiping a burgundy lipstick over her
lips, she puckered them and stood back.

Yikes.

Maybe she should get a good night's sleep and do
this tomorrow.

No, she'd promised Lexi she would tell him today.

Ugh. Consciences. Who needed them?

She drew her shoulders back. *Lord, I know You made
me strong enough to do this, but sometimes I get tired
of being strong. Will You be my strength?*

Someone knocked on the door. "Amy, are you in
there?"

Nash! Her pulse sprinted as she straightened her
shirt, trying not to panic. She went to the door.

"What are you doing here?" She drank him in, from

his cowboy hat to his plaid button-down, belt buckle, jeans and cowboy boots. His face was scruffy, like he'd forgotten to shave.

He stepped inside and closed the door behind him. Gently took her by the biceps. His jaw shifted.

"I love you." He stared into her eyes, and she spiraled into their intensity. Trying to get her head on straight, she blinked. More than once.

"I love you," he said again. "And I am not going to walk away this time. You were right. I didn't trust you but only because I never fully trusted myself. For the record, I *was* afraid my mother would hurt you—I grew up with abuse, and not just from her but from the men around us—but it went deeper. Part of it was Hank. Not the way you think, though."

She wanted to say something, but she held back. Instead, she savored his calloused hands on her skin, his light grip on her arms.

"When I lost Hank, I lost the one good thing in my life. And I think part of me believed I could never trust in anything good lasting forever."

Amy bit her lip. What he said made sense.

"So I left you. And I spent years taking risks, punishing my body, seeing how far I could go to escape the fact I wasn't with you. And then when I returned, you were so spectacular. I mean, I had a child in tow. And I'd never met anyone as generous and selfless and forgiving as you. You are too good for me. But I never stopped loving you, Amy, and this love—what's in my heart—is so much more than I can put in words. I don't expect you to believe me, but I would do anything for you. Please, tell me you forgive me. For leaving you back then. For pushing you away last night."

She inhaled deeply, shaking her head in wonder. "I love you, too, Nash."

"You really love me?" His body was close to hers.

"Yes." She nodded, unable to tear her eyes from his. "But I need you to hear me out about something."

His face fell, but he nodded. "Okay. Your turn."

Nash braced himself. He had a feeling he was about to hear something that would shatter his dreams.

"I realized something."

Here it comes. Take it like a man.

"You're Ruby."

He twisted his lips, frowning. "What?"

She nodded, her pretty brown eyes sincere. "You and Ruby—you're the same. Same eyes. Same forehead. Same mother. Same awful start to life. You both had terrible childhoods. Neither of you could trust the one person you should've been able to trust with your entire heart. And the look on Ruby's face the first time you tried to leave her here—the terrified, shattered expression? You had the same one last night, Nash. I'm not telling you this to make you feel bad. I want you to understand that, whether you know it or not, you share some of the fears Ruby's overcoming. The main difference between you and her is she got out when she was young. You've never had anyone you could truly trust."

He took off his hat, running his fingers through his hair. Amy was right. He'd put some of it together last night, but he'd never realized the issues Ruby was dealing with were issues he needed to deal with, as well.

"And, Nash." Amy took his hand in hers. "You can trust me. I know it's hard for you, so I'll be patient. I love you, and I'll never let you down. I'll never abandon you or use you."

This woman. His breath caught in his throat as he stared up at the ceiling. She slayed him. Just when he thought she couldn't get any better...

"Amy, I know I can trust you. With all my heart. With my soul." He reached into his jeans pocket and took out the box. Clumsily, he dropped to one knee, trying not to wince on the way down. *Please, God, let me not ruin this. Let her say yes.*

"Ten years ago, I bought the house and land I'm living on as a gift for you. I didn't tell you about it because I'd also purchased something else, and I wanted both to be a surprise." He opened the box and took out the ring. "Even though the surprise is a decade late, there is nothing in the world I want more than to be your husband. You've showered me with goodness, and I want to shower you with whatever your heart desires for the rest of your life. Will you marry me?"

Her jaw dropped and she cupped her hands over her mouth, her eyes filling with tears.

"Oh, Nash!" She pulled him up to stand. "Yes! I'll marry you."

"Don't you even want to see the ring?" He held it out to her.

Through her tears, she beamed, laughing. "Yes."

He slid the ring on her finger. From the way her eyes widened, he guessed she liked it.

"Wow." She held her arm out, hand up, admiring the large diamond. "That's some rock."

"And you're some woman." He tugged her closer and lowered his lips to hers. Perfection. Sliding his arms around her waist, he drank in her sweetness, dazzled at the thought he'd be kissing her every day for the rest of his life.

Finally, he broke free. They grinned at each other. No words were needed.

"So you know this means you're going to be a mommy."

Her smile arched like a brilliant rainbow. "I want to be Ruby's mommy."

"And how do you feel about adding more little cowboys and cowgirls as soon as possible?"

"As soon as possible. Nash, you have no idea how much I've longed for children. But if for whatever reason it doesn't happen, Ruby will be more than enough."

"I love you." He kissed her again. "You're really mine?"

"Forever." She wound her arms around his neck.

"Let's go tell Ruby."

Feeling lighter than a helium balloon, Amy held Nash's hand as they walked to Dottie's Diner to tell Ruby the big news. What if Ruby didn't want them to get married? Well, there was no sense in borrowing trouble. They'd find out soon enough.

Lord, You answered my prayers in the most spectacular fashion. Thank You! Please let Ruby be happy with our news. I don't want to bring turmoil to her life. I love her so much.

"After you, my lady." He held the diner's door open, and she sailed through under his arm.

"Miss Amy!" Ruby hopped off her stool and flew into her arms. Amy smoothed her hair and held her close. Ruby smiled up at her. "You didn't leave!"

"Is that what you thought?" Amy knelt. "I would

never go somewhere without telling you goodbye. But, Ruby, I don't have any plans to leave. I love Sweet Dreams. My life is here."

Ruby hugged her as if her life depended on it.

"Come on, let's get out of the way." Nash directed them to an empty booth. Once they settled, he rested his elbows on the table. "Miss Amy and I have something to tell you. We know it might bring up some emotions in you, so don't be afraid to tell us the truth about how you feel, okay?"

Worry wrinkled her little forehead, but she nodded.

"I asked Miss Amy to marry me, and she said yes."

Ruby's face transformed from scared to awestruck. "You mean Miss Amy will be my mommy?"

"Yes, RuRu, that's exactly what it means." Nash looked serious.

Amy turned to Ruby. "I know this is sudden, honey, so if you're—"

Ruby wrapped her arms around Amy's neck and began to cry. Amy patted her back, murmuring comfort. Was the girl happy or sad? Then Ruby lifted her head.

"I pray to Jesus every night that you'll be my mommy, Miss Amy. And He answered! You were right! He does answer prayers."

Amy was unprepared for the emotions swelling within her. This girl's love—it amazed her. *Lord, I forgot You're listening to more than my prayers. Thank You for answering both our prayers.*

"I love you very much, Ruby, and I can't wait to be your mommy." She kissed Ruby's cheek, and Ruby climbed onto her lap. "You're the daughter I've always dreamed about."

Amy met Nash's eyes, and from the looks of it, he

was having a hard time with his emotions, too. She reached across the table. He took her hand. And they smiled at each other.

God had saved His best for them all.

Epilogue

Today was no ordinary day, not for Amy Deerson, at least. Scratch that—Amy *Bolton*. She'd just married the man of her dreams and had become the mother of her favorite little girl in the whole world. Pausing in the church's entryway, she took advantage of the rare moment alone. *Thank You, God!*

The doors opened, and a September wind gusted, kicking up the back of her veil. Nash grinned, taking one step toward her and sweeping her into his arms. He easily carried her down the steps and to the waiting limo. Ruby had gone on ahead with Dottie and Big Bob.

"It's a good thing I've been working out with Shane, or I might have missed out on carrying my beautiful bride." He slid into the back seat of the limo next to her, shutting the door. Then he drew her close. "Finally. I've waited all day to be alone with you, Amy."

"That's Mrs. Bolton to you, hotshot." She barely noticed the countryside as they drove the short distance into town.

"Puddin', I don't care what you want me to call you as long as you're mine."

"Oh, I'm yours. You can't get rid of me." She couldn't believe how much her life had changed in the few short months they'd been engaged. She'd received the strike offs of her fabric line, and the final products would be finished in time for next May's International Quilt Market trade show. In the meantime, she'd started another portfolio to sell. Construction on Nash's training center was coming along nicely, and he would be opening it in the spring. She, her mom and Lexi had spent last weekend packing up Amy's personal items and moving them to Nash's house. Her house, now. She'd decided to turn the entire apartment into a quilting studio. She might even give sewing workshops there in the future.

"I feel like I'm forgetting something." Nash had a goofy grin on his face.

"What could you possibly be forgetting?"

"What it was like to not have you in my life." He kissed her. "Now I don't have to spend a single day without you."

"Oh, Nash…"

The limo stopped in front of the Department Store, Lexi's reception hall. Naturally, they'd hired her to plan the wedding, and she'd pulled off a spectacular event in a short amount of time.

"Does this mean I have to share you again?" Nash pulled a face.

"Yep." She gave him a quick kiss. "When we get inside, I'm going to find Ruby. I have something for her."

"You do?" He helped her out of the limo and tucked her arm under his. "What is it?"

"You can join us if you're curious."

"I am curious. But I admit I'll take any excuse to be with you."

They entered the building and applause erupted. Wade and Clint, clad in tuxedoes, rushed up, clapping Nash on the back and congratulating Amy. Only Marshall couldn't make it. His twin sister had gone into labor with quadruplets. Four babies? Amy didn't blame him for missing the wedding. She searched for Ruby, excitement growing when she spotted her. "There she is."

"I'll come with you." Nash's gaze burned with love. He excused himself and took her by the hand. The three of them climbed the grand staircase to the room Lexi had prepared for Amy.

"How did you like being the flower girl?" Amy knelt next to Ruby. The girl wore a white dress and a tiara like Amy's.

"I loved it! I sprinkled the flowers all over the aisle just like you showed me."

"You did a great job." Amy straightened, reaching for the box she'd brought over last night. "Now that it's official, I wanted to give you this."

Ruby held the large wrapped box in her hand. "What is it?" She sounded breathless.

"Open it." Amy smiled, hoping she would love it.

Ruby tore off the paper and lifted the lid. Bringing her hands to her mouth, she said, "Oh."

"Go ahead. Pick it up." Amy nodded to her.

Ruby held up the pink and purple quilt with the kitten pattern.

"I made it for you."

"It's the colors I loved, and it's got kitties!" Ruby drew it to her chin, rocking back and forth with a huge smile on her face. "I love it!"

She'd poured her love into the quilt, and it made her happy that Ruby appreciated it.

Nash put his arm around Amy. "Wow, I can't believe you made this." He crouched before Ruby. "What do you say?"

"Thank you, Mommy!"

Amy gasped in wonder. She really was a mommy now.

"You've given me the best gift in the world, Ruby." Amy kissed her forehead then hugged her. "And, Nash, you've given me the best gift in the world, too."

Nash drew the two of them into his arms. "You've got it backward. You're the gift, Amy. I will never let you go."

"Never, ever?"

"Never, ever. That's a promise I'll gladly keep."

* * * * *